The Noble Woman

M.L. Lexi

I0614655

Titles by M.L. Lexi

THE BLIND WOMAN
THE DETERMINED WOMAN
THE FORGIVING WOMAN
THE GUILTY WOMAN
THE UNFAITHFUL WOMAN
Coming Soon
THE COMPLETE WOMAN
THE FEARLESS WOMAN
THE GRIEVING WOMAN
THE LOYAL WOMAN

For every woman facing life's challenges
head-on and redefining herself in the process.

History repeats itself, but in such cunning disguise that we never detect the resemblance until the damage is done.
—Sydney J. Harris

Prologue

AS ROSA GAVE her heart and body to the man she loved, she accepted she would never see him again. Gianni sailed in the morning for France to marry Contessa Beatrice. That the man she loved more than life itself married another out of love for her, she supposed, was some form of consolation.

Unlike Gianni, Rosa was a realist and understood they were from different worlds. The harsh reality that had touched Rosa's life made her see everything in black and white, not through the rosy-coloured glasses Gianni did.

Their families were as different as the sun and moon and clashed like oil and water. His was blue blood through and through. Hers lived off and for the land. There was a line, and Gianni's family would never allow her to cross it. His royal blood would never meld with that of a simple Sicilian farm girl, no matter how fiercely he defied his parents. They would make sure of that.

"I want to make love with you, I do, but this is not a good idea, *amore*?" Gianni said, in the erudite Italian of the aristocrat.

Before he could turn away, she reached for his arm to stop him. "Tonight's our last night together. I'll never see you again, and I want to be with you," Rosa murmured in the farmworker's coarse Italian.

Gianni's shoulder-length black curls spilled over the handsome face with dreamy blue eyes. "Please don't cry, *amore.*" He pressed his face to hers and felt her tear land on his cheek.

"You don't have to do this. You shouldn't do this." He brushed the loose strands of hair from her face.

She was so beautiful, he thought, looking into the jade-green eyes set in a delicate face with skin the colour of burnt honey.

"I want to." Rosa looked at him with eyes that held innocence and optimism until he came into her life.

In the silence she left, the sea whispered secrets, and crickets sang a symphony. Soft beams of sunlight seeped through the old deserted house's cracks on the cliff overlooking the Mediterranean Sea. In the flash of white, dust drifted in the air like snowflakes. There was a tattered rug on the wide-planked floor. Walls, once buttery yellow, were washed-out. Frayed lace curtains billowed at the living room window. Colourful bougainvillea dripping from the paint-flaked pergola above them billowed in a soft summer breeze that brought the scents of sea and brine.

It was their secret meeting place where they met under cover of night and spoke of dreams and love.

"As much as it pains me to say, you need to remain true for the ... man you will in time ... marry." Gianni swallowed the bitter taste of the words. "I don't want to dishonour you."

Here was love, she thought, feeling the deepest sense of intimacy she'd felt for him, due in part to his selflessness, and in part, to the feel of his body pressed to hers. "I never want to forget you. I never want you to forget me."

"I'll never forget you. Nothing and no one will ever stop me from loving you," he vowed, brushing his lips over her mouth. "And I have our memories. They have a physical, almost realistic quality to them. They will be with me forever. And I have the stars," he said, for the nights they were apart, he looked up to see her beautiful face in them.

"Promise me you will never forget me because I will never forget you." Eyes glistening with tears were full of love for him.

"I promise." "You're my one true love. I could never forget you."

"Then love me tonight, Gianni." Her eyes swam when she lifted them to his face.

His heart wept for her for him. "I love you too much to dishonour you, *amore*."

Rosa reached for his hand, brought it to rest on her heart. He felt her heartbeat against his hand and his beat with hers. "I have never needed your love as much as I need it now."

Gianni pulled her closer, let his fingers trail a slow line down the front of her bodice to untie lace. Eyes on her, Gianni slipped the linen dress and chemise away, inch by inch, revealing soft, sensual curves.

His mouth brushed over her shoulders and neck to her lips. Untying the white kerchief around her head, Gianni loosened the long braid and let her dark hair tumble in waves over the milky white shoulders to her breasts.

With one long measuring survey, his eyes took in the long lines, the soft curves. "You are so beautiful. More so than what I had pictured in my fantasies these past six months."

"You thought of me like this?"

"Often. After all, I am a man, but I would never..."

"And I'm a woman." Taking his hands, Rosa pulled Gianni down onto the tattered rug. "Make it special, Gianni. Make it memorable."

Even as he felt something inside him breaking, in the abandoned house where they often hid from the judgemental world that didn't approve of their relationship, Gianni played his mouth over hers. Lingering, he took his time, as much for himself as for her.

His mouth and fingers set off to explore that which would be his only for tonight. He filled her with sensations that set her body aflame and brought her to heights she'd remember forever. Gianni made love with her for the first and the last time.

The pain throbbed in him like a deep, infected wound.

Afterward, her scent, mixed with his floating around them, Gianni held her as the tears flowed down her cheeks. "Please don't cry."

"I don't mean to, but you touching me in this way, I ... I never imagine it would feel as wonderful and beautiful. I didn't think I could love you more than I already do."

Gianni's fingers brushed over her tear-stained cheeks. Sensing the struggle brewing inside her, he looked into her eyes. "I'm sorry for hurting you as I am. I don't want you to be sad. I want you to be happy and for your life to be full of love and joy. You must find a man who will do so."

More tears spilled from her wounded eyes. "I love you, Gianni. I love you so much."

Gianni held Rosa as she cried out her sadness until drained and exhausted she slipped into sleep.

Watching Rosa looking peaceful in sleep, Gianni felt so small beside her. He was a coward. He wasn't half the man to the woman she was.

How could he leave her behind to marry another? Rosa was his world, his life, his air. At the thought of the life he was about to embark without her, he felt adrift, anchorless in a deep, dark ocean. Gianni hoped she'd remember tonight with fond affection.

Gianni regretted being who he was. He hated his family for putting Rosa through everything they had. He resented them for hurting her as they had and keeping them apart. As much as he hated to leave her, it was the only way to put things right because staying would cause her more pain.

Grieving for both, Gianni touched his lips to Rosa's, filled himself with her taste, her scent. Crying silent tears, he took her picture into his heart. "You are the best of me. I love you, Rosa. I always will," he whispered, setting the envelope by her side.

His cape swirling in the wind as he galloped off into the shadowed night, Gianni never looked back.

ROSA NEVER SAW OR HEARD FROM Gianni again, but she wouldn't soon forget him, for the contents of the envelope changed her life in unimaginable ways. And unbeknownst to her, it would do the same one hundred years later.

Part I

The Beginning

One ordinary encounter can lead
to a life of extraordinary things.
—M.L. Lexi

One

One Hundred Years Later

UNDER CLEAR BLUE skies and the warmth of a January, Sicilian sun, the Alitalia flight landed at the Fontanarossa Airport. The last time Alessandra visited Sicily was at the age of six with her parents. Yet, twenty years later, when the Airbus' wheels connected with the runway, she felt an immediate sense of belonging—a sense of home.

It was just what she needed.

Eyes rolling with the carousel as the luggage trickled out, Alessandra spotted the first suitcase. A large, strong hand from behind reached out, fingers wrapped around the handle over hers.

"Let me help you with that." He pulled the case off the carousel with ease and set it down at her feet.

He was even more handsome under the bright lights of the terminal. His short chestnut hair was neatly combed back. Dark, thick lashes haloed large, glacial-blue eyes set in a face with a strong jaw. His nose was too large for his face, but that seductive pouty mouth and bewitching dimples made up for it.

"Any more?" he asked, pulling his Samsonite off the belt.

Alessandra pointed to the duffel bag spinning toward them. "Thank you," she said when he pulled it off the belt.

His brain staggered under the green gaze she flashed his way. "It's the least I can do for such a pleasant flight companion. This is my card. My contact information is on there. I'm at your service."

Alessandra read the card. "Let's hope not, Daniel DiBlassio, Attorney at Law." The smile she flashed left him staring at her.

"My office is not far from where you're staying if you need anything, anything at all, I'm a phone call away." Daniel signalled for a porter. "I'd offer you a ride, but you said your aunt's friend is picking you up."

"Yes, so, I better get going. It was nice meeting you, Daniel DiBlassio."

"It was nice meeting you, Alessandra Cuomo." Their hands met, and Daniel held it longer than she expected.

"Well, goodbye," she said reluctantly, taking her hand back.

When Alessandra turned to walk away, Daniel's blue eyes weaved with her as she wound her way through the crowded terminal with the porter in tow. Daniel watched Alessandra hoping she'd turn for one last look before blending into the crowd. When Alessandra finally glanced over her shoulder, Daniel was gone.

As much as she wasn't in the mood for company or talking, Alessandra had to admit she'd enjoyed Daniel's company during the flight. Aside from Aunt Sofia, he'd been her first human contact since her world turned upside down. Daniel helped if only temporarily, to forget. He'd helped her cast aside the debilitating guilt and remorse that had consumed her for months.

And Alessandra couldn't deny he was easy on the eyes. The fit of denim against the tight butt was enough to make a girl giddy. Best of all, he hadn't looked at her with the flirtatious gaze of a man hoping to score a quick roll in bed.

As long as it had been since she'd seen that look cast her way or had a man's hands on her, now wasn't the time. To bring anyone into the hell that was her life wasn't fair.

Erasing all thought of Daniel from her mind, Alessandra absently tucked his business card in her jeans pocket and focused on locating her ride.

For the first time, she caught sight of her surroundings. Fontanarossa, the sixth most trafficked airport in Italy, was modern, designed, as everything in Italy was, aesthetically beautiful. Lustrous marble floors and polished steel gave the interior a contemporary look. Its distinctive façade, pyramid-shaped white steel beams and glass, wrapped the building in a layer of transparency and allowed streams of gold from a glowing sun to shower the terminal in bright light.

Alessandra remembered Daniel saying that the allies seized the airport during World War II—the first built in the region—to use as a military airfield. It was hard for her to imagine such a beautiful, harmonious space had a part in so much destruction.

Alessandra wound her way past the woman dressed in black, waving a handkerchief in the air, then lowering it to wipe the tears away. She and the porter skirted the family in saying their goodbyes to the newlyweds setting off on their honeymoon.

Dodging clusters of people and luggage crowding the terminal, she caught sight of the man with the large, doe eyes holding up the placard with her name. He was inches shorter than she was, and his face was weathered by sun and age, had lines that dug deeply.

"Hello, I'm Alessandra Cuomo," Alessandra said, over the announcements for incoming and outgoing flights drifting from speakers overhead.

"I can see you are Sofia's *nipotina*," he said, eyeing her over.

The last time he'd seen her, she barely reached his waist, but there was no doubt she was a Cuomo. She bore the traits handed down through the generations of Cuomo women. The spill of chestnut hair, the prettily sculpted nose, and the almond-shaped green eyes sprinkled with orange were so much like her *nonna*. The wide mouth and full lips could be used as a man-luring weapon, although she'd rarely used it for that purpose. Cuomo women didn't flaunt their beauty for male trapping. Never, no how, no way.

The one trait he couldn't attribute to genetics was Alessandra's height. She was taller than the generations of Cuomo women before her.

"Yes. I'm Sofia's niece. And you must be *Signore* Battista?"

He nodded. "I am Francesco, just Francesco." Removing his checkered cap, the rough, calloused hand that tilled the land for decades reached for Alessandra's offered hand. "Your *Zia* Sofia, umm, how you say?" Francesco searched his memory for the English translation. "Your auntie, she ask me to pick you up and take you to Villa Cuomo."

Alessandra's lips curled into a soft smile. "Thank you. It's very kind of you."

"Anything for the ah..." Francesco scratched through the puffs of white hair, "the granddaughter of *Signora* Cuomo. She a good friend."

Alessandra's eyes darted away from the red, bulbous nose that took up a great deal of his face. "Your English is better than my Italian."

Francesco's eyes bracketed with deep lines, pulling the thick eyebrows along. "Me and my Maria live in London for five years. We learn English there, but we don't speak it for a long time after we come back to Sicily. You have to be *molto* patient with us."

"I'll be patient if you promise to be patient with my broken Italian."

Francesco flashed her a tooth-gapped smile. "*Va bene, andiamo.*"

Alessandra's luggage loaded into the trunk of Francesco's Fiat, he helped her in before he rounded the hood and took his seat behind the wheel. With the expertise of an F1 driver, Francesco maneuvered his car through the maze of double-parked cars. Within minutes, he joined the traffic flow that took them onto the highway that ribboned along the coastline.

As the vista opened up, Alessandra caught sight of the rolls of thickly carpeted green hills where goats, sheep, cows, and horses grazed behind split-rail fences under a sun-washed sky. They drove past centuries-old towns. Stone farmhouses and sunbaked homes with flower-strewn balconies lined narrow cobbled streets brimming with children who played with abandoned pleasure.

Green hills dropped off to white sand and the Mediterranean Sea's rich blueness, its waters deepening in colour in the horizon as it melded with the sky as one.

Sandwiched between sand beaches, jagged walls of dark stone stretched for miles.

Everything she saw came together to form the quilt of her new home. A spear of the much-needed comfort she'd searched for months arrowed straight to Alessandra's heart.

Awestruck by the beauty coming at her and the history that spoke to her, she remembered her father's stories.

Sicily was home to thousands of small towns, each with its character, food, and unique dialect. The island benefited from the rich culture deposited by many powerful races as the Greek, Roman, German, Norman, and Spaniard, who'd invaded its shores and inhabited it since the eighth century B.C. Alessandra saw their influence in the Baroque and gothic architecture.

Where the road bordered on the wide crescent of beach, Alessandra saw the ribbon of white foam rolling and tumbling along the shore. She imagined that sun worshippers crowded its white sand to soak in the sun's rays during the summer months.

Winding the car through the snaking road, in charming broken English and with great pride, Francesco recounted the island's history. Alessandra absorbed everything Francesco said and felt a sense of pride and communion with her ancestry.

These were her roots, and she made a mental note to get to know as much as possible about her temporary home.

To Alessandra's disappointment, the fifty-minute drive flew by quickly. Before she knew, Francesco's Fiat bumped down Villa Cuomo's cobbled driveway.

Throwing the car in park, Francesco killed the engine. "Welcome to Villa Cuomo, your new home."

Alessandra was about to tell Francesco her stay was a temporary one when the sight of the small stone home snuggled at the end of the driveway drew her attention.

Francesco retrieved the luggage. "You expect a bigger house, si?" he said, noting the confusion on her face.

"Sort of. I mean, Aunt Sofia called it a villa."

"It was a villa, more *grande*. How you say?"

"Bigger."

"*Si,* bigger, but part of the house go," he burst fingers in the air, "in the war. Your *nonna*, she fills that area with trees and flowers to make things happy." Francesco waved toward the garden where weeds overran the lavender and lilac trees, and white, red, and pink bougainvillea overran the trellis in need of repair.

At the center of the garden, the fountain where water once flowed from the vase at the mermaid's hands sat idle. The stone basin beneath sat dry and choked with browning leaves. Alessandra made a mental note to make it functional at the first opportunity.

"Your *nonno* and *nonna* never get around to fixing the house. First, no money, then children and no money, then it become too late and your *nonna* alone."

Alessandra met the older man's eyes, and a moment of complete understanding and respect passed between them. The thought her relatives had the misfortune to experience the devastation of war firsthand was as foreign as the day felt long. Still, Alessandra's admiration for their determination and perseverance to come out survivors was boundless.

The Cuomos were survivors, had been for generations, her father told her. They didn't allow the darkness that touched them to define who they were. The garden was a clear symbol of their courage to press on with their lives.

A newfound resolve engulfed Alessandra, and she felt emboldened. For the first time in months, the prospect of a brighter future felt within reach. All the things that placed her in the world stolen from her felt attainable again.

"It can be pretty again. You make it pretty," Francesco said.

"Yes, I'll make it look pretty." Alessandra eyed the eighteenth-century home.

Towering green olive trees shaded the north side of the house from the burning sun and wind. A small balcony wrapped with an iron balustrade with hand-carved leaves jutted from above the front door. Knee-high, terra-cotta pots pitched against it spilled over with cheerful geraniums. Alessandra pictured her *Nonna* Teresa tending them.

The home's limestone façade was sunbaked golden. A heavy wooden door looked as old as the home it guarded. A pathway next to the house sloped to the field that spread for miles and burst with rows and rows of grapevines.

"Under there, you find the key." Francesco pointed to the mat on the stoop.

Alessandra fished the key, and setting it in the brass lock, opened the door to creaks and groans from hinges pleading for oil. Alessandra made a mental note.

The interior of the home was quaint and clean. Although bearing the scars from years of use, walls were washed in taupe and the tiled floor sparkled. Sunlight speared from the picture window lighting the room bright. A black, wrought iron staircase wound up to the second floor, and the kitchen was beyond the living room.

Antique oak furniture, older than her, was polished to a gleam. The couch and chair, upholstered in charcoal damask, were draped in a white and brown hand-crocheted throw.

Above the sofa, oil paintings of gardens and seascapes in bright colours that crowded the wall caught Alessandra's attention. The canvasses, a wash of bold and vibrant colours, were eight by ten inches in simple wooden frames. One depicted the home and land around Villa Cuomo. Others portrayed grapevines, while another was of a moonlit garden vibrant with colour.

The exquisite oil painting of a stately villa surrounded by acres of land boasting thousands of grapevines caught Alessandra's eye. It was the larger canvass of the bunch. Skirting the estate were miles of golden sand that verged on blue water. Inscribed at the bottom right-hand corner were the words *Mea Domus, Est Tua*. She made a mental note to find out what the Latin caption meant. Running her fingers over them, she felt as if she was touching the past—her past.

"Your *nonna*, she paint." Francesco managed a smile when he caught Alessandra eyeing the framed oils.

"She was very skillful with a brush," Alessandra said, wishing she'd inherited her grandmother's creative flare.

"Your *nonna*, she love to paint, and she very good, but I tell her she no Leonardo." Francesco's voice drifted from the top of the stairs.

"You mean, da Vinci?" Alessandra traced a finger over the paintings and felt a connection.

Francesco called out from the bedroom. "*Sì*, he my favourite painter." Heels clattered against steel when he started down the stairs. "Your luggage is in your *nonna's* bedroom. La prima porta, ummm..."

"Yes, first door," she jumped in when he went thoughtful.

Francesco nodded. "You relax, and I pick you up in three hours, at nine. My Maria, she make you dinner."

Alessandra's eyes formed into an apologetic smile. "I've troubled you enough for today, Francesco. Right now, all I want is to take a hot shower and get to bed. There is hot running water in the house, isn't there?"

"You have hot water, gas, electricity. See?" He flipped the switch on the lamp, making it bloom with light.

"I'm sorry about dinner, but it's been a long day." Alessandra stifled a yawn.

"Is no trouble. My Maria, she love to cook. Best food in Sicily." Francesco brought the tips of his fingers to his lips and burst them into an air kiss. "We marry forty-five years, and I still no tired of her food or her." He winked.

The sweet smile on his face and devotion in his eyes stirred memories of her parents. They'd shared the same sentiment for thirty years. In a few months, they would have celebrated their thirty-first.

"If you get hungry, my Maria buy you lots of food. You find in the kitchen. I go now, but I come back tomorrow morning. Cook and shop. It's all my Maria do." Francesco mumbled to himself, closing the door behind him.

Alessandra's eyes scanned the small, century's old home where generations of her family were born, triumphed war, endured famine, celebrated life, loved, and ultimately mourned death.

Feeling the centuries of history around her, she said, "It's perfect, absolutely perfect."

Two

THE AROMA OF brewed coffee stirred Alessandra awake. Groggy and disoriented with sleep, she fumbled in the darkness for the lamp switch. When her fingers fell on empty air, Alessandra turned heavy-lidded eyes toward the nightstand.

Confusion clouded her face when her bedroom lamp was nowhere in sight. Uneasy, Alessandra scanned the darkened room. Nothing was recognizable. She'd never seen the furniture, the ornate dresser with the large round mirror, or the dainty, white lace curtains framing the window.

With a jolt, Alessandra sat up in bed and eyed the room with eagle eyes. It took a full thirty seconds for recognition to set in. She let out a sigh of relief.

Raking fingers through her tangled hair, Alessandra's eyes floated out the window. The sky was tinted soft yellow and orange as the morning sun peered out on the horizon. A glance at the face of her watch told her it was five a.m. She damned the person who woke her with the temptation of caffeine so early in the morning. Murmuring a few choice words, she pulled the bedsheet over her head. Sleep didn't come.

Wide awake, Alessandra's mind raced as it had for months at first light. Staring up at the ceiling, she thought of her family. The graphic images that appeared on the front of newspapers and television reports flashed vividly.

The tug came, quick and painful, and Alessandra sat up in bed. Drawing her knees close to her chest, she let her head drop. Rocking and biting back tears, she prayed the images to stop haunting her.

She should have never insisted on seeing the mangled car. She should have listened to her aunt and officers McShane and Shaw when they advised against seeing the car. But she was her father's daughter. She had to see it, if only to disprove the sensationalized news reports and images, to sell airtime.

Alessandra wondered if there would come a time when the pain, the gruesome vision of her parents and twin brothers' death would fade from her mind.

Alessandra's dewy eyes came to rest on her grandmother's black and white photograph on the wall. The eyes that stared back were determined and resilient. They spoke to her.

Suffused her with newfound strength, Alessandra decided she wasn't going to allow emotions to take control of her anymore—not today, anyway.

Her aunt was right. She'd spent too much time brooding, and that was going to change here and now. Knuckling the tears away, Alessandra rustled herself out of bed.

"Jesus!" she cried when she tossed the bedsheet aside and felt the cold hit her naked body.

She was wearing nothing but her underwear. She didn't remember stripping out of her clothes and cringed at the possibility Francesco put her to bed.

Thought through, she dismissed the ludicrous idea, but the image of how that might have played out set her off into a fit of laughter. Alessandra chalked it up to jet lag and the long day she had yesterday. She wasn't what you'd call a seasoned traveller.

Pushing to her feet, she walked to the light switch. The room blooming with light, the sound of music came at her. It was faint and distant. Still, she scanned the room for the radio. No radio.

Had she turned a radio on? If so, where in the house had she done so? Her clouded jet-lagged brain wasn't cooperating.

"Think, Alessandra, think."

Her brain stopped rolling when she heard the sound of running water. The hair on her neck stood on end, and the need to protect herself kicked in. Alessandra looked around the room for something to use as a weapon.

She could use the bedsheet to—what?—strangle. Alessandra eyed her running shoes but passed on the idea when she played out the futile shoe-throwing scene in her head. The pillow? Too soft. The hairbrush? Too small. Nothing useful jumped at her.

Panic shut off Alessandra's air when she heard the slamming kitchen drawer.

Yanking the bedsheet off the bed, she wrapped it around her goose-bumped body. Slowly, she opened the bedroom door and poked her head out to scan the hallway before stepping out. Alessandra followed the sounds of music and running water.

Winding down the cold iron staircase, she crossed the empty living room to the front door. When it clicked open, panic choked her. Alessandra searched her brain. She didn't remember locking it, but she didn't remember much.

Alessandra made a mental note to check the locks every night before going to bed.

The sound of music grabbed Alessandra's attention again. She turned to the kitchen, where the ceiling light bloomed bright, and the coffee maker gurgled over a low flame. She sure as hell didn't do that.

She felt the clutch at her belly.

Making her way to the tiny kitchen, she noted the sturdy wooden table with four chairs neatly tucked in showed streaks of dampness where it had been wiped clean. One of the pea-green cupboard doors over the gold speckled counter showing years of wear was open. Alessandra's eyes drifted to the Zenith radio atop the ancient refrigerator, where a passionate Italian love song poured.

A shiver of fear snaked through Alessandra.

After some thought, Alessandra abandoned the idea of an intruder in her home. What kind of burglar took the time to make coffee, wipe the table clean, and listen to music while burglarizing the house?

This was Europe, though.

"Nah." She decided the logical conclusion had to be Francesco.

Presumptuous and intrusive, Alessandra thought, especially when he was doing it at the god-forsaken hour of first light.

As quickly as the irritation grating at her nerves came, it dissipated when she reasoned it was a goodwill gesture on Francesco's part. Helping one another was small-town psychology she wasn't used to. Regardless, she made a mental note to have a chat with Francesco about boundaries.

Alessandra called out for Francesco. No response. She called out again. The quiet sent an eerie chill up her spine.

"What have I gotten myself into?" she screamed in her head.

Tiptoeing to the rear window, Alessandra slid it open. The world was silent, but for the whisper of a soft breeze that brought the scent of sea and brine. Alessandra's eyes darted across the stone patio flanked with olive trees, and the pergola swathed in riotous red, white, and pink bougainvillea.

Beyond the patio wall, a vegetable garden cascaded toward acres of fertile field. Under the faint light of a rising sun as its fingers of light burst into the outgoing night sky, Alessandra made the silhouette of hundreds of grapevines lined in symmetrical rows like brave soldiers.

Brows frowned in confusion when she recalled her aunt saying the villa had been empty for a long while. She made a mental note to walk the grounds in the morning under a better light.

Continuing her search for Francesco, Alessandra caught sight of the long, narrow path leading down to golden sand and the sea that hemmed it. Its waters rippled in deep tones of black and blue. Beyond the crescent of beach, she saw the continuous long roll of foam fringed white lapping the shore. Listening more intently, she heard the hushed hum of the sea.

Lost in the moment, Alessandra took the picture in, let it instill the tranquillity she hadn't felt in a long while. She'd been on the island less than twenty-four hours, and she already felt better than she had in months.

She thought of her parents and brothers and felt a dull ache in her heart. She'd love to share the moment with them. She missed them terribly, but the sense of homecoming eased the aching loneliness.

It became clear to her then why her aunt insisted she make the trip. In the home of her ancestors, her healing would come to pass. Her tense shoulders loosened.

"*Scusi*?" The man's voice cut into thoughts.

Alessandra's body snapped stiffly with tension. Eyes filled with fear swirled to the man arched in the kitchen doorway. "Who ... who the hell are you? What are you doing in my home?"

He wore jeans, a buttoned-down white shirt, sleeves rolled halfway up, and loafers. Alessandra could see the trace of broad shoulders and the ripple of muscles against cotton.

He casually leaned a shoulder against the doorjamb. "Who are you?"

Alessandra's inherent need to protect herself had her scanning for the closest weapon-like object. Her shoulders sagged when all she saw was a wooden ladle. It would have to do, and she reached for it. Misjudging the distance between her and the counter, Alessandra tumbled forward. Instinctively, she threw her hands out to break her fall.

Lips, ripe with a smile, watched the bedsheet glide down her body to pool at her feet. Naked, Alessandra stood facing the inquisitive sea-blue eyes surveying her with appreciative eyes.

Worthy of a Michelangelo painting, he mused with a winged brow.

She was tall and fit with soft curvy lines that made a man appreciate the female form's beauty. The hard tips crowning milky, taut breasts made him grateful for the house's cold temperature. Her breasts weren't as large as he liked—a B-cup in his estimate—but beautifully sculpted. He gave them a pass. He eyed the black cotton panty against the delicate skin he imagined glowed like ivory by candlelight and continued his scan of the legs that seemed never to end.

Blood trumpeting in his veins, he imagined the things his mouth and hands would do to such a fine body. He could almost hear her whimpers as the pleasure geysered through her.

The moss-coloured eyes that stared at him with an expression alternating between alarm and embarrassment were captivating. She was a masterpiece, he concluded, feeling the punch of heat spread to his belly.

"Can I help you with that?" His lips stretched out in a smile.

"Stay away from me," Alessandra snapped, and wielding the spoon like a weapon, dove for the bedsheet on the ground.

"Or what, you'll stir me to death?"

Her eyes narrowed into angry slits, and she took an attack stance. If the spoon failed her, she determined to deliver a sharp kick to the crotch. A well-placed kick to their most treasured body part could incapacitate any man on contact and drive him to his knees.

"Don't come closer." Alessandra poised for attack.

"I'm sorry if I startled you." His relaxed drawl touched a nerve. "And I wish you wouldn't cover-up. You have a beautiful body. I wouldn't mind admiring it a little longer." His eyes roamed over her body, and as he visualized it. His insides seared.

Alessandra gripped the bedsheet tighter and, with a face like stone, measured him. His mouth was full with a bottom-heavy lip begging to be nibbled. His tanned face sported a fashionable stubble. Dark waves that spilled to chin length topped the casual beach-boy look, and she couldn't overlook the fit of those jeans. Her friends would rate him extra-yummy and ditto to that.

As difficult as it was to take her eyes off him, she shook herself back to reality. "Don't move," Alessandra warned when he raised his arm to reach into the cupboard.

"I'm reaching for a coffee cup. Would you like some?" His eyes darted to the gurgling coffee maker on the stove. "Freshly made." When she didn't respond, he went ahead and poured himself a cup.

"Who the hell are you, and what are you doing in my house?" Alessandra barked.

He rubbed a hand over the stubble on his chin. "Your house? Funny, I've lived here for years, and I haven't seen you before today. Do you have proof this is your house? I'm looking for the sugar bowl," he said when he reached back into the cupboard.

Heat flashed in the green eyes. "I don't have to prove anything to you, and what do you mean you've lived here for years? This is my grandmother's home. How dare you move in here without my family's consent?" Alessandra watched him lean back on the doorway and casually sip coffee.

"It's good coffee. You sure you don't want a cup?"

"I ask you again, what are you doing in my home?"

He noted her eyes turning a provocative shade of green. Very sexy, he decided. "You're not from around here."

"No, I'm not. I'm from Canada, where people respect boundaries and don't barge into people's homes."

He gave her a dimpled smile. "Ah, Canada, beautiful country, beautiful women. I've been there a few times, in Toronto and Montreal, on business. You don't have a French accent, so you must be from Toronto." When she didn't reply, he went on. "Canadian women are beautiful, which I think you are." He liked the way she blushed. "But that cold weather wasn't for my taste. I prefer the heat and sun. By the way, you'll need to get some sun on that body. It's too pale for my liking."

"You're delusional, and you need to get out of my house. Now."

"That may be a problem. You see, I live here. All my things are," he raised a finger upward. "I'm assuming in the bedroom next to yours because I don't remember sleeping with you. I'm sorry, but I had too much to drink at my friend's birthday party last night. You know Italians and their wine."

Eyes widened at the realization she'd slept in the house with this lunatic. "Jesus! You were here last night?"

"Mmm-hmm."

"Jesus!"

"Well, was I everything you've dreamed of?" he said, with a wicked wiggle of eyebrows.

"Jesus, no. No. We certainly didn't share a bed."

Tsking, he shook his head. "I didn't think so. I'd remember sleeping with you. I wouldn't forget that body. And you, well, you certainly wouldn't forget the pleasure I'd have given you," he said with an arrogant grin.

"I don't know what's worse, the fact you're intruding in my home, or that you're cocky enough to believe I'd sleep with you."

Painting a casual smile, his dimples fluttered to life again. "Oh, trust me, you will."

With a look of indignation, she snapped, "Get out. I want you to leave my house. Now." He didn't budge an inch. "I'm calling the police."

He eased off the door, jamb, signalled for her to pass. "Go ahead."

One hand clutching the bedsheet, and the other white-knuckling the ladle, Alessandra bound past him. In the living room, her eyes scanned for the telephone. Her shoulders deflated when she didn't see one. From the corner of her eyes, she caught sight of his pouty lips creasing into that cocky grin she wanted to slap off his face.

He lifted his shoulders let them fall. "Sorry. No telephone in the house." He waited for her next move.

"That's absurd. How do you live without a telephone?"

"I've done just fine without one. A telephone is an annoyance, and there's no need for such distractions when you have so much beauty around you." He cast eyes over her. "May I see your naked body again, please? I want to review the attributes once more before I consider sleeping with you. And this time," he twirled his finger to indicate she should circle her body.

"You're Goddamn insane."

"You don't like sex? I'm going to be upset if you say no." He waited for a beat for her response, but thinking better than to entertain his comment, she kept quiet. "I hope you were going to say yes because I'll guarantee to make it very enjoyable. I'll make it, so you vocalize your praise for me the entire time, and maybe a little afterward because there's nothing more I enjoy than to please a woman." He sang in the melodic Italian accent that flowed like a calm brook making her body liquefy into a raging hormonal puddle, and a wanton gaze replaced anger.

Stop it. You're supposed to be afraid of this lunatic, not attracted to him, Alessandra reminded the woman in her who hadn't felt a man's touch in months. But sweet and sour Jesus, the man was gorgeous, and that Italian accent was just, mmm-hmm. Alessandra couldn't remember the last time a man had brought her to her knees as she imagined he would.

What the hell is wrong with me? I'm pulling a Jekyll and Hyde.

It took a few seconds to temper the heat bulleting through her. Composed again and with the appropriate amount of feigned irritation in her voice, Alessandra said, "Let's get a couple of things straight. One. This is my home. Two. I wouldn't sleep with you if ... you were the last man on earth." She topped the comment with a snort of disgust.

"Challenge accepted," he said in response to her snarl. "By the way, my name is Luca Santini," he called out as she bound up the stairs and to himself murmured, "And I thought this was going to be just another boring day."

Three

BACK IN HER bedroom, a chair propped against the door, Alessandra reached for the T-shirt and jeans on the floor. Slipping into both on, she bundled the chestnut hair into a ponytail.

Agitated, Alessandra paced, mulling her next move. She didn't feel threatened by the man—a woman sensed these things—but she was alone in a foreign country. She didn't speak the language, didn't know the area, or had a telephone. Alessandra would address those issues at the earliest, but what was she to do until then?

As much as she'd bumped up the trust quotient on—what did he say his name was?—Luke, Luca, that was it, Luca Santini, she'd wait in her room for Francesco behind a closed door. She recalled him saying he'd be by in the morning, although he didn't say what time. She didn't have much of an option. Sitting back in her bed, stretched out legs crossed at the ankles, she set the wooden spoon by her side and waited.

Alessandra's thoughts drifted back to Luca. He didn't look like a drifter. And they sure weren't as fit as he was. Drifters didn't have his handsome good looks or wear Armani, but this was Italy. Everyone had a sense of style.

A cringe followed a gasp of embarrassment when the thought she'd exposed herself, mole on her breast and all, struck her. She could still see the faint line of concentration as he surveyed her. It took several dates and vast amounts of alcohol before she considered exposing as much skin as she had. And those hypnotic blue eyes stopped her from reaching for the bedsheet for a few short seconds.

"Jesus, what was I thinking?" Alessandra bolted to her feet.

The man could be a serial killer hiding in her home, waiting for his next prey, and she willingly made herself his next victim. Mind racing, heart pounding in her chest, she did what any trapped human being would.

She got up to tidy up the bedroom.

Every piece of furniture in the room was older than she was, but it was functional and polished to a gleam. The room was distinctively feminine. Walls were washed in pastel yellow, and hand-knitted doilies covered the two-night tables, chiffonier and draped the tuft chair's back. Artwork, painted by her grandmother, hung on the walls.

Alessandra dug into her suitcases and hung up shirts, jeans, and the one little black dress her aunt threw in—just in case. Alessandra questioned when her aunt supposed she'd find the need to use the very short, very low cut hope-to-get-lucky-tonight dress during her stay.

Alessandra tucked away tanks, T-shirts, socks, nighties, and underwear into drawers. She lined up running shoes, sandals, and patent slingbacks, which like the dress, appeared out of nowhere, at the bottom of the walnut armoire with the carved floral panels.

Alessandra set suntan lotion, cream, and make-up, on the vanity table next to the ornate silver brush with the matching comb and hand mirror belonging to her grandmother. The vanity table with its round mirror and tufted button chair brimmed with femininity, something Alessandra knew little about.

Alessandra stripped the bed when she finished unpacking and lay down fresh linen she found in the dresser drawer. She scanned the room. Satisfied, she crossed to the dresser crowded with framed photographs.

The pewter frames displayed several family photos. Alessandra looked over the faded black and white photograph of a handsome man resembling her father. The eyes that looked into the camera creased into a happy smile. Alessandra assumed the man to be *Nonno* Gino, who died of a heart attack while tending to his sheep in the field years before she was born. She remembered her father telling her he'd died, as he wanted, with his animals on the land he loved.

Alessandra eyed the black and white of the young, attractive couple on their wedding day. Her grandmother looked to be no more than a girl, and her grandfather didn't look much older than she did. Her gaze on her husband's face, the love radiated in her eyes. A tear spilled from Alessandra's eyes.

She saw the photographs of herself at five-years-old with the pink ribbon in her hair she wore until it frayed, at eight with a toothless grin riding her first two-wheel bicycle, and at eighteen in her graduation cap and gown.

Alessandra's emotions surged when she picked up the photograph of her parents on their wedding day. Both looked young, happy, and ready to take on the world. Next to it were photos of her twin brothers enjoying an ice cream at the fair, and on the pony, they insisted on riding in tandem. But it was the one of them standing by her side, happily smiling into the lens that pushed her to the edge and made the emotional upheaval she'd fought for months, push its way straight to her heart.

Incredible how one event could strip you of everything dear in your life in seconds, she thought, holding back the tears. She wasn't going to cry. She'd promised her aunt she wouldn't anymore. Besides, during the past months, she'd cried herself empty.

With nothing else to occupy her time, Alessandra sank onto the bed. Resting her head on her updrawn knees, she cast eyes out the window to watch a luminous sun shower the island in sunshine while she waited on Francesco's visit or murder to be committed by a gorgeous lunatic.

"*Scusi.*" At the unexpected knock on the door, Alessandra's heart leapt to her throat. Pushing off the bed, she took a ninja stance, the wooden spoon in her right hand. "I wanted to let you know there are fresh pastries in the kitchen, and I made a fresh pot of espresso for you." Luca's voice carried the musical, exotic musical Italian lilt that made her insides liquefy.

She was glad for the door between them that prevented him from seeing the unabashed arousal that set her cheeks ablaze." Go away."

"You should have some breakfast. It is the most important meal of the day. In Sicily, it's customary to have a fine cup of espresso and *cornetti* or pastries."

Alessandra couldn't remember the last time she had anything to eat. Her mouth salivated at the thought of food. "I'm not hungry, and I sure as hell don't want your food. I want you to get out of my house. For all I know, you're a murderer hiding from the police."

"I know you don't believe that. Murder is too messy, requires too much work, and it's too stressful. Not good for my complexion." Luca's words netted him a smile he couldn't see. "I'm going out to the field now, so you can eat without the benefit of my company," Luca said, and as an afterthought added, "Which by the way women enjoy."

"I don't doubt that for one minute," Alessandra murmured under her breath.

"Did you say something?"

"Yes. Get out of my house and take your *cornetti* with you."

"You're warming up to me." Luca leaned against the bedroom door.

"How do you figure that?"

"Your voice is not as high pitched now." Luca grinned when he heard something resembling a snarl. "Tell me, are you naked right now."

"I'm...." She stopped when she pictured his lips curving at her expense. "Get out of my house."

"It's clear you're not a morning person. We'll continue this conversation when you're in a better mood. I'll be back around lunchtime. Why don't you whip up some spaghetti for lunch? We'll share a bottle of wine and talk."

"Get out."

"By the way, I'm partial to anything cooked in wine." Luca's brows raise in appreciation at the string of oaths that followed. She was a talented orator.

Ear against the door, Alessandra listened to his retreating footsteps. When the front door closed, she stepped into the hallway. Eyes scanned right and left before she made her way down to the kitchen.

Wandering to the stove, she picked up the coffee maker and poured into the cup Luca left out for her. On the plate next to the pastry box, she set two very fattening cream-filled croissants. An audible hmm and an ahhh escaped her when the rich glory of it melted on her tongue.

Relaxed, Alessandra poured a second cup of coffee, and as she sat back to enjoy it, the click of the front door handle jarred her nerves.

"Damn it! I should have locked the front door," she chided. Back stiffened, she picked up the saucer in her throwing hand.

"Buon giorno."

A long breath of relief escaped her when Francesco cocked his head in. "I'm in the kitchen."

"My Maria, she send you fresh bread. But I see you already eat." Eyes rolled toward the pastry box.

"Thank you. I'll save it for later. Have a seat. Can I get you a cup of espresso?"

"I never say no to coffee." Francesco took a chair. "Ahhh, *cornetti* and *cannoli*."

"Help yourself." She reached into the dishrack for a cup and saucer.

"Luca buy for you?" He drew out a chocolate-filled cannoli from the box.

Alessandra dropped the coffee maker on the stove with a thud. "You know him? You know this, Luca San..."

"San-ti-ni," Francesco sounded out each syllable. "Everybody know Luca, especially the *ragazze*."

Alessandra swept a stunned gaze over at Francesco. "Yes, the ladies, and what do you mean everyone knows Luca?"

"*Si*, we like Luca." Francesco dug into his cannoli with fervour. Powder sugar drizzled from his lips like a winter snowfall.

"Were you also aware he's been living here, in my home?" Alessandra's tone was ripe with irritation, but whether Francesco chose to ignore it or was too distracted with eating wasn't clear to her.

"Luca live here for about five years. My Maria cleans the home for him." Francesco attacked the rest of his cannoli with gusto, missing the bewildered eyes staring at him.

"Five years and Maria is...? Does Aunt Sofia know?" she asked when she found her voice. At his nod, Alessandra shot a seething look Francesco took no note of as he took the last of his cannoli and chased it with coffee. "Why didn't anyone think to tell me? A little warning would have been nice." The words came out stronger than she intended, but the irritation swelled in pounding waves.

Francesco dusted the corners of his mouth with a paper napkin. "Your Aunt Sofia say you no come if you know."

"She what?" Alessandra said, pacing.

Her aunt talked her into travelling across an ocean to revive the centuries-old family villa from ruin while purposely holding back the knowledge of a stranger living there. This, Aunt Sofia told her, was the diversion she needed to help her snap out from her depression.

"I believed that duplicitous woman." Alessandra breathed in deep for control to contain her anger. She'd save it to unleash on her aunt at the first opportunity. "So he's been living here all this time, and no one did anything about it?"

"He's a *occupante abusivo*. Ah, how you say?" Francesco paused, thought. "This one, I don't know how to say in English. I get the dictionary from the car. My Maria, she find my dictionary when I tell her you no speak too much Italian."

Alessandra made a mental note to brush up on the language and then made a second note that her mental notes were becoming too many for her brain. She needed a pen and paper.

When Francesco returned, he flipped the pocket-size book open. "Here, she is. Squa ... squa..." He wrestled with the word before turning the dictionary over to Alessandra.

"Squatter." She read. "Wait, what? Luca's a squatter." Alessandra faintly remembered reading an article about squatters in European countries, but that was the extent of her knowledge on the subject.

"Squ-a-tter. Squ-a-tter," Francesco pronounced until Alessandra threw him a half-masted glare. "They move into empty house, live there, and only the owner can throw out. In Italy, squ-a-tter is normal." Francesco smiled, pleased with himself when the word flew smoothly from his lips. "This is why I tell your Aunt Sofia, she must come here."

Alessandra shook her head in disbelief. "This gets better and better. So, let me get this straight. Aunt Sofia has known about Luca for the past five years."

Francesco rose, went to the stove, and poured himself a top-up of coffee. "Your papa, he know too," he said and immediately regretted rousing the painful memory.

Alessandra caught Francesco's silent apology and threw him an understanding gaze. "Why didn't Dad or Aunt Sofia do something when you told them?"

"One, two-week visit do nothing. They must move back into the house and live here for months. They say no time to come for so long. They ask me to ... ahhh, ricotta cannoli."

"Francesco, please focus." Alessandra made a rolling hand gesture to speed him along when he attacked the pastry with enthusiasm.

Francesco wiped his mouth with the back of his hand. "I talk to Luca. He say he want to buy the land from your papa. I tell your papa and Aunt Sofia, but they say they no sell to him."

She threw hands in the air. "Why wouldn't they want to sell?"

"This you ask your Aunt Sofia. She explain to you."

Frustration edged into a grating annoyance. Alessandra had to speak with her aunt. The woman knowingly sent her into what Alessandra perceived as a battlefield.

She flew halfway across the world to turn her life off and erase all the bad that shrouded it, to jump into the middle of a precarious situation.

After losing her family, the paralyzing guilt drove her to blame herself for what happened. The guilt latched onto her like the jaws of an animal around its prey. It consumed her and ate away at her once-happy existence. She lost herself and lost control of her life. Right now, she needed emotional stability, and Luca Santini meant to de-rail her recovery by causing unnecessary stress.

Alessandra had to find out what her aunt got her into.

"Francesco, I need your help."

Francesco took in the remainder of his coffee, licked his lips. "*Si*. You tell me what you need."

"I need to use your telephone, and I need you to help me get a telephone installed."

Thick, peppered brows raised. "Sure. We go to my house."

"I don't know what my aunt got me into. At worst, I have a murderer living in my house. At best, I have someone who's going to become a huge boil on my butt," Alessandra murmured on her way out the kitchen.

"Luca, no murderer. He no boil either. He buy fresh *cornetti* and *cannoli*." With a shrug, Francesco helped himself to another pastry.

Four

FRANCESCO AND ALESSANDRA found Maria where he said she'd be—in the kitchen. Loose strands of greying hair spilled around a face dusted with flour. Her ample bosom bobbed as she pounded and kneaded the pasta dough on a marble slab. Her cheeks, ruddy from exertion, were like a beacon in the night.

Maria's nut-brown eyes by-passed Alessandra and went to Francesco, who sniffed the air to ascertain what to expect for lunch. The short animated exchange with her husband had Francesco scurrying out the kitchen.

Arched in the kitchen doorway, Alessandra scanned the room. The kitchen was compact and tidy. Walls were lemon yellow with oak cupboards that gleamed under a coat of wax. The room's focal point was a vintage cast iron gas stove, where burners flamed under a pot of boiling water and a skillet sizzling with chopped vegetables. At the center of the room, the ten-seat table showed the scars of use from hundreds of family gatherings.

Maria gave Alessandra her back while she covered the dough with plastic wrap. After setting the dough in the refrigerator to rest, Maria moved to the sink to wash sticky dough off her hands. She brought the wet hands up to her hair to paste the loose strands in place, then dried them on the white apron at her waist.

"Turn." Maria twirled a finger in the air.

Alessandra's brows drew together, forming that vertical crease between them that Maria thought was so much like her *nonna*. "I'm sorry."

"You turn." Maria's tone held a ring of authority, and Alessandra did while she scanned her from head to toe. "Francesco, right, you look like your *nonna*.

"You think so?"

Maria kept her eyes levelled on Alessandra. "You taller, but everybody in America taller. You eat lots of meat there. How tall you are?"

"Five-seven."

"You sit." Maria signalled a seat at the table.

"Francesco get biscotti," Maria said, setting down a steaming cup of espresso before Alessandra along with a sugar bowl and tiny spoon.

Alessandra opened her mouth to turn coffee and biscotti down but closed it. Maria was petite in stature, but she was a force to be reckoned with. A few extra calories and caffeine-infused nerves were easier to handle than saying no to the woman.

"She meet Luca," Francesco said when he stepped back into the kitchen. His arms were loaded with two jars of tomato preserves and a tin of biscotti.

"Ah, Luca." Maria remained lost in thought for a few seconds before proceeding to slam the flat of her knife on two cloves of garlic, startling Alessandra in the process. "What you think of Luca? *Bello ragazzo, si*?"

Alessandra gave a disinterested shrug, although her blood began to heat and swim when she thought back to the sapphire eyes, the dark, flowing curls, and the fit of those jeans.

"You no think he *bello*?" Maria waved the sharp knife in the air like a jousting knight.

"He is very handsome."

"You like him? Because I know for sure he like you."

"We've just met?"

Maria lifted a single dark eyebrow "Luca, like the signorine." Maria scooped chopped garlic onto the knife's blade and, with her finger, slid it off into hot olive oil. The sizzling garlic immediately filled the room with its aroma.

"Luca, like the signorine. A lot." Francesco concurred, pouring espresso into a thick-lipped cup. "She think he a murderer and a boil on her butt." Francesco grinned to himself, dipping a biscotto into his coffee.

"He too *bello* to be a murderer or a boil," Maria added chopped vegetables to the sautéing garlic. "But he the son of a Santini."

"And?" Alessandra watched Francesco munch on biscotti and wondered where the rail-thin man put it all.

"Sofia, no, tell you the story of the Santinis and Cuomos?" Maria turned to Alessandra, who responded with a shake of the head, and next to her, Francesco dived into the next biscotto triggering an oath-laced Italian rant complete with eye-roll and hand gestures. "All morning, I work to make fresh pasta and sausages, and he fill his stomach with biscotti before lunch."

"I can eat all." Francesco took the last of the biscotto before walking out of the kitchen.

"You no get married." Huffing an exasperated breath, Maria poured tomato sauce over sautéed vegetables. "What I say before he make me crazy?"

"Something about the story of the Santinis and Cuomos."

"Santini-Cuomo history very long. You must talk to Sofia." Maria added sausages, sprinkled salt and pepper, and lowered the flame on the bubbling tomato sauce.

"You got me curious and worried now."

"You no worry about Luca. He a good boy." Wiping her hands dry, Maria joined Alessandra at the table. "But his father not such a good man. His father is why your *Zia* Sofia ask you come to Villa Cuomo."

"I don't know anything about these Santini people. And I didn't come here to... I came to ... restore the property, and now I find this Luca living in my grandmother's house."

Maria rested a hand on Alessandra's when she leaned back in her chair and closed her eyes. "I know why you come, and I tell you, you no need to worry about Luca. He harmless. He just want to sleep with you. You no sleep with him already?"

Alessandra's mouth opened in a stunned O. "Of course not. I only met the man this morning," and exposed my naked body.

If Maria heard the indignant tone in Alessandra's voice, she overlooked it. "You will."

"I will not."

"Why, you no like sex?" Silence. "I hear he very good," Maria said, with a devilish wink.

A deep red flooded Alessandra's face. "Oh, Jesus!"

Maria slanted a stare of disapproval. "We no talk like that here."

"I'm sorry," Alessandra bit back the snort in her throat at the irony.

ONCE FRANCESCO ARRANGED FOR THE TELEPHONE installation at Alessandra's home, she dialled her aunt's number.

She breathed in for calm, but the moment she heard her aunt's voice, Alessandra's anger sprang hot. "You deceived me into leaving my home, my safe space, to travel thousands of miles and thrust me into a precarious situation without warning. You never thought to mention this Luca person was living at the villa, which by the way, is nothing of the sort. So you lied on all counts. And..."

Sofia let Alessandra flush her anger out of her system. "Feeling better?"

"Yes." With a huff, Alessandra fell back onto the couch.

"I know I wasn't completely honest, but would you have gone if I'd told you the truth?"

"No, but..."

"It's why I didn't tell you."

"Why would you put me into the middle of this? You know I'm not up to this."

"I would never have insisted for you to make the trip if I thought you weren't. You believe me don't you?" Sofia went on when Alessandra didn't answer. "As for Luca, he's a kind, warm-hearted man, and from what I understand, a gorgeous specimen."

The comment, which had Maria written all over it, netted a smile. "He is that."

"And apparently very talented."

"Jesus, Aunt Sofia, not you too."

"I may be old and long out of circulation, but I'm not dead, dear, and neither are you. I want you to remember that. By the way, you better not be using the Lord's name in vain around Maria. I know it's hard to tell, but like most Italians, she's a God-fearing woman."

"I got that lecture already."

Feeling now was the right time to tell Alessandra everything, Sofia did. "Luca is Antonio Santini's only child."

"And?" Alessandra sunk back into the soft cushions of the velvet couch.

"Antonio owns the Santini Winery Corporation, one of the oldest and largest wineries in Italy. The company is over one-hundred years old and worth billions. And the Santinis are the reason Villa Cuomo came into our family's possession."

Five

1882 – Gianni Santini

THE IRE IN Abramo Santini's eyes toward his son blazed as hot as the fire in the hearth before him. "You don't think I knew about you and the peasant girl. I know everything that goes on with my family and business. I let it go because I figured you were sowing..."

"Be careful what you say, Father. Her name is Rosa, and I love her." Gianni's eyes were intense and sober.

"You love her." Abramo laughed despairingly, cynically. "What do you know about love?"

"I'm not a child, Father. I'm twenty-years-old."

The rays of an early summer's sun having set for the day, the house came to life under the mellow light of dozens of candles on wall sconces and candelabras. The roaring fire crackling in the hearth made the living room with polished mahogany furniture, whitewashed walls, and gleaming marble floors cozily warm.

"It's difficult to tell you're a man when your actions are those of a child. What were you thinking by bequeathing that peasant girl the one-hundred-and-twenty-three acre parcel of land your grandmother left you? Goddamn it, Gianni, it's Santini land, and it always will be." Abramo slammed the whiskey decanter on the counter.

As Gianni suspected, his sister couldn't wait to betray him. He wondered how long it took her to run and tell daddy once she'd found the paperwork in his bedroom or what she got in exchange for sharing the information. Well, the joke was on them because he'd planted the seed to infuriate his father after Rosa told him Abramo threatened to fire her entire family from the winery.

"It's my land to do with what I wish." Gianni drank whiskey, felt it streaming down his throat.

"She's a simple peasant girl, and now by giving her this land, you have thrust her into our family, to remain connected to us forever." Abramo's tense fingers tilted back the tumbler, drank deep. He would have preferred a good glass of Santini wine to the Irish whiskey, but he needed to feel the burn on his throat.

Abramo thought his four girls would drive him to the grave, not his only son—his pride and joy. Hormones, however, turned young men into fools and their brains into mush. He was sympathetic to the boy. He knew well the starring a beautiful woman's smile set off in a man. It was what had drawn him to his wife, Aria.

"Rosa may be a simple farm girl, but she has more class than many of those that bear the Santini name." Gianni dared to slam his fist on the table in his father's presence.

Was it anyone other than Gianni, who was so much like him, to show such disrespect, Abramo would have reciprocated with the merited ferocity. "Not only is she a farm girl, but she is the daughter of our best vineyard manager. And she's sixteen-years-old."

"You married Mama at the same age." Gianni was quick to point out.

The boy had him on that one, but Abramo refused to be baited.

Abramo saw love in his son's eyes for the girl, not infatuation. Abramo doubted the feeling was mutual. Abramo reasoned the girl could only be interested in his son for his money like all the others. Women aimed to make Gianni their personal bank, and the boy was too naïve to see it.

As Abramo's sole male descendant, the boy stood to inherit Santini Winery. Abramo couldn't allow Gianni to throw his life, name, and money away on a peasant girl.

The Santini family roots went back to the House of Savoy, a regal lineage that dated back to the fourteenth century. They were a powerful, influential, political dynasty that produced popes, prime ministers, and tycoons who'd left an envied legacy. Abramo couldn't allow Gianni to jump into a relationship with a girl from uneducated, farming stock with so much history and prominent blood in theirs. Santini's blue blood couldn't meld with the ordinary.

Abramo's generation was responsible to the ancestors before them who had fought enemies and gave their lives to carry the Santini legacy. Regardless of how deeply Gianni was in love with the girl, it was a love Abramo wouldn't allow to come to pass.

"I will marry her, Father. I'm old enough to do so without your consent." Gianni's bold tone told Abramo he meant it.

Eyes on his drink, Abramo shrugged. "As you say, you're a grown man. You do what you like."

Gianni's brows furrowed. "Thank you, Father."

"But not on my coin."

"I don't want or need your money." Gianni spat.

"Fine, but do you think her family will see it the same way? They're all employed by Santini Winery." Abramo went silent to allow his son to weigh the implication of his words. For a long time, the only sound in the room was that of the hearth's crackling wood.

"Dismissing them only stands to harm you. The Cuomos are the best workers you have, loyal to you. You've said so yourself."

"They are, but you marry the girl, and everyone in her family who works for me will be fired." Abramo's stare bore into Gianni.

"You wouldn't dare?" Gianni shot a fulminating glare at his father.

"Every last Cuomo gone." Abramo calmly replaced the drunk whiskey in the snifter. "I may even throw her friends into the mix. All of them gone."

There was a new and fresh quiver of anger and hate beating at Gianni's chest for his father. It was never going to end. His father was always going to control his life. Worse, Gianni didn't doubt Abramo would make Rosa's life a living hell. As much as he loved and wanted to be with her, he couldn't thrust her life, or those she loved, into one of misery, which was what his father intended to do. Gianni could never live with that.

Why did he have to be born a Santini?

Gianni had never hated anyone as much as he hated his father then. His heart beat so thick with resentment in his chest it hurt.

Feeling as if he was fast sinking in quicksand, Gianni flicked eyes to his father. "You win. I'll do whatever you want as long as you leave Rosa and her family alone."

"I thought you would see sense." Abramo raised the glass to his son in toast.

"What do you want from me?"

"You will leave for France to marry the Contessa Beatrice on the next sail. She's a woman with an impressive regal lineage."

"Handpicked by you and mother."

"Yes, because we clearly can't trust your judgement. Her family has agreed to sign over to you the family's Burgundy vineyards and the Château d'André, a ten-thousand square foot palace, which will be your primary residence, as part of her dowry. You will manage the vineyards and, in time, bottle the juice under Santini label."

"It's always about the Goddamn business." Gianni stormed to the bar, poured Jameson into his glass.

"That 'Goddamn business,' as you eloquently put it, is what affords you the cozy lifestyle you enjoy."

Gianni slammed the bottle on the counter. "This may surprise you, Father, but I have no interest in any of it."

Caustically, Abramo smiled. "Spoken like someone who has it all. Do we have an agreement, son?"

Gianni drained his glass. The whiskey burned straight down to the sickness in his belly. "On a couple of conditions."

"I don't think you're in a position to negotiate," Abramo said, although he expected nothing less from his son. Gianni was from his loins, and negotiating was in the Santini blood.

"I will sail for France and marry the woman of your choice." Gianni refilled his glass and drank to wash the vile taste of betrayal down his throat. "And I will remain in France manning your vineyard, only if you give me your word you will not contest ownership of the parcel of land I want to leave Rosa. I also want you to have our lawyers legalize the transfer to her name. You will also vow to employ her family—for life."

Lazily, Abramo lifted an arm to drape it over the back of the Giltwood couch. "Those are quite the conditions."

"And you will agree to them if you want descendants. I am your only son, the only one who can produce the male heirs you so desperately want to carry the almighty Santini name and your legacy."

Well played, Abramo thought. He didn't see that coming and didn't doubt Gianni meant every word. Whether the boy wanted to admit it or not, he was his father's son.

Looking up to Gianni, Abramo smiled a little. "Agreed," he said, offering his hand to seal the deal. As Gianni clinched it, and as much as his planned script had worked and secured Rosa's future as he intended, he wondered if his father would stand by his word.

Six

ALESSANDRA SUMMARIZED. "SO Gianni was Luca's great-great-grandfather, which makes Rosa my great-great-grandmother."

"That's right, and the parcel of land Gianni gifted Rosa as an act of love is Villa Cuomo."

"Pfft, an act of love. He gave it to her out of guilt and married another out of cowardice." Anger for the Santinis clicked up a few notches.

"I think it was an act of love. Gianni loved Rosa, and my guess is he wanted to remain connected to her, and the land was how he thought to do so. As for marrying the Contessa, it was what he had to do to protect Rosa. Had Gianni not married her, the repercussion would have been severe for Rosa and the family. Santini Winery was the only employer in the town. Had Abramo fired Rosa and her family, they'd be doomed. Then, by extension, for fear of reprisal from Abramo, friends and distant family would have ostracised our family." Maria sighed.

"Gianni loved her too much to let that happen, and the only way he knew to manage the situation was to marry the Contessa. Being a Cuomo, Rosa would have supported and encouraged his decision to ease *his* pain."

Alessandra felt a deep ache for the heartache a sixteen-year-old girl suffered because of her station in life. Her heart ached for the great-great-grandmother she knew nothing about until today.

"That's so sweet and so horrible. Did she ever hear from Gianni again?"

"They say she never did."

They both fell into a reverent silence, imagining Rosa's sadness and misery for merely falling in love.

An ugly hard resentment floated deep inside Alessandra. "That's just..."

"That's life, honey." Sofia put in.

"I'm so glad things have changed since then."

"It hasn't, honey. Situations like Rosa and Gianni's aren't rare. They exist today and will in all walks of life. Today we tend to be more politically correct when dealing with such matters. Anyway, this is where you come in. I need you to secure Villa Cuomo."

"Secure? It's ours." When the silence lengthened, Alessandra pressed, "Isn't it, Aunt Sofia?"

"It's not, and don't forget it's yours now."

"Never mind that. You told me that generations of Cuomos have lived on the property for one-hundred years."

"They have."

"I don't understand."

"We don't have the deed to prove the property is ours. Whether because Rosa never got the legal paperwork or was displaced throughout the years, I'm not sure. Your father and I suspect Gianni's father didn't provide Rosa with the paperwork. Whatever the reason, we don't have a legal deed to prove the property is ours, and now we stand to lose it."

"But why? How?"

Sofia confirmed Luca five years ago moved into Villa Cuomo for no reason other than to cultivate grapes to use in Santini wine production. Sofia told Alessandra her suspicions that the variety of grape planted was valuable to the Santinis but that she had no proof.

"Your father and I believe the grapes Luca planted are no ordinary grapes."

"Why do you think that?"

"Luca offered to buy the land from your father for triple what it's worth."

"And you turned the offer down?"

"We did."

"That makes no sense. The villa hasn't been occupied since *nonna* died. You know what I mean."

"I do, but your father and I vowed to fulfil the promise carried out by generations of Cuomos on Rosa's behalf that the villa remains under Cuomo ownership."

Deep in thought, Alessandra hesitated for a moment. "You think Luca's squatting to steal the land? But why now? Why didn't Luca's father take possession earlier?"

"Public relations."

"The optics of throwing an old lady out of her home wouldn't have fared well for him," Alessandra concluded.

"That was our guess. Antonio Santini, your father believed, and I still do, doesn't have proof of land ownership. Otherwise, he would have taken possession already. So he's been planting all the necessary seeds to work toward it."

"So, I need to find proof the property was gifted to Rosa one hundred years ago. Easy." Alessandra released an exasperated breath.

"I don't know much about squatting laws in Europe. You'll need legal expertise to help you maneuver through this maze. And you'll need a good one since it's my understanding Luca is a lawyer."

"Wait, what?" Alessandra rose from the couch to pace the orderly living room. Could the man with the eyes so blue they looked transparent be so deceitful as to weave his way into taking her only valued possession? Her resentment skated into anger. "As soon as I get home, I'm throwing that perfectly carved ass out the door."

Although Alessandra snapped the comment with anger, Sofia said, "And I hear a tight, carved ass it is," to lighten the mood.

"Does Maria hold anything back?"

"Pfft, I'm only sharing with you what can be said in mixed company." Sofia snorted a laugh when she heard Alessandra begging not to say another word. "Anyway, you can't throw his butt out, honey."

"And why not?"

"Because you need him."

"Excuse me."

"For information. You need to find out about the grapes. You need him to tell you how long he's been on the property and why he's there. I know it's a lot to take on, but you can do this, Alessandra. I wouldn't have laid this on your lap if I didn't think you couldn't handle it. You're smart enough to outsmart the Santinis."

"I don't know."

"Think of Rosa. You wouldn't want to break our promise to her."

A short silence followed before Alessandra said, "Fine. I'll do it."

"Rosa and I thank you. I'm sorry for not being straight with you."

"I'm sorry for taking my frustration out on you."

"It can't be helped. You inherited the Cuomo's emotional instability." Sofia's snort of laughter was matched at the end of the line.

Alessandra told Sofia about Villa Cuomo and described how beautiful the island was. She told her about her sense of belonging from the moment she landed. Alessandra gave her aunt a condensed description of Maria and Francesco because they were too animated to summarize over a telephone conversation. She told Sofia of her first encounter with Luca, and both women had a good laugh over it.

"Use that experience to lure him into your lair. From what I understand, Luca does love the *signorine*."

"Aunt Sofia, you want me to prostitute myself."

"Of course not, but I do want you to use your feminine wiles to entrap him into giving you the needed information. Men who love the *signorine* as much as Luca does can be easily manipulated."

"You sound like an expert."

"How do you think I ensnared your uncle?"

Alessandra let out a laugh, and it warmed Sofia to hear her niece sounding cheerful again. "I'll do my best."

There was still more to discuss, but Alessandra cut the conversation there. Replacing the receiver in its cradle, Alessandra made a mental note to dig out Daniel DiBlassio's card when she got home.

Seven

FRANCESCO'S CAR FADING at the end of her driveway, Alessandra stabbed the key in the lock. Hinges creaked when she pushed the door open. She made a mental note to oil them.

Alessandra saw him the moment she stepped in. His hair, still wet from his shower, glistened around a tan face. His stubble of a beard, was freshly trimmed. Propped on the living room chair, his feet, crossed at the ankles, rested on the coffee table. On the one hand, he held Umberto Eco's *The Name of the Rose* and the other a glass of wine.

Did he have to look so damn gorgeous?

The blue eyes flicked up to Alessandra. "*Ciao*, did you enjoy your *passaggio*?" His melodic voice, warm and rich, flowed in concert with Pavarotti's Nessum Dorma, making her belly flutter.

"It wasn't a pleasure outing. I was out tending to ... business." Alessandra snapped with the anger from the conversation with her aunt, abruptly pulsing in her.

If Luca caught the cold chill in her voice, he didn't show it. His eyes were busy looking her over.

She looked damn sexy with those defiant green eyes sweeping over him. He liked her hair tied back but preferred it when it tumbled around her face as it had at their morning encounter. As much as he admired the fit of the tight Levi's, he liked her better naked.

"That's too bad. You should have been enjoying this beautiful day, but don't worry, we have many in Sicily. I hope you will take the time to enjoy them. If you like, I can show you around the town." Luca bookmarked his place in the book, set it down. "I just opened a bottle of Chianti. Would you like a glass?" Luca wondered how that tightly, puckered mouth tasted.

Luca surprised himself at the number of times he'd thought of her since that morning. He imagined how soft her skin would feel under his touch. The thought of how that curvy body fit with his had life spurting inside him. It had been some time since anyone set his blood on fire as she did.

"I don't want wine from you." Alessandra slanted an irritated look, prompted by his smugness.

Regardless of his drop-dead gorgeous appearance or how confident Maria and her aunt were, he was a good person, Alessandra had to maintain her focus. The simple fact was he was an unwelcome intruder in her home, possibly aiming to steal it from under her.

The thought made Alessandra's blood boil, and she said the first thing that came to her. "I want you out of my house."

"I know you don't mean that." Luca swirled the wine in his mouth, allowing the array of flavours on his palate to soak through.

The gesture spoke volumes to Alessandra. He was undoubtedly a man of social standing. She'd dated enough men to separate the cultured from the unsophisticated, and he was undeniably from the cultured classes. It begged to question why a billionaire vintner, lawyer, a man of privilege, was wasting his time squatting in her tiny home.

"Did you visit anywhere nice?" Luca's question came with that dimpled smile that pulled at the pit of a woman's stomach, but she wouldn't give him the satisfaction.

"No," she shot out with unusual sharpness.

The curt response made no impact on Luca. His mind was busy estimating how long it would take to get her out of her clothes and into bed.

"Would you care to join me for dinner tonight?"

"And why would I do that?" Alessandra's eyes blazed hot over him.

"Because I know deep down, you would love to have dinner with me." It pleased him greatly to see the quick jerkiness of her movements. It told him he made her nervous.

"You arrogant, presumptuous..."

"Ass." Luca finished at her hesitation. "It's good to express emotion."

"What makes you think I'm not involved?" The flush of heat flushed her cheeks when his eyes touched on her ringless finger. "I, ah, not wearing a ring means nothing."

"Your instinctive reaction to jam your hand into your pocket says otherwise." Luca watched her eyes pierce into him with the wrath of a predatory animal. God, he did like fire in a woman. "It's just dinner, the consumption of food unless you'd like to skip it and bring the night to a more exciting conclusion." The smirk twisted his lips.

Ugh, the arrogance. "I want nothing to do with you. What I want is for you to get out of my house. It's small enough for you to find the door," Alessandra barked and immediately regretted it, but the man could turn her from hot to cold in seconds.

"There's a great restaurant a few minutes from here. We could get to know each other over good food and a bottle of wine."

"No."

"You may end up liking me."

"Do you have any idea how irritating you are?"

"You may even end up begging me to sleep with you. In which case, I can guarantee you will end up liking me."

"Stop trying to get me into bed. I'm not going to sleep..." She let the sentence hang, refusing to fall into his trap.

Temper suited her, he thought. "I know, even if I was the last man on earth. Seeing as I'm not the last man on earth, logically, I still have a chance. *Si*?"

She had to admire his tenacity. Italian men, she thought with a roll of the eyes. "When hell freezes over," she said, with an icy smile as she bounded up the stairs.

"Challenge accepted," Luca called out after her.

EMOTIONALLY EXHAUSTED, ALESSANDRA FELL BACK ON her bed. Staring up at the ceiling, she tossed the information she'd been bombarded with in her mind. In the end, she settled on a hot shower to wash the day away was what she needed.

Under the spray of hot water, the idea came to Alessandra. Luca's invitation to dinner was the perfect chance to befriend and get to know him. Dinner was the perfect intimate setting to find out what made Mr. Boil-On-Her-Butt tick, and it was a better option than spending the night in her room.

"Excuse me?" she called from the top of the stairs.

Luca looked up from the book he hadn't read a word from since he heard the shower water run. Wrapped in a worn, pink bathrobe, her face flushing rosy, and the long ropes of wet hair clinging to her shoulder, he thought she looked stunning.

"I'd like to accept your dinner invitation."

Excitement stirred in Luca, but his response was one of casual disinterest. "All right. Meet me down here in an hour. Dress sexy."

"And why would I do that?"

"You don't want me to look sexier than you." Luca noticed the small smile that escaped her and considered it a small victory.

Eight

ALESSANDRA KNEW SHE was making a mistake by slicking into the black dress that hugged her like a glove and transformed her B-cup breasts into the swelled illusion she saw in the mirror. The Chanel number she'd saved for months was a third date outfit. It was the dress she reserved for the dates she hoped would lead to bedroom cardio. Not the message she wanted to convey to Luca, but it was the only dress she had.

Alessandra made a note on the pad she got from Maria to go shopping for a new wardrobe.

Mulling what to say to Luca, Alessandra dabbed perfume on her wrists, behind her ears, and absently down her cleavage.

Should she play it coy as her aunt suggested? *You seem so knowledgeable about grape farming. A city girl like me can learn a lot from a man like you.* Should she be duplicitous, as Maria suggested? *I know nothing about you, and I'd love to get to know you better.* Or should she be direct, like Francesco said? *What are you doing in my house?*

Alessandra elected to do none of those things. She'd let the conversation flow naturally. People were talkative by nature. They willingly told you everything if you expressed an interest in their lives. And getting a man to talk was simple, toss a sexual innuendo here and there, and he willingly bared his soul.

Dabbing fire-red lipstick, Alessandra took a slow, contemplative look at herself in the mirror. Her hair spilled loose around her face and shoulders. Men liked the sensual look of long, flowing hair, and she imagined Luca was that type. Alessandra gave off way more sexy than she wanted, but she'd use it to her benefit.

Luca felt the air change the moment she started down the stairs. A smile played across her face when his mouth fell open.

The long chestnut hair that tumbled in waves around her face, and the body-hugging dress tracing curves, stunned and dazed him. Legs that never seem to end spearing from a thigh-high hem shot a bolt of fire through Luca.

He'd had his share of women, but Alessandra was different. The hot punch of lust that came from the women Luca took to bed was different with her. With Alessandra, it was a jolt of unfamiliar but wonderful emotions. Alessandra made him feel in ways he never had.

Alessandra didn't only affect the part of him his mother referred to as his inept "lower brain." Alessandra made him feel like a giddy teenager melting into a puddle of anxiety and tension as butterflies swarmed his stomach.

"Do I out-sexy you?" Alessandra tossed her hair, sending waves of chestnut in the air. Luca search deep in his upper brain clouded in a thick fog for the words that didn't come. "The cat got your tongue?"

"No, ah, you, ah, look great." Luca didn't know what it was about Alessandra that turned him into a blathering idiot.

For a moment, she too lost her train of thought.

Seeing the power in the broad-shouldered build, the taut arms, and hard chest against powder-blue silk rendered her speechless.

When Alessandra found her voice, she said, "I'm glad you think so because it's the only dress I own right now."

"Excellent choice."

Alessandra's lips curving, she leaned into Luca. "Lead the way, Mr. Santini." Her mouth, a whisper from his ear, shut down his upper brain and activated the lower one.

"Yes. Yes, of course." Luca fumbled with the door handle. When he managed to click it open, he said, "I don't know your name."

"It's Alessandra Cuomo." The long lashes above the emerald green eyes that fluttered in his direction left him staring, frozen on the spot. "Are you coming?"

Men were simple creatures, Alessandra thought when Luca, unable to find his voice, hemmed his response. How right her aunt was.

Settled in the marshmallow-soft leather of Luca's Maserati, he set it in gear and pulled out of the driveway. "How do you like your visit to Sicily so far?"

"I love it. This is my first time back since I was a child, and it feels as if I never left." Alessandra rolled the window down. The scent of sea air blowing inland flowed into the car, and she could see a full moon begin its rise to replace the outgoing sun.

"Sicily has that effect. The sea, sun, weather, the people, everything about it is perfect, but I'm biased. How long will you be staying?" Luca turned right at Via Pompeo instead of winding onto the coastal road.

"I'm not sure yet. I have matters to sort out and will be sticking around for as long as it takes."

"Well, I hope your visit is a long one."

For her benefit, Luca wound the car through the town. Alessandra rolled down her window, craned her neck to take in the view of the seventeenth-century villas nestled amid low-lying mountains rooted in luscious green. She caught glimpses of the olive and almond groves at the foothill. Patches of wild borage and cape sorrel flowers painted the sloping green hills with blue and yellow.

Alessandra made out the ribbon of road that wound from the highest peak of the mountain and wound down to the base where a quaint chapel jutted out from between almond and olive groves.

"Those villas were once home to royalty. Many of the townspeople are believed to be their descendants, although they'd be hard-pressed to prove it," said Luca.

"Why is that?"

"In the early part of the seventeenth century, an earthquake triggered tsunamis that destroyed coastal towns and killed thousand people."

A flash of sadness crept into Alessandra's eyes. "My dad said he was a descendant from royalty. I always chalked it up to wild imaginings."

"You may be a princess."

Alessandra snorted a laugh. "Do I look like a descendant from royalty?"

"No. You're more beautiful than any royalty I've seen." Luca's comment made her cheeks heat. "Whether you are or not, you'll be treated like one tonight. My friend owns this place," Luca said, turning into *Nardello's* parking lot.

The air flowing through the car window was ripe with the rich scents of garlic, grilled fish, and the sweet-spicy scent of tomato sauce. "That smells heavenly."

"And the food tastes even better. Now you'll see how we do Italian food in Sicily. I hope you enjoy it," Luca said, with an endearing vulnerability Alessandra didn't expect.

The restaurant teemed with diners. Tables were filled with couples and families in animated conversation, punctuated with laughter flowed over the stream of accordion music. Candles spearing from wine bottles flickered on salmon-coloured tablecloths. Out on the patio, lanterns twinkling bright swayed in a soft breeze. The sound of foaming surf lapped the shore.

Dario, a gregarious, stylishly dressed man in his sixties, greeted Luca with a kindly smile and warm embrace before escorting them to the table overlooking a sea plunged in black. Snapping the RISERVATO sign off the table, Dario informed them their server would be out with their specially prepared meal and a Vermentino wine bottle.

The European sea bass was mouth-watering. The wine was smooth, richly fruity, with a delicate bouquet and the perfect pairing. At least that's what Luca told Alessandra. Once she took a sip and savoured it, Alessandra couldn't argue with the assessment. They easily drank the entire bottle between them.

Luca made no mention of the Santini name on their bottle's label or those at every table, and Alessandra didn't bring it up. She made a mental note to read up on the Santinis at the first opportunity.

"By the way, they'll be installing a telephone at the house this week." Alessandra took spoonfuls of tiramisu, oohed and ahhed without shame with an amused Luca watching on. "This is to die for." Taking the last of her dessert, she eyed his. "You going to eat that?"

Luca slid his plate to her. "It's too bad about the telephone. I like the quiet, but it's your home."

The glow of triumph in Alessandra's face would have had a better impact if her mouth wasn't full of tiramisu. "So you do acknowledge that it's my home."

She pulled back when he leaned in with his napkin. "You're dripping chocolate," he said and surprised him when she leaned in for him to wipe it clean. "Would you like another piece?"

"I do, but I think I've had enough for today."

The waitress dropped what she was doing and rushed to their table when Luca waved her over. After a brief exchange of suggestive smiles, Luca sang out an order for two cognacs and two espressos.

The waitress, on her way to the bar, Luca said, "Of course I recognize it's your home. I never said otherwise."

"Then why are you living in my home?"

"Your family wasn't making use of the land excellent for cultivating grapes."

"But why on my land?" Candlelight flickered in the intense eyes that gazed at him.

"For winemaking, of course."

"I understand it was for a purpose. My question is, why on Villa Cuomo land when you had no permission to do so?"

Her eyes turned that provocative shade of tempestuous green he liked as irritation set in. She needed to learn to relax, Luca thought. "But, I did have permission."

Alessandra's wine glass came down on the table with a thud. "Not from anyone in my family."

Luca remained silent while the waitress, never leaving his eyes, set their cognacs and coffees on the table. "Grazie, *amore*," he said, with a wink and a smile that had her giggling like a schoolgirl all the way to the kitchen. "Your *Nonna* Teresa allowed me. She was fully aware of what I was doing on her land."

"What are you talking about?"

"Your *nonna* allowed me to cultivate grapes on her land."

Dubiously, Alessandra glanced up at him. "She did not."

"Oh, but she did. I paid her generously to use her land and arranged for her to get a cut from the crop's sale. Your *nonna* and me, we were like this." Luca held tightly crossed fingers in the air. "Drink your cognac while it's warm."

"You're lying," she snapped and absently tossed back some of her drink.

"What would I benefit from lying to you?" He picked up his cognac, sipped.

"My family knows nothing about this." Alessandra's raised tone got her curious stares from nearby diners.

"Have more cognac. It'll calm you down."

"I don't need calming down."

Luca cocked a brow when nearby tables turned to stare at them. "Only your *nonna* and I knew. When I initially approached her with the plan, it took some convincing, but eventually, she warmed to the idea of cultivating grapes on her land. We made the deal contingent on me, agreeing never to make our venture public. Until now, I kept my promise."

Alessandra gnawed on her bottom lip. "Why wouldn't she want anyone to know?"

"Maybe pride or a sense of independence, what I know for sure is that it's what she wanted, and I complied."

"She needed the money to survive and didn't want to let on." Alessandra drank deeply to smooth her guilt.

"The money may have been how it started, but that's not how she felt years in. She kept telling me Rosa would have been happy with our alliance and to see the land put to use. Do you know who Rosa is?"

Alessandra nodded.

"Well, your *nonna* went about town strutting like a peacock when everyone praised her for her keen business mind and savvy management style."

"What do you mean?" Alessandra watched him spoon sugar into her coffee when she nodded.

"I went along with her in letting everyone think she was doing everything although it was me who hired the manager, the team of hired hands, supervised the planting and harvesting. In the end, she gained the staff and manager's loyalty with her cooking, and the nosy town's people were none the wiser."

"Thank you." Alessandra's tone was contrite at the thought a stranger came to her grandmother's aid when she needed it most.

"You were far away. An ocean between families complicates life. Besides, if I know your grandmother, she wouldn't have asked for your help. She'd see it as an intrusion in your lives and dependence on her part."

"That's no excuse. She was family, our family, and we should have done more." Alessandra's gaze was lost in the coffee in her cup.

The cacophony of sounds around them filled the ensuing silence. Wine glasses clinked over the sound of servers reciting the day's specials. Over the rattle of cutlery on china, a mother pled with her son to eat.

"Don't feel guilty. Your *nonna* was a formidable woman who needed to do things her way, on her terms. She wouldn't have taken a handout from you. She never took one from me or anyone around her."

"Thank you for saying that." Alessandra reached for her cognac, found the glass empty. Luca signalled the waitress for another round. "When she passed away, you moved in to maintain the crop. Was that when you contacted my dad to make him the offer to buy the land?"

Luca nodded. "He turned me down. I tried to contact him several times afterwards, but..." Luca went silent when the waitress approached the table with their drinks.

"When was the last time you called?" Alessandra said when they were alone.

"As recent as a few months ago, I..." He paused, sensing he'd stirred something in her, some struggle deep in her when darkness filled her eyes. "I'm sorry if I've said something to upset you," he said, falling into the silence she demanded.

For a long while, they sat listening to the ceaseless motion of waves riled up by a wind that had steadily picked up as the night wore on.

"My father, my entire family, was killed by a drunk driver several months ago," she finally said.

Sympathy stirred in Luca when the tears welled in her eyes. "I'm so sorry for your loss, Alessandra."

"Except for Aunt Sofia, my mother, father, and eight-year-old twin brothers, the only family I had, are gone." Luca could hear the loss in her tone. He saw the pain in her eyes. As tempted as he was to reach for her hand, he held back. "It's why I'm here. I decided to come to get away from the constant reminder of what happened, get my head back in order. The last few months have been ... difficult for me."

Luca set down his cognac, left his fingers on the stem to run up and down to keep himself from reaching for her hand. "And when you got here, to what you thought would be a sanctuary, you find me intruding your space."

"Something like that."

"I'm sorry. I never meant to cause you any stress or add to your pain."

"I told you to get out of my home."

"You did."

"Then why didn't you leave when I asked you to?"

"Because I know you didn't mean it." He noted her lips tightening into a long, firm line.

"Why would I ask you to leave my home and not mean it?" She gave him a scorching look. She'd bared her soul, and he dismissed her as quickly as she had.

"Because deep down, you find me irresistible," Luca said to lighten the mood.

"Is that so?"

"It's so."

"You're incorrigible." A soft grin followed Alessandra's feigned irritation.

"Incorrigible? That's a new one, and I've been called many things." His comment netted him a grin, but underneath it, he saw the pain in her eyes. "I'll be out of the house tomorrow."

Alessandra leaned back in her chair, gave him a contemplative look. She needed the solitude she'd travelled across an ocean in search of, but she also needed his help. Until she secured the property and got the crop information, she needed him to stay put.

"You can stay, but I have two requests."

"You want me to move into your bedroom tonight and make wild passionate love to you all night." Luca joked, masking his delight at her decision to let him stay.

She edged forward the candlelight flickered in the eyes that narrowed into slits. "I'm setting the record straight. Sleeping with you is never going to happen." She raised a finger to silence him when he opened his mouth. "Never. I have a feeling you have enough women to keep you busy. I want you to give me my space, my alone time when I ask for it. There are going to be times when I'll want to be by myself to work things through in my head."

"Done," Luca said, and with curious eyes, asked, "What's your second request?"

"You teach me everything there is to know about grape farming. I guess I should at least learn the basics seeing as my land is chock full of grapevines."

His response followed without the resistance she expected. "Farming is my passion. I'd love to teach you everything I know," Luca said, wondering how his father was going to react if he found out he was teaching a Cuomo Santini's best-kept secret.

Part II

The Middle
And suddenly you know:
It's time to start something new
And trust the magic of new beginnings.
—Eckhart von Hochheim

Nine

IT WAS ELEVEN in the morning when Alessandra rolled out of bed. Suffering from a wine-throbbing headache, she dragged herself to the bathroom. Throwing cold water on her face, she eyed herself in the mirror and saw the smile on her face.

Maybe it was a by-product of the wine consumed last night at dinner, but she'd had an enjoyable night. Luca had been a pleasant dinner companion and a great listener.

Alessandra couldn't remember the last time she'd been with a man willing to listen or talk about anything other than himself. She couldn't remember the last time she had a guilt-free time—since her family's death.

Brushing hair away from her face, Alessandra stared at herself in the mirror and saw a different woman. All the therapy she'd undergone in the months following the accident hadn't netted the positive results of one dinner with a sympathetic listening ear. She had Luca to thank.

The idea struck her, and she hopped into the shower. Drying herself, she bundled wet hair into a ponytail and threaded it through the red baseball cap. She slipped on a white T-shirt and red polka-dotted shorts and headed for the kitchen.

Alessandra fished eggs, cheese, and a selection of fruit from the refrigerator. That would do for the fruit salad and a cheesy omelette—the only thing she knew how to cook.

She'd serve the eggs with Maria's bread. That would make up for her lack of cooking skills.

The lace apron she found in the drawer fastened around her waist, Alessandra beat eggs, sliced apples, bananas, and grapes. She topped the fruit with honey and scooped it into two bowls. Next, Alessandra poured water into the coffee maker and spooned coffee. The coffee brewing, she slathered butter on four slices of bread.

"What's this?" Luca asked when he walked into the kitchen. He wore a white T-shirt and the trademark body-hugging jeans she'd come to appreciate more by the day.

"Lunch, my way to thank you for a lovely evening. I can't remember the last time..." I didn't feel guilty about enjoying myself, "I felt so at ease."

"I had a great time too, but this isn't necessary."

"It is, and don't get excited. It's only fruit salad and a cheese omelette, my only cooking skill." Alessandra swept a dimpled smile over her shoulder that set the butterflies in his stomach fluttering and head butting each other.

"Fritatta."

"I'm sorry?"

"In Italy, an omelette is called a frittata. Makes a fried egg sound more exotic, doesn't it?"

Alessandra let out a soft feminine laugh when she caught him eyeing the mess on the kitchen counter. "I'm what you call a don't-know-what-the-hell-I'm-doing-in-the-kitchen cook. I'm hoping Maria's bread and pastries will make up for my limited cooking skills. I have to tell you that woman can bake." She tossed the beaten egg onto the hot pan.

"And don't even get me started on her cooking. It's no wonder Francesco worships the ground she walks on. I would too if I was fed deliciousness every day." Alessandra warbled on in a perpetually good mood, oblivious to whether he was listening or not. He was.

Luca hung on her every word and took pleasure in her happiness. He especially liked the measure of life she brought to the house—to him.

"There's freshly brewed espresso on the stove. Why don't you pour us a cup?" She walked the fruit salad bowls to the table.

"I'm sure you make a mean frittata and fruit salad." Luca filled two cups with coffee, set them on the table along with linen napkins and cutlery.

"Oops, I guess I forgot to set the table. I can confidently make a one-hour long presentation to a room full of strangers, but my mind checks out with anything kitchen-related."

"Then, thank your lucky stars, I've been domesticated. My mother made sure of that from a young age. She never was, so she figured I should be for when I married her clone. She claims we marry our parents, and I am therefore destined to marry a non-cook."

Alessandra flashed him a smile. "My mother said the same, or at least she hoped I would marry my opposite since she could never domesticate me." Her voice broke, and Luca fell into the silence with her. "Take a seat and start on the fruit salad. The omelette will be ready soon."

Wanting her in his sight, Luca eased himself into the chair facing her. "Frittata."

"Sorry, the frittata." Alessandra sprinkled cheese on the frying eggs.

"Make it a good helping for me. I'm starved."

"You may not want such a large serving after you taste it."

Luca gave her a dimpled smile. "You're looking very sporty this morning."

"I thought I'd go for a run after breakfast. I do about three miles now. I stopped running after... I need to work up to the five I used to. I'm looking forward to running on the beach, next to sparkling blue water with waves lapping the shore and egrets squawking. It's a sense of calmness and peace I need right now. I'm sorry, I'm blathering." She was, but it was the first time in a long while she felt at ease sharing.

"You're not blathering, and as your housemate, I want you to feel you can talk to me whenever about anything."

"Anything?" The smirk on her face made him wince.

"Okay, not everything. I don't know how to handle discussions on women's delicates or split ends. I know nothing about that given I have such perfect hair."

Alessandra's laugh was full and rich. "Regardless, you may regret the offer, Luca." It was the first time she said his name, and it sounded like music to him.

She'd bottled up feelings and emotions in the past few months, which needed voicing. There were days she felt like a dam ready to burst, but with no one to open up to, the dam swelled inside her. Still, she reminded herself they'd just met. She couldn't verbalize every thought she had to a stranger, particularly one she may be going into a legal battle with.

"I know we've only known each other for a couple of days, but I'm here for you." Luca lifted eyebrows to drive the point home.

"That's kind and brave of you, but instead of talking, I run. I started up again a month ago. My therapist recommended it to help with my mental health and as a great stress reliever. It took some time to take her advice to heart, but when I finally did, it helped a lot. Running clears my mind. I'm used to running on busy sidewalks crammed with people, next to traffic and smog. A calm scenery will add to my sense of tranquillity."

"If tranquillity is what you need, tranquillity is what you'll get." Luca watched Alessandra absently run the spatula through runny eggs. "You seem to be scrambling the frittata."

"Oh, shit."

Luca took the spatula from Alessandra and walked her to a chair. "Have a seat. Start on your fruit salad, and I'll take care of the frittata." He held a hand up when she started to speak.

Luca spooned raw egg over the cracks. "There, it's now a frittata again. You're very much like your grandmother was, a strong, independent woman."

"How do you figure?"

"You've dealt with a lot and persevered. Many would have given up or broken down."

Alessandra set the spoonful of fruit down. "I did break down. I've been broken for some time. The nights are the worst. It's when I feel the emptiness most. Sometimes I have bad nightmares." Alessandra shut down, and Luca didn't press.

For the first time, Luca wished he could take on someone else's pain—her pain. He wasn't sure when it happened or how, but Alessandra got into his head, and he couldn't shake her out. Not that he wanted to, but he didn't know how to deal with the wave of unfamiliar, unmanageable emotions she unleashed in him. He knew how to handle the conniving, manipulative women, who tricked their way into his life and bed, but he didn't know what to do with someone as trusting and sincere as Alessandra was.

"Do you run?" she asked.

Luca shifted his gaze from the frying egg to Alessandra. "No, I'm up by five and out in the field by five-thirty, at the latest. During harvesting season, I'm out there throughout the night. I guess you could say that's how I get my workout."

And a good workout it was, Alessandra thought, sinking back in her seat and admiring the smooth line of muscling against cotton. "My compliments to the chef," Alessandra said, digging into the frittata he served her.

"How you handle the spatula makes a big difference."

Her lips twisted into an easy smile. "Luca, can I ask you for a favour?"

There was his name on her lips again, flowing like the murmuring waters of a trickling creek. "Anything."

"Would you drive me to the closest bookstore or library?"

"There's a library in town. I can drive you there."

"I'd run or walk there, but I don't know the town well enough to make the trek on my own, and I've bothered Francesco enough these past couple of days."

"It's no problem. Can I ask the purpose of your visit?" He scooped eggs and bit into buttered bread.

"I'd like to get Italian books to brush up on the language while I'm here. You know when in Rome and all that. I haven't spoken Italian in so long. I'm afraid I need some serious brushing up. I figured it'd be easier to communicate with Francesco and Maria." Alessandra took a bite of buttered bread.

"If you like, I can help you." Luca scooped eggs with his remaining piece of bread.

"I don't want to impose. You seem to have a lot on your plate." Alessandra set her untouched slice of bread on his plate.

"It's no imposition. I'm usually back from the field around this time. We can set aside some time every day. Say late morning."

"Sounds perfect. That way, I can get my runs in. If I don't get them in early in the day, I let them go by the wayside."

"All right, we're set." Luca emptied his coffee cup.

"Refill?"

"Please." Luca watched her wander to the stove. He could get used to her, to the routine of home life.

Alessandra made Luca feel a part of something wonderful and fulfilling, which made him feel as if he more than just existed. Something he'd been searching for years.

"There's so much I need to learn." She wrapped her arms around folded legs.

"You will. What are you interested in learning," he asked, wanting to know everything about Alessandra Cuomo.

"I'd like to learn how to drive stick. I had better learn if I'm sticking around for a while. I want to try my hand at painting. My grandmother had a knack for it. Did you know she painted the art hanging in the living room and my bedroom?"

"They were her pride and joy. I'll tell you all I know about your *nonna*."

"I'd appreciate that." Alessandra pushed eggs around her plate. "I'd also like to learn how to cook something other than eggs."

Luca looked into her eyes with a smile. "I can help you with that. I can help you with all of it."

"Thanks, and I know you're a cultivating expert and that you can teach me how to speak Italian and drive, but cooking."

"I love to cook, and I had the best teacher. My paternal nana was a great cook. My mother is much like you. Boiling water is a challenge." Luca caught the napkin she balled and tossed at him midair. "Nana taught me everything I know about cooking, and I'm more than happy to pass on to you everything she taught me."

Alessandra raised an appreciative brow. "I'm impressed, but I couldn't impose."

"No imposition. I'll enjoy it as much as you will." Luca's eyes held an expression in them that tugged at her.

"Then I'll take you up on your offer. No. I'm cleaning up. It's my thank-you lunch." Alessandra took the dishes from him and walked them to the sink. "Are you involved in anything other than farming this property?" Alessandra said casually as she set rinsed dishes on the rack.

Luca shook his head. "I love working with the land. I don't know if you know, but farming is a complicated science. Our forefathers made it look simple, but there's a lot of knowledge that goes into growing, particularly when it comes to a vineyard..." Luca cut himself off when he realized he was willing to tell her secrets his father wouldn't appreciate.

"I guessed as much. Last call," she said, waving the coffee maker.

"I'm coffeed out."

"I hope you have the patience to teach me what you know."

"I do. Besides, I'm guessing you're a fast learner."

Alessandra smiled guiltily. She was surprised at how much she was already regretting seducing him into her scheme to extract information. She had to remind herself she did it to keep a long-kept promise to Rosa.

Ten

LUCA WATCHED ALESSANDRA launch into a military-like assault on the uncompromising librarian who refused to recognize her as a resident of the town and denied her a library card. The two women were formidable opponents, and the fact that neither understood what the other said made the animated debate all the more compelling to watch.

There were hand gestures from the librarian. From Alessandra, there was eye rolling, accentuated with frustrated exhales. At one point, Alessandra emptied her purse's contents on the librarian's desk in search of proof. She came up empty.

People gathered to watch the Americana duke it out with the unyielding *Signora* Leone. Luca saw the trio of twentyish-year-old men exchanging money while two pointed to Alessandra and one to the librarian. The pièce de résistance came when Alessandra slammed the desk with her palms, and the librarian matched her blazing eyes dagger for dagger.

"*Scusi.*" Luca stepped in between Alessandra and the fiftyish woman behind the black, thick-rimmed glasses to the men's disappointing groans, but the argument now bordered on the physical. A flash of Luca's dreamy, long-lashed eyes, along with words accompanied by his liquefying smile, had the librarian withering into a sniggering teenage girl. "And that's how you do it?" he murmured in Alessandra's ear.

Eyes rolling heavenward, Alessandra snatched the library card from Luca's hand.

"Thank you, Luca. I appreciate your assistance." He mimicked her voice.

"Thank you," she snapped. "Did you offer to sleep with her in exchange for the card?" It wasn't how she'd meant to put it, but it was out now.

A pleased smile curved his lips at the jealous words camouflaged with anger. "For your information, I used my charm. I can be persuasively charming." He paused for her reaction, but all she did was give him her back as she turned to head walk away. "Don't you want to know what I said?"

"Nope." She walked into the third isle when he steered her there.

"Since you're so curious, I told her she, being as youthful as you, could understand your penchant to quell your curiosity about your new home by reading about it, and her books would help you do that."

With a dramatic eye roll, she said, "Lucky for you, there are gullible women to inflate your already enormous ego."

Luca pressed his lips together to suppress the smile. "It's not gullibility. It's a talent. You have heard that you can catch more women with flattery?"

"I think you mean you can catch more flies with honey than vinegar," she corrected, heading into the library's historical section with him trailing.

"Take the one next to it." Luca pointed to the book on Sicilian history. "I said what I meant. I coined the phrase. You know it's interchangeable."

The cocky expression she wished she could slap off his face jumped at her. "It is, is it?"

"Sure, it is. Try it out on me. Go ahead, flatter me."

"I'm good, thanks." Turning to walk away, she caught the eyes on them. A collection of women had gathered and was eyeing Luca like a sinful, delicious cannoli. "Friends of yours?"

She was jealous. A wicked grin spread slowly across his face. "The townspeople are very friendly." Luca gave the ogling women a wink that made them break out in girlish giggles. "There's a better dictionary than that one somewhere around here."

Alessandra's brows winged up. "They're not townspeople. They're ogling women. This one?" When he nodded, she pulled the dictionary off the shelf.

"Back to my quote, you can catch more women with flattery." Luca shirked when she tossed the book on top of the pile in his arms.

"Are you telling me you're swelled head leads you to surmise you're capable of flattering all these women?"

"You should try it sometime. It really works. I'll help you master it. Try flattering me."

Alessandra leaned into him. "I'm a slow learner. How about you help me master it over lunch? Buy me a pizza and a glass of wine." Her mouth, a whisper from his, made his breath hitch and his heart skip a few beats.

"Yes. Sure. Of course," he said, on command.

Amateur, she thought, pivoting toward the checkout counter.

Books checked out, Luca drove them to his favourite trattoria. Under the glow of a brilliant sun in the restaurant's outdoor patio, Luca and Alessandra shared a pizza and a glass of red wine. Appreciating each other's company, they spoke about nothing of consequence.

After lunch, Luca took Alessandra to a souvenir shop where he bought her a map. "I'll always be available to chauffeur you, but I thought it a good idea you familiarize yourself with the town's lay." Luca sat on the steps of the municipal building, and Alessandra followed suit. Unfolding the map, Luca pointed out the points of interest. "The town is small enough to access most places on foot."

"That's perfect, and thank you for taking the time to show me around."

"You don't have to keep thanking me." Luca met the wave of the women whizzing past on a Vespa. He smiled at the group of uniformed schoolchildren walking past them.

"You seem to have lots of friends."

Luca's mouth eased into a playful curve. "What can I say? I'm popular."

"And modest." She toed her flats off and flexed her feet.

"Are you tired?"

"No, and I'm having a great time. Thank..." She stopped when his left brow arched. "Why can't you let me say something without a commentary?"

"I was about to tell you I have too. Probably more so than you have," Luca said, thinking today was the best day in recent memory. Alessandra filled the loneliness, the void he'd felt in his life for a long time and didn't know how to fill. "You've made me see the town in a different light." He found it hard not to stare when the light breeze fanned her hair and sent the sweet floral scent of her shampoo his way. Drinking it in, he felt the hum of need burn.

Colour flooded Alessandra's face when she recognized the look of desire in the eyes that held hers. "Everything is beautiful here, and there's so much history, a prideful history," she said, to distract.

"We'll read up on it during your Italian lessons." Luca leaned back on his elbows, stretched his legs out. "After you rest up, we'll get a granita."

"A granita?"

"It's frozen flavoured ice with more emphasis on the flavour than the frozen. Sicilians invented it."

"I'd love to try one." Alessandra's expression of beaming excitement made Luca broadly smile. He wished the day to never end.

Eleven

1882 - Gianni & Rosa

GIANNI STEPPED BACK to study his work.

"It's beautiful. You're very talented, Gianni." Rosa admired the painting. Beautifully executed strokes of colour displayed artistry she envied.

The painting portrayed his home and the colourful gardens hemming it. At its core, the fountain of a goddess' eyes reverently gazing to the sky held secrets. Rosa could almost hear the sound of water spilling from the urn in her hands.

Gianni lay next to Rosa under the dense canopy of greenery and twisted branches of the olive tree swaying in a warm wind. The steady drone of sea waves lapping the shore filled the silence.

"You think so?" Propping himself on his elbow, he turned to face her.

"I wish I had your talent."

"You do. You paint as well as I do." Gianni loosened the scarf bundling her hair to let the long, dark curls tumble around her delicate face the way he liked it. She looked like a beautiful siren emerging from the sea. "It's yours, *amore*. I want you to have the painting."

"Really?"

"Really." Gianni leaned in for a taste of her mouth.

In one instant, he became intimate with the texture of her tongue. His needy mouth pressed more tightly, took, ravaged.

The kiss became desperate, needy, and she pulled back. "Is everything all right, Gianni?"

"I love you so much."

Rosa's eyes flashed a wild blue when he went sullen. "What's wrong, Gianni?"

"My mother says what I feel for you is infatuation. I rarely question her wisdom, but I do now." Gianni raised a finger to stroke her cheek. "Do you know how I feel when you are not with me?"

"I hope the same way I do. As if, there's no meaning to the day. As if, life did not matter. As if the sun, the moon, and the stars stopped shining. As if the oxygen has been taken from you. As if, I'm nothing without you."

Gianni nodded. "I've never been in love, and I don't know if these feelings are what everyone feels, but in my heart, I know I will always feel this way for you because these feelings are fierce in me." The hurt in Gianni's eyes should have been a warning of what was to come, but his voice was level and calm. "I love you, *amore*. I love you so much."

There was something so sad in his tone, and Rosa couldn't help but feel anxious. "I know, Gianni."

His throat went so dry he could barely speak. "You know I would never do anything to hurt you."

"I know that too, Gianni. Is something wrong?" Rosa felt the chill in her bones.

Gianni took a deep breath as he calculated how to tell her. "My father gave me his word he would stop threatening your family, stop his harassing them if..."

Nausea churned in her stomach. "If what, Gianni?"

"If I agree to marry a French Contessa called Beatrice." He watched her drift into a stunned silence. "And move to France."

"I see." Rosa's voice dropped to a whisper.

Gianni lumbered to the cliff's edge overlooking the spread of blue sea. "If I don't, you and your family will live a miserable existence. If I marry the Contessa, he vowed never to threaten you and them with unemployment or worse." His bitterness came through in his voice at the thought of his father's manipulation of their lives.

Rosa rose to join him. "I don't care. He can threaten me all he wants," the rebellious woman in her snapped, but she knew he was right.

"If I marry the Contessa, all that goes away, *amore*. You and your family will keep your jobs and never have to look over your shoulders," Gianni said, hoping to drive the point without having to tell her he'd already agreed to the marriage.

Along the water's edge, terns darted in and out with the roll of waves that hit sand then got sucked back in. A brilliant gold sun hung in the western sky. In a few hours, they would watch it descend and be replaced by a white moon. It was a sight Gianni watched with Rosa time and again, and he couldn't imagine not sharing it with her ever again.

Quietly for a time, they stood side by side, only the sea moving.

Gianni touched Rosa then, had to. Her hands were like ice. "I don't want to leave you, but you know this is what

I must do. If I don't, he'll make it his mission to make everyone's lives, including yours and mine, a living hell."

She looked at him with devastated eyes. "I know."

He looked down at their joined hands. "I leave tomorrow."

She let that sink in before eyes drenched and vulnerable looked up to him. "I understand. I do, Gianni," Rosa said, to ease the pain, anger, despair she saw in his eyes, and because she did.

They were from different worlds, with breeding that set them apart. There were restrictions, which Rosa tried to understand that dictated how to feel and love. There were rules, which compelled their worlds never to come together. Rosa knew this day would come, but she never imagined it would hurt this much.

The hurt in Rosa's eyes added to the pain Gianni felt in his heart. "I will always love you."

"And I you." Rosa felt him brush the tears off her cheeks as his flowed down his face.

"Rosa, I..."

She glided her lips to his to stop him from talking. She couldn't love him more than she did then. To sacrifice himself, move to a foreign country and start a life not of his choosing was a life sentence no one deserved. And he willingly did it for her and her family's wellbeing.

She never imagined she could hurt so much for the man she would never see again or hate as much as she did the man who drove them apart. Saying goodbye would be the hardest thing she would ever do. Vowing not to waste time mourning his loss until then, Rosa took Gianni's hand and walked him back to the deserted house.

"Let's make our last hours memorable."

Twelve

UNDER THE BOUGAINVILLEA covered patio, dripping with colour overlooking the sea that stretched to the horizon until sapphire waters melded into one with the sky, teacher and pupil sat at the cast iron table. Filling her lungs with morning air and exhaling in frustration, Alessandra winced at the mispronounced words as she read aloud.

"Relax. Enjoy the language, the sound of it. Until you do, it'll feel like a chore, and it shouldn't. Italian is the language of love. It was meant to flow off your tongue like a symphony."

Alessandra's brows snapped together. "But..."

"No buts. Read another paragraph. Before you do, close your eyes, take a deep breath, and exhale the bad."

"It's hard to relax when all I'm doing is mispronounciating everything." Alessandra sighed when Luca cocked a brow. "Now I'm mangling my mother tongue."

"Picture me naked." Luca's smile, full of mischief, made Alessandra snort a laugh. "I hope you're laughing at the suggestion and not at the naked image of me flashing in your head because, and not to toot my own horn, I look great naked." At that, she broke out into a fit of uncontrollable laughter. "Relaxed now?" When she nodded, he said, "Read the next paragraph."

Alessandra did, and the words flew out like an orchestrated melody. "I did it."

"You'll be speaking Italian in no time."

"You're a great teacher."

"You're an eager student. Now, can you tell me what made you laugh so hard? On second thought, I don't want to know." Luca pushed to his feet, setting a couple of doves to flit from one olive tree to another to continue their serenade. "I think you've earned a glass of wine."

"I'll get it."

"I will, while you read the next sentences out loud."

In the kitchen, Luca poked his head in the refrigerator and chose a bottle of Valpolicella. He'd made sure not to bring Santini labelled wine into the house for fear of prompting questions he wasn't ready to answer—not yet. Luca wanted to get to know Alessandra without the imposition of his complicated life.

Luca uncorked and poured chilled wine into two glasses. With a wistful expression on his face, he flicked his eyes out the window. The patio, flooded with morning sun, circled Alessandra as she ran her finger over the passage she read. He watched the frustration on her face replaced by a smile of accomplishment when the words flowed from her lips with ease.

Luca etched the scene in his mind.

Alessandra brought life to the house and meaning to Luca's life. He saw everything in a new light, and he had her to thank for that. Luca lost his way when he went to work alongside his father as his corporation's lawyer.

Law was his father's dream, not his. Everything Luca did was to please his father.

Being born into the Santini name came with demands—so many demands. The expectation to maintain the Santini image, reputation, and legacy dating back centuries was taxing.

The Santini name opened doors, but in equal measure, slammed them shut. Unlike his father, who was a proud Santini, Luca would have traded the name in a snap if it meant he could live his life the way he wanted. Uncomplicated and undemanding where happiness, not money, was the driving force was how he wanted to live it. It was the reason he was at Villa Cuomo, tending to the fields rather than practicing law at the Santini Winery Corporation.

But even the lands he loved hadn't brought Luca the satisfaction or fulfillment he sought. Alessandra had.

In a matter of days, she'd changed Luca's life, and for the first time, he felt happy, fulfilled, and complete. Alessandra gave Luca purpose, brought meaning to everything he did. Luca never thought such completeness was possible or existed.

The conversation with his father resonated in Luca's mind. The knot at the base of Luca's stomach, one that had been there since meeting with him, squeezed tighter. Regardless of what his father believed, the facts were Luca couldn't do what he asked. As formidable a man as Antonio Santini was, he wouldn't get what he wanted.

This time Luca wouldn't allow his father to succeed.

Luca had to figure out a way to keep Alessandra from his father's reach. He wasn't going to allow him to hurt her as he hurt everyone who got in his way. Luca determined to do anything necessary for Alessandra, even if that meant going up against his father because he was falling in love with Alessandra.

Thirteen

ESCORTING THE TECHNICIAN out, Alessandra picked up her newly installed telephone and called her aunt.

After giving Sofia a detailed summary of her dinner conversation with Luca, the air hummed for a spell as emotions churned in Sofia. "I didn't know, but Mama was as stubborn as she was proud. She'd never turned to us for help."

"Luca said as much."

Sofia heard Luca's name spoken with a quiet pleasure. "You're not sleeping with him, are you, Alessandra?"

"Jesus, Aunt Sofia."

Sofia dismissed the defiant denial. "Well, are you?"

An ocean between them and the woman could reduce Alessandra to a quivering child. "No. For one, I've only known the man for a few days."

"And two," her aunt prodded when Alessandra hesitated.

"He's not my type."

Sofia's snort came loud over the telephone line. "Luca is everyone's type."

"You really have to stop talking to Maria." Alessandra huffed a breath.

"Why would I when the woman is better than the National Inquirer."

"Can't deny that," Alessandra muttered.

"By the way, I've wired you thirty-thousand-dollars. So, go ahead and set the appointment with the lawyer and call me once you've talked to him."

Alessandra closed her eyes and let her head fall back on the back of the couch. She was up for the fight. She just didn't want Luca to be the cause of it. Feeling as limp as her spirits, Alessandra reasoned he couldn't be that callous. Luca couldn't be set on taking her property from under her. And it wasn't because she was becoming emotionally attached to Luca, as Sofia claimed.

She wasn't, was she? Nah, she definitely was not, Alessandra told herself. Luca was the type of man she detested, pompous, arrogant, a womanizer.

But, maybe, just maybe, a roll in the sheets with Luca wouldn't be so bad. It would be purely a sexual thing, she told herself, two sweaty bodies tousling under the sheets. There would be no emotion, just raw, unadulterated sex between consenting adults. Alessandra sighed at the thought.

It wouldn't be so bad if all Alessandra were doing were scratching an itch she hadn't scratched in seven months, twenty-hours, and fifteen minutes. Jesus! Had it been so long she had the count floating in her head?

Still, the thought of her hands on the powerful arms and the hard chest she'd sketched beneath cotton sent a shiver of delight through Alessandra. She drew a sharp breath when she drifted into thoughts of his pouty lips and skilled tongue possessing her.

Sweet and sour Jesus, she needed a night with a man.

Stop it, stop it, Alessandra told herself. She needed to stay focused to be able to make rational decisions.

Alessandra mulled, giving Luca the benefit of the doubt. She debated laying out her concerns to him before pulling Daniel in. After much debate, she opted not to. As much as Alessandra's gut feeling told her she could trust Luca, Sofia was right. They didn't know Luca well enough, and this was too important to rely on instinct alone.

Villa Cuomo was her inheritance, her legacy, and she needed to safeguard it. Villa Cuomo represented a heartfelt tribute to a woman by the man who loved her. It meant a promise carried out by the generations of Cuomos, and Alessandra wasn't about to become the first to violate Cuomo law. Alessandra wasn't about to break with tradition.

Alessandra didn't believe Luca was spiteful. Luca had spoken of her grandmother with fondness, but maybe Sofia was right. They didn't know Luca well enough. Human beings were capable of lying, cheating, and deceiving for far less than a plot of land.

Alessandra dug out Daniel's card and dialled. She was glad when Daniel's secretary put her right through. Had she not, she may have hung up.

"*Pronto, sono* Daniel." His voice boomed confidently at the end of the line.

"Hi, Daniel, this is Alessandra Cuomo. I'm not sure if you remember me."

The glow of delight on his face was swift. "Of course I do. I'd never forget such a delightful flight companion?" he said because telling her he hadn't been able to get her off his mind wasn't a suitable segue. "It's nice to hear from you. How are you enjoying your visit?"

"It's been great, thank you. I'm sorry to bother you, but I need to take you up on your offer. I've run into..." Doubt, confusion, and guilt clutching at Alessandra, she wavered.

The hesitation in her voice had Daniel setting his cup down with a clunk. "Is everything all right, Alessandra?"

"I need legal advice."

"Whatever you need, I'm here for you."

Daniel's assuring words were the comfort she needed to set her angst aside. "I'm glad to hear it because I have nowhere else to turn."

"Where are you staying?" He pencilled the address as she rambled it off. "You're not far from my office. How about I take you out to lunch, and you can tell me everything?"

"You don't have to go out of your way. I can come to you."

"It's no trouble. I was heading out to grab a bite to eat." Daniel tossed the salad into the garbage and reached for his car keys. "I'll pick you up in fifteen minutes."

AT THE SOUND OF WHEELS CRUNCHING on gravel, Alessandra nudged the curtain aside and watched Daniel roll the Fiat into the driveway. Luca was out, and Alessandra was glad of it. The last thing she wanted was for the two men to run into each other. Chance was Luca knew Daniel or of him. Luca seemed to know everyone.

Alessandra watched Daniel slide out of the car. In the stylish black suit against a white shirt and silk tie, he looked handsome and authoritative. His neatly combed coffee-brown hair crowned a face the colour of burnt-honey.

Daniel's seductive full lips above the bewitching deep, cleft chin curved when Alessandra stepped outside. "Hi."

"Hi." Alessandra flashed him a smile that shot a flash of heat to the pit of his stomach.

The few days on the island had shaded Alessandra's skin darker, making the forest-green eyes appear more luminous than Daniel remembered. Her hair flowed like silk around an unpainted face. She wore jeans, a peach blouse, and running shoes. She looked stunning, and for a long while, he stared.

"Do you mind if we get going? I'm starved," Alessandra said, not wanting to risk Luca from appearing out of anywhere.

"Sure. I gather you're not a gardener," he said, gazing over the garden overflowing with browned leaves as she slid into the passenger seat.

"I'm not. I kill everything I touch. I want to get the fountain working, but I'm not sure I'll be here long enough."

"When you're ready, I've got a guy that can help you with the gardening and the fountain."

"I'll keep it in mind," she said, watching Daniel gear the car to drive.

Over the ten-minute drive to Dante's Pizzeria, Alessandra and Daniel exchanged small talk.

Walking into the pizzeria, over the hum of conversation, Daniel requested a patio table overlooking the sweep of sea, which today shimmered with tiny diamonds and foamed against the white sand. The smell of sea fought with the inviting aroma of oven-baked pizza.

After ordering a medium pizza and a bottle of wine, Daniel turned to Alessandra. "I hope you like pizza."

"Who doesn't? The food here tastes so amazing. I'm enjoying foods I don't necessarily like." Alessandra's eyes followed the flight of a tern as he expertly fished lunch, and with fish snagged between its beak, set in flight across the clear sky.

"Would anchovies be one of those foods?"

A salty breeze wafting inland made Daniel's dark hair just a bit shabby, and Alessandra thought the look suited him. "How did you know?"

"It's a staple of Sicilian cooking, whereas, in the west, it's considered an acquired taste." Daniel thanked the waitress when she set the wine glasses down. "So, you're enjoying your stay."

"I am. I've already fallen in love with the island." She described in detail her visits to the various points of interest without bringing Luca into the conversation.

Daniel set his glass down when her expression turned solemn. "What's wrong, Alessandra?"

"I need your help, Daniel."

"You have it." Daniel rested a hand on Alessandra's and was pleased when she didn't pull away. "What is it you need help with?"

"It's about Villa Cuomo," she said after the server set the pizza down and moved to the next table.

"The place where I picked you up." Daniel set a slice of pizza on her plate and his.

"Yes, I'm afraid I stand to lose it. I need you to help me save it." Alessandra felt the muscles of her stomach tighten. She took a swig of the wine in her hand. "I may be blowing this out of proportion."

"Start from the beginning and tell me everything." Daniel took a generous bite of pizza, gestured to her to do the same.

Feeling confident, Alessandra picked up her pizza slice and, in between bites and sips of wine, told Daniel about Rosa, Gianni, and the property under Cuomo ownership. Alessandra's heart sank when she told Daniel of her suspicion of Luca's alleged betrayal.

"That's quite the story. What makes you suspect Antonio Santini wants the property or that he even knows about it?"

"My aunt thinks everything adds up and leads to that." Alessandra went silent when the waitress approached the table to check on them. When they were alone again, she continued. "She says that men like him possess they don't give."

"She's right about that."

"My grandmother supposedly signed an agreement with the Santinis to allow grape cultivation on the land."

Daniel wiped his mouth and picked up his wine glass. "How long has the cultivation been taking place?"

"Aunt Sofia surmises it's going on two decades."

"If there was an agreement between your nonna and the Santinis, it could be construed as a legitimate business transaction."

"I'll see if I can dig up the paperwork," Alessandra told Daniel about finding Luca at the villa. She explained Luca was the one who'd planted the crop and looked after the vineyard.

"That adds a level of complication to the situation. How long has he been living in your home?"

"Maybe five years."

"That's a long time, but at least he's gone now." Daniel watched her wrap her hands around the wine glass. "He's gone, isn't he, Alessandra?" He watched the sidelong glance with disbelief. "He's living in the house with you, now?" Daniel posed the question more out of curiosity.

Alessandra answered with a murmured, "Yes, in separate rooms, of course." She was compelled to clarify when Daniel's judgemental brows lifted.

Whether in separate rooms or not, it was a troubling notion for Daniel, who hadn't been able to get her off his mind.

Daniel had read about Luca in the multitude of articles written about him. He had seen the photographs portraying him as the Italian playboy who enjoyed living the sweet life. Resentment churned in Daniel at the idea of Alessandra becoming an addition to Luca's long string of women he paraded on his arm.

"I need to pick Luca's brain. I need him to teach me everything he knows about the grapevines he's planted on my property. My aunt thinks it's not your average grape."

Daniel drained part of his wine. "I see."

"Is that going to cause a problem? I mean legally."

Drowning in the sea-green eyes full of worry, Daniel set to put Alessandra's mind at ease. "We'll figure it out."

"So, you'll help me, Daniel? You'll take my case?"

The thought of Luca and Alessandra sleeping under one roof gave Daniel the resolve to say, "I will. I'll do my damnedest to do whatever necessary to secure your property. My question to you is how far you're willing to go?"

"I'll do whatever is necessary to secure the property. I have a promise to keep."

"Good. Leave this with me for a few days. I'll do some digging and call you when I've put a strategy together."

"Don't call me." She gave him Maria and Francesco's number. "Leave a message there, and I'll get back to you."

Fourteen

FOR THE UMPTEENTH time, Luca checked his watch. Alessandra left for her run ninety minutes ago before the rain began to come down in blinding sheets, and she hadn't returned. Worried, Luca paced the patio, following the path of the past hour.

Alessandra didn't have to answer to him, but he couldn't help and worry. She still didn't know the town well enough to disappear for such a long stretch. As thunder rumbled and lightning lit the sky, Luca couldn't believe the woman was crazy enough to persist with her run.

Luca breathed a sigh of relief when Alessandra came into view. Silhouetted through the downpour of rain, she was difficult to make out, but it was her stride her movements. He'd watched her for days and knew them well. That was her long, lean frame pressing on in the rain. Those were her long, long legs.

As Alessandra struggled to make it up the slippery, worn, sloped path leading to the house, Luca noted she was soaked to the bone.

"Running out in the rain, that's discipline." Luca's calmest voice came forward for fear of inciting the argument her eyes told him was ripe for release.

Alessandra heard the hint of concern in his voice but walked past him without uttering a word. The lingering guilt and remorse from her meeting with Daniel, the anger from her conversation with her aunt, was too raw to enable Alessandra to say the right thing.

Toeing wet running shoes off, Alessandra stepped into the kitchen, leaving puddles in her path. Deciding this was one of those alone-me moments, she demanded Luca stayed behind. His mother hadn't raised a fool. He knew better than to place himself in the line of fire of an angry woman.

Alessandra ducked into the refrigerator for a bottle of water. Uncapping it, she took a long swig and cast eyes out the kitchen window. Watching Luca idly stare at the falling rain, Alessandra thought back to the conversation with Sofia. The anger for the Santinis bubbled hot, but Alessandra quelled it.

She'd keep her guard up, but Luca had been kind, considerate, and eager to help her. He shouldn't be held responsible for the actions of his ancestors. Our ancestors' sins were ours to bear, but it wasn't who we were. Alessandra pressed fingers to her eyes. She had to put emotions aside for Rosa's sake.

Putting on an apologetic face, Alessandra walked out to the patio. "Do you think the rain will let up soon?"

The question caught Luca by surprise, and he cautiously entered into the conversation. "It'll pass in an hour."

Alessandra took the towel Luca offered, wiped her face dry. "Are you busy today?"

He had a million things to do. "Free as a bird," he said because she looked too good wet to say otherwise.

Alessandra walked to the cast iron table, scraped back a chair, and planted her wet behind. "Would you drive me to the supermarket?" She patted her legs dry.

The idea of spending the day with Alessandra put the sparkle back in Luca's eyes. "Of course, but it's a market."

"As long as I can pick up toiletries, a hat, and suntan lotion." Alessandra bundled her wet hair into the towel.

"It sounds as if you're planning to spend time outside."

"I thought I'd start going with you to the field in the next couple of days."

Under an unwavering green gaze, she gauged his reaction and was surprised when Luca said, "Sure, if that's what you want."

"You don't mind?"

"I told you I'd teach you everything I know, and I will." Luca's words led hope to soar in Alessandra's heart. He wasn't the man she'd formed in her head. "After shopping, do you have time to grab a late lunch?"

"I'd like that." Alessandra rose.

"There's, umm, ah, all right." Luca stumbled over the words when his eyes lasered in on the clinging wet fabric, mapping the taut mounds and erect nipples.

His eyes were on her for seconds but long enough for the spear of pure lust to arrow straight to his loins. The erection came fast, and Luca swirled to give her his back.

"I'll go get ready," she said, wondering what it was about women's breasts that turned men into a quivering mess.

ALESSANDRA'S GUILT WASHED DOWN THE SHOWER drain, she dressed in jeans and a shirt, tied her hair into a wet ponytail, and was downstairs before Luca. Her eyes darted up to Luca when heels clanked on the stairs as he made his way down fifteen minutes after her.

"Well, this is a first." Luca's eyes registered surprise.

"What is?" Her eyes followed him down.

The tips of his curls, still wet from his shower, clung to the nape of his neck. He brought with him the smell of soap and man, and lust, hot and sharp, speared into Alessandra. Jesus! She'd jump him there and then if she could, but that wasn't in the cards, and she shook the thought from her head.

"You having to wait for me. Normally it's me waiting on my date." Luca folded his shirtsleeves to the elbows.

"One. This is not a date. It's a shopping trip. Two. I've never been one to fuss. I can get ready in fifteen minutes flat. I've been waiting for you for just as long."

Luca raised an appreciative brow. She wore no makeup, a green shirt, which brought out the magnetic eyes he couldn't get enough of, and jeans, and she looked centrefold-worthy. "You look great."

"You clean up nicely yourself."

"It's why I took so long to get ready," Luca said, eliciting a smile. "Shall we head out on our date?"

Knowing his words were meant to goad, Alessandra remained silent as he shrugged into his leather jacket.

A LIGHT DRIZZLE FOLLOWED THEM TO the market. By the time they got there, the sun rained down gold from a sky as clear as glass.

The market pulsed with energy and sounds. The air was crowded with the squawks of haggling patrons trying to get the best prices. The variety of offered goods struck Alessandra.

There were farm-fresh produce and seafood displayed on rustic, wooden crates. There were breads, cheese, pasta, and wine vendors strutted their wares. The nut vendor put on a show with the array of Sicilian almonds, olives, and pistachios.

Colourful tarpaulins lent to the essence of the boisterous, electric atmosphere of the market. Hurtled cries from vendors pitching their wares to customers wending their way from stand to stand in search of the family's dinner were hard to miss. Alessandra relished every moment.

Luca knew many of the vendors and introduced Alessandra to them. As the introductions were made, each offered a taste of this or a sample of that. All nodded without hesitation when Luca told them she was a friend and should be treated as such.

Luca and Alessandra wound their way to the market's general merchandise area. There, she chose a wide-brimmed straw hat with a black silk ribbon. Luca gave her a slow, intimate survey when she moved her shoulders with gentle elegance as she modelled it for him. Nodding his approval, Luca told her she looked like Audrey Hepburn in Breakfast at Tiffany. The comment got him an unexpected flirtatious wink.

While Alessandra filled her shopping list, Luca stepped away long enough to pick up art supplies. He bought canvasses, paints, and brushes, everything Alessandra needed to try her hand at painting. Luca planned to surprise her when they got home.

The shopping trip, something Luca detested, turned into an enjoyable experience. Alessandra seemed to make the mundane new and exciting.

It was one p.m. when Alessandra and Luca made the short walk to Fellini's for lunch. The restaurant and its patio were packed with the lunch crowd. Couples with heads close together clasped hands or raised glasses in toast. A group of chatty tourists took over the long family-table by the wall, and business-professionals crowded the remaining tables. Many of the diners enjoyed mouth-watering dishes while sipping on wine.

The perky host with the flowing dark hair and hourglass body led them to a table out in the patio with a graceful sway of her hips. From the intimate eye exchange between her and Luca, Alessandra deduced they knew each other well.

"Just for you, Luca." Perky flashed Luca a flirtatious smile as she fanned herself with the RISERVATO sign she lifted from the table. "And this is your menu," she said, setting the linen napkin on his lap and ignoring Alessandra altogether. "The usual bottle of wine?"

"Si, grazie, amore," Luca fixed a grateful smile that made Perky liquefy.

"I'll let Luisa know." Giving Luca one last scan, Perky sashayed back to her host stand.

"A friend of yours?" Alessandra eyed him from beneath the brim of her hat.

There was deep satisfaction when Luca detected the tinge of jealousy in her tone. "Let's call her an acquaintance." He had lots of them.

Since puberty, women had fascinated Luca. A big fan of their curves, femininity, and softness drove Luca to hone his skills in the art of seducing women and had become a master at it. It didn't hurt that the media had labelled him as Italy's most desired billionaire-bachelor.

But since Alessandra came into his life, his interest in women faded. Luca wasn't sure when or how it happened, but Alessandra was now the only woman who captivated his interest.

"Mmm-hmm, an acquaintance," Alessandra hummed, wondering what level of intimacy qualified as an acquaintance in Luca's books. From the way Perky eyed Luca, they had crossed the acquainted bar long ago.

"Are you cold?" Luca asked when she followed her question with a shiver.

"A chill from my wet run this morning is setting in."

Shrugging out of his leather jacket, Luca draped it over her shoulders. The lavender scent from her hair assaulted his brain, and he staggered to compose his next thought.

"I know you think our February temperature is balmy in comparison to Toronto weather, but promise me to dress more warmly next time you go running under a rainstorm."

There it was again, the undercurrent tone of concern. As much as she wanted to shield herself from it, it touched her. "What do you recommend?"

"Would you like to share a Margherita Pizza? It will pair perfectly with the bottle of dry rosé Luisa is bringing." When Alessandra lifted a curious gaze at him, Luca said, "I'm Italian. I know my wines."

"Yes, wines."

Alessandra sat back to watch Luca's interaction with Luisa as she shamelessly flirted with him while he sang his order in Italian. The order placed, Alessandra watched the petite beauty sway her curvaceous assets for Luca's eye-over.

"Another 'acquaintance,' Alessandra highlighted in air quotes, "I presume."

"I eat here often. There's no need to be jealous. I'm here with you, not them."

"You certainly think a lot of yourself to think that I'd be jealous of you garnering the attention of an impressionable young girl."

"Well, aren't you?"

"Pfft, not in the least."

"That's too bad because I hoped you would be."

"Well, dream on." Alessandra's cockiness drew an appreciative laugh from Luca.

"Did you enjoy your shopping trip?"

Her tough façade was replaced with a smile. "Very much. Thank you for taking me."

"My pleasure." Luca broke off when the waitress set two long-stem glasses down then turned the bottle toward Luca for his inspection. When he nodded, with a dimpled smile, she poured him a sample. "It's perfect, *amore, grazie*." Luca shot her a smile that sent her tumbling into love.

"It's not nice to tease a young girl." Alessandra pointed out when Luisa managed to get her liquefied legs back to solid form and walked away

"Who says I'm teasing." Luca gave Luisa a wink when she turned for one last glance before disappearing into the restaurant.

"As I was saying before, we got derailed from the grown-up conversation. There's a layer of pleasure to everything I do here, which I haven't felt in months. I'm not sure why that is."

"I have the same feeling, but for me, it's since I've met you. You make everything interesting and an enjoyable experience, and I appreciate that." Luca tilted his glass, the red liquid sloshing dangerously to the edge, at the two women taking their seats at the table next to theirs who called out a "*Ciao*" to him.

Alessandra shot him a sidelong glance. "How could you say that when you have so many acquaintances?"

Luca's eyes lit with laughter. "They're just that, acquaintances. They don't make things special for me as you do."

Despite herself, Alessandra blushed. "Now you're just trying to flatter me to get me into bed."

"There's nothing more I'd like. However, that's not why I'm saying it. I truly enjoy spending time with you. And would it be so bad if we end up in bed?"

Smiling at him from beneath the brim of her hat, Alessandra leaned in. Her mouth a whisper from his, she said, "Not for you."

Luca couldn't help but smile. "I'd dedicate the entire night to pleasing you."

"Keep enticing me and..." Alessandra let the sentence hang when she thought better than to answer.

"Tell me you were going to finish the sentence with, 'you're bound to end up in my bed tonight.'"

The comment got him a roll of the eyes. "That's not going to happen any time soon."

"The wine is very good." Luca signalled for her to try it. She did. "You underestimate my persistent nature."

Alessandra traced a finger around the rim of her glass. "I don't. I sense you're used to getting your way, and when you don't, it becomes a cat-and-mouse chase for you. You, Mr. Santini, underestimate my indifference to your persistent nature."

Humour hit Luca's eyes. God, he wanted her. "Well, then I'll just have to do my damnedest to break that indifference. I really hate you to miss out on experiencing the best sex of your life. So, challenge accepted."

"Cocky and modest. Can I ask you a question?"

"Anything."

Alessandra broke off when the waitress approached their table with their steaming pizza. Alone again, Alessandra was about to ask her question when a woman called Luca's name.

Luca turned in the caller's direction and, catching sight of the woman walking towards him, shot to his feet to take her into a tight embrace and kiss her. The kiss wasn't a long intimate one, but Alessandra could tell it was heartfelt. Alessandra was struck with a pang of jealousy that surprised her.

Resting a diamond-clad hand on Luca's shoulder, the woman keenly surveyed him. "You look wonderful, *amore*."

"And you look as beautiful as always." The sound of their laughter inexplicably assaulted Alessandra.

"You know flattery will get you everywhere." A perfectly manicured finger playfully tapped Luca's chest.

"What brings you to this part of town?" There was love, sweet and real, in Luca's voice, and a stab of jealousy struck Alessandra again.

"If you called me more often, you'd know we're spending a few months at the villa," she griped, pinching Luca's cheek.

"I'm sorry. I've been busy, but you know you're my special girl." Luca circled an arm around her thin waist and pulled her in.

"Don't try to get out of this with flattery." The woman's glare was chastising, but her tone was pure warmth.

Alessandra eyed the woman Luca seemed intimately familiar with and wondered how many acquaintances he had and how he managed to keep track of them.

When Luca turned to Alessandra to make the introductions, the faintest of smiles touched his face at her obvious irritation at the woman garnering his attention. He'd seen that look many times before, but coming from her meant something. For a short moment, he relished in it.

"Luca, don't be so rude, and introduce your friend," the woman said, skimming a gaze at Alessandra. The girl was a beauty.

"I'm sorry, Alessandra Cuomo, Laine Santini, my mother."

Alessandra rose to her feet and reached for Laine's diamond-clad outstretched hand. "It's a pleasure to meet you, Mrs. Santini."

A woman of taste and means, Laine Santini, although in her mid-fifties, looked ten years younger. She was inches shorter than Luca with honey-gold hair that tumbled over her shoulders. She had an aristocratic face with arctic-blue eyes and rounded lips painted in bronze lipstick. In a white Versace dress, Laine Santini looked the picture of elegance, and everything about her screamed sophistication.

"It's a pleasure to meet you, Alessandra." Laine's smile bore an uncanny likeness to her son's. "I hope I'm not intruding."

Alessandra released her grip on Laine's hand. "Not at all," Alessandra said in her practiced Italian.

"Mom's from New York. You can speak English to her."

"That suits me better, seeing as your son has just started to teach me the language."

Laine curiously probed her son. "Isn't that interesting?"

"He's a great teacher, patient. At least he is with me. But you'd need to be because sometimes I can be quite the challenging student." Alessandra gave Luca a dimpled smile, and Laine didn't miss the intimate gaze her son returned.

Laine studied her son with a mother's keen eye. Based on the tenderness in his eyes, Laine deduced this girl wasn't a lustful desire triggering his lower brain. He was smitten with the girl, and it pleased Laine.

At thirty-six, Luca was getting too old to lead the playboy lifestyle that he'd fallen into since his youth. Laine was ready for grandchildren.

"Safe to assume you're the young lady who's been taking up my only son's attention, so much so he can't spare a few minutes to pick up a phone to call his mother."

"If I have, I'm sorry." Alessandra's heartfelt apology charmed Laine.

"Don't apologize, dear. I'm happy you have him focused on something other than," the tarts he involves himself with, "grapes. Have you known each other very long?"

"Not too long. I'm new in town. Your son's been kind enough to help me assimilate to my new home."

"I see, and where are you from?" Laine asked, and Alessandra gave her a brief history. "You've moved here permanently?"

"No. I'm here to take care of some family matters. Once that's done, I plan to head back home." The hint of sadness that washed in Alessandra's eyes told Laine there was more to her story.

The girl was genuine, Laine concluded. She wasn't like the plastic-faced women who threw themselves at her son. Laine was pleased by that. Luca needed a woman in his life who saw him for the kind, loving person he was, not for the name he bore or his bank account.

"Mom, please stop interrogating Alessandra." Luca's firm, unyielding gaze at Laine made her raise a perfectly formed brow.

Protective, Laine thought. That was a first. "I'm getting to know your friend."

"Would you like to join us for lunch, Mrs. Santini?" Alessandra's offer got a wide-eyed distressed look from Luca.

"Thank you, dear, but we're meeting friends for lunch, and we're already running late. Your father should be somewhere around. I lost him back at the wine stand. Be a dear and go find him for me, Luca." Laine looked over her shoulder at her son, whose focus on Alessandra made him deaf to her words. "Luca, close your mouth before the bugs get cozy in there, and go find your father. Now." Both women watched Luca, like a chastised boy, walk away. "No matter the age, men are like children."

MINUTES LATER, LUCA RETURNED WITH A man who bore a resemblance to him in every way. Alessandra pegged him to be in his early sixties. He had olive skin, and his hair was the same dark richness as Luca's, with wisps of steel-gray woven at the temple. There were creases around the eyes and mouth that gave men his age a distinguished air. His eyes, the same deep, rich blue as Luca's, were cold and hard. An imperious air about him projected confidence that said he always got what he wanted, and failure wasn't an option.

"You found him." Laine rose, and Alessandra stood with her. "This is Luca's friend, Alessandra," Laine said when her husband gave Alessandra the same dismissive look he gave to Luca's women. "I'm sorry, dear, what was your last name?"

"Cuomo." With a direct, knowing look, Alessandra offered Antonio her hand. "Nice to meet you, Mr. Santini.

"Nice to meet you." With piqued interest, Antonio pumped her hand.

She was a looker, with the type of natural beauty that turned men into puddles of weakness, but she didn't tick any of Luca's boxes. Her classic oval face wasn't covered in colour, and neither were her lips. Her hair was tied back in a ponytail, with strands that escaped its hold and hung in disarray around her face. She exuded charm and innocence, but the glint in the green eyes held a quiet fire that could sear if stoked.

Antonio didn't doubt Alessandra already had Luca rolling over like an obedient puppy. He knew his son's weakness for beautiful women too well, and the puppy love gaze in Luca's eyes told Antonio all he needed to know. The girl had already gotten under his skin—if not him.

Luca was going to let him down—again. Once more, he'd have to take control of the situation. He didn't have the ruthlessness of a Santini. The boy was weak. He'd allow Alessandra to manipulate him with her feminine wiles and let him down—again.

"Excuse me." Antonio turned his piercing gaze away from Alessandra and pulled Luca aside.

Over Laine's voice, Alessandra heard Luca's faint, muttered denials in Italian. Although she didn't understand the exchange, Alessandra could tell from the frustrated look on Luca's face none of it was particularly pleasant. When Luca joined them, the distressed look on his face confirmed her suspicions.

With an abrupt and perfunctory good-bye, Antonio closed Alessandra and Laine's conversation and whisked his wife away.

"Your mother is lovely," Alessandra commented, taking her seat.

Shaking off the sick feeling his father left in him, he followed suit. "She's great. I'm crazy in love with her. My father is more of an acquired taste, one that takes some getting used to," he said by way of apology. "What did you and my mother talk about?" he asked, turning the subject matter.

"Girl talk." Alessandra took a bite of pizza.

Luca gave her an arched look. He couldn't remember the last time his mother had spoken more than a polite, forced word to the women he'd introduced to her, let alone had so-called girl talk. "I've never known her to girl talk before."

Alessandra mulled that over. She might be able to use Laine as an ally if it came to it. "You haven't introduced her to the right women before me."

Luca considered and ultimately decided she was probably right.

"By the way, she invited us to Villa Santini for lunch. You're supposed to give her a call to confirm the date and time." Alessandra set a slice of pizza on his plate, reached for a piece for herself. "Close your mouth before the bugs get cozy in there."

"Girl talk and lunch invitation." Luca mused in awe.

His mother took a liking to Alessandra. His father was a different story. Luca's hands went to tight fists when he heard his father's ultimatum in his head.

How could he hurt Alessandra as his father demanded?

Fifteen

LUCA KNOCKED LOUDLY on Alessandra's bedroom door.

"Leave me alone. It's five in the morning." Alessandra's groggy voice snapped. When the knocking persisted, Alessandra swore, with fervor.

Luca choked back a laugh. "This was your idea. Now get your butt out of bed. We leave in half-hour."

Alessandra's body screamed for more sleep, but she rustled herself out of bed. "The sacrifices I make for family," she mumbled.

Wrapped in pink terry cloth, Alessandra opened the bedroom door, and there he was. Christ, it was five in the morning, and the man looked perfectly gorgeous in jeans and a white T-shirt. He smelled of her lavender soap, his hair was neatly combed, and the dark stubble was neatly trimmed.

Brushing the mop of hair from her face, Alessandra wiped sleep out of bleary eyes. "You're enjoying this, aren't you?"

"More than I care to admit."

Alessandra's eyes narrowed. "Good to know I'm your source of entertainment."

"I appreciate it. Oh, come on." Luca reached for her arm when she started to walk away. "You'll feel better after you shower."

"Bite me."

"Can do."

"Shut up."

Luca's grinning eyes followed her to the bathroom until she slammed the door. "By the way..."

"I said, shut up." The words came from behind the closed bathroom door like daggers.

"But..."

"You need to shut up already."

"Suit yourself." Luca leaned back on the wall. His lips curved when she broke out into the collection of muttered oaths. "I tried to warn you to let the water run awhile before you hop in." Luca's lips curved when the string of more colourful expletives followed. The woman had a talent, he thought, laughing all the way to the kitchen.

Fifteen minutes later, in a T-shirt and newly purchased overalls, she walked into the kitchen, scented with freshly brewed coffee. Her wet hair clung to her skin in a way that made him want to trace the dampness with his lips.

"Feeling better?" Luca set a steaming coffee cup on the table.

"No," she barked, walking past him to the refrigerator, leaving her shampoo's scent—strawberries, he thought—in her path.

"You aren't a morning person."

Round eyes narrowed to thin slits. She wanted to hurl so many choice words, but she wouldn't give him the satisfaction. "Not when you wake me up at five in the morning. No pastries."

"It's too early. The bakery doesn't open for another hour." He was sure that if she had superpowers, she'd have disintegrated him into fine sand. Luckily for him, he had the superpower of phase-out. And that's what he did when she launched into her rant.

"How am I supposed to function on an empty stomach? I need sustenance, and why must we go out this early in the morning? The vines will still be there at seven, eight, and nine."

Alessandra talked out, Luca said, "We need to get out as early as possible for several reasons. For one, at this time, it's still cool enough to work. Even though it's late February, the Sicilian sun is relentless. Once out, it becomes unbearable. The cooler early morning temperature allows us to work longer hours and without the benefit of the little critters that come out during the sunlit hours," Luca added, tucking back a smile when her coffee cup stopped mid-way to her mouth.

"What critters?"

"Bees, wasps, snakes, that sort of thing, but you don't need to worry unless you have type O blood. Do you know your blood type?"

"No, why would I?"

"Well, I guess we'll find out once out there." Luca watched her contemplate and recoil as she did. When the smirk twisted on his face, she threw the kitchen towel at him.

"You're enjoying this way too much."

"Mmm-hmm."

"It's still dark out." Alessandra's eyes darted out the kitchen window, where a dark sky twinkled with stars.

"We have diesel-powered lights set up. You'll be able to see just fine." He set his empty coffee cup in the sink. "You ready?"

"Not really, but let's get this over with." Alessandra took in the last of her coffee and started for the door.

Eyeing her backside in the overalls that defined it so well, he said, "By the way, you look great."

Heated eyes burning into Luca, she griped about the early hour and everything that came to her mind for the eternal walk to the field.

Christ, the woman could talk. Realizing there was nothing he could say to shut her up, Luca resorted to tossing in the random "I completely agree" or "Mhmm" to keep his end of the conversation.

"This is all yours," Luca said, rendering her silent. Luca exhaled a breath of relief.

Alessandra gazed at the rolling hills overflowing with vines. Rows upon rows of vines heavy with fruit spread for as far as the eye could see. Each tree clung to what Luca referred to as vine training systems. Standing amid her field, her appreciation for the work he'd put into her land grew tenfold.

"How many plants are on the property?"

"Just over one-hundred-thousand vines."

"That's extraordinary." Alessandra gaped in shock.

"Come on." Taking her hand, Luca walked her deeper into the field. "It's a lot of fruit, but each acre produces about three-hundred gallons of juice or a little more than one-hundred and twenty cases of wine."

"Wow," Alessandra murmured reverently, skimming fingers over leaves and fruit. "You did all this for my grandmother?"

Luca nodded. He didn't mention the increase in value to the property because of the Florentia grape he'd planted on her land, not because he didn't want her to know, but because money didn't play into the equation. What he saw before him was something he'd brought to life, and it filled him with a great sense of accomplishment.

"Impressive, I don't know what to say." Filling her lungs with cool air pungent with the smell of rich earth, Alessandra bent down and took a handful. Fisting soil in the palm of her hands, she felt the connection with Rosa. It was then that Alessandra understood Gianni's sentiment of communion between Rosa, him, and the land. "It feels magical."

Alessandra's words, the tone in which she said it shot a wave of contentment through Luca. "That's how it feels to me," he said, thinking she understood him as no one had. No one touched him on as many levels as she did.

In companionable silence, they surveyed the field for a moment.

Alessandra fell in step with Luca as he introduced her to the workers and manager. "I planted a lot of these vines with my own hands." Luca's pride beamed from twinkling eyes. "And I'm going to teach you everything I know."

Luca had Alessandra pruning, planting, fertilizing, and digging her hands into the soil that brought her close to her ancestors. Luca prattled on about acid and sugar levels, plant cuttings, and so much more.

Luca could talk about grapes, the land, and farming without running out of something to say.

Two weeks later and Alessandra thought he'd be talked out. Luca wasn't. In his excitement of the captive audience he had in her, Luca dismissed every warning his father had issued and told Alessandra the truth.

The grapevines on her property were a unique hybrid to the Santini Winery Corporation called Florentia.

Sixteen

"HYBRID?" ALESSANDRA STARED at Luca. "What are you saying, Luca?"

"The vines on your land are one of its kind developed by the Santini Winery Corporation and proprietary to them."

Alessandra's eyes huge, her lips parted in shock, she gaped at Luca. "Aunt Sofia was right," she murmured under her breath.

"Your land has the perfect soil and weather conditions to test it, and Villa Cuomo is small and obscure enough not to raise attention. Me being the corporation's lawyer wouldn't either. It was why my father put me in charge." Blue eyes serious, he stared at her while she processed the information. "You don't want to know who my father is."

"I already know who he is." Alessandra looked into his eyes. "I know who you are."

Luca's brow winged. "You've known all along?"

"No. My aunt only told me about you a few days after I found you here. It turns out she knew you were here all along and didn't tell me for fear I wouldn't make the trip." She scooped soil and dipped the pH test strip. "You know who I am." She showed him the stick.

"It's a pass. You can go ahead and plant the cuttings in that soil. Plant them deep enough." Luca handed her the plants. "And, yes, I know who you are."

"So, you know what your father wants from me."

Luca nodded. "Press the soil around it."

She patted earth around the roots then sat back on her heels. "Are you going to help him steal the land from me?"

Luca's eyes changed, sobered. "What? No. Of course not. Why would you say that? He wants me to talk you into selling it."

The lit, unwavering eyes that fixed on hers told her he was telling the truth. "Do you know your father well?"

A frown creased his brow. "Of course I do. Why?"

"Do you believe he'd steal the property from under me?"

The squint lines around his eyes were deep now. "No. No, why would he? Why would you ask that?"

"Because my aunt thinks so and because after all this work you've done, I can't sell you the property. I'm sorry, but I can't. I need to go. Francesco and Maria are expecting me for lunch."

"I can drive you." Luca offered, needing the conversation not to end there.

"Thanks, but I need to clear my head. I'll run the distance." She dashed off before Luca could get a word in.

FLEXING AND STRETCHING IN FRONT OF her neglected garden, Alessandra determined Luca wasn't lying. If his father was planning to take the property, he knew nothing about it. Or didn't he?

Holding her foot against her right buttock for a count of ten, Alessandra thought about her deceit. Spying and tricking Luca into giving her information unnerved her. She was piling lie after lie like a Jenga tower. She wasn't built for lying, but she couldn't tell Luca she was heading out to meet Daniel, not going to Francesco's place.

She reached for her left foot, held it against her left buttock. Holding it for a count of ten, Alessandra pondered the idea of taking shears to the trees and the bougainvillea sprawling wild in the garden. She'd love to bring the fountain to life. Her grandmother would like that.

Bringing her knee up, Alessandra wrapped hands around it and pressed it to her chest. Luca was neither malicious, vengeful, nor spiteful. At least, that's how Alessandra saw him, but she couldn't detract from her plan. Her aunt was right. She needed to get the deed to Villa Cuomo in her hands.

Alessandra took one last look at the garden before she got underway. It and the fountain would have to wait. For now, she had bigger fish to fry.

Clearing her mind to a blank canvass, Alessandra wound her way through narrow streets. Everyone was quick to offer a smile or wave. Her mouth and eyes smiled at the laundry hanging overhead, flapping in a soft March breeze under a brilliant sun that was so much a part of the town.

Alessandra ran past the group of boys practicing their footwork with a football as spectators cheered on. There were tourists scanning maps, plotting their next destination. Some flipped through dictionaries in their attempt to communicate with servers at the outdoor cafés. The *piazza* brimmed with mothers pushing strollers or couples out for an early afternoon walk.

Alessandra relished every moment.

Forty minutes later, Alessandra walked into Dante's Pizzeria. Wonderful scents steamed out when she opened the door to the restaurant.

As if sensing Alessandra's arrival, Daniel's eyes flickered over to her when she stepped onto the patio. Daniel thought she looked nothing short of spectacular in shorts, a red sweatshirt, and a flushed face. But it wasn't until she removed the red ball cap and let dark hair spill out like a flowing waterfall that his stomach jerked with that feeling that bordered on need.

Daniel had needed like this once before, long ago, and hadn't been struck with the feeling since. Daniel didn't think the feeling would hit again, but Alessandra stirred emotions he'd buried long ago and thought no woman could revive. Alessandra made him feel alive again.

"I'm sorry I'm late. And I'm sorry I'm dressed so casually," Alessandra added, on seeing him looking handsome and stylish in the double-breasted chocolate-brown suit, blue silk shirt, and tie.

Daniel shot to his feet, pulled the chair out for her. "You're right on time, and you look great." Daniel signalled the waiter to bring a bottle of water. "If it's too cool for you on the patio, we can move inside."

"This is perfect," Alessandra said, enjoying the breeze sweeping over her damp body.

"I didn't know you ran." Daniel watched the server pour water from the bottle into a glass.

"Running has been an obsession since high school, but I'll confess that I walked the last bit just to make sure I wasn't a complete sweaty mess when I got here." Alessandra drank deep.

"Let me get you another bottle of water, or would you prefer something stronger?"

"*Aqua, per piacere*," Alessandra told the server Daniel waved to the table.

"I didn't know you spoke Italian."

"Ordering water is simple enough. I've been trying to learn the language by reading Italian books." Alessandra cast eyes to the stretch of green-blue sea, verging against a darkening sky threatening rain. "It's pretty here."

Daniel's eyes on her, he watched the soft breeze whiffle through her hair. "Very."

"I smell rain in the air. It's a special gift of mine," Alessandra added when Luca's eyebrows raised in wonder.

"The forecast calls for a thunderstorm tonight, clear skies for tomorrow. You know that gift can make you a star with farmers and make you a millionaire."

"So, I've been told." By Luca, Alessandra wanted to say but thought better than to inject his name into the conversation. She'd sensed Daniel wasn't a fan of Luca or the Santinis. "Dark skies or not, I never tire of this view."

"You get the same view from your house, don't you?"

Alessandra nodded. "From my patio and out my bedroom window. It's spectacular during sunrise, but I love it best at night when the moon is floating on the horizon, riding over darkened waters. It's when I hear the sea whisper. Smell it. It's when shadows move behind the trees, and cicadas sing. It's soothing."

"You're a romantic," Daniel said, with reverence imagining her in the middle of the scene she'd painted.

"Isn't every woman?" Alessandra shot him a look from under her lashes.

"I suppose."

"You mentioned you have something to discuss with me." Alessandra's head jerked up at the screech of a flock of gulls in flight overhead.

"Yes. I did some digging in the archives and didn't come up with much."

"That doesn't sound reassuring."

Daniel reached into his briefcase for the folder. "Digging up files dating back one hundred years isn't going to be easy. In those days, transactions were sometimes done on a handshake."

"What does that mean to me, Daniel?"

"It means I'm going to have to dig a lot deeper, and by that, I mean dig into historical records and documents to come up with something that will show a negotiable interest in your family's favour. I need to find something that shows why your family was under the assumption the property was theirs. It can be something as simple as a handwritten note from the Santinis to the Cuomos. That alone would prove your family was under the assumption of ownership. Do you know of any such documents in your possession?"

Alessandra shook her head. "I'll speak to Aunt Sofia, and I'll go through the papers I found in my grandmother's bedroom."

"You do that, but I also suggest..." Daniel hesitated.

"Tell me what needs to be done, Daniel. I'll do whatever you think necessary."

"We need to hire a historian, someone whose expertise is sifting through the archives for historical data. I have someone who's done excellent work for me in the past. I have to warn you he doesn't come cheap. I can waive my fees, but he needs to be paid." The eyes that stared back at her were a clear, unalloyed blue.

"Go ahead and do what you think is necessary." Alessandra made a mental note to call her aunt and have her transfer more money. Dipping into the inheritance to fulfill Rosa's wish was a cause worth the expense. "And, Daniel, I appreciate your offer, but you will bill me for your time."

Daniel capped the Mont Blanc, set it on the table. "All right."

Alessandra drained the remaining water. The ice rattled against the glass when she set it down on the table. "I'm starting to wonder if any of this is necessary anymore."

"Why do you say that?" When the server set the bowls of minestrone on the table, Daniel pointed to her glass. "More water?"

She shook her head. "Luca has been helpful and transparent in sharing information. I'm doing this because my aunt insists I locate the deed."

"I see."

Misreading the flicker in his eyes as concern instead of resentment, Alessandra clarified. "I've gotten to know him over the past few weeks, and nothing leads me to believe he's out to steal my home."

Jealousy conflicting with lawyerly responsibility stirred beneath the composed shell, and Daniel eased into his response. "Trust is not a lawyer's forte, and I'm going to side with your aunt. All I can tell you, Alessandra, is that I've crossed the Santinis in the courtroom on a couple of occasions, and they're manipulative, devious people who will do whatever's necessary to win."

"It's hard to believe Luca is like his father. He's kind, and..." Alessandra stopped when she thought she'd said too much.

She was falling for Luca. Daniel sucked a breath to calm his bitterness because telling Alessandra that all Luca wanted was to get you into bed was out of the question.

"I have to agree with your aunt." Daniel held up a hand when she started to speak. "It's a good idea to get a copy of the deed in your hands. It's never good to leave things to chance. I'll get the historian working right away."

Alessandra heaved a sigh that sounded like regret. She, not Luca, was the manipulative, devious one.

Seventeen

1882 - Abramo

"YOUR SON IS refusing to marry the Contessa until I provide him proof of the deed bestowing the property to the girl." Abramo crumpled Gianni's letter and tossed it into the fire casting warmth and light in the living room.

"He becomes my son when he displeases you, and you did make an oath to him, Abramo." Aria studied her husband's profile.

He was a handsome man, aristocratic-looking, but what she most admired was the ruthlessness, which always got him what he wanted.

"Wine?" When Abramo nodded, Aria rang for the servant. "And I'm guessing my son has now found out about his betrothed's so-called tarnished reputation."

"The Contessa's tarnished reputation, as you call it, is why her parents agreed to the generous dowry. Had she not gotten herself in the family way by spreading her legs to the gardener..."

"Stable boy," Aria corrected.

"I don't care if it was the village idiot. The point is, had she not gotten herself pregnant, we wouldn't have been able to negotiate the acquisition of the Burgundy vineyard in exchange for marriage. God love youthful defiance." Abramo watched the logs in the marble fireplace crackled with flames when he added firewood onto the fire.

"Don't be so crass, Abramo, or take so much pleasure in the deception you partook in that steered your son into a loveless marriage. Gianni will not only be raising another man's child, but he will be married to a branded woman." Aria waved the servant at the door in. When he swung the door open, the aroma of rabbit stew and baked bread flowed into the room and mingled with the smell of wood smoke. "Bring a glass of wine for Mr. Santini and a cup of coffee for me." Aria dismissed the servant with a wave.

"Lest you forget it was you who concocted the scheme?"

Aria sunk into the Queen Anne chair. "My sole purpose was to draw Gianni away from Rosa, not take pleasure. You know as well as I, he's deeply in love with the girl and would have married her had we not sent him away. How would it have looked to have a Santini married to peasant stock?"

"Well, what we have done seems not to matter because your son is refusing to marry the Contessa. If he doesn't, the deal is off. The girl is swelling up by the day. He needs to marry her now, or we will not get our hands on the Burgundy vineyard."

"Or the château."

The comment meant to stir Abramo's blood hot had. Aria could be combative and antagonistic and knew how to get under her husband's skin. Aria also knew it was why Abramo loved her—and how he liked her in and out of bed.

"The château is the icing on the cake, but you know damn well what we both care about is the vineyard. That vineyard will increase our production output by fifteen percent, making Santini Winery the third largest wine producer in Italy. It's a stepping stone to becoming number one in Europe."

Abramo was accustomed to winning. Every decision he made for his business was calculated, and the thought of losing the Burgundy vineyard made his heart quicken and his mind race.

"That there is your problem, *amore*." Aria walked to the window.

"What? What is my problem, Aria?" Abramo's voice growled as blazing eyes watched the remaining two pages of his son's letter burst into flames.

"Calm yourself, *amore*, and I will point out your lack of foresight. Gianni is in love with Rosa. His thinking right now is irrational since the wrong organ is manipulating his brain. I must say you men are all quite alike when you're around a pretty girl. And stunning she is. I can see how easily it was for Gianni to have fallen for her."

"I don't take note of such things when I have you." Abramo's eye fixed on Aria's heaving breasts spilling over the black silk bodice. She looked good enough to eat.

"Of course, you don't." Aria nodded at the servant to enter when the knock at the door came. "You need to address that irrationality. Quell it." When their drinks were served, Aria said to the servant, "Tell Cook Mr. Santini, and I will be eating dinner one hour late. Leave us."

"I have no idea what you're saying, Aria," Abramo said in a low growl.

She loved the way the curling flames of the fire flickered in his eyes. "For someone with the brain the size of the universe, you're very inept when it comes to matters of the heart, *amore*." Aria grinned when he groaned. "It is simple. You need to tell Gianni what he wants to hear."

"Your son demands proof, and I don't want that girl or any of her family on Santini land." Abramo shot back with a sniff.

Aria walked toward him with gentle elegance, bringing her perfume's discernible scent and the ostensible force of herself. "You tell Gianni what he wants to hear and Rosa what he wants her to hear."

"Aria, please just say what you mean."

"You are going to see that lawyer we pay a hefty price to right now."

"Why would I want to speak to Horatio?" Abramo swilled wine for calm. The drink festered uncomfortably in his stomach.

"Because you're going to instruct him to tell Rosa that she and her family can move into the derelict property we own. You know, the one with the house in disrepair overlooking the Mediterranean Sea you acquired and have yet to put in operation." Aria waved a hand when she saw Abramo's outburst brewing. "Have Horatio tell Rosa she and her family can move in, rent-free on the condition they do all necessary repairs to make the house livable and till the land. You will pay the taxes and expenses related to the land in order..."

"To ensure it remains our property, and while there, we get them to ready the land for farming. We'll have them turn it into the vineyard we planned all along at no cost to us. And getting Horatio, a reputable lawyer, to put this in motion will give it the appearance of legality."

With a delicate touch, Aria smoothed her husband's lapels. "That is exactly right, *amore*. They are peasants, ignorant of the law. Horatio will then contact Gianni and tell him the Cuomos have been ... situated. No, he will tell him they have moved into Villa Cuomo. The name gives it that personalized touch, don't you think?" Pleased with herself, Aria smiled.

"And since Gianni promised no contact with the girl, and my boy is a man of his word, he'll never know the truth."

Aria lifted a perfect brow. "Now he's your boy."

"He is, and you are my brilliantly scheming wife." Abramo kissed her deeply. As always, she roused the man in him, and he trailed kisses down her neck to the exposed swell of her heaving bosom as he thought to do the entire conversation.

"No, Abramo. This will keep until you return. Right now, you get yourself to Horatio's office. It should take you no more than an hour. I'll have them get the carriage ready while you go up and change." When disappointed eyes rose, Aria gave him a wink, "I'll be waiting for you in bed in nothing but my diamond necklace."

Eighteen

ALESSANDRA'S HEART RACED, and her chest tightened, making it difficult to breathe. The locked words in her throat eventually escaped in a loud, panicked voice.

"Get out. Get out."

Someone else screamed, or maybe what she heard was the screeching of steel on steel. Sounds and smells, fear and anxiety melded together. It was all becoming too confusing. It was all happening so fast.

"Get out. Get out of the car now."

A sheen of sweat layered Alessandra's face as the mangled car's image and the limp bodies raced in her slumbering mind. The vision of Nathan and Gabriel's small bodies crushed against the car's front seats made Alessandra's lungs contract.

Alessandra saw her mother's body slumped like a rag doll in the front seat. Shards of glass that had rained over her were stained red with blood. Her mother was as still as a stone.

Her father's body sandwiched between the steering wheel, and the front seat was vivid in her mind. His face was painted crimson from the blood spilling—from where she couldn't see.

Blood, thick red, flowed like a river spilling over its banks. But it was their eyes, wide, listless, and lifeless as they stared back, that assaulted Alessandra. Alessandra jolted up in bed.

Alessandra's heart pounded like a jackhammer in her chest.

Her breath heaving and strangled, Alessandra screamed, "Mama, Daddy, Nathan, Gabriel, I'm coming." She couldn't get them out. "Someone help me. Please, please help me get them out of the car."

Alessandra's cries pierced the silence and streamed through the murky shadows and into Luca's room, icing his skin. Bolting out of bed, Luca stumbled into his jeans. Heart thudding, he darted to Alessandra's room. Her face was marble-white as she rocked back and forth against the all too familiar fear and pain. Whimpering like a child, the stream of hot tears poured down Alessandra's face.

Luca's mind went blank with panic.

Alessandra screamed out for help again.

Shaking the panic off, Luca's mind cleared and deduced Alessandra was asleep. He remembered reading somewhere that you shouldn't shock a sleeping person out of a deep trance and moved to gather her in his arms to soothe and comfort.

Alessandra struggled to break loose while continuously apologizing. "I'm sorry, I'm so sorry for letting you down. I couldn't save you, Mama. I'm sorry I didn't do anything, Daddy. I'm sorry, Nathan, Gabriel. I'm so sorry I didn't save you."

Refusing to release her from his embrace, Alessandra succumbed to Luca's hold and burrowed her damp face into his chest. Trembling, Alessandra clung to Luca as he shushed and caressed her hair.

Teary eyes tilted up to Luca, and he met them with warmth and compassion. "I was in the car with them. I was the only one left alive. I saw them dead. I saw their slumped bodies. There was blood everywhere. So much blood. It's all over me." The scene played back vividly in her mind.

Luca took hold of her hands when she started to wipe herself. "There's no blood."

"It's all over me. It's red and thick."

"There's no blood, *amore*." Luca chained his arms around her to keep her still.

"I can't reach them. I can't save them. I can't do anything. Everything is going dark for them. I'm alive. They're not." Alessandra pressed her face into his bare chest as the tears of guilt burned her eyes.

The pain in Alessandra's voice, the tears dripping onto his chest, pulled on Luca's heart. He would have done anything to erase that dread in her eyes. "Shhh, they don't blame you for what happened."

"I'm alive. They're not." Alessandra's chest heaved in agitation. Her voice shook with pain and anger as guilt swirled inside her. "Get off of me." Alessandra pushed him away, but Luca held on tight.

"It wasn't your fault. Your family understands that. They understand it was an accident, and you had no control over it." The hand that stroked her hair was as tender as a gentle breeze, and Alessandra succumbed.

The warmth of Luca's body against hers offered the comfort Alessandra needed. Slowly she eased out of sleep and heard Luca's voice, strange and foreign, shushing her.

"I should have died with them. I shouldn't be alive." The anguish in her voice made Luca's chest constrict. "I've tried to join them twice, but I couldn't go through with it," Alessandra confessed in her moment of angst.

Stunned, Luca stared lifelessly, shock glazing his eyes.

Luca brushed the tangled hair from Alessandra's face, looked into the vulnerable eyes. "Your family would never want you to do that. They'd want you to live. They love you, and if you love them as much as I know you do, you will live for them." There was kindness and concern in his voice. "You will carry their legacy, their memories. You'll do that for them. Promise me you will."

Alessandra gave him a silent nod, and Luca drew her in for a tight hug. She heard his heart beating, listened to the gentle rhythm of his breath. The rise and fall of his chest soothed. His scent, male and potent, floated into her, and she breathed it in. She wanted to touch life and have life touch her.

Alessandra's lips were on his. She scraped her teeth lightly over his bottom lip. Pleasure hummed in his throat when she traced his lips with her tongue, dipped inside to tangle with his. God, she tasted so good. His bottom brain concurred.

Her kiss was intense, desperate, needy. As her mouth lingered on him, she increased intimacy. Parting his lips with her tongue, she heard him suck a breath.

Tasting her stirred hunger and want in him, and before he could stop himself, he responded to her invitation and tangled his tongue with hers. His mouth, hot, skilled, and greedy, fused with hers, fed her need to feel life.

Her lips were velvet-soft, sweet tasting. She put an ache of need and want in him Luca didn't know what to do with. At that moment, all he wanted was the taste of her to flow in him.

Luca pulled away.

"I want to be close to you." Alessandra's pleading words floated in the darkness.

Luca rested his forehead against hers, "There's nothing more I want than to be with you, but not like this, not now."

Alessandra clutched at Luca. "I want you to hold me and make it beautiful and hopeful and comforting."

His heart clenched when the eyes full of pain looked into his. "I wish I knew how to free you from this pain and take it on myself."

"You can." Alessandra brushed her lips to his. The heat hit him like a sucker-punch to the stomach and made his body come alive.

He'd wanted this for so long, had patiently waited for her—something he'd never done until her. He'd desired her in that instinctive, primal need men have to mate with a woman the moment they met. But soon realized she wasn't just any woman, and now that Alessandra was finally in his arms and all Luca wanted to do was to make love with her.

He wouldn't.

Luca kissed her. His lips on hers felt as perfect as he imagined they would. Alessandra was perfect. In that instant, as sure as the night was dark, Luca fell in love. There was nothing in the world more real to him than the love coursing in Luca's heart for Alessandra.

But now wasn't the time. If Luca let himself go, he'd resent himself, and Alessandra would resent him. He let the thought circle in his head. When it took root, with his heart pounding and his hormones demanding, Luca pulled back.

"I'll stay with you until you fall asleep."

"But..."

"I'll be right here, beside you. I promise I won't leave you." Tucking Alessandra under the blanket, he spooned his body against hers and enveloped her in his arms.

With the sound of the incoming rain drumming on the roof and window, Alessandra fell into sleep. For the first time in months, she slept deeply and dreamlessly.

Nineteen

WRAPPED IN HER grandmother's ratty robe, Alessandra stood framed in the doorway watching the man who'd flat out rejected her rummaging through her refrigerator for eggs and butter. He was the first man who turned her down after she practically threw herself on him.

Goddamn him, and how dare he?

After weeks of chasing after her, the lobbed sexual innuendos and advances, she'd offered herself to him, and he turned her down. Flatly refused her.

Instead, he'd offered her unconditional support, the words, and the comfort she'd needed. He'd lay next to her with only a thin layer of cotton between them and held her while she cried out her shock. There was no judgement, no demands, only unconditional support.

How was a woman supposed to react to such selflessness but open her heart and let him in? He was stealing her heart from under her.

Alessandra couldn't allow it to happen. She might be entering into a legal battle with Luca, and fraternizing with the enemy—in bed nonetheless—wasn't helpful.

But God, aside from the fact he'd done and said all the right things, he looked great.

Alessandra watched Luca fish the makings for a frittata from the refrigerator. Aside from the fact he looked drop-dead gorgeous in the white T-shirt sculpting his chest, the snug jeans, and the tousled hair, there was nothing more attractive than a domesticated man.

Alessandra had seen Luca doing what he was doing then many times before, but this morning it felt different.

Sensing Alessandra watching him, Luca turned. "*Buon giorno.*"

"Hi." Alessandra tilted a long-lashed gaze up to him that froze his brain.

"I wanted to surprise you with breakfast out on the patio. It's a beautiful day, and I thought..."

"Thank you for last night." Alessandra stepped forward, kissed him on the cheek.

Though he felt the urge to kiss her, he didn't. "There's nothing to thank..."

"It's the first time in months I slept soundly. When I woke this morning, I didn't feel as anxious or scared as I usually do. I felt wonderfully calm, so, yes, I have a lot to thank you for. So, again, thank you for being there for me." She gnawed on her bottom lip. "I, ah, think I said some things I shouldn't have. Somethings I've never told anyone but my therapist. And you probably think I'm..."

"Hurting a lot."

He understood her so well. A pleasant warmth flooded Alessandra. "Only you and my therapist know," she reiterated.

"Your secret is safe with me, but only if you promise that if the thought crosses your mind again, you'll talk to me about it. Better yet, you'll turn to a professional." The eyes that stared back were caring in their gaze, and at that moment, Alessandra felt a bond, a connection she'd never felt with anyone.

"I promise." Alessandra tucked a strand of hair behind her ear. The gesture made with unease was sinfully alluring.

"I'll be there for you whenever you need someone to talk to and for as long as you want me to be. Do you want me to be in your life, Alessandra?" Warm eyes met hers, and the shame consuming her slid away.

"I do, but..."

"I want you in mine." Luca traced the curve of Alessandra's cheek with his finger. "I can't stop thinking of you. You're in my system, in my head, and I can't shake you out," he said, awestruck by how much she'd come to mean to him.

"Don't say that. You don't know me. What you saw last night was just a sample of how broken I am."

"We all have issues we're working through."

Alessandra hunched her shoulders. "My issues are ginormous. My emotions are a tangled mess, and my head is scattered. I deal with PTSD, nightmares, and so much more. I don't want to visit that on you. And there are things you don't know about."

"I have my own baggage." His father's words drummed in his head. *Get her off the property by any means necessary. If you don't, I will.*

"You can't ask too much of me."

Luca pulled her in, chained his arms around her. "I won't."

In the folds of Luca's arms, Alessandra felt safe. Alessandra felt the comfort she needed. Luca was the rightness missing from her life all these months. Against her better judgement, Alessandra reached for his hand. Twinning fingers with his, she led him to her bedroom.

CHEERFUL SOUNDS OF TWEETING BIRDS AND rolling surf fluted through Alessandra's bedroom window as Alessandra shed her robe.

"Have you ever wanted something so badly you thought you'd burst? That's how I feel about you. It's how I've felt these past weeks since the night I met you," Luca said.

"That's because you've been floating that unfortunate naked image of me in your mind since that morning."

"I have cherished that image since then, but that's not why. I've wanted you from the moment I saw you because you fill my life with oxygen, and when I breathe it in, I feel as if you're filling me with something I've lacked all my life."

"Don't say that, Luca. You barely know me." Alessandra pulled away, but he caught her arm before she turned to go.

"Maybe I don't, but I know enough that I want to be with you. I know that every day shines brighter when you're in it. I know that I ache when you're not with me. I know I want to make love with you and make you feel life again, make it as hopeful and wonderful for you as it once felt. I know I want to do that for you, no strings attached, regardless of the consequences."

Alessandra wasn't expecting that. She had to meet the only man who wanted emotion to flow with a roll between the sheets. "Christ, Luca. I liked it better when you were the arrogant, cocky, annoying horndog grating on my nerves. I know how to handle him." She caught sight of the unmade bed, where he'd spent the night holding her—just holding her. What was he doing to her?

"Horndog?" His brow shot up, and she met it. "If it's sex you want. I'll give you that. I'll do anything you want me to." The irony of the moment, he thought. What was Alessandra doing to him?

"I do want to feel life. I haven't felt alive in a long while, but I'm not ready for ties or a commitment. I want to be with you, but no strings attached. I thought that's what you wanted."

Sensing the struggle inside her that had nothing to do with the moment, Luca slid his fingers under her chin, turned her to face him. "All right, if that's what you want. It's what I'll give you."

"It's all I want because I can't give you more. I'm going to hurt you, Luca."

"It's a risk I'm willing to take." Luca brushed his lips to hers with a gentle passion that made her tingle all over.

Alessandra tore away from him. "I'm serious."

"So am I."

It went quiet in the bedroom. All they heard was one another's breathing. "I felt a connection with you last night. I want to be with you, but I..." can't allow you to cloud my judgement and derail me from doing my duty. "Sex, Luca. It can't be anything more."

"If that's what you want. It's what I'll give you."

"I mean it, Luca."

"Me too." Luca crushed his mouth on hers when she opened it to launch into another argument. His kiss was gentle, tender, but it left her breathless. Alessandra tried to ease away, but her weakened legs and craving body cemented her where she stood. "I want you."

And Christ, she wanted him. Alessandra wanted him more than she wished to admit. It scared her. Luca set off emotions she hadn't felt before or knew how to control, but she'd made a promise to her family one she had to keep. Having Luca in her bed wasn't going to be conducive to fulfilling it. But God, her body hungered for his touch.

Alessandra was going to regret it, but Luca was in her head, her system, and she couldn't walk away from him. "Just sex, Luca."

"Just sex."

"No emotions, no expectations, no commitment."

"Tick, tick, tick," he said, wondering what in the hell was happening? Those were his words, his sentiment, what he expected from the women that slid into his bed. "You have my head swimming in crazy." He leaned in to kiss her, but she wiggled free.

"Promise me, Luca."

"I promise."

On his vow, Alessandra's hands streaked over the broad shoulders, under his T-shirt. The feel of his flesh under her hands set his skin on fire. Luca sucked in air, hissed it out.

In one quick move, she slipped his T-shirt off. Sweet and sour Jesus, she screamed in her head. He was beautiful. His body was tanned, trim, and hard as steel. This was a body hardened, defined by backbreaking labour. There was something sensual in that.

She took in his scent, musky and sultry. It breathed life into her. Her eyes told him just that, and Luca's mouth came down on hers. His kiss, frantic, needy, greedy, filled with desire, left her breathless.

"I've never needed anyone as much as I need you." Luca's arms chained Alessandra possessively.

She tilted her eyes up to the ones blue as sea and ocean. "Luca, just..."

"Can I see what's underneath that nightgown?" Luca interjected to shut her up.

Lace curtains billowed in a soft breeze carrying the pungent peaty smell of damp earth from last night's rain. The sounds of a waking morning filled the room. Under beams of sun spilling through the open window, Alessandra's smiling eyes met his as she slid the satin straps off her shoulders.

"Your turn." Her fingers skimmed down to the snap of his jeans.

Alessandra let out a long appreciative sigh at the lithe, bronzed body ready for her. He was perfect. This was perfect, she thought, melding her naked body to his. The glorious warmth of his skin against hers made her purr like a contented cat. Scooping her into his arms, he carried her to bed.

His mouth came down on hers with the sharp edge of need and passion. Kissing her long and deeply, he swallowed her soft sighs, the quiet moans as she floated and dissolved in his arms.

Luca's hot, hungry mouth streaked down her neck, over her shoulders to her breasts. Filling his mouth with them made her body, made her come alive. Christ, there was nothing like this feeling, Alessandra thought. She wanted as a woman wanted, and arching her body, she drove her breasts deeper into his mouth.

Luca's erotic slide of his tongue over her nipples down her belly was maddening. The man wasn't kidding when he said he had skills.

Sharp blades of arousal cut deep into her when his tongue trailed up her thigh, into the heat to her core. The shocking ripples of pleasure bulleting through her made her sing his name on a frenzied shudder.

His name on her lips made his heart drum in his ears.

Wave after delightful molten wave of heat washing over her, the orgasm burst powerfully, violently. The moment she thought it was over, his strokes went deeper. She gasped more out of shock than stunned arousal when he drove the next orgasm to swell in her.

She'd heard of the illusory multiple orgasm theory but had never experienced it firsthand. No one had made her soar over that precipice of sensational pleasure more than once. A few times, her limited dramatic skills had been put to the test, but here was Luca persisting with tongue and mouth.

When he made the pleasure whip through her for the third time, her eyes flew open, and she bucked her body against him. The tension she'd bottled up for months flowed like a giant sea swell, and she cried out his name like a prayer.

"Dear. Holy. God."

Luca straddled her damp, slaked body. "I hope that means I did right by you," he said, toying with her lips.

"Mmm-hmm," she hummed between breaths. "That felt wonderful and right and perfect." She framed his face with her hands. "Take me, Luca. Make me yours."

This wasn't just sex without emotion or expectations or commitment anymore, Luca thought. Flying on the notion, Luca took Alessandra's mouth for a passionate kiss and lovingly claimed her.

The connection he felt with her was a first. He felt complete.

He wanted, as a man wanted. Moving in her, he held on, drawing out the moment he didn't want to end for as long as possible. His pulse beat wildly, his heart thundered in his ears. He relished every stroke, every second inside her.

When his breaths became strangled, she joined him, rocked with him in rhythm. He fought to catch his breath as the quiet power built up in him. He moved with her until his self-control snapped and filled her.

For a long while, washed in the glorious warmth of slaked bodies and the inescapable emotions neither had felt before, they lay together in complete silence.

Rolling off her onto his side, Luca met her gaze. There was something raw and powerful in a woman who got deep under your skin in the best possible way. She was the best of him, and he loved who he was when he was with her.

"You make me feel whole and complete. I think I'm in..."

"Don't say it, Luca."

"It's the first time I've felt this way. I never imagined it would hit this fast or this hard. I feel like shouting it from the rooftop, and I'm going to say it. I think I'm in love with you, Alessandra Cuomo." He took that fast leap off the edge without a parachute and floated with it. Enfolding her into his life and saying the scariest words in man's lexicon felt damn great.

"You promised." Tears streaming from her eyes, she buried her face into his chest.

"I'm sorry I said anything. Please, don't cry, Alessandra."

Tugging her closer, his familiar scent slid into her, and the tears came faster. "You can't fall in love with me. You agreed. I'm going to hurt you. You heard what I told you last night. I'm broken right now, and I come with too much baggage." There was despair in her voice.

Luca held her hand to his cheeks. "You could never hurt me, and I've told you everyone has baggage."

"I will hurt you, and my baggage is an emotional one that cuts deep and affects me so deeply I thought of hurting myself. It's not something I want to burden anyone with."

Wiping tears from her cheeks, Luca looked into the pained eyes. "It's not a burden to me if it's your pain. Please, let me in, Alessandra. Let me be there for you."

The eyes that looked at her were full of love and compassion. Everything that dragged her down to the dark place she'd been drowning with the weight of her anger, hate and guilt for months dissolved.

How could she cast aside the man who made her feel safe, the man wrapping her complicated life into a neat parcel with his offer of love and understanding? Luca was the rightness she'd searched for months.

On a sigh, she rested her head on his chest. "I want to let you in, but..."

"If you hurt me, I'll pack my ego and be on my way. No questions asked. I promise."

Alessandra wondered how long it would be before he'd leave her.

Twenty

LUCA AND ALESSANDRA spent the rest of Sunday in bed. In between pleasant conversation, falling into a perfect rhythm, they explored heated bodies, fusing until passion, raw and real, poured out in violent eruptions.

It wasn't until early evening that they made their way to the kitchen in search of food. Together they whipped up a meal of bocconcini salad and grilled Paninis. Dinner spread on the patio table overlooking the blue waters of the Mediterranean, they ate and shared a bottle of wine.

Everything seemed different, appeared brighter, felt settled to Alessandra. For the first time in months, Alessandra looked forward to the future. Luca resurrected the feeling of hope and the confidence she'd lost.

Alessandra owed him the truth.

Biting into the last of her panino, Alessandra flicked eyes to Luca. "I'm electing you, our official panino maker."

Luca set his fork down. "Your salad was Michelin star rated."

Alessandra let out a soft, girlish laugh. "I do make a mean salad."

"Would you like more wine?"

Alessandra held her glass out. "You seem to have all the qualities a woman wants, and I'm guessing there have been lots of women who've wanted them. Why is it you're still single?" She asked, watching him over the rim of her glass.

"I haven't met the right girl. Until now, that is," he said, brushing his lips to hers. She smelled of the lavender soap they'd shared in the shower.

"You probably say that to all your conquests."

"I do." His admission netted a look of shock. "But with you, I mean it." That turned the mouth opened in a stunned O into curved lips.

Enjoying their wine, as the first scatter of rain falling over the sea began to move inland, they spoke. Alessandra mused how nice the comfort and familiarity of talking about nothing in particular but meaning so much felt.

"The rain is going to pick up soon. We better head inside, or we'll end up getting soaked." Luca started to clear the table, but she stopped him.

"I, umm, need to tell you something." The need for honesty was essential. They had crossed the friendship line into lovers, and the dynamics had changed.

Sensing the seriousness in her tone, Luca sat down. "All right. You can talk to me about anything," he said, sensing her anxiety.

"It's about Villa Cuomo."

"What about it?"

"As of this December, you'll have used the property for your crops for twenty years, uninterrupted and unchallenged."

A frown creased his brow. "And?"

The sound of rain and lashing winds filled the stretch of silence as Alessandra gathered her thoughts. "According to my, ah, lawyer." The burn of guilt rose in her chest when his shoulders tensed. "He claims you can take legal claim to the land, my home, under squatter's rights since technically you now meet the occupancy time."

"I see, and when did you hire this lawyer?" The shock was still filtering into his system, but he kept an even tone.

"Soon after I got here. Finding you in my home..."

"Made you assume I was a squatter out to take your land," he finished with a levelled tone as he watched her walk to the window.

Alessandra stopped and stared. Darker clouds filled the sky, and the sea was restless. "When I found out you were a lawyer, I reached out for legal advice." She hesitated for a moment, watched him considering the angles. "I know you cared for my *nonna*. That in my books counts for tons, but I know so little about your personal life. Everything I know, I've found out second hand. You know second-hand information comes with judgement. In the three months, we've been housemates, you've volunteered zero information about yourself. Not that I have either, but..."

Seeing her struggling for words, Luca reached out to close his hand over hers. "You're right. I haven't been forthright, and I'm sorry if I made you feel threatened in your own home." The air hummed between them while he took a moment to compose his thoughts.

"My title is Vice-President of International Affairs, but I'm not a lawyer, not in my heart. Becoming a lawyer was my father's dream. I love working with the land. Being able to turn a seed or cutting into a plant feels like an accomplishment. Nurturing its growth and watching it transform into life brings me joy. Agriculture is not for everyone. It's hard physical work, long hours, and it's a complicated science, which I have a knack for."

Wounded eyes demanded support, and she said, "There's no question you have a talent for it and that you have a love for the land. I mean, you just need only to look out there to know. Have you ever told your father?"

"You met my father. You think I'm able to talk to him. I'm thirty-six years old, and my father still controls my life. I've done what he expects of me for my entire life, what I'm told to do. He's chosen my likes and dislikes, directed the course of my life. And you don't contradict Dad." Frustration bright and sharp in Luca's eyes, he let out a deep sigh.

"I haven't told you much about myself or family because, well, they're complicated." Luca ran a frustrated hand through his hair. "I didn't want to complicate your life more than it already is."

Alessandra rose, kneeled next to him. "You took everything in my life unconditionally. I want to do the same for you."

"My life is complicated, Alessandra."

"Unconditionally," Alessandra repeated.

Luca took the time to pause and reflect. He was about to open the Pandora's Box filled with secrets and unpalatable truths about the Santinis that would inject conflict into their relationship as it always had and always would. Until now, he hadn't cared because, until Alessandra, he hadn't loved and losing her terrified him.

"My family owns the Santini Winery Corporation, one of the oldest and most prestigious wineries in Europe. Our history and lineage date back to the House of Savoy. It's very blue blood, very regal, and my father is deep into it. Dad believes history makes the man, and what we do in life becomes our legacy. He's not wrong. I, too, believe in that. The only difference is that my father is willing to attain it at any cost." Luca took the glass of wine she handed him, drank to wet a dry throat.

"Santini Winery was started a century ago. Generations of Santini built the company into the dynasty it is today. My father has been the most successful at managing the business worth billions. He doubled revenue in the first ten years of taking over the company by brokering the right relationships in the United States, which helped him break into that market and harness distribution channels. It was a challenge, but when my father sets his mind, it gets things done—at any cost. Once that market was in his pocket, he needed to maintain its momentum." Luca rose to walk to the edge of the patio.

"That's when he came up with the idea of introducing a line of specialty wine processed from a unique grape, a hybrid he developed—after years of research. It cost millions to develop, and cultivation had to be done under cloak and dagger to keep the competition away. A handful of farms were sourced to carry the project forward. Villa Cuomo was one. It met the necessary criteria. It was privately owned, small enough not to raise attention, and met the soil conditions to farm the Florentia grape. There are only a handful of people entrusted with the process. You're now one of them."

Through the rumble of thunder, rain lashed, torrential, and unforgiving on water and land and found its way onto the patio. Reaching for her hand, he pried her to her feet and led her into the kitchen.

Settling at the table, Alessandra watched Luca reach for the coffee maker. "That means your father wants you to take on a farming role."

"I should explain. I've taken over the management of the private farms that cultivate the Florentia not because I was assigned the task but because I fell into it. Your grandmother wouldn't deal with anyone other than me." Luca set the percolator on the stove over a full flame. "My father approached her with an offer to buy the land. He offered her a tidy sum. It would have allowed her to live her retirement years in luxury, so he assumed it was a done deal." He set coffee cups, saucers, and sugar on the table.

"Regardless of how good a deal, it was my grandmother refused to sell." Alessandra's voice rose to compete with the rumble of thunder overhead.

"That's what happened. My father isn't used to dealing with people who can't be bought. He believes everyone can be, and to a certain extent, he's right. People are generally greedy, and when you throw someone with deep pockets willing to spare no expense to get what he wants, it changes the dynamics. It makes the process simpler, but that wasn't the case with your grandmother. She couldn't be bought at any price. He'd never come up against someone like her and treated her as an adversary. Rather than..." Luca hesitated, trying to find the right words.

"A stubborn old woman set in her ways," Alessandra offered.

Luca smiled at the apt description. "Exactly, so in the end, all he did was piss her off and made her more determined not to sell."

"She had her reasons."

"It was her prerogative. It was her land." Luca poured coffee into their cups and sat next to Alessandra.

"I assume that's when you came into the picture. You walked in with the dreamy, blue eyes and the handsome face to sweet talk a lonely old woman."

"You make me sound like a..."

"Sex god," she finished with a wink. "You are, *amore*."

Luca flashed her a sheepish smile. "Anyway, I'd been around a vineyard for most of my life. I knew how her land was going to be used. It could have been that I cast a spell on her or that I was an ambitious whippersnapper—her term—that endeared her. Either way, she took an instant liking to me."

"I can understand why." Alessandra grinned, pleased her grandmother approved of him.

"I think it was because I treated her as a human being, not as a business deal. In the end, she told me she'd be happy to bring the land back to life that she'd let me use it on the condition I never allow my father to set foot in her home or speak to her, and I remain as her only contact. Her requests met, she signed on the dotted line, and we began planting the vines you see today." Luca's eyes cast out the window to the land where rain fell on hundreds of trees standing in a series of rows that his work and dedication had brought to life.

"How long does the contract give you access to the land?"

"Your grandmother renewed it for another ten years a few months before she died, but it became null and void on her passing." Luca picked up his espresso, drained it.

"So you have been squatting on the land."

"Technically, no. As per the lease, payments continued to be paid into an account. I figure eventually, a relative somewhere would pop up, and I'd turn the account over. I've already signed the account over to you. It's at the Banca Centrale. I'll take you this week if you like."

Surprise flashing in her green eyes, she dropped the coffee cup down in its saucer. "Why didn't you tell me this before?"

"I wanted to enjoy my time with you as Luca without having the Santini name or my family's complications come into the equation. I wanted you to know me for who I am. Not for the name I bear or who my family is."

Alessandra thought of the staggering implications that came with such a powerful name and so much wealth.

Alessandra saw first-hand how women fussed over him. Until now, she thought it had to do with his Adonis looks. She wondered now whether the money and the Santini name triggered the adulation. Alessandra imagined the mental gymnastics his mind went through every time he met someone.

Lightning lancing the sky and the touching sea drew Luca's gaze out the window. He saw a cruise ship unhurriedly sailing through the lashing rain and leaving a trail of smoke from its stack.

"Do you see me differently now that you know who I am?"

Alessandra brought her hand to Luca's cheek, "You don't think very highly of yourself. While thinking you were a squatter out to take my land from under me, I was drawn to you. Therefore, logically speaking, being who you are makes no difference to me. If truth be told, it scares me to death to know what I know now."

Luca flicked a muddled gaze at Alessandra. "What do you mean?"

"I'm the type of woman who gets chocolate on her face eating tiramisu. I allowed a stranger to see me naked by way of introduction. I come into your life a broken woman. All qualities, which I'm guessing, are unacceptable in your world. I wasn't bred for the circles you take for granted, and I sure as hell wasn't built to deal with the drama that comes with such a prestigious name. Those are only a few of the reasons why it scares me to death."

Women were willing and eager to roll on their backs for him and do anything necessary to pull him into their web. By Alessandra's reasoning, the Santini name, with all its money, prestige, and influence, was a drawback, not the profitable gain women targeted for. Alessandra was willing to take Luca, as he was, failings and all. That was why Luca was falling in love with her.

"There's not a thing I'd change. You're perfect as you are." Luca tucked the loose curl behind her ear. "Do you know why your lawyer thinks I can take claim of the land?"

"Not exactly. He's out of town for a few weeks. I'm supposed to meet with him when he gets back to discuss his findings."

"Would you mind if I attend the meeting with you? I want to talk to him and understand why he's making the claim."

Alessandra rose, sat on his lap, and without hesitation said, "I don't mind at all."

Warmed by Alessandra's response, Luca pressed his forehead to hers. "All right then, set up the meeting. By the way, what's his name?"

"Daniel DiBlassio. I met him on the flight from Toronto. He's a nice, trustworthy man."

He hoped "nice and trustworthy," translated to old. Making a mental note of the name, he refrained from asking the probing questions whipping around his head. Luca understood Alessandra's need to keep Daniel from him but wondered how many times they'd met, when, and where.

Luca shook away the thoughts crowding his mind when it dawned on him it was jealousy eating at him. Another new feeling Luca didn't know what to do with. What was this woman doing to him?

Mistaking the tangle of emotions that passed Luca's face for annoyance, Alessandra cursed herself. "Don't hate me for what I've done. We'll meet with Daniel together, and we'll sort this out."

Looking into her eyes, Luca said, "I could never hate you, and we will sort this out. I promise you it was never my intention to take your land. I would never allow that to happen. I hope you know I'd never hurt you."

"I know that now. Just as you should know, I'm grateful to you for being there for my nonna and me. I don't care what your last name. All I want is to be there for you as you've been there for me. I want to make you feel as happy and loved as you make me feel." Alessandra sealed her remark with a passionate kiss.

Luca's love for her evolved into something deeper, something he hadn't anticipated. It took a firm hold of him, consuming every fibre of his being. At that moment, he knew he'd never love another as he did her.

Love flowing through him, he blurted out, "I love you, Alessandra." Feelings on the table, he thought, and there was no going back.

Alessandra brushed her lips over his to ease the panicked look on his face. "I love you too, Luca."

Twenty-One

ALESSANDRA PROMISED LAINE to get Luca home to spend time with her son. Now minutes from Villa Santini, Alessandra regretted making the promise.

"You have nothing to be nervous about. My mother's taken a liking to you, which doesn't often happen," never, actually. "So, she's clearly smitten." Luca veered the car past the slower traffic.

"It's not your mother I'm worried about. I sensed animosity from your father when we met at Fellini's."

"You misread him." It was difficult to say the words with confidence when, at that moment, Luca's father was the reason for his own anxiety. "Besides, it's my mother you have to win over. You know, I'm her little boy." Luca's all teeth grin made Alessandra laugh, and he thought he heard relief in it.

"It's pretty here in the spring," Alessandra said, watching pastoral green hills blooming with spring roll past. Budding colours heralding the season sprouted in the vibrant fuchsia and pink wood sorrels and gladiolus painting the landscape. The green, thick carpet beneath them glinted with dew. Groves burst with hundreds of flowering almond and olive trees, and fragrant rosemary bushes scented the air.

Luca drove past sleepy villages with stone houses, and steepled churches tucked in the hills' hollows as if hiding from the world. To the west, mount Aetna's snow-covered peak rose to a dramatic height against a blue sky. Grapevines stretched to the base of its jagged rock.

"It's beautiful all year round," Luca said, driving past the cast iron gates fashioned with welcoming gods. "That's Dionysus, the god of the grape harvest and wine," Luca explained when her brows creased. "And this is Villa Santini." He announced, killing the car's engine next to the fountain with the goddess reverently gazing at the sky as if guarding it.

The ten thousand-acre estate that made up Villa Santini was jaw-dropping. Thousands of vines in perfect symmetry for as far as the eye could see coexisted with green hills and miles of sun-bleached sand. Gardens sprouted pink and purple clover, yellow lilies, and blood-red poppies and scented the air with their fragrance.

The façade of the stately home was white brick with Baroque tones. Tall windows glinted under a late morning sun. Towering doors of deeply carved oak wide enough to accommodate a herd of elephants stood at the top of a red flagstone staircase. From balconies, bougainvillea wound through iron balusters and cascaded like a colourful waterfall.

Alessandra stepped out of the car, breathed in the scent of the sea and mowed grass. "To say this is impressive is an understatement."

"This land dates back over five generations of Santini's." Luca reached for her hand and led her up the steps through the front door.

The foyer was the size of her home. High ceilings, marble floors, and a curving staircase edged in black iron floated to the second floor. French doors opened to a luxurious living room with plush sectionals, Murano lamps and an exquisite

Monaco coffee table. A black stone fireplace was the centrepiece of the room, as was what Alessandra assumed to be the original da Vinci above its mantelpiece.

The overwhelming sensation of money was everywhere.

Luca walked Alessandra down the long hallway where walls lined with framed paintings of authoritative-looking men followed them into the kitchen bright with sunshine.

The aroma of roasting chicken scented the air. White cabinets lined tan-washed walls. Beneath them, polished black counters gleamed.

Luca snuck up to the matronly looking woman tearing lettuce into a bowl and took her into an enthusiastic embrace. "*Ciao, Moma.* You're looking younger and more beautiful every day." He pecked her on both cheeks.

"It's not nice to tease an old woman." A girlish blush flooded Moma's lined face as she swept fingers through the swirl of peppered hair. "Now, let me look at you. A healthy glow on your face, meat on your bones and ... happy," she said approvingly, turning to Alessandra, whom she assumed was the reason for the grin on his face. "You do that?" Moma asked in Italian.

Luca let out a booming laugh. "Moma is a shy one."

"I just want to know if she's the reason for the grin on this beautiful face." Moma pinched Luca's cheek.

Luca slid an arm around Alessandra's waist. "Yes, she's the reason for the smile. Moma, Alessandra Cuomo. Moma's the love of my life. She's taken care of me since I was a baby."

"It's a pleasure to meet you, *Signora* Moma." Alessandra's Italian was almost flawless.

"It's nice to meet you," Moma said to Alessandra before turning to Luca. "Your mama is out on the terrace. I'll bring you each a glass of chilled Florentia wine."

Luca mirrored the old woman's smiling jet-black eyes. "Now, you can taste the wine your grapes produce," he whispered in Alessandra's ear.

"I thought the wine was sold only through pre-orders, and you'd be hard-pressed to find a bottle out of season."

"Yes, but my father holds back a few cases for himself."

"Well, go on. Take the young lady out to the patio." Moma waved a hand.

"We better do as she says." Luca took Alessandra's hand. "By the way, her name is Mona, but as a child, Moma was how I pronounced it, and it stuck."

"By any name, she seems like a lovely woman, devoted to you," Alessandra said, although the affection in Luca's eyes for Moma told her the remark was unnecessary.

Stepping aside, Alessandra walked out the French doors onto the slate terrace. Under a striped canopy with a view of the swimming pool, hemmed by manicured gardens overlooking the white curve of beach and blue waters, Laine sipped wine. Diamonds glinted at her ears and fingers, and a wide-brimmed hat covered the gold spun hair. Her skin was bronze against the white sundress. Even in the casual dress, and suede flats, Laine looked like a woman of taste and means.

Laine tipped down the black-rimmed sunglasses and jumped to her feet. "You're here. You're actually here."

"By the way, don't even breathe a word that you know about the Florentia grape or that I've taught you everything about our most well-guarded secret," Luca murmured.

Laine drew Luca into a motherly embrace. "Thank you for bringing him," she mouthed to Alessandra.

Pulling away, Laine took an assessment of her son. "You look wonderful, *amore*. I've never seen you so relaxed, and..." Laine hesitated, studying her son.

"Happy." Moma finished Laine's thought setting wine and glasses down. "He's happy. Not his usual miserable self."

"Yes, happy. You're absolutely right, Moma."

"Aren't I always?" Moma poured the wine, handed Luca and Alessandra each a glass. "I'm going to be very busy in the kitchen getting lunch ready, and I don't want any further disturbances. Understood?" Moma shot them a look that made Laine, Luca, and Alessandra flinch.

"Understood." All three said simultaneously.

"She's lucky I can't boil water and that I love her as much as I do." Laine turned to Alessandra. "It's nice to see you again, dear, and don't you look lovely and spring-like." Laine pecked Alessandra on the cheeks.

Alessandra didn't get the usual air-kiss, but the whole two-cheek deal Luca noted.

"Close your mouth, Luca. The birds will mistake you for a feeder," said Laine.

Alessandra giggled at that. "It's nice to see you again, Mrs. Santini, and thank you for inviting me to your home, which is lovely."

Laine waved Alessandra to the chair next to her. "It's my pleasure, dear. It's nice to have female company."

Eyes wide, Luca watched in awe as his mother and Alessandra chatted. They smiled, laughed, and complimented. His mother's hand reached out to touch and hold Alessandra's, for God's sake. The scene of the two women he loved embracing, connecting sent shockwaves through him. Luca was sure he was experiencing an out-of-body experience.

Laine turned to Luca. "Close your mouth and refill our glasses. You like the wine, Alessandra?"

"It's the best I've ever tasted."

"Then don't be shy to drink as much as you like. We are in Italy, where wine is consumed like water." Laine raised her glass, and Alessandra met it.

"Italians do love their wine,"

"And their food and lovemaking," Laine winked at Alessandra, then tilted her gaze to a dumbfounded Luca. "*Amore*, if you drop that bottle, you know Moma is going to take you over her lap and spank you. I may just enjoy it. I haven't seen that butt over her lap in some time." Both women burst out laughing, and Luca's eyes scanned the area looking for the four horsemen of the apocalypse.

Alessandra's smile faded when the uneasiness crept up her spine, and she struggled against the intimidating nerves that set in when Antonio Santini stepped onto the terrace.

The picture of righteous indignation, Antonio offered Luca a stiff hand. "Son."

Luca met the offered hand with a forced smile. "You remember, Alessandra?"

"I do." Antonio turned his gaze to her.

The girl was breathtakingly beautiful, but every woman on Luca's arm usually was. Alessandra's beauty, however, was natural and wholesome, a rarity from the heavily painted, plastic-faced women who paraded in-and-out of Luca's life. Any man could be drawn into her web—particularly his son—Antonio reasoned.

And there was no doubt Luca was bedding her. The look in his son's eyes spoke of love and intimacy. Maybe Laine was right about Luca being in love with the girl, Antonio thought. Still, he wasn't about to let his guard down as easily as his son or Laine had.

Too often, Antonio found people capable of masquerading behind forged façades to get at their wealth. Alessandra could very well be playing Luca to get at his money. The women in his life were all jockeying for a position in the Santini fold. Antonio's sixty-six years on this earth had taught him that women were more cunning than men when it came to protecting their interests.

"Have a seat." Antonio imperiously waved Alessandra down.

Coiling fingers around her wine glass to stop them from shaking, Alessandra nervously said the first thing that came to her mind. "You have a lovely home."

Antonio flushed with pleasure and with hawk-like eyes, asked Alessandra, "What would you say if I told you that all this would someday be Luca's?"

Laine opened her mouth to chastise her husband's arrogance but closed it when Luca, sensing his father's hostility toward Alessandra, jumped in like a warrior to defend. The fierce look in Luca's eyes confirmed what Laine had suspected all along. Luca was in love with Alessandra.

"Don't start, Dad, or..."

"That's all right, Luca. It's a conversation." Knowing the question had a deeper connotation, Alessandra wasn't about to pass up the chance to respond. "I'd say it's something to look forward to. It's a stunning property. Who wouldn't want to live here?" She paused a beat to compose her anxious thoughts. "But at the same time, it scares me to death."

Alessandra's unexpected comment piqued Antonio's interest. "How so?"

Alessandra's confidence surging, she said, "It's a huge responsibility for one person to bear."

"But it's just a house, land." Antonio's voice, like her gaze, remained steady.

He's enjoying this. "Maybe I'm reading too much into it and understand this is coming from someone who doesn't come from your world of money and privilege, so it's difficult for me to understand the machinations of it. To me, this is not just a house and land, but so much more."

Intrigued brows raised. "How is that, Miss Cuomo?"

"Alessandra. This is Santini history, a legacy you're handing your son with the expectation to carry until the next generation. It's something that has come to fruition because of your work and dedication and that of your ancestors to make it what it is today. I'd be terrified to have to be accountable for such an enormous financial and moral obligation." Alessandra thought of her obligation to Rosa and the overwhelming responsibility she felt to keep a promise.

Impressed with Alessandra's insight, Antonio gave a subtle nod of respect. "But there are perks that come with such a demanding job or 'obligation' as you call it. You get to play and live in magnificent homes like this. You get wealth and the prestige that comes along with it."

And grow so out of touch with reality that you've alienated your only son to the point of losing sight of the wonderful man he is, Alessandra thought.

"You're telling me you're not sidling up to Luca to reap the benefits that come with the Santini name?" The smug look on Antonio's face made her blood simmer.

Luca was about to put an end to the caustic and inquisitorial conversation when his mother gave him a subtle head shake. There was more to Alessandra than the deep-green eyes led you to believe, and Antonio needed to be shown that first hand.

Alessandra shot Antonio a fiery glare that could have thawed the North Pole. "With all due respect, Mr. Santini, I don't 'sidle up' to anyone and my friendship, loyalty, and love can't be bought—at any price. I'm very selective of the people I allow into my life. It would be you, Mr. Santini, who'd be grateful to me if I decided you're good enough to allow you to 'sidle up' to me." Alessandra's burning eyes caught what she thought was a smirk of admiration on Antonio's face, but it didn't deter her.

"In your world, wealth is a measure of success. In mine, it's a person's character. Integrity can't e bought. It's your identity. It's what we're judged on regardless of our origins, gender, the colour of our skin, or financial standing." Alessandra let her words hang in the crisp silence for a moment. "And if truth be told, Mr. Santini, how often do you enjoy what you reap? For example, how often do you enjoy this home?"

Antonio drank wine to help him wash down the taste of bruised ego. "I don't spend much time here."

"Why not? You'd be hard-pressed to find a more perfect utopia." Alessandra turned to look out to sea, where the water was a pale green near the shore and a deep blue beyond it.

"I'm out of town often," said Antonio.

"Working?"

"Yes."

"Then it's not as much of a perk as you make it out to be."

"My wife enjoys it. She spends a lot of time here." Antonio pointed out.

"She'd enjoy more if you were here to share it with her, and as much as you think you're doing it for your family, they may wish you weren't. As you're shortening your lifespan in favour of your company's bottom line, you're minimizing the time you spend with your family and driving them away in the process. But it's a double-edged sword, isn't it, Mr. Santini? You can't have all this without putting in the sacrifice, the twenty-four-seven schedule. Without that demanding work ethic, you'd have none of this." Alessandra's eyes and tone remained unshaken.

"A privileged lifestyle doesn't come easy or cheap. Inherited or not, sacrifices must be made. Don't get me wrong. I don't mind hard work or reaping its rewards. However, I do mind sacrificing my life and family because, in the end, family is all you have, and alienating them is not worth the price of success. Your family won't be around forever, Mr. Santini, and neither will you. By the time you realize that it may be too late to make amends. So you see, Mr. Santini, getting all this, as beautiful and as valuable as it is, doesn't entice me in the least."

Luca's admiration and respect for Alessandra growing ten-fold, he murmured, "Checkmate," while Laine whispered, "Well done."

Alessandra sunk back in her seat and measured Antonio over the rim of her wine glass. "No disrespect meant, Mr. Santini. I was answering your question."

As Antonio opened his mouth, Laine cut him off. "Let's head into the dining room to enjoy this wonderful lunch Moma's prepared," Laine said, sliding an arm through the crook of her husband's. "Don't be angry with yourself, darling. There's a lot more beyond that pretty face you didn't bargain for. The girl has a brain and character. I'd say an admirable one." Laine's observation netted her a grunt and scowl.

"Do you still believe she's using her feminine wiles to exploit our son? Because if you ask me, I think it's our son who's working on drawing her into this lair of ours, and I think the girl has no interest in getting involved with the lot of us."

Twenty-Two

THE NEXT FEW days were one of those rare and wonderful interludes life throws your way, which made everything seem perfect. For the first time, Luca and Alessandra understood what love meant and believed their future was filled with promise. Until...

"I'd like to see you on my return in a couple of weeks, son." Antonio's authoritative voice came at Luca over the telephone. "I want an update on where you stand with the takeover of Villa Cuomo." Antonio hung up before Luca could get a word in.

The conversation left Luca's stomach knotted, and he couldn't shake the feeling.

LUCA WATCHED ALESSANDRA FOLLOW THE CURVE of the beach. Long, lean legs pressed down on the sand. With each step, he saw the power in them. Her skin glistened with a film of sweat. The ponytail swung like a pendulum in rhythm with her strides.

"What's this?" Alessandra asked at the sight of the towel spread on the sand and the picnic basket.

Shielding his eyes from the sun, Luca watched Alessandra perch her sunglasses on her head. "I've been moody these past few days, and I wanted to make it up to you. With the beach to ourselves, I thought I'd surprise you with brunch."

"You have been on edge lately, but I understand it has nothing to do with me and everything to do with the upcoming meeting with your father." She ran the back of her hand against her sweaty forehead. "You still don't know what it's all about?"

With a straight face, Luca shook his head in response. Keeping secrets from Alessandra was what had him stressing and his stomach twisting in tight knots. How could Luca tell Alessandra his father wanted an update on where he stood in taking ownership of Villa Cuomo?

"How about you take your mind off the call and enjoy this wonderful brunch." Alessandra eyed the spread of cold cuts, fruit salad, espresso coffee, Maria's bread, and pastries.

"You're right, let's. In a few weeks, when summer rolls in, this place will be jam-packed." Luca reached into the cooler for a water bottle, turned it over to Alessandra watched her hold it against her neck before uncapping it and taking a long swig. "You hungry?"

"Starving." Alessandra sat next to him.

"What would you like to start with?"

"I'll take a bowl of fruit salad." Alessandra took off the baseball cap, fanned her hair with her fingers.

"You were longer than usual on your run." Luca spooned salad into a bowl, drizzled honey on top.

"I met a fellow runner. She took me through the town and areas I haven't been." Alessandra gave him all the details about her new friend and their run. "She's staying at a beachfront B&B thirty minutes from here. She invited me to dinner, but I wasn't sure if we have plans." She tucked her tongue in her cheek, and as she'd hoped, Luca smiled.

"What time is she expecting you?"

"Sevenish."

"I'll drive you."

"You don't mind?"

Luca shook his head. "I know you need a girlfriend to brag about my sexual prowess to."

Alessandra's eyes lit with laughter. "It's nice to have a woman to talk with."

"I know." His lips skimmed hers. "Just be kind when you talk about me."

"No need for that, my sex god."

Luca's eyes, warmly blue, smiled. "Are you enjoying your runs on the beach, or are you still doing it for the therapeutic benefit?"

"Both. I enjoy running, and how could I not take advantage of the beauty around me?" Alessandra gazed at the silky waters reflecting the sky like a mirror. "I have the beautiful Mediterranean Sea steps from my home and perfect weather. Running in such peaceful surroundings helps me deal with ... everything."

It had been months since the accident—was that the right word for something so destructive?—and the slash of pain and anger still occasionally surfaced and shot straight to her stomach and flipped it over. The man, who'd struck her parents' car was drunk, had blown beyond the legal limit, and that was no accident. Alessandra often wondered how the legal system meant to protect them could only slap a meagre six-year sentence for killing her entire family.

Alessandra toyed with the fringe of the spread. "I had a lot of anger and hate. My emotions were in turmoil. I was sleeping my days away. I realize now that sleeping was a conduit to bottling up my emotions. I needed to expend that bad energy, and running does it."

The pain and anguish in her eyes palpable, Luca reached for her hand as if the contact triggered transference. "I wish I could take all the hurt from you."

Alessandra set the bowl and spoon down and turned her eyes to Luca. "You have. My runs have contributed to my mental state's betterment, but that's only a temporary fix. You're the one who's helped turn my life around. Meeting you is the best thing that has happened to me. I didn't think I could love or feel love again. You changed that." Soft lips pressed to his in gratitude.

"I've done nothing. You've done it yourself. You're a strong woman. You just needed time. We all would, after such a tragic life-changing event." Luca skimmed his thumb over the honey dripping from the corner of her mouth.

"I told you I'm not classy material."

Luca responded by brushing his lips to hers, sweetly, tenderly. "You're perfect the way you are." She smiled at that and fell into the silence he left. "You haven't woken up screaming in weeks."

"Knowing you're lying next to me has helped keep the nightmares away."

Luca watched her eyes focus on some distant point. "What's wrong?"

"I've wondered at times if maybe I've pushed you into this, that we may be moving too quickly." As much as being with Luca felt right and perfect, comfortable and safe, the thought often crossed her mind since asking him to share her bed permanently.

Luca cupped her chin, lifted her face to meet his. "You haven't pushed me into anything. I love lying next to you at night and waking up to those beautiful green eyes every morning. I want to be with you every minute of every day. I've never felt about anyone the way I feel about you. Truth be told, I thought it was me pushing and putting unfair demands on you."

"You should know by now I don't do anything I don't want to. I enjoy the time we spend together and being with you. I'm everything I am because of you, and I love you for that."

Emotions swirled in Luca's eyes. Alessandra spoke from the heart. Her words weren't laced with the contrived prattle he was used to hearing from the women who passed through his life.

"You can't imagine how happy you make me." He kissed her with a passion that evolved into something deeper every time their lips met.

Alessandra met the blue eyes aimed her way. "Ditto."

"Now, how about I give you something to brag about to your friend tonight? Join me for a swim. I brought your bathing suit down, but I'd rather you didn't waste time changing."

Luca shed T-shirt and jeans to expose powerful shoulders and a hard body that tapered down to narrow hips. The orange Speedo set off the skin the colour of burnt-caramel.

The man's body was glorious, Alessandra thought, her eyes never leaving him as he walked through the foamy froth crashing on the white sand and dived in.

Toeing her running shoes and socks off, Alessandra followed him into the water.

Twenty-Three

ANTONIO'S FOCUS NEVER left the paperwork in his hand when Luca walked into his study. He wore a navy, hand-tailored Brioni suit that made him look elegantly suave and authoritative.

"I'll be a moment, son. Pour yourself a drink."

The usual tension his father set off in Luca made his shoulders knot tight, and he made a beeline for the bar. Pouring himself two fingers of scotch, Luca took it in too quickly for pleasure. Luca refilled his glass with a generous pour and walked to the window.

Sun poured bright when Luca pushed the shutters open. There was an exotic flair to the blend of steel blue water, green from the trees, and the medley of colours from the gardens. That glorious view was why his father converted the family room into his study.

The memories, as clear as water, swam back. Flashes of Luca playing with his Legos and Tonka trucks while his father, behind his Cocobolo desk, went over the mounds of paperwork that rarely shrunk came at him. Luca idolized his father and vowed he'd sit behind the desk, running the family business as he did then.

But as Luca got older, his admiration for Antonio waned into resentment as his father took control of his life. Antonio steered him to study law at his Alma mater. He coaxed him to socialize in their circles of wealth and snobbery to cultivate the necessary connections.

As much as Luca enjoyed the privileged life Santini money afforded, he never felt fulfilled, felt lost. That is until, at his father's insistence, he learned the business from the ground up, he sent Luca to Villa Cuomo.

A young sixteen, Luca learned to respect the lands that brought them wealth and power. Remembering the first time he dug his hands into rich earth and planted his first cutting into Villa Cuomo soil, Luca smiled. The experience gave him a wonderful sense of satisfaction and accomplishment and opened his eyes to a new world. One Luca wanted to become a part of.

To work with the land, outdoors and not sit in a stuffy office heading meetings with self-serving, entitled corporate types who'd, thrust the knife in your back if you didn't dodge at the right moment was what Luca wanted. Selling the idea to his father was an uphill battle, and the thought of letting his father down wasn't in the cards. As Antonio Santini's only son, there was no escaping the responsibility of carrying on the family business.

Luca tried his best to fulfill his duty to his family, the firm, and his father, but he couldn't muster the passion needed to lead the company and its thousands of employees. It wasn't for fear of failure or lack of leadership skills. Luca was a Santini, after all, and the ability to command was in his blood. It was because Luca didn't have it in him to put the company ahead of everything and everyone and make it his only priority, as his father expected. Santini Winery was his father's world, not his.

The click of his father's briefcase shattered Luca's thoughts. "Have a seat, son." Antonio's tone was business-like and cold.

Luca sat at the guest chair, glad for the distance the massive desk put between them.

The desk, polished to a shine, was orderly with everything in its place. The OUT basket was stacked inches higher than the IN. A two-line black telephone sat at exactly a forty-five-degree angle. Next to it, a leather-bound holder held a selection of Montegrappa pens. Orderly and organized was his father's way.

Luca took half of his drink as he mentally prepared to enact the script written long ago that both players knew well. Although the ending was a predictable one, each would utter the words repeated over the years.

"When are you going to get into the office to do some real work, son?"

"I am working, Dad. I'm overseeing the vineyards."

Antonio brought steepled fingers to his chin. "Last I checked, planting didn't require legal expertise."

No matter his age, his father could make his balls shrink to grape size. "It's what I want to do, Dad."

"You have an Oxford-trained legal mind, Luca, and you need to put it to use if you're to take over the company."

"I'm not ready to take over yet, Dad," or ever, for that matter.

"You weren't ready at twenty-eight, at thirty, or thirty-two. You're now thirty-six. I was running the company at..."

"Twenty-one, I know, Dad, but I'm not you. I need more time."

The script played out on cue. His father would huff a breath of dismay, and as was always the case, Luca would leave deflated, feeling ashamed and guilty, like a complete failure. He'd resent his father.

Luca wondered why he bothered to come. He was thirty-Goddamn-six years old, a grown man who should have control of his life.

"The harvest at Villa Cuomo will produce quality grapes for us this year?" Antonio asked in the same authoritative tone he employed with his staff.

"It will, on schedule and in the expected volume." Luca drank deeply, hoping the effects of the alcohol would settle in sooner than later.

Antonio sank back in the marshmallow-soft leather chair. "You believe the typicity of this year's Florentia crop will reflect our past vintages?"

"You know there's no simple way to measure typicity, especially on such a new variety of grape, but I'm confident this year's crop will offer the signature characteristics our customers have come to expect." Luca's voice boomed with confidence.

"Good to hear. You've been closely monitoring the ten vineyards we cultivate the Florentia."

"I have, particularly now that we're getting closer to harvesting time. In the coming months, I'll be making trips more often to the farms, but based on the reports I'm getting, the farms will produce the estimated juice volume and meet every requirement. It's all in here." Luca set the report down on the desk.

"Excellent work, son." This was a change in the script. Wide-eyed, Luca stared at his father. "But we still need to increase output. The Florentia wine is in great demand. We're fetching up to five thousand dollars per bottle, and I'd like to continue to capitalize on that. I'm looking to increase production. It's why I wanted to see you." Antonio slid the manila folder across the desk. "I'm looking to purchase this parcel of land. It's an existing vineyard in the Tuscany region."

Luca reviewed the aerial shots of the property with interest. "This is far bigger than the existing properties, and it won't be privately owned. It doesn't meet the scope we set of using small privately-owned land to fly under the radar."

"No, it doesn't, but at this point, we've grown too big to be able to persist with that strategy. This vineyard is already in place and meets our needs."

"Looks like a good fit, Dad." Feeling more at ease with his father, Luca relaxed his attack stance. "We can bottle the juice generated by the existing crop this year and put in place a conversion program to cultivate Florentia grape only by the fifth year."

"That's what I was thinking." The boy had the brains to lead Santini Winery, Antonio thought. If only he could get his head out of his ass long enough to concentrate on the company.

Luca started to speak when the click of heels on marble cut into the conversation. Both men swung eyes to the raven-black-haired woman sashaying toward them with instinctive grace.

Her hair fell in wisps around a delicate, alabaster face. The coal-dark eyes that gazed from under thickly mascaraed lashes had a slumberous look. Her mouth, traced in wine-red, was like a beacon—or warning. The white Armani suit that hugged the curvy body and breasts spoke volumes of the wealth she had no qualms in flaunting.

"Nice to finally put a face to the voice, *Signore* Santini." Her voice rumbled with a confident tone.

Antonio rose and met the offered hand. "Likewise, *Signorina* Donatella, I'd like you to meet my son, Luca."

"Elisa, please. It's nice to meet you, Luca. Your father has told me so much about you. I feel as if I already know you." Holding out her hand for Luca, she eyed him with predatory eyes. He was yummier in person, she mused. The fun they could have together.

"Can I offer you a drink, Elisa?" Antonio rose, made his way toward the bar.

"Whatever you're having is fine." The sureness in Elisa's tone told Luca she was the type of woman who had men tripping over themselves for her attention.

"Elisa is Charlie Donatella's daughter and his real estate advisor on the Tuscan property I mentioned. She's here to oversee and negotiate our purchase price. Her father asked for seventeen million dollars, which I agreed to, but Elisa has other ideas." Antonio poured brandy into two glasses.

"And what might they be?" Luca turned to Elisa.

Killer blue eyes, Elisa thought, wondering what it would be like to have him underneath her. "I believe my father is underselling the land by three million dollars. The property is in the prestigious Chianti Classico region. It's not only a historic landmark but famous for the Chianti wine it produces." Elisa took the offered glass of brandy from Antonio, sipped. "Besides, what's a few million to Santini Winery?" Her tone was sugar-sweet as she honed in on the ring-less hand. Although that wasn't a deciding factor, it would make the chase a more respectable one.

Antonio laughed Elisa's comment off. "If I went around giving our money away, that wouldn't make a prudent businessman."

"But it would get you this property." Elisa crossed long-tone legs allowing the split on her skirt to ride high on a creamy, white thigh. Both men appreciated the gesture. "What do you think, Luca? About the property, I mean."

Snapping out of his testosterone-induced trance, Luca said, "I'd have to see the property and run soil samples before I'm able to give you an opinion either way." He was sure the heavily mascaraed eyes on him undressed him.

"Of course." With a flutter of her lashes, Elisa slid a cigarette between moistened lips. "Light?"

Antonio retrieved the matches from the top desk drawer and slid it across the desk to Luca. "This is where you come in, Luca. You have a keen eye and appreciation for the land."

The cigarette burning red, Elisa wrapped her hand around Luca's and blew out the match's flame with rounded lips. "Thank you."

"Luca?" When Luca snapped out of his trance, Antonio continued. "Elisa's is asking for three million dollars above her father's price, and I want you to determine if it's justified.

Take a trip to Florence to assess the property. Test the soil, tour their much talked about wine cellar."

Luca remained silent, unsure he'd heard correctly. "You want me to assess the property for you?"

"I do. I want you to determine if the investment is financially viable. Are you up to it?" Raising the brandy glass to his lips, the ice clinked against crystal.

"I am. I'll make the necessary arrangements as soon as possible," Luca said with an enthusiastic tone.

A thin streak of white smoke plumed from Elisa's lips curled then disappeared into thin air. The gesture entranced both men. "I look forward to working with you, Luca. Let me know when you set a date for your visit. I'll make sure to make myself available. I'd like to give you a personal tour of the grounds myself. You will be my guest," Elisa said, with the subtlety of a venomous cobra.

Luca thought he heard the hiss from her lips, and his inner guarded signal flashed on. Elisa was the type of cunning, conniving woman he'd come to know well. "I wouldn't want to impose, Elisa."

As much as she liked hearing her name on his lips, she would have preferred him crying it out in a moment of passion. "You wouldn't be imposing. I know the property inside and out, and we have plenty of room. Besides, it would be good for you to reside on the property for the duration of your visit. It'll give you easy access to ... everything." Eyes full of mischievous intent rested on Luca.

Luca swallowed hard. "Sure. Okay. Yeah, I'll let you know the details."

How delicious, she thought, detecting the trepidation in his tone. That made the chase that much more exhilarating. "I'll courier the land surveys and the paperwork for your review in the next couple of days. And, Luca, please don't hesitate to call me with any questions. I'll make myself available to you twenty-four-seven." Elisa handed him her business card.

"My personal number is on there. I look forward to doing business with you, gentlemen." When Elisa rose, Antonio and Luca did too.

"As do I. It's no secret I'm interested in the property. However, I'm not willing to pay more than it's worth." Antonio offered his hand, and Elisa reached across the desk to pump it.

"I'll prove to you it's a sound investment." Elisa turned to Luca with an outstretched hand. I look forward to seeing you again, Luca. Gentlemen, it's been a pleasure. I'll see myself out." With the cool façade of confidence, Elisa sashayed out the room with Antonio and Luca's eyes following her.

"I bet you her bite is as venomous as her bark." Luca sat and took the last of his drink.

"You're not wrong about that." Antonio settled back in his chair. "Try to get this deal finalized as soon as possible. I want to get their crop in our possession before the harvesting season. We'll be paying cash for the deal to speed things along and entice Charlie. Without the bank's involvement, I'm sure we can talk Charlie into giving us possession right away."

"It'll take some time to get the legalities in order, but I can get the deal closed by early summer. Does that work for you?" Luca found it difficult to mask his excitement at the responsibility entrusted to him. This was what he wanted to do.

"That's perfect. Keep in mind the additional three million Elisa is asking is not a far stretch for us, but I can't let it get around we're overpaying for our land acquisitions."

"Why is Charlie selling?"

"He wants to retire, and I'm guessing viper woman's talents don't extend to running his wine division."

"What about his son?" For the first time, Luca enjoyed what he felt was a conversation of equals with his father.

"He's focused on their construction division. It's profitable and growing. I'd like this deal to be the catalyst for building a good relationship between the Donatella's and us since I'm interested in taking his vineyards and his winemaking business off his hands before word hits the market. I don't mind throwing Elisa a few million dollars to grease the wheels since it's clear she's in charge of selling their real estate holding. A woman like her speaks the language of money. Still, I want you to consider all those factors when assessing the property."

"Understood, and, Dad, thank you for this opportunity. I won't let you down." A hint of Elisa's lingering powdery perfume hit Luca when he pushed to his feet.

"We're not done yet, Luca. I wanted to talk to you about Villa Cuomo."

Luca's enthusiasm flatlined. "What about it?"

"Have you made the girl the offer?"

Alessandra's story of Rosa and Gianni stirring in the back of his mind, Luca said, "She's not going to sell, Dad."

"Then, we'll have to resort to less civil tactics."

Luca's spine stiffened, as did his voice. "What does that mean? I don't want you to..." Luca cut himself off, thinking it better than to finish his thought.

"To what, Luca?" Antonio kept direct eyes on his son. "I gave you one simple task. Talk the girl into selling the property to us. And as usual, you haven't been able to generate the desired result, which means I'm going to have to step in and do your job."

"Believe me when I tell you she won't sell, to us or anyone, at any price. She has a good reason for not wanting to do so. Please, Dad, leave her alone." Luca's tone was a pleading whisper.

"You're already sleeping with her, aren't you? How many times have I told you that business and pleasure mix as well as oil and water?"

"It's not like that, Dad. I..." Luca's voice trailed, and his father thought he saw affection, love in the eyes that stared back.

"You know damn well I can't. For one, we need the land. If you were more involved in the business, you'd know we're buying every farm where the Florentia is cultivated. We've been generous to our landowners, and they've been willing to sell. No one has put up the resistance we've faced with the Cuomo property. What's hysterical about this whole situation is that the property is rightfully ours. It's Santini land, and I want it back. Up until now, I've played it your way. I've tried to do the right thing with no results. So, now the gloves are off."

Luca threw a cautionary glare. "I'm warning you, Dad. Leave Alessandra alone. Don't do anything you're going to regret."

The fulminating glare Luca gave his father before slamming the door behind him told Antonio all he needed to know. Alessandra Cuomo wasn't a casual roll in the sheets. His son was in love with the girl, and Antonio would have to take matters into his hands.

Twenty-Four

LUCA'S MEETING WITH his father left a metallic taste in the back of his throat that lingered for days. He wondered why he wasn't immune to the tinny taste by now.

In the past few weeks, Alessandra looked happy and settled. She had a new friend to do what women loved to do—whatever that was. She was settling into her new home, and their relationship was blooming. The nightmares hadn't plagued her for a long while. It was the happiest Luca had seen Alessandra, and he was damned if he was going to inject pain into her life. Not because he loved her, but because she'd had enough heartache for a lifetime.

Luca was stuck in a difficult situation. Regardless of their turbulent relationship, Antonio was his father. Luca, however, was no longer the man he was a few months ago. Alessandra changed him. He was no longer the man who did what was expected of him.

Alessandra settled the unsettled in his life. She brought contentment where none existed. Alessandra gave him meaning and purpose. She'd chosen him to give her love to, taught him how to love, and felt loved. He'd do anything to protect Alessandra, even if that meant going up against his father.

Luca studied Alessandra as she ran the spatula through the eggs in the frying pan. "You seem distracted."

"I'm wondering if I should go see Daniel on my own today. I don't want to bring you into... I don't even know what this is yet, but I do know I don't want to tangle you into the middle of it." Alessandra watched Luca reach into the cupboard for cups and saucers.

"I'd like to go with you, but if you don't want me to, I won't." Luca poured coffee into his cup and returned the other to the cupboard when Alessandra waved the offer down.

"It's not that I don't want you to come with me. It's that I don't want to pit you against your family. That's not my intention." Alessandra topped plates with eggs, bread, and butter and walked them to the patio table.

"You're my family now." The words felt good to hear, but they didn't assuage Alessandra's distress. "You're not the cause of anything. I wouldn't have asked you to schedule the appointment with your lawyer if I thought otherwise."

"I..."

Luca cut her off by brushing his lips to hers. "Please, don't worry. You're not going to come between my family and me. I promised your *nonna* and you, I'd do whatever it took to safeguard your land, and I intend to do just that. Understood?" When the piercing blue eyes didn't leave hers, Alessandra nodded.

"Why is this land of so much interest to your father? It's a small parcel in comparison to the sizeable vineyards your family owns." Alessandra forked eggs.

"Aside from the fact the Florentia is sacred to him, the demand for its wine has exceeded expectations, and he has to keep up or lose the market. Securing the crop on your land is essential." Luca chased his bite of toast with coffee.

"But, I'm committed to selling you my crop and using my land."

"I know you are, but..." he paused to consider. In the end, he opted for the truth—partially. He wouldn't tell her his father claimed Villa Cuomo as Santini land. "My father's in the process of buying all the properties where the Florentia is cultivated. Yours is the only farm he hasn't secured."

She set her fork down with a clatter. "Everyone sold their property to your father. I don't stand a chance, do I? One way or another, your father will take my property."

"Not if I can help it. I'm on your side. It's why I want to meet with Daniel. You believe me, don't you?"

"I do. Not that I'd consider selling, but no one has made me an offer." She watched Luca idly move his eggs on the plate. "Luca, talk to me."

"I'm supposed to make you an offer, a generous one, but knowing about Rosa and Gianni and your family's promise, I decided it wasn't a conversation to have."

"And now he's blaming you for not getting the deal done." Alessandra rose to pace. "That's what's been bothering you all this time." When Luca nodded, Alessandra let out a deep sigh. "I'm sorry I've put you in such a compromising position. Does your father know I have no intention to sell the crop on my land to anyone else? I'll sign anything he wants promising that."

"I've told him."

"Then, why can't he leave my property alone." Frustration setting in, Alessandra began to pace the patio with Luca's eyes following her.

"I think your land carries much more than a valuable crop."

"What? What could be more valuable?"

"Its Santini history."

"But it's my land, handed down through the generations of Cuomos. It's all I have left of my family, of meaning."

Luca watched her run fingers over the foliage spilling into the patio. He saw the trepidation in her eyes, and a flash of anger for his father bubbled hot in Luca. "It's why I'm going to do everything I can to ensure you don't lose your land even if it means going up against my father."

"No. This is my battle, and I don't want it causing you to fall out with your family." The roller coaster of anger and guilt left her head throbbing.

"You're my family now, and it's *our* battle." He nudged her to sit on his lap. "I don't want you worrying about my father. I can handle him," he said, but both knew he could never go up against his father.

"But..."

"No buts. We, as in you and me, are going to deal with this. I'll never allow anyone to hurt you."

She mattered too much to allow his father to sweep in and take advantage of her. Villa Cuomo wasn't his father's land to take. Alessandra may not have the paperwork to the property, but for a century, the land had been in Cuomo hands. They had tended it, nurtured it, and she didn't deserve to be treated like a thief.

Luca wondered what made his father the callous, self-serving man he was. They had money, power, influence, and taking over a few acres from an innocent woman, in

Luca's eyes, was a cowardly assault. He wished he could talk to his father, have a son to father talk, but they'd grown far apart over the years, and the notion was an unrealistic dream.

"I don't want to cause a rift between you and your family. Family, regardless of how difficult they are, is still family. They'll always be there for you."

"And you won't be?"

Alessandra touched a hand to his cheek. "I'll always be by your side."

"And I'll be by yours," Luca said, taking her into a deep kiss.

HE WAS GLAD SHE'D TALKED HIM into taking the assignment, not only because of the fringe benefits she offered him, but because these two were like rabbits. In the one week, he'd surveilled Luca, he and his woman friend put on quite the show. Luca and his woman friend—whose name he found out was Alessandra Cuomo—had done it in the water, by the olive tree, and on the patio. Once, Alessandra imparted her oral expertise on the breezy, bougainvillea-dripping terrace, and he happily clicked his Nikon to memorialize the event.

He could make a ton of money selling the shots to the tabloids, but he wouldn't. His client was imparting her own oral expertise on him, and that woman could suck the nails off concrete.

Click, click, click. He got a clear shot of Luca undressing Alessandra and she him right there on the patio.

He wasn't sure if his client appreciated the photographs as much as he enjoyed taking them, but she'd told him to get all he could on Luca. Alessandra was a pleasant by-product of his surveillance. She was a beauty and talented.

Click, click, click. He snapped Alessandra straddling Luca as he pierced her, filled her.

When Luca wasn't on top or under the woman, they did everyday mundane things: shop, spend time in the vineyard, reading, and driving lessons. The two were inseparable.

When he'd reported that to his client, it put a damper on the evening, luckily, but he turned the night around, and they ended up in bed anyway. Her anger that night made it for the most tumultuous tumble between the sheets he'd experienced. The woman was adventurous.

To quell his curiosity of the woman who'd captivated the attention of the most sought after bachelor in Europe, he'd checked Alessandra's background. Aside from the fatal accident that claimed her family, her life was average and very middle class.

Click, click, click, his finger was quick on the camera as he photographed Alessandra riding Luca like a wild stallion.

The camera flashed on Alessandra as she tossed her head back, and her breasts lifted high when the orgasm shot through her. That one was for his collection.

Twenty-Five

"WE HAVE SOME time to spare before we meet with your lawyer." Luca paralleled parked the car in front of the Banca Centrale. "I thought we'd take care of the bank account I mentioned. Also, I'll introduce you to the bank manager. It never hurts to have connections at a bank." Luca stepped out of the car and rounded the hood to Alessandra's door.

It was noon, and the sun rode high in the sky. Restaurant patios and cafés were thick with diners. Luca bade a *buon giorno* to the woman pushing a cooing baby in a stroller walking past them. Across the street, a group of tourists studied the map in their hands until their petite honey-blond-haired friend called out for them to join her at the café where she'd snagged a table. Within seconds, all six disappeared through the glass doors of the Aroma Café.

"My mother's favourite boutique is a couple of blocks from here. I want to take you there after our business at the bank is done." He held a hand up to silence her. "I want to treat me to some lingerie."

"I didn't get the memo on you wearing lingerie." A teasing smile played across her face.

"You won't accept gifts from me. So, I figured you'd accept a gift as long as it was for me. And believe me, this is for my benefit. I'm thinking of a black and a red Chantilly lace babydoll with matching garter belt." Luca let his imagination run. "You'd look magnificent in lavender too."

"I don't know whether to be flattered or worried you're so well versed in women's lingerie."

"I can't shake the image of you in them from my mind, so you're going let me buy me all the lingerie I want." He flashed her a wicked grin, and Alessandra couldn't help but laugh.

THE MOMENT THEY WALKED INTO THE bank, everyone—particularly the women—fussed over Luca. After a short conversation with the petite brunette behind the receptionist desk, she escorted them to the manager's office.

Sitting across from the mid-fiftyish, impeccably dressed *Signore* Marciano, Alessandra felt his metallic-gray eyes studying her. Were it not for the enormous comical nose with the flaring nostrils that seemed to inhale every ounce of oxygen in the room, Alessandra would have found him threatening.

In her learned Italian Alessandra, understood when Luca told *Signore* Marciano she was to be treated like a Santini. In a firm tone, Luca told *Signore* Marciano no information on their visit or the signing over of the account to Alessandra was to be shared with Santini Winery. All future correspondence, Luca instructed, was to be mailed to Alessandra at Villa Cuomo.

"Aren't you curious to see how much money is in the account?" Luca asked when Alessandra tucked the envelope into her purse.

Alessandra shook her head. "I trust you."

Luca's brows smoothed. "We better get going if we're going to make the appointment with your lawyer."

FEELING THE CLENCH IN HER GUT, Alessandra, with Luca, stepped into Daniel's office. The office was larger than Alessandra expected. Daniel employed two lawyers, a legal aid, and two secretaries.

The space was stylishly serviceable. Floors were gray-streaked marble, and dove-gray painted walls were decorated with impressive diplomas. There was a long comfortable leather couch with a matching chair and white lacquer table in the waiting area.

The secretary escorted them to the largest of the three offices. A floor-to-ceiling bookcase packed with legal books covered one wall. Bright sunlight poured from the two unblinded windows. The room, like Daniel, evoked authority and professionalism.

From behind the rosewood desk, Daniel bolted to his feet. "*Ciao*, Alessandra," he said, with a smile, she read friendly to Alessandra, but much more to Luca.

"It's nice to see you again, Daniel. Did you have a good trip?" Alessandra's voice held an intimacy that tightly set Luca's jaw.

Luca watched Alessandra and Daniel in conversation. The familiarity between them and the glint of delight in Daniel's eyes made a storm brew inside Luca. Jealousy, resentment, possessiveness, whatever it was, Luca couldn't shake it off.

Alessandra never led him to believe Daniel was anything more than contracted legal help, but from their close interaction—particularly Daniel's—Luca saw much more between them. Irritation ground on Luca's nerves, but he bit it back. Luca trusted Alessandra, but the ardent look in

Daniel's eye told him he needed to keep a close watch on the man.

"Daniel, I'd like you to meet Luca Santini." Alessandra's abrupt turn sent her chestnut waves tumbling over her shoulders. The irritation in Luca clicked up a notch when he caught Daniel feasting on her.

"I wasn't aware you were bringing anyone with you, Alessandra." Let alone a Santini.

"I asked to be brought. Alessandra and I will be dealing with this together." Luca laced a protective arm around Alessandra's waist. "It's nice to meet you, Mr. DiBlassio."

Daniel didn't fail to miss the warning move. "Please, call me Daniel." He signalled the guest chairs.

Fanning his feathers wide, Luca took Alessandra's hand and threaded fingers through hers. Daniel would have remained unaffected by the gesture if Alessandra hadn't responded in kind and curled her fingers with Luca's. Resentment tightened in Daniel's belly.

Tall, good-looking, brimming with confidence and loaded to boot. How was Daniel to compete with that? Daniel would have kicked Luca's ass out of his office in a heartbeat if Alessandra hadn't shot him that silky smile that tugged at him.

"A question before we proceed. For the record, Alessandra, you're authorizing disclosure of all information of this case to Luca?" Daniel asked more out of curiosity than as a matter of record.

"You can speak freely in front of Luca, Daniel. As he said, he's helping me with this matter." Alessandra's emotions for Luca dancing in her eyes drove a layer of resentment in Daniel. He forced himself to clear his head, to find the much-needed calm.

"You're the client," Daniel said in a detached tone that mystified Alessandra. "If I understand correctly, you're also in the legal profession." The question was directed at Luca without the benefit of meeting his eyes.

"Not practicing. I haven't practiced law in a few years. I've been tending the land at Villa Cuomo and supervising several other farms in the region. I think I better explain." Luca offered when Daniel's brows furrowed.

Luca told Daniel his sole reason for moving into Villa Cuomo was to safeguard and maintain the unique crop after Alessandra's grandmother passed on. Luca let Daniel know of his many failed attempts to purchase the land. In detail, Luca told Daniel his agreement with Alessandra's grandmother.

"The last lease was signed a few months before she passed away, but that contract became null and void on her death," said Luca.

"And now the two of you live together at the Villa?" Daniel asked, wondering if their living arrangements had crossed into intimacy.

"We do," she nodded with a loving smile that drifted to Luca and made something inside Daniel break.

"So, you have your personal belongings at Villa Cuomo?" Daniel asked Luca, regretting the question as he asked it.

"Aren't these questions rather personal, Daniel?" Alessandra's failure to conceal her disapproval told Daniel what he didn't want to know. They were sleeping together.

"No, they're not, Alessandra," Luca assured her with a squeeze of the hand. "To answer your question, Daniel, yes, I've had my personal belongings at the house for over four years. And I know where you're heading with this, but my intention was never to steal the property from Alessandra. As mentioned, my only reason for moving into the vacant home was to tend and manage the crop."

Daniel wondered how long it took the sonofabitch to move in on Alessandra. "But you did move in without the owner's consent." Daniel's voice, as Alessandra perceived, was accusatorial.

Luca defended himself when he saw the shadow of doubt cross Daniel's face. "I know it all sounds questionable, but my intentions are anything but. I'm as concerned as Alessandra of Santini Winery, who has a vested interest in the property."

"It's not questionable to me." Alessandra's fingers curled tightly on Luca's hand, and Daniel pictured himself driving his fist through Pretty-Boy's face. He let the satisfying image of a toothless Luca wash over him until Pretty-Boy's voice cut the thread.

"By the way, as a matter of full disclosure, I'm currently an employee of the company in a Vice Presidential capacity." Luca watched Daniel make a notation in the file.

"Let me lay out the facts I've uncovered, which should give you a better understanding of where you stand, Alessandra. I found documents, which prove the Santini Winery Corporation and not Gianni Santini, as your aunt claims, owned Villa Cuomo." Daniel capped his pen, sat back in his chair.

"There's no deed to the property registered with the municipality under your great-grandmother's name or any member of the Cuomo family. There are also no registered endowments, wills, or other legal documents that would establish some form of ownership for the Cuomos." Daniel noted the colour draining from Alessandra's face and regretted his abrupt attack triggered by jealousy.

"But you said in those days transactions were sometimes done on a handshake." Alessandra's head was starting to spin.

"Don't worry, Alessandra." Luca tried to assure her, but Alessandra looked past him to Daniel with panic in her eyes.

Alessandra's nerves sagging on the edge of fear, the constant ringing phones, clattering keyboards, and jovial collegial conversation drifting from outside Daniel's office became a drill in her head. "You need to do something, Daniel. This is my home."

Her pleading words made Daniel feel the tug. "I promise you I will do everything I can to protect your interest, Alessandra, but we can't deny the facts. You're correct in what you say about the handshake agreement. Still, we need documents if we're going to discredit the Santini Winery Corporation of ownership. By documents, I mean a negotiable interest, which drove your family to presume the property was theirs. It can be something as simple as a signed handwritten note from a Santini to any Cuomo. That alone would drive the point of expected ownership. Do you know of any such documents in your possession, Alessandra?"

"I don't. I came up empty when I went through the stack of papers in my grandmother's bedroom. I'll speak to Aunt Sofia again," Alessandra said in a desperate voice.

"Do that. In the meantime, I'll have the historian dig deeper. Alessandra, you know..."

"It's going to be expensive," she finished.

"Money's no object," Luca was quick to add.

"In the interest of what we're trying to accomplish, and seeing as you're a blood relation to the Santinis, and affiliated to the Santini Winery Corporation..."

"It would be in Alessandra's best interest if Alessandra pays all billable hours and associated expenses herself." Luca jumped in to explain when he saw Alessandra's questioning gaze. "Any trace of funds infused by me into the case may compromise the case, *amore*."

Luca's loving term of endearment lanced Daniel through the heart, but he pressed on. "That's right, Alessandra. This is your call."

"Tell Daniel to go ahead and do what needs to be done, Alessandra. We'll figure something out," Luca said when Alessandra slipped into the momentary silence.

"Don't you see, Luca? I don't have Santini money. Old money has very long tentacles. Do you know how much of an investment this process will require and to what outcome?" She shot Luca a look of real pain.

"I'm not going to lie to you, Alessandra. I can't even venture to estimate what the costs or the outcome will be. I can tell you with one hundred percent certainty I will put forth my best effort on your behalf. And my previous offer to do this for you on a pro-bono basis still stands." Daniel's tone was steadfast, and Alessandra knew he meant every word.

Mulling the thought over, Alessandra looked over to Luca and back to Daniel. The insurance money her parents left was all she had to fight this battle. It was substantial to her, but pocket change to the Santinis. It would barely cover the initial costs because knowing Antonio Santini as she knew him now, he would drag this out until he broke her.

Alessandra thought of her father and wondered what he'd do if he were in her shoes. "Do what needs to be done, Daniel. And as I told you before, you go ahead and charge me for your work because you're going to give me everything you've got to keep my great-great-grandmother's land under Cuomo ownership," Alessandra said, with resolve.

Pleased by her renewed tenacity, Daniel said, "All right then. There's one issue of concern that needs to be addressed at the soonest." Daniel sorted through the stack of paperwork in her file. Hating to upset Alessandra further, he'd deliver the last of his bad news, like medicine, in one fast dose. "Were you aware that Santini Winery has been paying all utilities water, hydro, gas, including taxes?"

Luca stiffened. "I wasn't. Dating back to when?"

"Two decades."

"You're certain." For Alessandra's sake, Luca made sure to sound calmer than he was. "The contract never stipulated payments, and I never authorized the corporation to assume them."

"Quite certain." Daniel laid out the proof before Luca. "Please understand this information came to me through, we'll call it, creative means."

Luca nodded his acknowledgement as he studied the paperwork. "This was done without my knowledge or consent. It never occurred to me to check with Alessandra's grandmother. I assumed she was paying them, and she must have assumed I was." Luca's explanation sounded plausible to Daniel.

"What does this all mean?" Alessandra's panic was immediate and total as confused eyes scanned the documents spread out on Daniel's desk.

Daniel fixed his gaze on Luca, and Luca understood he was permitting him to explain it to Alessandra.

Luca said nothing for a moment as he tried to quell the seething anger coursing through him for his father. There was no doubt his father was behind it. Antonio's sense of entitlement and blatant disregard for everyone but himself repulsed Luca. At that moment, he regretted being his son.

"It means the goal was to take your property from you all along," Luca was forthright. Alessandra had a right to know the truth.

Alessandra's brows slammed together. "How?"

The truth, Luca told himself. "By the corporation paying utilities, primarily the taxes, they can take the property through adverse possession. They can claim squatter's rights on the day following the twentieth year of occupation." Luca simplified for Alessandra.

A deeper crown of confusion creased Alessandra's face. "I still don't understand."

"A squatter is required to continuously and uninterruptedly openly use or occupy the squatted land for twenty years to claim the property. By paying all utilities and taxes, which the Santini Corporation has done, they would legally meet the requirement to take possession of the land coming January."

Alessandra gaped at Luca. "But, you had a contract with my grandmother."

"Yes, but that could easily be dispelled since your *nonna's* no longer with us and unable to confirm it ever existed. With no other member of the family or anyone else for that matter knowing about it, it wouldn't be difficult to bury those documents if you wanted to." Luca explained.

Alessandra met Luca's gaze. "But you're here. You know about it. You can clear this up."

Luca took her hand. "I will."

There was an uncertainty in his eyes that made her say, "You can't. Even you've told me that no one has ever crossed him. Your father is bigger than the two of us. I'm going to lose my home. I'm going to be the first generation to let my great-great-grandmother down." Alessandra's body deflated like a punctured balloon.

Guilt pricked at Luca's conscience. "No, you're not. I was involved in the deal. I'll produce the lease documents for Daniel. I'm sure you'll find copies somewhere in your house. One way or another, we'll get this sorted." Luca squeezed her hand. To Daniel's delight, Alessandra tugged it away.

"Your father's made sure to cover every angle. I don't have the money to fight your family. They have deep pockets. I'm going to lose my home." She laughed despairingly, cynically. "I know it's not much in comparison, but it's my legacy. It's all I own."

"My father will not get his hands on this property, not if I have anything to say." With a defiant look on his face, Luca turned to Daniel. "You and I will get this sorted."

For Alessandra's sake, Daniel pitched in, "You can count on me. I will certainly do whatever I can to help you, Alessandra. I wouldn't mind winning one against Santini Winery. No offence."

"None taken. I want you to fight hard," Luca said. "Please don't worry, *amore*. It'll be fine."

Daniel felt the bottom drop out from under him when he saw the deep-rooted love in Luca's eyes for Alessandra. It was a love strong enough to turn a son against his father. He would have done the same for Alessandra was the role reversed. Christ! He'd offered to work with the man who'd stolen her heart from under him to make her happy.

Daniel had gone up against Antonio Santini on two occasions and found him a formidable opponent who spared no expense to win. Each time Antonio Santini had beat Daniel not because the Santini Winery Corporation had a solid case, but because they played hard and dirty.

Luca turned to Daniel. "First thing I'm going to do is to get you the signed lease agreements. Second, we're going to have utilities, taxes, anything pertaining to the property switched over to Alessandra's name."

"That's a good start. I'll have my secretary get you copies of the affected accounts." Daniel pressed the intercom and dictated his instructions to his secretary. "Alessandra, let me know if you manage to find anything of interest from your aunt. I'll contact the historian first thing. I promise you I'm going to do everything in my power to help you, Alessandra. And with Luca's help, I think we have a good chance."

Both men turned to Alessandra with reassuring looks, and both secretly wished the sentiment resonated true.

THE MAN WROTE IN HIS NOTEBOOK.

Visit bank, duration thirty minutes,

Visit the boutique, duration thirty-seven minutes.

Visit the lawyer's office, duration forty minutes.

He didn't know where Luca and Alessandra were heading next, but today was one of those mundane days both seemed to enjoy so much. He'd lost interest in the surveillance after Luca and Alessandra's breakfast sexual escapade when honey and whipped cream were thrown into the mix. Keeping his interest roused after that had been difficult.

He scanned the gold Rolex on his wrist—an incentive gift from his employer—and decided he'd stop his surveillance then. He had enough on Luca Santini to give his employer. He'd grab a bite to eat at *Fellini's* for lunch and review his report. It was his last one due for delivery that day. He insisted on hand delivering it. Hopefully, his employer would be as keen on the use of honey and whipped cream when he proposed it.

Twenty-Six

ALESSANDRA'S MIND FLOATING on thoughts of losing her home, she remained quiet on the drive home from Daniels' office.

"What time would you like me to pick you up?" Luca stopped in front of Maria and Francesco's low-rise, where she'd asked him to drop her off.

"I'll have Francesco drop me off—whenever." Alessandra was out of the car before Luca could say anything.

Luca hoped this was an alone-me-time moment. Just as well. He, too, needed time to himself to temper the surge of anger washing over him for his father, and he required alcohol—lots of it. With that thought, Luca steered the Maserati toward Villa Cuomo.

Ten minutes later, bumping the car along Villa Cuomo's driveway, Luca parked the car. The moment he stepped through the front door, he heard the silence. The house felt cold and empty of life without Alessandra.

Luca didn't like the feeling.

Luca reached into the kitchen cupboard for the unopened bottle of scotch and a glass. The scent of sea and mist hit him when he stepped onto the patio. Luca took a swig of scotch and looked out beyond to the horizon. The sky exploded crimson, and gold from an outgoing sun and the sea was a mirror.

Luca's gaze lowered to the empty chair across him, and his muscles tensed. The silence that hovered was torturous.

He couldn't allow that to persist. Luca picked up the bottle and poured scotch into his glass.

Luca missed Alessandra, but he understood the feelings of anger and betrayal swimming in her. He understood that right now, she needed to distance herself. Still, when she asked him to drop her off at Maria and Francesco's because she needed to be with family, it hurt deeply.

Luca prayed Alessandra's anger would dissipate, and she'd make her way back to him.

Alessandra had been right all along. His father was out to take her property. Luca thought of Antonio's treachery, and he quivered with rage. His father could hurt him all he wanted, but no one touched Alessandra. No one.

Luca swilled scotch, hoping it would smooth him out, but it did nothing of the sort. He re-poured, drank it, and poured again.

This time, his father was in for a shock because he wouldn't sit back as he usually did and let him throw the punches. Until now, he'd compartmentalized his life. He'd kept the life his father wanted for him and his desires separate.

Luca wasn't doing that anymore, and he was going to lob back. Not because the fury simmering in Luca emboldened him, but because his deep-seated need to protect Alessandra did. Alessandra was worth fighting for, and Luca was going to fight for the woman who'd brought joy and love into his life. For Alessandra, Luca would give up his fortune, his inheritance, and he'd tell his father just that.

Luca threw his head back and watched the pair of gray turtledoves jump together from branch to leafy branch in harmony. Luca watched them chirping to one another. He wondered what they said, what plans they made, what secrets they shared.

The jade eyes full of love Luca woke up to every morning flashed in his mind. Luca heard Alessandra's laughter, thought of how she brightened his darkest nights, and brought meaning to his life. His life was no longer the vacuum it once was because of Alessandra. She made Luca feel in ways he never had before. Alessandra had made him believe in love and himself.

Luca imagined the two sitting side by side on the little patio, looking out to the blue water watching the sunsets for all eternity.

Luca drank deep at the thought that may now be a dead notion.

Luca thought of the beauty that came from their lovemaking that morning. Waking up ravenous for a taste of Alessandra, their bodies came together, and it felt as new and exciting as the first time. It always did. Afterwards, their bodies nestled close together Luca felt a sense of wonder at how well they fit together.

Luca remembered every whispered word, every touch. Alessandra's scent was embedded deep in him as if it was a part of him. Luca couldn't imagine making love to anyone but her or sharing the feelings she'd awakened and fueled in him with another woman. Luca couldn't imagine sharing his bed with another woman—ever.

Luca thought of the day Alessandra reached for his hand and walked him to her bedroom and into her bed. Alessandra claimed Luca filled her with a sense of comfort and completeness. That Luca helped her find her way, but it was Alessandra who did that for him.

Alessandra was now as essential as the air Luca breathed. Luca couldn't imagine his life without Alessandra in it. The mere thought of it cast a dark cloud over him. Luca's heart gave one hard thud as the twisting arc of loss hit him.

Luca needed Alessandra in his life. They were hardly two separate people now. Without Alessandra, Luca was nothing, and nothing and no one mattered.

Now, Luca stood to lose Alessandra.

Luca's temper flashed at the thought his father was out to hurt Alessandra and shatter the life he was building for himself. His world was tilting back to what it was before Alessandra came into his life. The thought of going back to the loneliness, the emptiness, and the vacuum that was his life before Alessandra drifted into his life, terrified Luca.

He couldn't lose her.

In the solitude of the patio, Luca wiped at tears he hadn't realized were falling.

LUCA FELL INTO AN EXHAUSTED SLEEP, but before long, the scotch-induced headache roused him. Eyes groggy with sleep looked around the room, trying to make out his surroundings. Luca tried to sit up in bed, but the drumming at his temples prevented quick movements.

Bleary-eyed, Luca stared at the bedside clock's face until blurred numbers loomed full. It was three a.m. Slowly, Luca turned toward Alessandra's side of the bed. Panic filled Luca when he found it empty. Luca scanned the room in the darkness for Alessandra and felt a cold fear seep through his bones.

Alessandra didn't come home. She wasn't going to be coming home tonight or ever, Luca thought.

Luca's chest constricted. In a quick flash of despair, Luca called out Alessandra's name.

There was no response.

Without regard for stabbing pain at the base of his skull, Luca bolted to his feet. Through a sandpaper dry throat, he called out for Alessandra.

There was no response.

The strangling fear choked Luca. He bent down to snag his jeans off the floor. Luca swore when nausea rose in his throat, and his head shot darts of pain in revolt of his sudden movements.

Stepping into his jeans, Luca bounded down the stairs and into the living room. It was as empty and as dark as he felt. Luca's heart pounded in terror.

He should have gone looking for her when she didn't make it back last night, Luca told himself as he took the stairs two at a time. But no, he was too busy drowning his sorry-ass pity in scotch.

But that was what men did Luca tried to justify. Women cried, men, drank, or punched, or destroyed property, or... Christ! How much did he have to drink—a bottle, two? From how Luca felt, Luca thought it was an entire case.

Stop it with the self-serving pity, Luca told himself. You have to find Alessandra.

With the sense of loss suffocating him, Luca darted across the kitchen to the window. Luca's face brightened when he saw Alessandra on the patio. Under the moon's silver light, her chin rested on bended knees, and she contemplatively gazed up at the star-filled sky.

Barefoot, Luca stepped onto the patio. The air was ripe with the scent of orange blossoms and the sound of cicadas in serenade. In the background, he could hear the steady roll of waves tumbling onto the shore. Luca's throbbing head welcomed the soothing sounds.

Alessandra flickered eyes to Luca when he sat across her. She smelled the alcohol pouring from him.

"Are you all right?" Luca said nothing else, allowing her time to answer,

She didn't.

On a long frustrated breath, Luca pushed back his rumpled hair and felt his head explode into a wave of blinding pain. Willing the pain away, he said, "I'm sorry, Alessandra. I'm so sorry for all of it."

"I know you are."

"You know I'd never do anything to hurt you."

Alessandra nodded.

"How long have you been out here?" Luca said because the silence lengthened.

"Since I came home."

"I panicked when I woke up and didn't find you next to me."

"I'm sorry, but I couldn't sleep."

"My first thought was that you decided not to come home last night."

Sensing the panic in Luca's voice, Alessandra said, "I didn't mean to upset you."

"I hated the feeling that assaulted me when I woke up and didn't see you next to me or knew where you were."

"I needed to think."

Luca looked beyond them, where the moon glowed white and rode over the water, leaving a trail of light in its path. "Are you regretting meeting me?"

Alessandra looked up from tired eyes. "Not in the least. Why would you say that? Do you want me to get you an aspirin?" she said when he rubbed a hand to his temple.

Gently, he shook his head. "I've brought an added layer of emotional instability and difficulty to your life." Luca tilted bloodshot eyes to a velvet black sky twinkling with spatters of light. "It's beautiful and serene this late at night." The air hummed between them for a moment. "You know I'm crazy in love with you."

"And I love you. That's what makes all of this so difficult."

Luca held his head between his hands, hoping to steady the ceaseless pounding. "I had way too much to drink last night."

Alessandra's eyes fell on the empty scotch bottle. "I can see that."

"Jesus, is that all I had? It feels like I drank an ocean of the stuff."

"Wine drinkers shouldn't venture into drinking so much liquor in one sitting." There was humour in Alessandra's eyes. "Are you okay?"

Luca started to nod, stopped. "You know I would never hurt you."

"I know, and I'm sorry about what I said in the car about Maria and Francesco being my family." Alessandra's laid a hand on Luca's stubbled face. "You're my family. I hate your father, not you, for doing this to me, to us. I didn't want to feel this way again. I needed time to think, to work out emotions I didn't want to surface again. I didn't want to hate again, but I can't help but loathe him. Yet, as much as I detest him, I can't in good conscience pit you against your father. I'd never allow you to pit me against my family."

"One. Your family is not trying to steal your land from you. Two. You haven't pit me against my father. It's my decision, my choice."

"Answer me this. Would you be standing in my corner if the two of us weren't together?" The split-second hesitation confirmed Alessandra's theory, and something squeezed inside her. "See what I mean? And that's not to say you shouldn't because I wouldn't expect any different. It's your family and whether you have a difficult relationship with your father or not, there's an unspoken emotional attachment that can't be overlooked."

Luca couldn't deny the truth in what she said, but she was such an important part of his life now, and he'd be damned if he was going to allow anyone—family or not—to hurt Alessandra. If that meant going up against his father, so be it.

Luca loved Alessandra as he'd never loved before, and not having her in his life was not an option. The pain at the mere thought of going through life without her rippled through Luca like a toxic stream.

"I love you, Alessandra, and I'd do anything to protect you. But I also don't want to add more anguish to your life. If it makes life easier for you if I wasn't in the picture, I'll leave." Luca's heart tightened.

"You not being in my life would make it easier." Alessandra knelt before him. "But that's not what I want. I want you in my life. I don't think I could stand it if you weren't in it. You're the air I breathe, the reason I wake up in the morning with a smile on my face. You're the man I love touching me, emotionally and physically. You're the man I'm crazy in love with. But I don't think I could live with myself if I were the reason for breaking your mother's heart, for causing a rift between you and your father."

Luca's anger for his father bubbled like a boiling cauldron. If anyone was causing a rift, it was his father—between her and him.

Luca signalled her to sit on his lap. "You're not the reason for what's going on between my father and me, and you're certainly not the one breaking my mother's heart. Fathers and sons have different types of relationships that women don't understand. Sons are expected to prove their worth to their father's. It's a demanding relationship, at times, adversarial. Whether good or bad, it's the way it is. And as for my mother, she's tougher than she leads on." Luca cupped a hand under her chin. "Understood?"

"I do." Alessandra's smile was sad.

"Then let me do what needs to be done to save the land that's rightly yours, and I don't want you for a moment to feel guilty."

Alessandra nodded. "All right."

"Now let's get me a handful of aspirin and you to bed. It's been a long day for both of us."

Twenty-Seven

LUCA THREADED SINEWY arms into Ferré silk. "I'm going to have to fly to Florence to inspect the Donatella property in a few weeks. I'd like you to come with me."

Alessandra gave it some thought. "I'd love to, but I don't think it's a good idea. This is your opportunity to prove to your father this is what you were meant to do, and I shouldn't be injecting myself in the middle of it."

Luca kissed Alessandra on the tip of her nose. "Haven't I told you you overthink everything?"

"You don't agree with me." Alessandra pointed over to the dresser for the belt he searched.

"I do, but as I've told you, I'm only going to spend a couple of days on the Donatella Estate inspection. We can spend the rest of the week together. Florence is beautiful in May."

"I imagine it is, but I'm going to stand firm on you doing this on your own. It's what you need to do. But I'm going to add visit Florence on my To-Do-With-You list."

Liking the thought, Luca smiled. "All right."

"Daniel called while you were in the shower. He said the historian came up with something he wants to show us. He'll be in the area and can pop in around noon." She watched Luca loop his belt in place.

"I won't make it back in time, and I'd rather not put this meeting with my father off. Can you reschedule?"

"I told him you'd say that, but he's going to be out of town for the next three weeks, and he didn't want to postpone showing what he has until his return."

Of course, he doesn't. Jealousy clutching at Luca, he put on his best poker face. "I think it's a good idea to see what the historian has uncovered sooner than later so we can come up with the plan of attack."

Alessandra lay down on the bed, propped herself on one elbow and watched Luca roll his sleeves to the elbow. "Daniel did say he's found some interesting bits of information, which will give direction for our next move."

"Good. Make sure to tell me every detail of your meeting when I get back." Luca took her mouth into a deep kiss he hoped told her how much he loved her. "If you're going swimming before Daniel arrives, don't put on the tiny white bikini."

The lift of her brow conveyed her amusement at the comment, but she didn't know men, as well as he did, Luca thought.

FROM ALESSANDRA'S PATIO, DANIEL WATCHED HER dive into blue water and surface. Tipping her head back, she brushed wet ropes of chestnut hair to expose the beautiful darkened face that captivated him before she dove again. Stroke after stroke, with a swimmer's fluidity, Daniel watched Alessandra glide through the glass-smooth water.

Mesmerized by the woman who'd captivated his attention months ago, Daniel followed her with unblinking eyes. It wasn't until Alessandra stood in knee-deep water that Daniel's heart leapt to his throat.

Daniel marvelled in awe as Alessandra walked across shallow water onto the white sand. Her body, a buttery glow glistening under the sun against the tiny, white bikini, detonated a grenade of need and want in his system.

Eyes cemented on Alessandra, Daniel watched her slip on the T-shirt and shorts. There was a gasp of appreciation when white cotton clung tightly to the wet skin. The longing, desire, and maybe a touch of lust dormant for months swelled. Daniel wasn't sure which emotion fuelled the fire in his belly, but it was blistering hot.

Daniel felt the arousal, the physical thrill, whenever he laid eyes on Alessandra. It had been so long since he'd felt that well of need rise inside in him. He'd almost forgotten how alive it made a man feel.

Daniel wanted to taste Alessandra's lips, taste her, and feel her body under his. Daniel wanted to feel the luxurious waves of sensation a woman like Alessandra stirred in a man when he was inside her. Daniel tingled at the thought.

Yet as much as Daniel relished the thought of him and Alessandra being together, it was a fleeting one. Daniel recognized he never stood a chance against Luca Santini and the privileged life his money offered. As much as Daniel believed Alessandra was the money-hungry sort, Luca offered financial comforts he never could, and she deserved the best.

When Alessandra began her climb up the path to the patio, Daniel sat at the cast iron table. Waiting for Alessandra's arrival, Daniel felt like a giddy teenager full of hope and anticipation.

"Ciao!" Daniel rose. He'd shed his jacket and tie and buttoned-down his shirt.

Surprise registered on Alessandra's face when she met Daniel's smiling eyes. "Hi. Am I running late? I wasn't expecting you for another half hour."

"I'm early. My last meeting didn't go as long as I expected, and you were close by, so instead of driving back to the office, it made sense to head this way." Daniel rambled on. "I just got here. Your front door was open, and— I can leave and come back at a later time." Daniel warbled on some more when he caught sight of her wet T-shirt, sketching the erect nipples.

Alessandra crossed her arms and wondered what it was about breasts that made men babbling idiots. "That's not necessary. Give me a few minutes to change."

"Sure. Take your time."

"Would you like some coffee or wine?"

"Wine sounds good."

"Will it be considered billable hours if I get you to open a bottle while I change?"

Daniel laughed. "It's on the house. Point me to the bottle," he said, following her into the kitchen.

"Bottle's in the refrigerator. Corkscrew's in there." She pointed to the cutlery drawer then to the cupboard above for the glasses. "If you're hungry, there's fresh homemade bread in the breadbin, cheese, olives and cold cuts in the refrigerator."

"Sure, I'll put a charcuterie board together. It'll be ready by the time you come down. On the house."

"Good because I'm starving." She gave him a dimpled smile that made his insides simmer.

Fifteen minutes later, wet hair smoothed into a ponytail in a lavender shirt with the sleeves rolled to the elbow and slim-fitting jeans, Alessandra joined Daniel on the patio. Taking the seat across him, she took a sip of the red he'd poured.

"It's wonderful, isn't it? It tastes of strawberries and roses with a trace of medium bitterness and just enough complexity," she commented after savouring the wine.

Daniel raised an appreciative brow. "A true wine expert."

"Luca's been educating me. Before coming to Sicily, the extent of my wine knowledge was white or red."

"Italians love their wine. Sooner or later, you become an expert." The floral scent of her shampoo flowed into him, stoking the fire in him.

"This looks great." Alessandra reached for a slice of cheese.

Daniel layered bread with cold cuts and cheeses. "Share?" he asked when he'd piled everything into a thick sandwich. At her nod, he set a triangle on her plate.

"You told me you lived with relatives in Toronto and went to school there, but you've never told me why you moved back to Sicily? Not that anyone needs an excuse to move to paradise." Alessandra touched her nose when she caught him staring. "It's beet-red, isn't it?"

Daniel nodded. "It looks painful."

"It is. First-degree sunburn. My nose always seems to get the worst of it. I have a balm I dab, but I didn't want to sit across from you with a white clown nose."

Daniel smiled and segued into answering her earlier question. "I moved back a few years back to care for my widowed mother after her cancer diagnosis. She died shortly after." Daniel's eyes focused on some distant point as if rooting through memories of her. "By then, I'd fallen in love with the island all over again."

"I'm so sorry for your loss, Daniel." Alessandra's eyes were tender in apology. "Are you an only child?"

"I have an older sister. She's married with two rambunctious boys five and seven. Unfortunately, I don't see them as often as I like. My sister and her husband live in Florence. They're professors of art at the university. When they're not spending time with their children or teaching, they restore artwork. My sister came down to help with my mother, but I sent her away after a couple of months. I thought she needed to get back to her family."

"You're a good son and brother." Alessandra took the last of her sandwich, chased it with wine.

Biting into the last of his sandwich, Daniel shrugged. "Share another one?"

"All right." She folded her legs. Her chin resting on her knees, she watched him assemble the sandwich. "You practiced law in Toronto?"

"I did." Daniel set half of the sandwich on her plate, refilled her glass. "I was a partner with Sheindlin and Johnstone."

Alessandra arched a thin brow. "Running with the big boys and as a partner, no less. Aren't you a bit young?"

"I did okay." Daniel's modesty didn't surprise her. It was who Daniel was, Alessandra thought. And she was right because he wouldn't go on to tell her he was the youngest partner recruited or that he first-chaired the two landmark class-action lawsuits against the tobacco industry.

Daniel didn't mention he spoke several languages, and because of that, he represented Sheindlin and Johnstone in trade deal negotiations with Venezuela, France, and Brazil. Daniel didn't mention any of it because it wasn't important.

"This must be a step down."

"I see it as a life-enhancing decision," Daniel explained when Alessandra's brow furrowed. "Working with Sheindlin and Johnstone was great for a while, but in time I came to realize the stressful fourteen-hour seven-day workweek was shortening my lifespan. I still do substantial work for their European branch, but it's on a consulting basis, not as a partner, which allows me to work the hours I want and enjoy my life." Daniel tossed back an olive.

"I travel a bit, but the work is not as demanding, and the trade-off is certainly worth it. My quality of life is far better than it ever was. Now, if I want to leave the office early to meet with a client to share a glass of wine over interesting conversation, I can do just that." Daniel raised his glass to her in a toast. "What about you?"

"I was in marketing. I put in the outrageous schedule that earned me the position that came with the corner, windowed office. I'd gained the ears and respect of the organizational chart's upper echelon. Then tragedy struck my life, and it all became a fruitless endeavour. Life is fragile."

"It is, so you came back to Sicily to rescue Villa Cuomo, which by the way, except for the garden out front, is impressive," Daniel said with a teasing grin.

"I should do something about that, but it's the least of my worries." Alessandra's gaze drifted past Daniel to the spread of sparkling blue water. "Rescuing the villa wasn't even my primary purpose. I needed to get away." The tug came quick and painful. Alessandra wondered if there would come a time when it wouldn't. To Alessandra's surprise, she told Daniel about the accident and her descent into depression without a second thought. "Villa Cuomo was the perfect sanctuary."

Hearing the loss in her tone, seeing the tangle of emotions in her eyes, Daniel wanted to hold her. He wanted to whisper assurances in her ear. Swept away by the thought circling his mind, eyes ripe with emotion echoed the depth of his feelings for her in the loving gaze that stared back.

Until then, Alessandra hadn't known Daniel felt that way about her. How did she not see it before now? It was as clear on his face as the sky above them was blue, and her expression transitioned into awkwardness.

The flush rising to Daniel's cheeks, he said, "I'm, ah, sorry, Alessandra. I didn't mean..."

"I'll make coffee." Alessandra pushed to her feet.

"Stupid, stupid, stupid," Daniel muttered under his breath as he watched Alessandra dart into the house.

Alessandra gave herself and Daniel some time to regain their composure before she reappeared with the coffee. He remained silent while she poured espresso coffee into two thick-lip cups.

"Do you take sugar?" Alessandra asked with a smile of kindness and understanding.

"One, please." Daniel watched Alessandra add the sugar and stir.

Alessandra set the cup before him. "You mentioned you have something to show me."

Grateful for the diversion Daniel said, "I have information the historian found, which I think you'll appreciate. By the way, were you able to find anything of interest?" Daniel's tone more relaxed, he set the file folder on the table.

"I found a whole bunch of love letters from Luca's Gianni to Rosa. They're sad. Gianni was hopelessly in love with Rosa, but their bloodline kept them apart. He wanted her to run off with him, but she wouldn't. Rosa told him she couldn't cause her family more suffering or leave them to deal with the misery his family would inflict if she did. It was somewhat of a Romeo and Juliet scenario." Alessandra retrieved a letter from her shirt pocket and handed it to Daniel.

"I did find this letter. The only one that references Gianni's intention to give Rosa a parcel of land as an apology for what his family had put hers through."

Daniel unfolded the letter, yellowed from years of storage, and read. "Gianni tells Rosa he intends to give her a piece of land from the home he loves as much as he does her, but he doesn't come out and say it outright or give specifics. Gianni doesn't say where it is or give specifics." Daniel folded the letter, returned it to the envelope. "One thing is for sure. He's clearly in love with her."

"And she with him." Alessandra's expression nostalgic and sad she recounted Rosa and Gianni's story.

For a moment, Daniel looked up to watch sunbeams slash through the olive trees when birdsong burst from its thick greenery. "They had to have kept their relationship secret."

"What are you thinking?" Feeling relaxed in Daniel's company again, Alessandra brought up her knees and circled them with her arms.

"I wonder how Rosa and her family explained to the townspeople the acquisition of acres of prime cultivating land, which would have raised eyebrows. I mean, Campesini or farmers wouldn't have had the financial means to own so much land. Even if they had, the ruling classes would have fought it. The nobility was interested in maintaining their power and privilege. If they allowed the average Campesino to own land, they'd lose their standing as noble landholders." Daniel stacked the dirty dishes, set them to one side to clear the way for the paperwork he spread out.

"I didn't know. I hate rich people." When Daniel drew brows together at the irony of her statement, Alessandra pivoted with, "You mentioned you have something to show me."

"Yes, surveys." He pointed to the paperwork. "Unfortunately, the historian found a deed on file, which states the Santini Winery Corporation as the owner, but..."

"Are you sure?" Alessandra dropped the coffee cup with a thud into its saucer. "It's possible the agreement was made on a handshake. You said so yourself."

"I did, but with a deed registered on file to Santini Winery, that will be difficult to prove."

Alessandra's breath caught in her throat, and her mind circled like the eye of a tornado at the notion she'd lost Villa Cuomo. Nerves bouncing, Alessandra rose to pace.

"How is telling me you've found definite proof Villa Cuomo doesn't belong to my family good news? We've kept the property under Cuomo possession for Rosa for one hundred years, and it stops with me. I've failed her."

"Please calm down, Alessandra. There's more I need to show you." Daniel pointed to the second survey on the table. "The historian dug up this land survey, which he thought meant something. After reading the letter and hearing your story, I think he was right. Now it makes perfect sense." Daniel drew the letter out from its envelope again, read it aloud.

"Here Gianni says, 'I want to give you the land that is close and dear to my heart, that is a part of my home, and that I truly treasure. It's where my roots lie, where my ancestors and history originated. It's the least I can do for causing you so much pain.'" Daniel went on to explain when Alessandra's brows knit in confusion. "I believe what he's talking about is part of what the Santinis now consider their summer home."

"What are you talking about, Daniel?"

"When he says, 'It's where my roots lie, where my ancestors and history originated.' I believe he's talking about the home he was born in."

Alessandra's brow creased into a frown. "Daniel, please stop talking in riddles."

Daniel went quiet as he divided, calculated numbers on the pad he drew from his briefcase with Alessandra anxiously watching. "The historian was right. The numbers work out perfectly. You've told me the land inherited was one hundred and twenty-three acres. You've been consistent about the acreage size, which I believe came down from the generations of Cuomos. This right here is exactly one hundred and twenty-three acres." Daniel pointed to the survey.

Alessandra studied the document. "But this is a survey of Villa Santini."

Daniel nodded. "I think the land Gianni Santini gave Rosa was part of the Villa Santini estate."

Alessandra shot up erect in her seat, "You're shitting me."

"I, uh, wouldn't... shit you," Daniel said hesitantly, drawing a grin from Alessandra. "Indulge me. This copy of the land survey the historian uncovered, which dates back to the early part of the nineteen hundreds, states that Villa Santini comprises only six hundred and fifteen-acres."

"Only?"

"I say only because it later grew to ten thousand acres. They must have bought the additional land later on. Anyway, take a look at the will the historian dug up."

"It states that Grand-Duchess Vittoria Gastone." Alessandra frowned at the unfamiliar name.

"She was married to the Grand-Duke Massimo Santini. They were Gianni's grandparents."

Alessandra read. "Grand-Duchess Vittoria Gastone deeds the property to her five grandchildren."

"That would be Gianni and his four sisters," Daniel explained. "If I do the math, six hundred and fifteen acres by five work out to one hundred and twenty-three acres, exactly. Villa Cuomo is one hundred acres." He pointed to the survey drawn from municipal records. "In the world of coincidences, that rates too high to be one. The land Gianni gifted to Rosa was his portion of Villa Santini, not Villa Cuomo. And Gianni's lot known as lot 262.049 is dab smack in the middle."

Her mouth rounded to a wide O. "You're shi ... kidding me."

"I shit you not," Daniel said, with the sense of triumph he felt, not at the strike against the mighty Antonio Santini nor at the notch it put on his belt, but because of the smile that filled Alessandra's face.

"This is amazing news. Thank you, thank you," Alessandra cried out and absently leaned in to peck him on the cheek.

The kiss was quick, a one-second contact of lips to cheek, and as innocent as two friends greeting one another on a busy street. Yet Daniel couldn't help but revel in it. As the fire that hadn't burned in him for some time did so then, he wondered if Alessandra knew the effect she had on him.

Until Alessandra walked into his life, memories of the woman who'd stolen his heart haunted him, not as often or with such a heavy heart, but Daniel thought of *her*. Alessandra made Daniel forget. Alessandra made it, so Daniel was able to move past the woman who'd ruined every relationship for him.

Until Alessandra, no one had been beautiful enough or perfect enough. Alessandra was all that and more. She helped him heal, but Alessandra was as unattainable as the stars.

"There are so many questions. Why would my relatives be living on this property—for a century no less? Why would they consider it their land if it weren't? It's all so confusing," Alessandra said.

"Unfortunately, we haven't come up with all the answers, but I have a theory I've just now pieced together. Would you like to hear it?" Daniel proceeded when Alessandra nodded.

"This is speculation, of course, but my guess is there was a deal struck between Gianni and his father. Gianni agreed to marry the contessa if his father allowed him to deed the property to Rosa. However, the Santinis..." Daniel paused. How did he word arrogant bastards delicately? "They're creative when it comes to protecting their interests. You don't get to be as successful and wealthy as they are by adhering to the rules. Anyway, there is no way Gianni's father would have given Rosa a piece of Santini history. So once Gianni was out of the country, his father tricked Rosa into taking Villa Cuomo."

"If the Santinis are as ruthless as you claim, there has to be a document somewhere stipulating to the use of the land by the Cuomos. I can't see them allowing my family to live on the land for a century or justifying it without cause."

"You're right, but it could also be said people's memories are short, and information sometimes is not passed on. That the Cuomos were on the land for so long, it became known as theirs is a strong possibility."

"Possible, but for Antonio Santini to come after the land now, he must know something about their ownership. Luca told me every move his father makes is calculated. He knows this land is his, and he wants it back. Daniel, we need to find the proof I own the parcel at Villa Santini."

"We will."

"Jesus, this is surreal."

"Did you know the beachfront that borders Villa Santini's ten thousand acres is privately owned?" Daniel watched Alessandra set aside her cup of coffee in favour of her wine glass.

For a long while, drinking wine, Alessandra aimlessly stared into the horizon, watching egrets sail across a staggeringly blue sky. Until now, she hadn't seen the collection of boats gliding on the shimmering water. Locals entertaining tourists who wanted to take in a day of fishing or soak in the sun, she thought.

"It was impressive."

Daniel's brows winged up. "You've been to Villa Santini?"

"We were there a few weeks ago. We had lunch with Luca's parents. It's a beautiful property." Alessandra's comment riled Daniel's interest. She'd been invited into the Santini circle to meet the parents nonetheless. The thought her relationship with Luca went deeper than he imagined saddened him. "Show me again, Gianni's lot."

Daniel traced the outline on the survey with his finger.

"If I read this survey correctly, the parcel we're talking about takes up half of the mansion, a nice chunk of beachfront, and a portion of the vineyard."

Daniel allowed a satisfied smile to escape. "Congratulations. Now, all we need to do is prove it. It won't be easy, but we'll do it."

"Funny. I've been accusing Luca of squatting on my land when it's my family and me, the squatters."

"It appears that way. What may play in your favour is if we prove you've been doing it with the owner's consent and the fact you've been doing it for a century may just give you ..."

"Undisputed claim to the property." Alessandra finished his thought.

"That's correct, but..." Daniel hesitated.

"But what, Daniel?" Alessandra's tone sounded frustrated.

"That may now be debatable, seeing as, by the end of the year, they've been squatting on Villa Cuomo for the legally required time. I'm guessing Antonio will counter with that fact."

"Which leads me to believe that Aunt Sofia was right. Antonio has been orchestrating this for the past two decades."

"Do you think Luca purposely moved into Villa Cuomo? With a Santini living on the property, particularly a direct descendant, as Luca is, Antonio would lay claim to Villa Cuomo more easily." Daniel threw out partly as a legal point, but mainly to paint Luca in the worst light possible.

"It's not what he told me. I never thought... You don't think..." The words tapered off to an injured tone he now regretted instigating.

"Ignore what I said. I was thinking aloud. Don't worry, Alessandra. I'll come up with proof of your ownership. Once I do, you'll claim it and use it as a bargaining tool to secure this property too." The incentive was an attempt to lighten the mood he'd purposely darkened. "I'll fix it. Are you listening to me, Alessandra?"

"I am," Alessandra said, but her mind was miles away.

Twenty-Eight

1882 - Rosa

BEING BULLIED AND taken advantage all her life by the aristocracy who employed them and ruled the land made Rosa strong. It made her a fighter. It was what brought Rosa to Abramo Santini's front door for the second time in months.

The first time Rosa dared to come was when Gianni first set eyes on her. Her impassioned outburst about the unfair hours demanded of his workers left Abramo speechless—for the first time. It also left Gianni intrigued and with the desire to get to know the girl with the fierce eyes who dared to challenge his father.

Rosa's pulse galloped, and her heart beat fast, but she didn't turn away and continued to knock. The scent of fried sardines and freshly baked bread came at Rosa when the front door opened.

"I need to see *Signore* Santini," Rosa told Celestina, the girl who'd discarded their long-time friendship when she became employed as the Santinis maid. "Right now," Rosa demanded, blocking the door with a mud-covered shoe when Celestina tried to slam it in her face.

"You're getting mud everywhere, Rosa," Celestina snapped.

"I'm not leaving until I see him, Celestina."

"You will never change. It's why you will always remain a peasant," Celestina said, in the simple dialect of the *Campesino*.

Rosa's eyes lowered to her muddy shoes. "Drip, drip, drip."

Celestina huffed a breath. "Fine, wait here."

"I will, but don't you close the door," Rosa told the stern-faced Celestina and watched her walk down the hall until she paused at the second door on the left and knocked.

A moment later, a haughty Celestina escorted Rosa down the same path. "You couldn't have washed up or in the least changed out of your work shoes before you came?" Celestina's eyes latched onto the trail of muddy shoe prints Rosa left. "Now, I'm going to have to scrub the floor again."

"I'm sorry," Rosa said, wondering if Celestina's eyes cracked a smile anymore. This was what the Santinis did to your soul—they broke you. They drained you of the good in you.

"You mind yourself. This is not your peasant kin you're talking to." Celestina cautioned, opening the door to the study.

Rosa was about to remind the girl who wore the Santini housemaid uniform with arrogant pride that she came from the same roots when Celestina closed the door behind her.

The smell of wood smoke from the fire scented the air of the stylishly masculine room. Bookcases of dark wood overflowing with books and artifacts from Abramo's foreign travels flanked the stone fireplace. Above it hung a portrait of Gianni's grandmother, the Grand-Duchess Vittoria. Rosa felt her dark eyes following her, judging her.

The carved, desk in front of the picture window framed in burgundy velvet damask was polished to a shine. Rosa could almost smell the sweet perfume of beeswax. The long couch, wing chairs, upholstered in the same fabric as the curtains, and an ornately carved coffee table sat atop a gleaming marble floor.

"My maid tells me you work in my vineyard and insist on speaking to me." Abramo's voice was steel in the silence of the room. The glug, glug as he poured a glass of red Santini wine into a crystal glass, the only sound that drifted in the silence he left.

Abramo's eyes on Rosa, she felt the room closing in as if the oxygen was sucked up. Rosa thought she was going to faint. Rosa sucked in a breath to steady herself.

"I work in your vineyard. My name is Rosa Cuomo," she said, although he knew damned well who she was.

Abramo stopped his drink mid-way, stared at the girl with the testicles he wished his son had. She spoke polished Italian. No doubt, his son's schooling.

Her hair was bound in a red and white checkered scarf. The dark curls that escaped its hold spilled around an ivory face. The shoes at her feet and hem of the linen skirt were soiled with mud she'd traipsed through picking grapes in his vineyard. Her white pinafore needed a wash and pressing. Even in her shabby state, she was a delicate beauty, Abramo thought.

"I wish to speak to you." Rosa would have liked nothing better than to run away, but she wouldn't. She was there on a mission, and she would see it to the end.

"I'm very busy."

"So am I," she dared to say. "I have fifteen-minutes. If I don't return to your vineyard on time, I will lose one hour's pay, which I can't afford."

Abramo took his time sipping. "What is it you want?"

She measured the distance to the door. If her legs could carry her, she would have fled, but she dug into her inner strength and said, "Your lawyer came to talk to me yesterday."

Abramo sat at the high-backed brocade chair and sipped on wine. "And?"

Rosa sucked in air, breathed it out. "Both you and he think I will idly sit by while you trick me into believing you're being charitable to my family and me."

She was a brazen one. No one but his Aria dare speak to him in that terse manner. He could see why the boy was attracted to her. Gianni, like him, liked fiery women.

"I have no idea what you're talking about."

Eyes burning fierce fixed on Abramo. "My family and I will take residence into what you're calling Villa Cuomo. We will tend and farm the land and turn it into a profitable vineyard but under my ownership." To his sock, Rosa held a hand up to stop him from interrupting. "You will stop harassing my family, relatives, and friends and threatening them with job loss. They have done nothing to you. Your qualms are with me, but since you forced Gianni to leave the country, that should no longer be a point of contention."

Abramo watched the faint flush of pink riding on Rosa's cheeks, and his expression became blandly amused. "Quite audacious of you to make such a statement when I'm allowing you to move into..."

"A home in total disrepair and land that requires backbreaking work to bring to life. And our reward is to become unpaid custodians."

Abramo's jaw clenched, the ungrateful bitch. "I'm allowing you and your family to live there at no cost," he tossed back because he, not a seventeen-year-old peasant girl, would have the upper hand in the discussion.

Emboldened by how she managed to rattle him, she pushed on. "It is not at no cost if you are expecting us to repair the home and turn the land into a viable business for you. And I commend you on the use of the 'Villa Cuomo' name. Did you truly think I would be awed by having your lawyer throw the name into the mix?"

Abramo should be angry at the ungrateful bitch, but he couldn't help but admire the girl. She had more gumption than many of the men on his payroll.

Setting the wine glass on the chair's arm, Abramo left his fingers on the stem to run up and down. "You don't have to accept the offer, *Signorina* Cuomo."

"Not under your conditions, I won't." In the hallway, Rosa heard footsteps followed by the sound of a brush against tile. Her eyes darted to her feet, where a layer of mud pooled onto the gleaming marble. Celestina wasn't going to appreciate that.

"Suit yourself. This is what I get for trying to help your kind. It's why you're all living in poverty." The arrogance in his tone and eyes fuelled the anger in Rosa and shot a burst of confidence.

"My kind understands you are attempting to pass off the offer of Villa Cuomo as a gesture of goodwill when in reality, what you want is for us to manage and build it up for you and distract from the issue at hand." Alessandra fixed defiant eyes on Abramo.

"You're speaking in riddles, Signorina Cuomo." Abramo rose in a fluid motion. He wasn't a tall man, but that didn't diminish his imposing presence. "As I've told you, my time is valuable." Abramo opened the door and stepped back to allow Rosa passage.

She didn't budge. "I think you will find time to listen to what I have to say." Rosa's lips pressed into a long, firm line. Her hate for Abramo for taking Gianni from her resonated strong and fueled her determination to make him pay. "You will advance the money necessary for the materials to repair the home, which to you is a pittance. My family and I will put in the manual labour. We will till the land and turn it into a viable vineyard, but we will manage it ourselves and sell you the crop at market price. Lastly, you will have your lawyer transfer ownership of Villa Cuomo to me."

Abramo let out a derisive, cynical laugh. "Stop wasting my time, *Signorina* Cuomo. I will have the maid show you out."

"The maid's name is Celestina, and I'm not done. And I believe I'm being most reasonable. You see, *Signore* Santini, I have a signed letter from Gianni." You remember your son Gianni. The man you coerced into moving to another land to marry a stranger because my blood trickles poor instead of blue. "The letter states he wishes me to take ownership, not supervision of lot 262.049." Rosa saw Abramo's eyes deepen in colour, and she determined the parcel was clearly of importance to him.

"He left it the night before he sailed. I couldn't bring myself to read it until recently." Rosa's eyes filled with a combination of grief and pain, "Luckily, I did."

The fury he'd barely held in check spilled. "Where is that letter?"

Rosa was pleased by his reaction. Until then, she wasn't sure the letter had any value. "It is out there hidden in one of the trunks of the many trees on the island, or possibly buried beneath green grass, or sunk into the deep blue water. No matter where it is, Gianni, three others, and I know of its existence." Rosa lied without a blink and prayed he wouldn't search her pinafore's pockets. "If anything happens to me, they will recover it and do what must be done."

"Goddamn it, you are not going to bribe me or get your hands on Santini land. You will turn that letter over to me." The order vibrated hot with temper.

Abramo's emotional outburst baffled Alessandra. Why was he so interested in the unlivable house and land he'd left uncared for years? As far back as Rosa could remember, the lot he called Villa Cuomo sat unused and neglected. Unless...

"I give you my word I will not claim the land I rightly own, which by my estimation is worth far more than Villa Cuomo." Rosa's mouth lifted at one corner when Abramo's eyes, hot and hard, told her she'd guessed right.

The land Gianni gifted her wasn't Villa Cuomo. Rosa wondered which parcel from the stores of land the Santinis amassed on the island it pertained to. Either way, it was clear lot 262.049 was of great significance to Abramo Santini.

"You know I can fire the whole lot of Cuomos. Last, I checked your entire family works for me. I should have fired all of you when I had the opportunity to do so." His abrupt bark penetrated through the thick walls to Celestina, and she dropped the pail and spilled water everywhere.

Rosa didn't flinch or bat an eye. Instead, the corners of her mouth quirked up because that would add to Abramo's aggravation. Rosa took great pleasure in knowing she'd transferred all the tension and anxiety she'd walked in with to Abramo. It was liberating to feel emboldened.

"You will fire no one, and you will meet all of my demands. Do we have a deal, *Signore* Santini?" Her voice cut the air between them like honed Damascus steel.

"Not until I get that letter."

"I'm sorry, but I can't do that. I need to hold on to it for collateral." Under no circumstances should you turn this letter over to my father. It's your only guarantee, Gianni wrote in the letter.

"Did you hear what I just said about firing every last one of you?" Abramo's eyes were slits.

"You're not getting the letter. So, do what you must, but I will also. I could see my entire family and me settling into lot 262.049." Rosa gave each number separate weight for effect. "Do we have a deal, *Signore* Santini?"

Discarding his wine glass, Abramo poured scotch into a tumbler, took it in in one swallow before turning to Rosa. "I will do as you ask once I have that letter in my hands."

"You can ask as many times as you want. You're not getting it, but I understand business is tit-for-tat. So tell you what, *Signore* Santini. You don't have to deed Villa Cuomo to me, but you will meet all other demands along with continuing to pay my family a yearly salary and allowing us to live on the property in perpetuity." Rosa was glad she had listened to Gianni when he spoke about the law he studied.

"You're insane. Why would I do that?"

Rosa aimed an earnest look from beneath long lashes. "Because you have my word that as long as you keep your word, I will never produce Gianni's letter and agree to sign the letter for your lawyer. You know the one Gianni requested confirming you've deeded the property to me, so he..." she sighed, low and quiet, "goes ahead with your plan to marry the contessa."

Abramo slammed the empty glass in his hand on the bar. The shattered pieces rained to the floor. "Fine, you have a deal."

"Please keep in mind if you go back on your word, I will have no choice but to produce the letter and make a claim to lot 262.049," Rosa repeated, to drive her point home while she made a mental note to research the municipal archives to match lot number to property. "Keep your word, and you will never see me again."

With the subtle flicker of firelight playing over Abramo's defeated face, he said, "You have my word."

Rosa stopped at the door. Her eyes calm and direct on him, she said, "I love Gianni more than anyone could love another human being." Her words came out slowly, each one a drop of pain, and with that, she closed the door behind her.

Twenty-Nine

AS THE LIMOUSINE wound its way to Villa Donatella, Luca wished Alessandra were there to share in its beauty with him.

Nestled amid the Tuscan hills, Villa Donatella, with its stonework, balconies, black shutters, and towers, gave it an old-world European feel. Luca caught sight of the vineyard-covered hillsides, the olive grove, pool, tennis court, and magnificent gardens abutting the colossal home. Villa Donatella was a Tuscan splendour, romantic and charming.

Elisa supplied Luca with documentation dating Villa Donatella back to the eleventh century. Documents showed Villa Donatella was originally an Etruscan settlement that the Romans later claimed. No doubt, the area was steeped in history, but as fascinating as that was, Luca's only interest was the rich soil and crops on Villa Donatella's land.

Luca already planned to extend the vineyard to encompass the land verging the home currently used as parkland. He'd already decided to leave the olive grove intact. He'd come up with a profitable option to present to his father for consideration.

Luca had yet to decide what to do with the fifteen-bedroom villa the Donatella's called home. Luca was mulling the thought of turning many of the bedrooms into residences for the migrant workers during harvest season and renting others to permanent staff. The revenue would sustain the enormous home. Luca considered the idea as he rang the doorbell.

A maid in a black and white livery led him past the timbered ceiling, gray tiled foyer through tall carved doors into the living room. Vases atop ornately carved tables spilled with fresh flowers. Velvet upholstered tufted sofas, and chairs filled the room with tall, wide windows flanked with burgundy velvet drapes.

From the living room balcony, Luca looked out to the rich green landscape. He thought of Alessandra, wishing she were there to share in the experience.

After Alessandra turned down his invitation to join him, Luca proposed it again, but she insisted he needed to do this on his own. This was the first olive branch his father extended, she'd told him, and Luca needed to seize the moment to prove that managing the vineyards was what he was meant to do.

Alessandra was right. She always was, Luca acknowledged. His only regret was that the last couple of weeks had been hectic, and he hadn't given Alessandra the attention she deserved. He'd make it up to her on his return. Lunch at Fellini's then, a visit to Tina's Boutique for a couple more of those lacy teddies he liked, followed by a romantic night. Luca would also set time aside to sit down and go over Daniel's findings.

The thought of Daniel made Luca recoil. He'd seen the look on Daniel's face the day they met in his office. It was a lustful look of desire. A primal male reaction to a beautiful woman Luca could handle. It was the look of affection, possibly love, that intimidated Luca. As much as he trusted

Alessandra, the man in him told him he couldn't trust Daniel.

"Welcome to Villa Donatella." The sultry voice cut into Luca's thoughts, and he turned to Elisa walking toward him.

The provocative dark eyes curved with a smile and lips painted fire-red spelled danger. Raven-black curls framing the alabaster face bounced with every step. She wore slim-fitting jeans that hugged curvy hips, and the thin silk of her blouse exposed the rose, lace bra beneath it.

The stunned gleam in Luca's eyes put a smile on Elisa's face. Men were simple creatures, she mused, offering her hand. "Did you have a good flight?"

"Ahhh, yes, yes. Fine. Your property is more beautiful than I envisioned." Luca reached for the floating hand that waited to be taken.

Liking the rough, masculine feel against her skin Elisa tightened her grip on Luca's hand. "Thank you. I trust our car picked you up on time."

"Everything was perfect." Luca snatched his hand back when he felt Elisa's thumb tracing the contours of his knuckles.

If the abrupt move offended Elisa, it didn't register on her face. "Please have a seat." She signalled the couch as she eased down in the chair. "Do I make you nervous, Luca?" Elisa's eyes brazenly scanned him from head to toe.

The full lips she'd thought of ravaging with hers since their first meeting pursed in fear as the killer blue eyes nervously blinked. Elisa's eyes scanned the hard body rippling against the white cotton shirt. Elisa wanted that tight body under hers and decided she'd have it before his visit was over. Whether Luca wanted to or not was of no interest to Elisa.

"Of course not," Luca said, feeling a gut fluttering fear wash over him.

Round sultry eyes stared at Luca as Elisa connected light to the tip of her cigarette. "Would you like to freshen up before we begin the first part of your tour?"

"That's not necessary. When will your father be joining us?" Luca watched rounded lips blow a stream of smoke into the air.

"Papa regrets he can't be here. My brother summoned him to New York. It was all very last minute. I'll be your hostess for the duration of your visit." Elisa fluttered heavily mascaraed lashes.

Luca's shoulders tensed. He suspected Elisa purposely changed his trip date to ensure Charlie wasn't there.

"I'm more than happy to show you the property and take care of your ... every need." Elisa's voice was a soft hiss. "I thought we'd start by taking a tour of the vineyard, the area of most interest to you. I've arranged for the manager to meet us there and make himself available for any questions you have. How's that sound?" Elisa twirled a lock of hair on her finger.

The prickle of anxiety made the hairs on Luca's neck stand on end. "Ah, sure, okay. I want to get started now."

Elisa put the cigarette out. "Whatever you want, Luca," she hummed. Although her sugary tone had Luca weary, the primordial man in him couldn't help but take an eyeful of her well-rounded assets as she turned to lead the way.

TO ELISA'S DISAPPOINTMENT, THEY SPENT MOST of the day, treading through the vineyard. Luca was only interested in seeing and learning everything about the crop of Sangiovese grape indigenous to the Chianti Classico region.

Luca inspected the grapevines and soil. He talked to the farmhand, posed questions pertaining to irrigation, fertilization, cuttings, and yields. Luca questioned the lateral trimming and leaf thinning and spent hours talking about nothing but grapes. Through it all, Elisa managed to muster feigned interest by hanging on to Luca's every word as if it was his last.

When after the sixth hour of grape talk, Luca asked to be shown the ageing cellars, Elisa was thrilled to lead him to the oaking room. Elisa was pleased when Luca's brows winged in appreciation of the Slavonian oak barrels.

"Papa demands the best for our *Vinissimo* wine. These barrels were installed twenty years ago. All our ageing cellars are equipped with Slavonian oak." Elisa added as a selling point.

"Impressive. Do you know how long your father ages his wine?" Luca thumped his knuckles against the wood.

Elisa slid her arm through the crook of Luca's to lead him to the sampling barrel. "You know those are trade secrets of each vintner. That information will be provided when we close the deal." She handed Luca a glass and urged him to loosen the spigot to pour.

"When we close the deal?" Luca held the wine to the light. "You're very sure of yourself."

"I usually am," Elisa purred.

"What if I told you I have some reservations?" Luca took in the wine's scent with a trained nose.

"Then, I'd ask you what they were and what I need to do to unreserve them." Elisa edged forward, brought the red lips inches from Luca's mouth. Having inflicted the desired effect, Elisa cupped Luca's hand and brought the glass to her mouth. "It tastes wonderful," she said, running the tip of her tongue on wine-soaked lips.

The liquid warmth spread in Luca's belly. Before he knew it, Luca went steel-hard. Pleased to feel the bulge against her leg, Elisa rubbed herself against him until the expression of lustful hunger clouded Luca's eyes.

He was so wonderfully simple, Elisa thought. "What do you say we head back to the house?" She pulled back and started for the stairs. "I've arranged for a bottle of our 1974 *Vinissimo* Chianti to be uncorked for your enjoyment. Afterwards, I have a surprise for you."

The lump that lodged in Luca's throat caused him to choke on his wine. "A surprise?"

The uneasiness in Luca's voice amused Elisa. "I thought I'd take you for a traditional Tuscan meal at my favourite restaurant."

Nothing about you is innocent. "I'd prefer to turn in early. It's been a long day."

"You're the boss." Elisa gave Luca a wink.

Thirty

THE BOTTLE OF Chianti was exceptional. Luca ended up sharing three glasses with Elisa, all while having a seemingly normal conversation about the property and Donatella's winemaking division. Through it all, to Luca's surprise, Elisa remained professional. At one point, Luca wondered if she was the same woman who minutes earlier set out to seduce him. The woman could turn from hot to cold without effort. Unpredictable, Luca decided—the most dangerous type of woman.

Elisa watched Luca take the last of his wine. "Refill?"

"I've had enough." He set his glass down.

Elisa's gaze didn't falter as she got a cigarette burning. "There's a glass left in that bottle. Finish it off with me." She exhaled a thin cloud of smoke with an indefinable hint of sensuality that telegraphed warning signals.

Luca pushed to his feet. "Thank you for the company and wine, but I think I'll turn in now. I have paperwork to review and a few calls to make."

"The chef's about to serve dinner." She brought the cigarette to her mouth, inhaled.

Luca was starving. He'd been savouring the ripe scent of broiled salmon and roasted peppers floating in the air, but Elisa's predatory eyes told him the safest place was in his room—behind a locked door. "I really should get to those reports before I get to bed."

Elisa flashed a sweetness Luca didn't believe she owned. "I'll have a tray brought to your room along with the remainder of this bottle. I wouldn't want you thinking I'm a bad host."

Luca could do without the wine, but nodding was simpler. "You're a perfect host, and thank you. Good night," Luca said, with Elisa's eyes following him out the door.

In his room, Luca undressed and stepped into the hot spray of water to shower the day off. Wrapped in the complementary white bathrobe, Luca walked to the sitting area where the food tray and the wine bottle delivered while he was in the shower sat on the coffee table. Sitting on the couch, Luca ate and scanned the room.

The bedroom was stylishly masculine with high ceilings and tall windows flanked in crimson velvet. Gold framed Titian, Giotto, and Botticelli oils hung on smoke-gray walls. There was an eye-catching hand-carved desk and sturdy sleigh bed set before a fireplace. In the dark rosewood armoire, his clothes hung in a neat line.

Dinner consumed, Luca spent the rest of the evening working numbers. Although Luca planned to spend another half-day inspecting the property, he'd seen enough to determine it was a worthwhile investment. Luca placed a call to his father to tell him they should proceed with the purchase.

Business taken care of, Luca picked up the bottle Elisa had sent up and poured its remnants. The fruity taste came with a dark and mysterious sweet flavour, but Luca saw no need to discard the glass.

Sliding under the bed cover, Luca reached for the telephone and called Alessandra. This was their first night apart, and he needed to hear her voice. Needing was a great feeling, Luca thought and having the person you needed answer the telephone on the half-ring was an even better feeling.

Twenty minutes later, Luca hung up with Alessandra. Just as well, the effects of the fourth glass of wine were strong in him, and the day suddenly struck hard. All Luca could think was sleep. He needed sleep, Luca thought before his head went swimming into dreams of Alessandra.

THE SOFT ILLUMINATION OF MOONLIGHT STREAMING through the window lit the room. Watching Luca in sleep, Elisa listened to his breathing, watched him.

Dark curls cascaded over the refined face bearing the vestiges of privilege. His fashionable stubble was freshly trimmed. The smooth scar on his chest amid the dark hair added a touch of mystery.

Everything about him spoke of money and privilege. The aura of power may not have been discernible then, but Luca was the heir to an empire worth billions. Looks, raw masculinity, and a powerful name, he couldn't be more perfect. Elisa breathed in the heady scent of man and power and felt the throbbing between her thighs. Power was intoxicating. Just thinking of it made her hot and damp.

Elisa sent the silk robe slithering to the floor. She wore nothing but the diamonds around her neck. Sliding her naked body into bed, Elisa watched Luca in sleep. She held back the urge to skate her fingers over the curves of his chest, to run them down, his belly and below the sheets.

He was magnificent. She had to have him.

There would be no intimacy or emotion. Elisa needed none, wanted none. That was reserved for the man she loved. Guilt clutched at her heart, and her eyes welled at the thought of him.

Composed again, Elisa thought of Alessandra. Lucky bitch. Not only did Alessandra get to share her bed with a virile, male specimen, but she'd managed to nab the richest and most desired bachelor in Europe.

The sting of jealousy rammed Elisa's gut.

Nothing came easy to Elisa. She had to work hard for everything. Proving herself to her father had been a lifetime struggle for Elisa. All her life, Elisa had to compete with her brother for their father's attention and love. It was why Elisa jumped at the opportunity to handle Villa Donatella's sale to the Santinis when her father proposed it. She'd prove to her father she was as capable and as deserving of his pride and love as her brother was.

From the moment her father handed her the task, Elisa set off to know everything there was about the Santinis—particularly Luca. Not wanting to leave a stone unturned, Elisa took it upon herself to surveil Luca, but after watching him lovingly paw Alessandra, she had to stop.

After some research, Elisa enlisted the investigation services of Tomas Burgos. A former Santini employee with an axe to grind Tomas would be invaluable.

Tomas initially declined to take Elisa on as a client, but simple female persuasion changed his mind. Tomas was simpler than most, and it took little to turn him into her lap dog.

Coercing Tomas with unbridled sex had him singing like a canary. As Antonio Santini's ex-bodyguard, Tomas had first-hand knowledge of the personalities and attitudes that gave her insight into Luca and the family dynamic.

Taking the time to listen to his post-coital blathering after regrettable sex was the price Elisa had to pay to get to know the Santinis. But it was invaluable information, which led her to determine a woman's lures could easily manipulate the younger Santini. More importantly, Tomas's prattling led Elisa to believe the younger Santini could be influenced into buying the property at her inflated price.

Once Elisa had the necessary information, she discarded Tomas like an old dishrag. Why waste her time with a lowly detective when she had a billionaire in the wings? Tomas wasn't happy when Elisa told him as much, but she had to put a stop to the endless phone calls and his grating vows of affection.

As if the Gods were listening to Elisa's prayers, they smiled down on her from the moment she met with Antonio because he immediately steered her to his son.

There had been a moment of doubt in Elisa as to whether she could handle the younger Santini when she first saw the photographs of Alessandra Cuomo. Elisa wasn't sure why Tomas thought the photos, including those of their sexual escapades, would benefit the cause. However, a picture was worth a thousand words and the photographs gave her a perfect understanding of what Luca liked.

At first glance, Alessandra intimidated her. Before Alessandra, no other woman had, but Alessandra was a natural beauty. Alessandra never had a trace of paint on her face, never wore designer labels, and the eyes as green as jade, Elisa had to admit, held a charming innocence.

Eventually, though, Elisa decided Alessandra's wholesomeness couldn't compete with her expertise. The art of seduction, sexual gratification, was what Elisa knew best.

It was beyond Elisa's realm of understanding why Luca was drawn to such an ordinary woman, but she was glad. Alessandra's plain goodness would play to Elisa's benefit. Elisa had much more to offer Luca than the girl-next-door he was bedding ever could. Elisa was skillful at pleasuring men, and someone like Luca would be highly appreciative of her talents.

Elisa brushed her lips to Luca's. Rousing him out of sleep, Elisa returned a sultry smile when his groggy gaze landed on her naked body. Luca's startled blue eyes watched the voluptuous body, hard nipples on firm mounds, and the shaven V between her legs as she straddled him.

Perfumed female flesh ambushed Luca, pushed him to that jagged edge of need when she rubbed against him, as she knew he wanted her to. Luca's reaction was immediate, and Elisa felt him go steel hard. The pressure building up in him, Luca clamped a hand over Elisa's wrist.

Elisa's pulse leapt when she saw possibly panic, surely need and desire slip into Luca's eyes. "I'm not going anywhere, *caro*. I'll take care of him," She looked at his face, looked into his eyes as she lowered herself to take him through the wet heat deep inside her. "Relax, gorgeous. I'm taking you for a long, enjoyable ride."

There was no tenderness, no emotion. There were no whispered words. There was no taking in each other's tastes or scents, but in Elisa's eyes, wanting was wanting, and she revelled in the sight of his clamouring body as he gave in to her.

Elisa rocked, drew him to desperation. A glorious smile spread on her face when his body shuddered, and he erupted in climax and filled her.

Thirty-One

LUCA SHIFTED RESTLESSLY in sleep. In the deep recesses of his mind, something didn't sit right. The disturbing image of Elisa's naked body on top of him as he thrust himself in and out of her assaulted him. Even in sleep, Luca felt the cold, clammy beads of sweat forming on his brow.

His mind circling with the repulsive image, Luca shot out of sleep. Through heavy-lidded, bleary eyes, he scanned the room, glaring far too bright under the sunlight pouring from the window. Luca took a steadying breath when he found himself alone and chalked the imaginings in his head to a nightmare and the spectacular morning hard-on he had going.

Feeling the sandpaper dryness in his throat, Luca tried to remember how much wine he drank. Four glasses of wine wouldn't have the punishing effect he felt on an expert drinker like him.

Steadying his pounding head between firm hands, Luca's eyes caught sight of the tray with the steaming cups of coffee. It was then he saw her. Luca's hard-on flatlined. Without a stitch on, her raven-black hair tumbling in loose waves over bare shoulders, Elisa framed the doorway in a provocative pose. The sight slapped the hangover and colour out of Luca. Thicker beads of sweat surfaced on his brow.

"*Buon giorno*, lover boy," Elisa purred, the expression of sexual gratification on her face had his stomach roiling.

Luca ordered himself to calm down and take stock of the situation, which felt too surreal to be true. But the realization that the sexual encounter wasn't a bad dream sucker-punched him in the stomach, making nauseous bile rise to his throat. The mere notion of Elisa and he tangling in the sheets burned like acid, and the sharp talons of guilt clawed at his chest.

Cursing to himself, Luca shook his head with each, "No, no, no, no, no," he cried out.

Elisa's eyes clung to Luca in amusement. "Now, is that any way to greet the woman who made you moan in ecstasy? You are a boisterous one, *caro*." Elisa walked toward his bed, the sparkling three karats at the end of the gold chain around her neck, the only thing she wore.

"Christ, so we..."

"We did."

"Jesus."

"That's what you moaned each time. You were magnificent, and if I do say so, I was too."

Shock and revulsion washed over Luca when the image of Elisa's naked body on top of him shot out from deep within the recesses of his memory to poison his mind. Guilt and anger at himself viciously clawed at him and built so much tension his head began to pound, blurring his vision. Tittering on the edge of despair, Luca pressed fingers to his temple, where the headache was now felt like jabbing pins into his skull.

Elisa shot him a sympathetic look. "Would you like me to relieve you of that tension headache?" She bit down on her bottom lip.

Luca's breath hitched. "Get out. Leave my room, and leave me alone." His tone was as deflated as his life suddenly felt.

Look at him, devastated, Elisa mused. After the fact, they always were. When they had to run home to their wife, fiancée, or girlfriend, their guilt got the better of them. Sometimes Elisa wished she didn't take so much pleasure from their misery. Well, welcome to the club.

"There's nothing to feel ashamed about. You're a virile, single man. I'm a sexual, single woman. It was hot, wild sex between two adults who appreciate ... indulging in sexual pleasure. Nothing more. No one else needs to know about what took place, but I have a favour to ask in return for shall we call it my ... discretion." Luca's full attention on her now, she said, "All I ask is that you give serious consideration to purchasing the property."

Luca stared with an icy glare. The meaning behind her words unmistakable, Luca quivered with righteous fury. "You seduced or drugged me or whatever it is you did," he rubbed at his temples, trying to remember, but came up blank, "to blackmail me into buying the property?"

Elisa tsked. "Caro, blackmail is such an unmusical word and as for drugging you. Look at me. Why would I need to do that."

"You did something. I don't know what, but you did."

"I did. I provided you with entertainment to relax you so you'd see things in a more positive light. I hate to point this out, but the sex was consensual. If you recall, I was leaving when you pulled me back." She saw him digging deep into non-existent memories. "So, *caro mio*, that burn you feel has nothing to do with me and everything to do with you."

Her words threw an anvil to an already drowning man. "Get out," Luca spat.

Elisa's lips puckered into a pout. "But I was hoping we could take a shower together. There are so many more things I'd like to do for you."

"Get out. Now," Luca shouted with remorse and regret eating at him.

"As you wish. Breakfast will be served in thirty minutes. Afterwards, we'll head out to finish the tour of the estate before my driver takes you to the airport." Elisa's words said without a trace of empathy for the crushed man before her.

"I'm done with the tour. I'm leaving for the airport as soon as I pack." His voice thundered with fury.

"You're the boss." She threaded her arms into her robe. "Remember, you can trust me to keep your secret." She locked her lips with the imaginary key. "But it is up to you." Elisa reminded before leaving the room.

When the bedroom door slammed shut, anger bubbled into despair and anger.

Thirty-Two

LUCA MADE A quick stop at the dining room on his way out. "Our lawyers will be in touch to finalize the purchase of Villa Donatella at your asking price with the agreed stipulation."

"That's wonderful news. I know it's early, but what do you say we open a bottle of Cristal to celebrate?" Elisa reached into the cigarette holder, took one, and lit it.

Hot rage burning on top of cold fury, Luca barked, "The last thing I want is to be near you."

Elisa studied the burning end of her cigarette. "This is the thanks I get for..."

"Being a conniving, manipulative bitch."

Elisa tutted. "I was going to say for offering you a great deal and great entertainment." She gave him a wink. "Hopefully, next time we meet, you'll be in a better mood."

"Our paths will never cross again. Not if I can help it." Luca stormed out.

Oh, but they would, she thought, exhaling smoke through rounded lips.

There was no doubt in Elisa's mind, the sale would go through, but she didn't anticipate there would be no haggling over the price or that it would happen so swiftly. But then Luca had to do everything in his power to keep their "shared interest" from reaching Alessandra's ears.

Elisa saw the depth of guilt in his eyes when Luca threw her out of his bedroom. A man wouldn't be consumed with as much guilt as Luca was without love being at the heart of it. Alessandra Cuomo was undoubtedly a lucky woman.

Elisa was struck hard by a wave of envy.

ELISA WAITED BY THE TELEPHONE FOR her father's call. This was one conversation she was looking forward to having with Charlie.

Since Luca's departure, Elisa itched to relay news of the sale at her asking price. Maybe now Charlie would be as proud of her as he was of her brother.

Her success in securing the land deal proved she was capable of running the business as well as her brother—if not better. Elisa would have proved it sooner if Charlie had given her a chance when she'd asked to take over the wine division. But Charlie told her she'd lead the company into financial ruin.

Although Elisa wasn't surprised by Charlie's denigrating response, and as much as she should be used to it by now, it nonetheless drove a stake through her heart. Charlie's disdain for her went as far back as Elisa could remember.

Charlie never said so, but Elisa knew he blamed her for her mother, his wife's death. How her father could blame her was something Elisa never understood? Her mother had died giving birth to her. Elisa couldn't be blamed for the hemorrhaging that took her mama's life.

Many were the days Elisa wished she'd died on the operating table in place of her mother.

Charlie provided for Elisa. He gave her a life of privilege, the material things that provided her with a life of comfort. Elisa would give it all up in a heartbeat for the one thing she wanted most, which she craved—his love. Once, Elisa wished Charlie would tell her how much he loved her. It wasn't as if Charlie couldn't say the words. He said them often enough to her brother.

Elisa worked hard to make him proud of her. She worked twice as hard as her brother did. Yet all she got was rebuking. Elisa was also his child and deserved the same amount of love and praise from him as her brother got.

Elisa gave up the man she loved, the only man that managed to knock down the walls she'd erected around her and love her for who she was because he wasn't—as her father put it—Donatella worthy. He didn't come from their elite circle of wealth. Elisa hadn't cared about his roots. He'd given her the one thing she craved, what she never got from her father or brother—love.

He'd loved her as she'd never been loved, but Charlie put an end to the relationship when he found out. Charlie told Elisa he'd disown her if she married him, cut off her financial support. She'd lived without love all these years, but she'd never lived without money. The choice was a simple one for Elisa to make.

When Elisa found out she was pregnant, her only option was to disappear. For seven months, she took refuge in the sleepy village on the northeast shore of Lake Brienz in Switzerland with the spectacular view of the ice-blue lake and the white-capped Alps. Living amongst the population of two thousand who didn't know her, she gave birth to the boy she opted not to see before handing him over to his adoptive family.

Elisa gave up so much, yet nothing she did was ever good enough for Charlie. Today was different. Today was the day when it all changed. Once Charlie found out what she'd managed to do with the Santinis—people her father revered—he'd be proud of her.

Elisa knew the property was worth seventeen million at most. The fact Luca didn't attempt to talk her down from the twenty million price tag told her she could get a good price for the wine division, which she suspected Antonio wanted. That deal would net Charlie a quick sale, and she could now hit Luca up for an additional five million, which she'd direct to her bank account. Elisa decided she'd talk the Santinis into a cash deal. Santini pockets were lined in platinum, and writing a one hundred million dollar cheque took no effort.

She picked up the telephone on the half-ring. "*Ciao,* Papa." Elisa's tone was euphoric as she looked out the window to a darkened sky. Hills, covered in rows of green vines, shimmered under the drizzling rain. "Are you enjoying your holiday?"

"It's been a very hectic week here in New York. Why I let you talk me into attending this building convention with your brother is beyond me. How did Luca's visit go?" Charlie Donatella's voice was laced with the irritation she'd become accustomed to.

"It went splendid, Papa. Luca left a few hours ago. Before he did, he told me they were buying the property at my asking price."

"Very good," Charlie said, and Elisa was thrilled to detect the approval in his tone. "He liked what he saw."

"Luca loved the estate, Papa. He was impressed with the ageing cellar, particularly with the Slavonian barrels."

"I thought he would be. The Santinis like to use the best woods for their wines. When do they want to close the deal?" Charlie asked, and Elisa's lips curved into a wide smile when she thought she heard him dismissing her brother in favour of their conversation.

"Luca told me he wants a quick closing, sixty days at most."

The patter of raindrops struck the window, and soon after, lightning lit the sky.

"That means they will be taking possession of this year's harvest." Charlie's tone took an irritable turn.

"Yes. They want to put out the juice under the Santini label. It was the only stipulation they placed on the deal." Elisa's voice became subdued.

"But that's not what I told you I wanted, Elisa. I told you I wanted to put out one last batch of *Vinissimo*." Charlie spat the words in frustration. "I should have never given in to Antonio's request to put you in charge of this deal."

Elisa's stomach twisted with the tension her father always managed to instill. "It wasn't you who decided I manage the sale?"

"Of course not. I knew you'd mess up it."

"Well, I got them to meet my full asking price, which is three million dollars more than you'd asked," Elisa said defensively.

"Elisa, those weren't my instructions. I gave you specific..."

"Meeting my price tells me they're interested in buying the entire wine division from us, Papa. And I'm sure I can get above your asking price." The quiver of exasperation was audible in her voice as she fell back against the wall for support.

"Antonio will make a play for our wine division regardless. It's well known he's on the market to buy all the land he can get his hands on. This is not what we discussed, Elisa. You never follow instructions. It's exactly why I can't trust you with business matters."

"But, Papa, the Santinis are willing to pay cash for the deal. They'll cut you a cheque, and the money's as good as in the bank."

"You may have sold it for three million above my asking, but you lost me a bundle. I wanted to capitalize on the revenue from this year's crop."

Elisa felt her chest compress as if one of their barrels fell on her. She'd seduced two men, given them her body to get the task done, and now Charlie was telling her it wasn't good enough. "But, Papa."

"Stop arguing with me. I should have let your brother handle this from the onset." Elisa heard the faint conversation over the receiver as her father, in a disparaging tone, recounted the story to her brother.

"But, Papa," your son wouldn't have been able to do for Tomas or Luca what I did to get you the sale Elisa wanted to scream, as the tears burned in her eyes.

Charlie said, "I should never have entrusted you with such an important task. We'll have to go ahead with the sale on their terms now that you've promised, but your brother will take over from here on." The last thing she heard was the click of the telephone in her ear.

Elisa's sagging body slid down the wall to the floor like the droplets of rain against the window. Curled in a fetal position, she cried.

Cried out, red-rimmed eyes went hard, and her stomach rolled with the anger she felt. Fucking Luca played her, and he was going to pay dearly.

Thirty-Three

THE SICK DREAD churning in his stomach, Luca asked himself the same question over and over. Why? Why? Why would he do such a stupid thing To Alessandra, of all people? She was the only woman who'd loved him for who he was and not because he was a Santini, which was why Elisa seduced him.

Luca was used to women like Elisa, but he had no idea what to do with someone as sweet and loving as Alessandra. How was Luca supposed to right this? How was he to explain there was a momentary lapse of control and common sense? How did you explain to the woman you loved that his action was a physical reaction to measured stimuli.

The lines and folds on Luca's face deepened as the nightmare he'd set in motion by sleeping with Elisa slapped him. Luca turned lost eyes out the window of his Lear jet. Aimlessly, he watched snow-white clouds drifting in a shockingly blue sky. Luca saw Alessandra's face in them.

Luca let the only woman he'd ever loved, the woman who'd brought joy into his empty life, down. Luca couldn't venture to guess how he was going to handle this mess. Luca rolled his shoulders to ease the tension, which felt like a vice.

How was Luca to explain he had no recollection of seducing Elisa to his bed? How was he to explain he'd tried to stop her but then proceeded to sleep with her anyway? How could he talk Alessandra into believing it meant nothing to him? Luca was almost sure Elisa drugged him—or maybe that was wishful thinking on his part.

Luca wasn't sure.

Luca wasn't sure of anything anymore. The only thing Luca was certain of was that telling Alessandra the truth was going to cause a hurt he never meant to inflict on her. Worse, it could send her spiralling back into depression. She'd made so much progress in the past few months.

But not telling Alessandra the truth was something that would remain hanging over Luca's head and between them. There would always be a lie at the heart of their relationship, and it wasn't how Luca wanted it to be. Alessandra meant too much to him.

Luca brooded over the thought Alessandra already had enough pain in her life to last a lifetime. Hadn't he told her he'd willingly take her pain to spare her from it. Yet here he was, inflicting undeserving pain on her simply because he couldn't control himself.

There was no doubt in Luca's mind that Elisa set out to trap him, but it came down to him in the end. Luca knew what the bitch was all about, and still, he remained in her home after he found out Charlie wasn't there.

Guilt gnawed at Luca with sharp blade-like teeth as the feeling of descent into the endless pit of dashed hopes washed over him.

Luca rubbed his hands over his face. He sacrificed all that was good in his life for a roll between the sheets with a conniving, self-serving bitch who seduced him for no reason other than to sell him a piece of land.

Rage for himself ate through Luca. He allowed what happened to happen.

Luca didn't want to lie to Alessandra. He loved and respected her too much, but the truth was innately unpredictable. Everyone demanded it, but no one knew what to do with it.

What would Alessandra do with this truth?

Luca's throat closed in on itself at the thought he stood to lose her. The plane's cabin, with its luxurious comfort, deep-recline leather seats, and ankle-deep pile at his feet, suddenly felt constricting.

Luca wasn't the same man he was a few months ago. Because of Alessandra, he knew now what love was and what being loved felt like. Luca was no longer the carefree man who'd have brushed the incident with Elisa off as one of his many "encounters." Alessandra changed him, and Luca didn't know how to deal with it all.

Exhaustion, guilt, and remorse conspiring against him, Luca's head began to throb.

"Please fasten your seatbelt, Mr. Santini." The stewardess instructed. "We'll be landing in fifteen minutes. I've arranged for your car to be waiting for you on arrival. The captain wanted me to advise you that there is a storm looming. It should hit shortly after we land."

You're not wrong about that, Luca thought.

Thirty-Four

BY THE TIME Luca left the airport and maneuvered the car onto the highway, the first rumbles of thunder sounded, and bolts of lightning lit the sky white. Not long after, ominous black clouds opened to let the rain pour thick and heavy. Rain washed over Luca's windshield like a raging waterfall making it difficult to see the road coming at him. The car shimmied in a sudden gust of wind, and he righted it. Not that he cared if he died.

Luca couldn't begin to fathom what he'd say or how he'd say what needed to be said to Alessandra. All Luca knew was he'd tell her the truth and that he'd say it before they got into bed that night.

A river of fear flowed through Luca at the thought of the what-ifs. What if once he told Alessandra everything, she didn't forgive him? What if Alessandra gave up on him, on them? What if Alessandra chose to end it?

What if? What if? What if?

The car shimmied on a sudden gust of wind, and Luca righted it before ending in a ditch.

Luca didn't know what he'd do if Alessandra walked out of his life. She was the only woman who'd made his joy flow as deep as the ocean and his troubles as light as the clouds. Alessandra understood him, and Luca loved her.

At the thought of his life without her, an unbearable pain cut Luca with the ferocity of the silver streaks crackling the stormy sky.

FORTY-FIVE MINUTES LATER, WHEN LUCA pulled into Villa Cuomo's driveway, the battering rain was down to a drizzle. The air was heavy with moisture, and dew skimmed the ground and hung from leaves.

The lingering smell of rain in the air followed Luca into the house. Setting his bags down, Luca called out for Alessandra. When no response followed, panic bulleted through him. Calling Alessandra's name, Luca took the stairs two steps at a time. He made a mad dash across the short hall to their bedroom. Luca's heartbeat quickened when he opened the door, and Alessandra's sweet scent was the only thing that rushed at him.

Luca's panicked voice called out to Alessandra with urgency as he went from room to room. Alessandra was nowhere to be found. Panic leapt at Luca's throat, and his mind became scattered. It was minutes before he honed in on sound judgment. Alessandra wouldn't know about him and Elisa. The thought calmed edgy nerves, and Luca determined Alessandra might be out for her daily run.

Stepping out to the patio, Luca scanned the beach and spotted her in the distance. Relief came in waves, and the knot in Luca's stomach loosened like an open fist.

Alessandra was soaking wet. The long strands of hair weighed down with rain, and her shirt and shorts hung unflatteringly on her tall frame. Yet, she'd never looked more beautiful.

Alessandra's face radiated with a smile when she caught sight of him. She picked up her pace. The distance closing between them, Luca's heart thud, and fear bubbled in the back of his throat. Luca thought of running away and keeping his indiscretion to himself. What Alessandra didn't know wouldn't hurt her—or him.

No, he wouldn't run away. Luca wouldn't hide behind a lie. He'd face Alessandra and tell her everything.

"I'm glad I came home. I've missed you so much." Alessandra lunged herself at Luca, and meeting his lips, sank into the kiss that told him how much she had.

"Not as much as I have you." Luca kissed her back tenderly, letting her know how happy he was to see her. "What do you mean came home?"

"When it started raining, I stopped off at my girlfriend's place, but she was out, so I came home." Alessandra pulled back. "I've gotten you all wet."

Luca drew her back in and took her lips with his. "I don't care. I want to hold you."

"It's so good to have you home. I don't think I could have made it another day with you away."

"Me neither." Luca took her hand, twined his fingers with hers. The connection set off memories.

The image of their first kitchen encounter came at him. Luca recalled the first time he'd curled up next to her and watched her in sleep. Luca thought of all the times they'd sat on the patio, sharing a bottle of wine as they watched the sun slip out of the sky. He remembered the first time he kissed her and made love with her, and love unexpectedly rolled through him in one fast unrelenting wave. It had been the most extraordinary connection he'd felt.

"You look tired." Alessandra looked into the shadowed eyes.

"You have no idea how good it is to be home." With a gentle touch, Luca brushed a wet strand of hair behind her ear. "I love you so much."

Hearing the weary aura of sadness in his tone, Alessandra asked, "Is something wrong, Luca? Wasn't your father happy with the results of your trip?"

Luca turned his gaze up to see a sun dancing between layers of dark clouds. "Everything went well," he said in a low voice.

"I'm so proud of you." Alessandra brushed her lips to his to seal her admiration. "I'm going to grab a quick shower. I'll be down in a few minutes to make us lunch unless you'd like to join me for some fun water activity," she offered with a mischievous wink.

"As enticing as that sounds, you're, umm, probably starving. I'll ah, make lunch." Luca stammered.

"No one looks after me like you do." Alessandra flashed a smile before the screen door closed at her back.

LUCA AND ALESSANDRA ATE A LUNCH of spaghetti Carbonara paired with a bottle of red. During their meal, Alessandra caught Luca up on the goings-on of the past couple of days. Throughout her animated conversation, Luca didn't say much.

"You look tired. I'll clean up, and you go get a few hours of sleep," Alessandra said, figuring the Florence trip had been demanding and what he needed was rest. "If you don't mind, I'd like to borrow your car."

"It's your car now," Luca said.

"My car?" Astonishment had Alessandra's eyes round and wide.

"Yes, your car. I was going to surprise you later, but since we're at it." Luca dug into his pants pocket for the keys.

"I can't take such an expensive gift."

"Sure, you can. I'm getting a new car. The lease is up, and I planned to buy it out for you." Luca set the keys on the table without a trace of guilt in his eyes.

"Still, it's a Maserati."

"And it's yours." Luca waved a hand to silence her. "It's yours."

"Thank you," Alessandra said, gliding her lips over his. "I'm going to take my car to make my first trip alone to the market. On the way back, I wanted to stop by Francesco and Maria's place. That'll give you time to rest up." Alessandra piled dirty dishes.

"All right."

The flash of sadness in Luca's eyes was hard to dismiss, and Alessandra said, "I don't have to go out. I can stay with you." She carried the dishes into the kitchen, and Luca followed with the empty wine glasses.

"I'll be fine."

Setting dishes and glasses into soapy water, Alessandra turned to study Luca. "If you're sure."

He nodded. "As you said, I need a couple of hours of rest to recharge. It's been a long two days."

Alessandra reached for the keys on the table. "All right. I'll wash those when I get back."

Luca caught her arm before she turned to go. "I love you. Never forget that," he said, brushing his lips over Alessandra to fill himself with the taste of her.

"Ditto," she said as his eyes followed her out the front door.

Thirty-Five

THE MOMENT ALESSANDRA pulled out of the driveway Luca went upstairs. He needed to rest his brain.

Throwing the door to their bedroom open, he stood for a long while. Luca couldn't bring himself to set feet in the room, let alone soil their bed with his betrayal. Alessandra deserved better.

Luca closed the door and made his way to his old bedroom. He lay on the bed and shut his eyes, hoping to erase everything that happened—if only for a couple of hours. Luca's racing mind wouldn't allow sleep to come and he lay there aimlessly staring at the ceiling.

Seeing Alessandra made everything real, and Luca had to fight the sensation of loss when it assailed him. For the first time in his life, Luca felt scared. Not a feeling Luca was familiar with or one he wanted to entertain.

The love Luca felt for Alessandra changed everything in him. Alessandra's love shaped him, and having her in his life was the only thing that mattered to Luca.

The twist of temper flared in Luca at the sheer stupidity of his actions. He jeopardized everything dear to him and betrayed Alessandra for a few minutes of lustful sex with a woman he detested. The fear Alessandra may decide their time together had come to pass when he told her the truth made Luca's stomach roll.

Luca bolted to his feet and anxiously paced the room.

For a fleeting moment, the thought he should sweep the incident under the rug and pledge an unspoken vow of fidelity from that moment on crossed Luca's mind. It's what he would have done in the past without a second thought. But Luca wasn't that man anymore. Alessandra changed him by sharing her love and giving it freely without taking.

Needing to fill his lungs with air, Luca crossed to the window, threw it open. He cast eyes to a sky turning from black to blue. Trumpeter finches outside his window celebrated the imminent change with a buzzing nasal trill.

Luca tipped his head back, closed moist eyes shadowed with exhaustion. Luca would never be able to look Alessandra in the eye with the lie hanging between them. It would mar everything good that existed between them.

Alessandra told him he brought life back to her, but she'd done that for him. The best moments in his life had come from loving her, and now Luca stood to lose her. Rattled by the thought, a flutter of anxiety rippled through him. Every muscle in his body tensed.

At the sound of the car pulling into the driveway, Luca's stomach jerked. Nausea billowed to his throat. Wiping his eyes dry, Luca made the dreaded walk down the stairs to face Alessandra and his uncertain fate.

"I'm sorry. Did I wake you?" Alessandra closed the front door with her hip.

"I was already up."

"Did you get some rest?" Alessandra asked when she thought the shadowed eyes looked more tired now.

"I did." Luca reached for the grocery bags in her arms to deflect from the guilt eaten at him.

"Set them on the table. I'll put the groceries away. While I do that, you uncork this bottle of Santini cabernet I picked up." Following him to the kitchen, Alessandra reached into the bag, drew the bottle out. "I thought we could enjoy it out on the patio now that it's cleared up and turned into a beautiful day."

"All right." Luca never met her eyes.

Groceries unpacked and stored, Alessandra joined Luca on the patio. She picked up the glass of wine he set out for her. "You Santinis make a great bottle of wine." Alessandra smacked her lips together at her first sip.

"Thank you." Luca's subdued voice caused Alessandra to gaze into the troubled eyes she'd seen since his arrival.

"Luca, what's wrong? You know you can talk to me about anything." She gave him a tug of insistence. "Please, Luca, talk to me."

Luca set down his wine glass and absently let his fingers run up and down on the stem. "I do need to talk to you," he said and reached for her hand. "You know I love you more than life itself. And you know I would never intentionally do anything to hurt you."

Alessandra's throat tightened, and her stomach quivered. "I know."

"I've done something I regret, very much, and..." Luca took a breath to steady himself, "That I need to tell you about." His voice barely registered a whisper, but the words reverberated in Alessandra's head like a nuclear explosion.

Her insides hitched, but Alessandra's eyes remained calm when she tilted her face up to Luca. "All right."

"There was a woman at the estate in Florence. The owner's daughter, her name is Elisa Donatella." The metallic taste in the back of his throat intensified. "She stepped in for Charlie when his son called him to New York to attend some construction convention. Anyway, she's the one who showed me around the estate. We spent most of the day together, and that night she wanted to take me out for dinner. I didn't think it a good idea, so I headed straight to my room. She was..."

"Very beautiful," Alessandra finished, feeling the pressure on her chest when her heart began to pound. Luca hadn't mentioned her during their telephone conversation.

"She's not as beautiful as you are. I was going to say brazen. It's why I skipped dinner and spent the rest of the night in my room working on the report for my father. Once I finished it, I called him to tell him we should proceed with the purchase. Afterward, I called you." Luca stretched his hand across the table, reaching for hers. "I had to hear your voice before I fell asleep."

Alessandra exhaled a breath of relief. There were so many thoughts roiling through her mind then, and none was as innocent as what Luca just shared.

"Luca, you're going to be dealing with women, beautiful women, from time to time. Considering we comprise fifty-percent of the population, that's unavoidable. I don't expect you to avoid them altogether. No sane woman would."

Her thoughtfulness punched him in the face. "I'm not finished with my story. Elisa snuck into my bedroom late at night. She must have had a key because I distinctly remember locking my door. Anyway, I woke up to..."

Alessandra inhaled sharply when Luca hesitated.

"I found her on top of me ... naked." Luca could see Alessandra snap straight in her seat.

"But you sent her away." Alessandra pressed a hand to her stomach when he refused to meet her eyes. "Luca?"

"I did. I asked her to leave my room," Luca said, after a floating silence.

Alessandra exhaled a long-held sigh of relief. "You don't know the thoughts that went through my head. Thank you, Luca, for telling me, for respecting me enough to have this conversation." Luca was tempted to end the conversation there until she said, "But more importantly, for making me feel that I matter so much to you to tell me the truth."

Those words slapped him into shame, and although every instinct told him not to say anymore, Luca did. "She didn't leave." Luca went silent for fifteen-seconds as the weight of shame settled on his chest, pressed down so hard he could barely breathe.

Alessandra's mind raced off in a dozen directions. "What do you mean she didn't leave?"

Luca glanced away, betraying his guilt, and she struggled with the dozen roving thoughts.

"What happened, Luca?"

"Please, believe me, it was nothing." Luca felt himself drowning.

Alessandra's fingers tightened on her wine glass. "What are you saying, Luca?"

Luca drank wine to wet his dry mouth. "It meant nothing, Alessandra. It was purely sexual," he blurted, and he couldn't take it back. There was no emotion involved, Luca wanted to tell her, but the damage was done.

The wrenching pain slammed into Alessandra, and even as the hand of betrayal reached into her chest and ripped her heart out, she remained silent.

"You have to believe it meant nothing, Alessandra," Luca repeated when the silence suffocated him.

"You want me to dismiss the fact you slept with another woman as a 'purely sexual' act?" Alessandra's tone was wrathful, and the tears clung to her lashes before they slid down her cheeks.

Luca rubbed at the tension in the back of his neck. "Please don't cry, Alessandra" Luca reached out for her hand, but she snagged it with a vicious tug.

"Don't touch me," Alessandra hissed, flushed with rage and an ache eating at her like acid.

A river of regret flowed through Luca at what he was doing to her. "It meant nothing, Alessandra. You have to believe me."

"Tell me, Luca, is that supposed to excuse you?" Her anger becoming more resilient, Alessandra quivered.

Everything seemed to wash over him at once: remorse, regret, fear, and hate—at himself. "No, no, it's not supposed to excuse me. I ... I need you to understand it meant nothing. Nothing," he repeated, hoping the word resonated as strong in her as it did in him.

Alessandra's eyes swept a blazing glare over Luca. "How would you react if it were me saying I'd slept with ... with

Daniel?" Alessandra said the first name to come to mind. "How would you feel if I'd jumped into Daniel's arms hours after I'd made love to you?" Her barked words aimed to cut him as deep as he had her.

Luca's hands balled into fists at the mere thought of Daniel lying next to her naked body, kissing and touching her. Luca shook his head to block the vile image that was too much to contemplate.

"I'm sorry. I'm so sorry." Luca's voice trembled, and his eyes sheened with tears. "I love you so much. I would never intentionally do anything to hurt you, Alessandra."

"And yet you have." Alessandra tore her hand away when Luca reached for it. "Don't touch me." Alessandra's voice remained steady and strong, even as the pain sliced her. "How could you say you love me after what you've told me? If you love me as much as you claim, why would the thought of sleeping with another woman entice you? I would never dream of betraying or disrespecting you by sleeping with anyone else. Do you know why, Luca?"

Luca said nothing.

"Because I love you so much that you're all I need and want in my heart, life, and bed. I willingly opened up to you, Luca. I let my guard down and allowed you into my life, heart, and home. Into my bed."

Her words made him feel small, like a heel. "If I could take it all back, I would, but I can't. All I can do is apologize and tell you how very sorry I am for hurting you, Alessandra. You're the only woman I want. The only woman I've ever loved. You have to believe me."

"Don't you see Luca? That's clearly not the case. I'm not the only woman you want. If I were, you wouldn't have found the need to take anyone else into your bed. Intimacy is too important to me to share with anyone other than you, Luca, the man I love and whom I thought loved me. After all, of our whispered thoughts and shared emotions, I could never think of sleeping with another man." Tears swam into Alessandra's eyes.

"I bared my soul to you and shared my innermost secrets. I shared my pain, my joy, my dreams, and love with you. How could you even think of rolling in bed with another woman simply for the sake of what, Luca? A few minutes of sexual pleasure. You sacrificed us, everything we had together, my trust, and my love for you."

The bitter resentment at the notion that he'd felt the need to find comfort in the arms of another woman swelled into an uncontrollable fury in Alessandra. It filled Alessandra with overwhelming sadness.

When Alessandra burst into tears, Luca filled with panic. "I'm sorry, Alessandra. I'm so very sorry," his voice grew feebler with each word.

"You've already said that, Luca. It didn't help the first time, and it's not helping now. I can never trust you again." Alessandra's voice sounded drained.

The threat of another woman seducing Luca was always present in the back of Alessandra's mind. How could it not be when women were constantly throwing desirous looks or sexual innuendo his way without regard for her?

"You can trust me, Alessandra."

Pushing to her feet, Alessandra walked to the edge of the patio. For a long while in silence, she stared at the still waters. Sunlight danced on the surface, and a handful of sailboats glided along its glass-smooth surface.

Alessandra watched the herons shrilling to one another before majestically taking flight. Her tear-soaked eyes soared with them. It was a sight Alessandra loved one that Luca made memorable for her, and which now, no matter how hard she tried, she'd never see in the same way again.

No, I can't." The patio revolved, and her broken heart with it. "I want you out of my house."

The words punched Luca like a steel-fist in the face. "Please, Alessandra, don't end what we have. I can't bear to live without you in my life." Luca's pleading words rang out like those of a whimpering child.

"I can't either, but..."

"I'm sorry to have hurt you, but I had to tell you, Alessandra. Don't you see? I didn't want my..." Luca stammered, thinking of the right word, indiscretion, tryst, one nightstand, infidelity? Luca couldn't bring himself to say any of them. "I didn't want this hanging between us. I couldn't live with myself if I'd kept this from you."

Wiping the tears from her cheeks, Alessandra turned to face Luca with an expression akin to understanding. "I know, but don't you see? This will always be hanging between us. I can never trust you again, and because of that, there could never be an us again."

Luca suddenly felt as if he was sinking deep underwater, gasping for air that never came. "Don't say that, Alessandra."

"You've marred every memory, every shared moment, everything good that was us." Alessandra's words stung like salt in an open wound.

"Please, don't say was." Tears blurred his vision.

"It is, was, Luca. You breached my trust, and that's irreparable. There's nothing you can do to mend that." Alessandra's anger was replaced by an overwhelming sadness that tore at her heart. "You'll need these." She dug into her jeans pocket and set the car keys on the table. "I don't accept guilty conscience gifts."

"I promise I'll make it up to you. Please don't end what we have. You mean too much to me. I'm nothing without you." Luca begged, watching Alessandra walk away.

Alessandra stopped at the patio door. "I'm nothing without you either. I've never known a love like the one I shared with you. But, Luca, if I mean so much to you, you wouldn't have betrayed me, disrespected me, us." Her back to him, the tears streamed down her cheeks. With a heart she imagined could never be unbroken, Alessandra said, "I want you out of my house and out of my life. And don't think of coming back."

The sound of the screen door slamming shut behind Alessandra sent a torturous echo in his ears. At that moment, Luca's world caved in on him. The thought of life without Alessandra was inconceivable. His life would never again feel as complete or as perfect as she'd made it.

His heart would never love another.

Thirty-Six

DANIEL WASN'T HAVING a good day. He'd spilled his coffee over his notes and silk tie. To make matters worse, when he went to refill his cup, the pot was empty. After an exhaustive search through the kitchenette cupboards, he found the coffee beans. The struggle became real when the coffee grinder succumbed to a grating death when he switched it on.

Daniel's arsenal of oaths depleted, he started toward *Signora* Russo's desk. He'd have a word with her on the merits of keeping a bag of ground coffee in stock. Steps from his secretary's desk, Daniel scrapped the idea. As efficient as *Signora* Russo was, she was equally as menacing when you tampered with "her" kitchen.

He'd crossed that battleground once before. Daniel couldn't remember on what issue, but he could recall almost losing his hearing when she went off on him. Daniel was too fond of his sense of hearing to risk it. Daniel walked away from her desk and back to his office.

To distract himself from the effects of caffeine withdrawal, Daniel picked up the telephone and dialled Alessandra's number. At the first ring, Daniel willed the Gods not to make Luca answer the phone. Today Daniel couldn't handle being civil to the man who moved in to scoop Alessandra from under him.

Daniel blamed no one but himself for how things turned out. Had he the testicular fortitude to say what was on his mind to Alessandra before they went their separate way at the airport, Luca wouldn't be living in her home or sharing her bed. But no, he had to let his fragile ego hold him back from inviting her out for dinner.

Daniel hadn't summoned the courage to say anything during the entire flight or their stopover in Rome. Had Daniel mustered the nerve to invite Alessandra out for a meal or a drink, he, not Luca, would be in her life.

A simple question—Can I see you again?—packed so much fear in Daniel he'd let the only woman who'd stirred his blood after all these years walk out of his life. Alessandra was the only woman who'd managed to set the long-repressed feelings in Daniel free, and he'd let her slip through his fingers. Daniel's cowardice allowed Mr. Moneybags to step into the picture with no chance of self-combusting out of the picture anytime soon.

Daniel let the phone ring for longer than he usually would. He'd been trying to reach Alessandra without luck since his return from Spain. When on the tenth ring, Alessandra didn't answer, Daniel thought of doing what he should have done ten days ago. He called Maria, but Maria wasn't forthcoming, and her feeble eluding led Daniel's imagination to run away.

A gut-fluttering feeling of panic overtook Daniel when he redialed Alessandra's number, and she didn't answer. Bolting to his feet, Daniel picked up the car keys off his desk and rushed out of the office.

Daniel's mind racing as fast as his speedometer, he steered his car through the narrow streets to Villa Cuomo.

Daniel sighed a breath of relief when he didn't see Luca's Maserati in the driveway.

Jumping out of the car, Daniel knocked on Alessandra's door. An uneasiness assailed him when his knocks went unanswered. Automatically, Daniel reached for the door handle and was glad when it clicked open. Stepping into the foyer, the humming motor of the ancient refrigerator filled the eerie silence.

"Hello, anyone home?" Daniel's voice echoed in the silence. The unnerving chill clawing at him, he called out again. "*Ciao*, Alessandra, it's Daniel."

The sick ball of uneasiness dropped like lead in his stomach, and Daniel darted up the stairs. Stopping at the first doorway, Daniel's eyes scanned the room. It looked as if a tornado hit. Drawers hung on the brink of teetering off their hinges, hangers were strewn on the tiled floor, and the bed was unmade. Next to the dresser, two suitcases sat opened, clothing and shoes haphazardly packed in both.

His mind racing, Daniel dragged a hand through his hair. Stay focused, Daniel told himself and turned toward the second bedroom. No Alessandra. Daniel darted down the stairs, through the living room to an empty kitchen. As he was about to succumb to despair, he caught sight of Alessandra out the kitchen window. Sitting at the patio table, her face was buried in the crossed arms that rested on bent knees.

Daniel opened the screen door. Its creaking hinges announced his presence. "Hi. Your front door was opened, so I let myself in," Daniel said from the doorway. "I've been calling you for days." In the ensuing silence, her whimpering sobs echoed thunderously in his ears, and he rushed to her side.

"What's wrong? Talk to me, Alessandra." Daniel came down to eye level. "Please, look at me. What's wrong, Alessandra?" His voice tinged with genuine concern pulled at her, and the tangle of chestnut hair rose slowly. The red-rimmed eyes that met his burnt a hole in his gut.

"Everything," Alessandra said between sobs.

"What's happened?"

"He hurt me, Daniel. He hurt me so much." Tears dripped through the words.

The anger in his eyes blazing to nuclear-red, Daniel took a careful survey of Alessandra. "What did he do to you? So help me, God, if he laid a hand on you, I'll fucking kill him. I'll kill that sonofabitch."

The impulsive statement made with a ripe violence Alessandra didn't expect startled her, and she rushed to correct. "Luca didn't lay a hand on me."

With a breath of relief, Daniel brought his hands to brush unruly hair out of her face. "What happened, Alessandra? What did he do to you?"

Shadowed, tear-stained eyes met Daniel's anxious gaze. "He shattered my world, my trust. He dismissed everything we've shared, everything we've built, my love. He betrayed me, Daniel. Why would he do that? Why did he have to sleep with her? All I did was love him."

The pain resonating in her eyes cut into his heart. "I'm so sorry, Alessandra."

That Luca was the cause of her pain didn't surprise Daniel. The man was known for discarding women at the drop of a hat. Luca didn't know what commitment and loyalty meant if it bit him in the ass. Daniel couldn't expect any different from a Santini. Taking and discarding was what they did best.

With a mixture of anger and wounded pride, Alessandra snapped, "I told him to leave. I don't want to see him ever again. I started to pack his things days ago, but I can't bring myself to finish. I want nothing of his in this house," Alessandra said, her voice rising, hardening.

Daniel's expression remained calm, but his hands fisted in anger, nails digging into his palms. "I'll pack his things, Alessandra," he blurted, stunning her and himself. "You don't have to deal with it. I know how difficult and painful this is for you." The sympathy and understanding that stirred in Daniel's eyes reached deep inside Alessandra, and she fell into him.

His arms chained around Alessandra, Daniel shushed and rocked, whispered words of reassurance.

"Don't." Alessandra pulled from Daniel's embrace. The fury in her eyes demanded distance now, but the pain in them was strong and raw, and he pulled Alessandra back. "Don't touch me. You're all the same." She fought him with all her strength, but Daniel held onto her until she went limp and gave in to him. Cradled in his arms, Alessandra sobbed.

"Shhh, it's going to be all right." Strong hands tenderly framed her face and looked into her eyes. "I promise you, Alessandra, it will be all right."

The words did nothing to assuage the pain slamming down on Alessandra. "It's never going to be all right again. I'm never going to love again."

Cupping her chin, Daniel raised Alessandra's face to meet his. "It will take time, but I promise you will love again."

"I gave everything to him, gave myself to him." Alessandra's mind drifted to memories now marred by Luca's betrayal. "Christ! I opened up to him, and without a second thought, he succumbed to the first woman who offered her body to him."

Daniel was on his knees now. "I'm sorry he hurt you, Alessandra. You of all people don't deserve this, but you'll get past this, and you will love again."

"How would you know? You're a man. You were put on this earth to hurt."

"I would have never hurt you." Daniel's tone, rather than the words said in assurance as much as a statement of fact, spoke to her.

For a long few seconds, their eyes held, and a moment of complete understanding flashed in her eyes. Here was love, Alessandra thought, and although she couldn't reciprocate the feeling, she would cross that line. Consequences and logic be damned. Alessandra would take from Daniel because she needed to. Because what she needed then was to feel desired, wanted, and loved, and Daniel would do that for her.

Without warning, Alessandra crushed her needy mouth to his. Her mouth hot and demanding, her scent wildly feminine made Daniel's blood run hot. Her fingers tangled in his dark shock of hair, his mind floated to the fantasies of him and her that had filled him since the day they met.

The kiss lasted seconds but left Daniel dazed, trembling with need. As much as he wanted to give in return, sensing her vulnerability and brittle state, Daniel pulled away.

"Alessandra," Daniel started to say, but she plunged into the next kiss with moist lips and tongue weakening his defences.

The woman in her was pleased to feel Daniel's body respond. For one quick moment, Daniel lost interest in logic and gave in. His hands tangled in the wild mass of hair as his mouth crushed down on her. Parting her lips, he joined their tongues in rhythmic dance until she was a part of him.

The kiss was intense and memorable, everything Daniel imagined it would be, and everything she needed it to be then.

Alessandra skated her fingers over the impressive breadth of shoulders, down the sinewy arms to his chest. Blood bubbled under Daniel's skin. The feel of her fingers as she unbuttoned his shirt was electric. Daniel wanted her more than Alessandra could imagine, but not under those circumstances and not in her fragile state.

"Not now, Alessandra. Now is not the right time." Although affection and regret came through in his voice, Alessandra heard derision and repudiation in her fragile state.

Humiliation pulsated into anger, and Alessandra tore away. "Get off of me."

Inside Daniel's gut, the knot of guilt tightened when he realized how he made her feel. Daniel gripped her arm when she started to walk away.

"Don't touch me." Tears burning and blurring, Alessandra tried to tear loose.

Inches from her, Daniel gazed into the eyes filled with hurt and humiliation. "I want to be with you, believe me, I do. I've fantasized about being with you every day since the day we met. You're beautiful and desirable. There's nothing I wouldn't give to be with you, but not like this." Daniel skimmed a finger over her wet cheek. "When was the last time you had a good night's sleep or a meal?"

Alessandra shrugged her shoulders in response because she wouldn't tell him the truth. She wouldn't tell him there had only been exhausted sleep that left her feeling listless and hulled out. Alessandra wouldn't tell Daniel it had been as long since she'd had anything decent to eat.

"Let's get you to bed. While you rest up, I'll make you something to eat. Do you have any sleeping pills?" Alessandra shook her head. "I'll go to the drugstore."

"Don't go. Don't leave me, Daniel."

The fear in her voice unmistakable his response came quickly. "I won't."

"Promise."

"I promise." Daniel squeezed her hand in reassurance. "I'll stay with you for as long as you want."

"Thank you." She brushed her lips to his in gratitude. The warmth of his breath, his lips ensnared her in a web of comfort. Needing a man's touch, she took his hands and rested them on the swells of her breast.

That took Daniel by surprise, but she kindled need, dazed him. It took all of Daniel's strength to tug his hands away. "Ah, let me, umm, how does spaghetti sound?"

"I don't want spaghetti. I want you."

Daniel took calming breaths. "No, you don't."

"I want you to want me."

"I do. Christ, I want you so badly. I have since the moment I lay eyes on you."

"Then take me, Daniel. Make me feel desirable." The eyes that met his spoke of a need to be wanted, to be touched. Seeing the yearning in his eyes would make her feel like a woman again.

Her eyes fixed on Daniel, she slid the thin straps of her nightgown off her shoulders and sent it slithering to the floor. Daniel swallowed hard. A satisfied smile played across her face as the wide blue eyes feasted.

She was more beautiful in the flesh. Daniel wasn't prepared for the assault of hunger and need that swelled in him with tidal-wave force when he took in the fluid lines, the supple curves. The stark contrast of the red lace against golden skin made him ache. It pleased Alessandra to see the need in Daniel's eyes.

Alessandra's hands framed his face. "Want me, Daniel."

"I want you, badly, but..."

"Show me how much." Alessandra brought his hands to touch her again. The warmth of her skin stole the oxygen from his lungs.

The wanting was there, a deep churning that made him long to touch, to taste, and take. Lost to yearning, Daniel ran his hands down smooth curves. Her skin was soft as down and as hot as lava. Filling his hands with her breasts, Daniel left his thumbs to roam over the pink tips until they hardened. The thrill of pleasure was so intense she let out a gasp of panicked need, and he flew with the sensation.

Working his mouth to her ear, he whispered, "I want you so very much," with a hunger in his voice that shot delight through her.

Alessandra's smile spreading, she reached for his hand. As she started to lead him into the house, Daniel scooped her in his arms and carried her upstairs to her bedroom.

Streams from a late afternoon sun poured through the open window, lighting the room gold. The scent of the sea and roses that claimed the room was strong.

Laying her on the bed, he skimmed eyes over her. None of the fantasies he'd conjured, the longing that speared through him when he had, was as powerful as the hunger he felt for her now.

He looked into her eyes. "You're stunning. I've ached for you daily since the day we met. You believe me?" The glint of need in the dusky eyes, the unabashed arousal in them spoke truth, and she nodded. "I want so badly to be with you." Daniel's words sent her ego soaring, and she held out a hand for his.

His eyes never leaving hers, he stripped out of his clothes. Her breath caught and shuddered when she caught a glimpse of the powerful body she never imagined under the conservative suits. His arms were strong, his shoulders broad. His body was the luscious colour of burnt caramel and as solid as a brick. It was a body made to be admired.

In one easy leap, Daniel straddled her. His mouth fused to her before his tongue explored because he knew she wanted him to and because it was what he'd dreamt of doing.

He felt her tremble when his moist lips roved over her body with butterfly kisses.

Her eyes fluttered close, and her breath hitched when his mouth swallowed her breasts. When he nipped at the hard tips with his teeth, he drove her breath to hitch and her body to quiver.

Arching her body, she drove her breasts deeper into his greedy mouth. Filling his mouth with them, Daniel feasted delicately, tenderly. Every touch was a separate thrill that made her come alive. Every stroke of his tongue made her feel wildly feminine, desired, and wanted.

"Now. Take me now."

His heart thundering in his chest, he rolled on top of her in one fluid motion. His mouth was on her, kissing with a ferocity that left her breathless. His gaze on hers, he ran his hands down to her hips, skimming fingers over the red lace that still covered her.

"Oh, God," she cried out in arousal against his caressing fingers.

Her heart took one hard leap into her throat when he slid his fingers under lace. She was hot and lusciously wet. She gasped for air when he replaced fingers with mouth and tongue.

His tongue glided and devoured, driving her to delirious moans of pleasure. Music to his ears, he thought.

The ripple of pleasure flooding her made her mind float to wonderful places seconds before her body demanded to be taken over the edge.

Her breaths came in fast, frantic gasps. "Now. Now."

He hoped she cried out his name, but this was about her, and he dedicated himself wholly to her. His tongue slid over hot, pink flesh with urgency until her body arched to the swells of blissful shocks. The orgasm struck quickly, violently. Her nails pressed into his back when the eruption burst, and the pain slipped away—if for the moment.

Two aftershocks of sensation followed, her body stiffened, and her toes curled with each before she cried out.

Alessandra's body slaked, her pride and dignity on the mend, slumberous, green eyes looked up at him.

"I won't if you don't want me to," he said, even as his need to be inside her swelled.

She heard the quiet desperation in his voice but was sure that if she told him to stop now, he would. Here was love, she thought, pure and true. Daniel was in love with her, and she was using him to stroke her hurt ego.

She knew that, and he did too.

Guilt clutching at her, Alessandra wondered whether she was doing the right thing. She was attracted to him physically, but that was the depth of her interest in Daniel. But he'd restored what Luca had sapped from her. But she didn't feel what she saw in his eyes for her, what she'd felt in his touch. Alessandra tossed the arguments in her head.

The thought of using Daniel made Alessandra's stomach hurt. "Daniel, I..."

He touched her lips with his to silence words he didn't want to hear. "I understand." The humbleness in his voice, the need in his eyes, squeezed her heart. As he started to lift himself off her, she took his arms. "You don't have to do this."

"I want to."

"Are you sure?"

Her nod drove emotions long buried stirred in him. Love surging in his heart, Daniel never took his eyes from her face as he thrust into her.

Swallowing each catchy breath, slowly, tenderly, he moved inside her, cherishing every moment of their union. She was his, was all he could think as hot flesh slapped hard against hot flesh.

Then there was only pleasure. The pure and simple joy of losing everything he felt and swamped with love, he emptied into her.

He'd tell her how much he loved and cherished her, but those words wouldn't be said today.

Thirty-Seven

IT WAS A great summer morning. The greatest, Daniel thought.

Sunlight burst through the bedroom window like fairy dust. From deep within the branches of the olive trees, the piping song of birds drifted. The woman lying next to him in bed was Alessandra, and she was as real as the morning sun was bright. No dream he'd conjured up had made Daniel feel as happy and complete as he felt then.

Indeed, it was a great summer morning.

Alessandra's scent slid into him, prompting the memory of their lovemaking into his thoughts. The tasted of her lips, the kisses they'd shared, how perfectly their bodies came together came at him. Daniel shifted so he could see her face. Listening to the rhythm of her heartbeat, his heart swelled. He, not Luca, lay next to her.

Losing himself in the moment, Daniel never wanted it to end.

Daniel didn't know the whole story, but his need to protect Alessandra from Luca was strong. He'd misjudged Luca. Daniel had seen love in Luca's eyes for Alessandra and thought it was real. He should have known better. Luca was his father's son, a Santini, and hurting people, taking and discarding, was what they did.

Daniel wasn't going to allow son or father to harm Alessandra. He'd protect and watch over her. He'd be by her side for as long as Alessandra would let him. If she allowed him, Daniel would love her with the intensity of a burning sun.

Daniel hadn't thought of another woman until Alessandra walked into his life. The first time they met, Alessandra took his breath away. Her indelible image etched in Daniel's memory, Alessandra had filled his dreams, his every thought for months.

Daniel brushed his lips over Alessandra's forehead and rustled himself out of bed. He'd make a light breakfast and serve it in bed. God knew when she'd last eaten a good meal.

Snagging his pants off the floor, Daniel stepped into them. With a blissful smile on his face, Daniel wandered down the hallway. He came to a dead stop at the top of the stairs when he saw Luca closing the front door behind him.

Luca's eyes narrowed into thin slits at the sight of Daniel. Shirtless, his hair tousled, and the expression of sexual gratification on his face stabbed Luca in the heart. Luca's mind hazed. He closed his eyes, pressed them tight, hoping when he opened them, Daniel would be gone.

Daniel was still there when he opened his eyes.

Luca's mind racing, he wondered how many nights Daniel had spent with Alessandra since he left. The thought that her refusal to see or talk to him was because she'd already found his replacement in Daniel struck him like a poisoned bullet. Luca's eyes went turbulent at the thought of Daniel moving into *his* home, taking over *his* life, and sharing Alessandra's bed.

Fear that he'd lost her forever sprang hot to Luca's throat, and anger roiled inside of him—at himself. The hurt he'd caused Alessandra made her seek comfort in the arms of another man. It made Alessandra share her bed and body with another.

Luca closed his eyes as the pain stabbed him.

He wasn't surprised Daniel was the man that offered Alessandra the comfort she needed. As much as Daniel respected boundaries, Luca knew he'd be by Alessandra's side the first opportunity he got.

"Is she all right?" Luca asked when he found his voice.

"No, she's not." Anger edged Daniel's voice.

The ache in Luca's heart at the underserved pain he'd inflicted on Alessandra choked him. "I need to talk to her."

"She's asleep." Daniel took a protective stance when Luca looked past his shoulder in disbelief. "She needs to be left alone. It's the first restful sleep she's had in days."

Luca's face held a mixture of remorse and regret. "Will you let her know I was here, that I need to talk to her?"

Daniel nodded, and after a pause, said, "You hurt her, her pride. You broke her heart. You shattered her world, the one she was trying to piece back together. You caused her unnecessary pain that's made her fragile again. That's inexcusable."

The thought Alessandra confided in Daniel burnt a hole in Luca's gut. "Stay out of it. You don't know anything."

"I know enough to say she did nothing to deserve it. That all she did was give to you." There was fury in Daniel's eyes, a sure sign of his love for Alessandra, Luca determined, and his throat closed tight enough to choke. "Whoever she is, I hope she was worth it because she'll never stack up to Alessandra. No woman does."

An absolute silence hung in the room. For a long while, both men locked eyes, each willing the other to perish, but Luca knew Daniel wasn't going anywhere anytime soon. The fear he'd lost Alessandra forever sprang hot to his throat. For the first time, he felt lost and alone. With a dull acceptance burning in his eyes, Luca left the home where he'd, found love, and now lost it.

THE HEADY SCENT OF MAN AND sex came to Alessandra when she opened her eyes. The guilt and remorse were like two vicious, heavy blows to her gut.

What had she done? How could she have lured Daniel into bed, knowing how he felt for her? Lured, Alessandra mulled. That was the apt word because it was precisely what she'd done. Lured and used because she wanted to feel desired—or possibly to get back at Luca. Alessandra tried to talk herself into believing it was the former, but she knew better.

How could she do it to Daniel? Alessandra chastised herself. Daniel was a wonderful, giving, and caring man. Daniel was a good friend, and she'd used him to inflate her injured ego.

The high song of morning birds broke outside the window as Daniel walked into the room with the food tray. Bare-chested, his hair tousled, Alessandra stared. How had she overlooked his stunning good looks all this time?

God, what was she thinking, Alessandra told herself?

Her thought process was so off and so wrong. She should be reflecting on her actions, contemplating her poor judgement, drowning in guilt. But good God! He looked great.

Daniel's sapphire-blue eyes flashed Alessandra, a smile that made her stomach clench. "*Buon Giorno*. I hope I didn't wake you."

Shaking her head, Alessandra pulled the bed sheet high enough to cover her naked body when modesty suddenly became an issue. "I, ah, must look a mess." Warily, she brushed a hand through the sleek cap of chestnut hair.

"You look beautiful." His compliment made her cheeks tinge red. "This is for you." Daniel set the tray of food before her. Scrambled eggs, freshly made coffee, buttered toast, and at the center of it, a pink rose speared from a Perrier bottle. "I snipped it off your rose bush. I hope you don't mind."

How perfect could this man get? Guilt turned Alessandra's expression sheepish. "Of course not. That ... this is very thoughtful."

"I thought you could use something to eat." Sensing her discomfiture at being naked under the bedsheet, Daniel handed her the robe on the chair.

Alessandra slipped into it when he turned his back. "I'm decent."

When Daniel spun to face her, Alessandra was gathering her hair into a ponytail. "I hope you like your eggs scrambled."

"Everything looks perfect."

Daniel wished they could dispense with the formality meant to be shared between acquaintances, not two people who'd shared a night of lovemaking.

Alessandra kept her focus on the eggs she idly moved around with her fork, but both knew her mind was filling with words she didn't want to say but would. "Thank you for … last night. You were… I enjoyed sharing it with you."

Sensing the but coming, Daniel said, "You don't have to explain, Alessandra. I know exactly what last night was." Daniel's quiet words masked the raw disappointment that rammed his gut.

There was a softness in Alessandra's eyes now. "I need … time."

The pain stabbing at his heart, Daniel fought to keep his face composed. "I understand, I do, Alessandra," he said, wishing he didn't have to.

The guilt all but swallowing Alessandra, she said, "No, it's not fine. I know how you feel about me, and I shouldn't have taken such liberties with your emotions to dull my pain." Her words were laden with regret.

"Don't apologize. I'm not sorry it was me you turned to, and I have no regrets." Daniel's kind tone stung Alessandra.

"I wouldn't have turned to anyone else." The jade-green eyes that looked up to Daniel told him she meant it. Still, he couldn't help but feel like a consolation prize. "I'm sorry, Daniel."

He picked his shirt off the floor and eased it over toned arms. "As I said, there's no need to apologize, Alessandra. And I want you to know I'm here for you. You can call on me day and night for anything, even if it's to talk."

Why in God's name did he have to be so understanding? She didn't deserve his kindness or friendship. A shock of remorse assaulted Alessandra's conscience, and she lashed out. "Jesus, Daniel, stop being so understanding. Treat me like the manipulative, conniving bitch I am, who thinks only of herself."

Daniel heard the guilt in her voice, quivering waves of it. He sat at the edge of the bed. "You're none of those things. You needed a friend to console you and make you feel feminine and wanted." Alessandra eyed him with wonder. "I hope I did that for you."

She sighed deeply. "You did, but…"

"I loved being with you, Alessandra." His mind weaved to how good she'd made him feel when she took his hand to lead him upstairs, and each time she'd received him in bond. "And I'll make myself available to you day and night if you ever need my therapeutic services again." He joked to infuse levity into the conversation that was becoming difficult for him.

A soft smile came over Alessandra's face. "I know. As I know, you'll always be there for me. That and the fact you were here for me last night means the world to me, Daniel."

"I'm glad." The air hummed between them as he took the time to qualify whether to tell her. "Luca was here," Daniel said in the end.

"I heard what you said to him."

"Oh," Daniel said, pleased she hadn't felt the need to speak to Luca herself.

"And you were right. What he did to me was inexcusable, and although I won't forgive him anytime soon, I love him too much to forget him and move on so soon."

"I know."

"I need time to figure things out in my head." Alessandra's voice held sadness.

"I know," Daniel repeated.

The expression on his face spoke volumes to Alessandra of the depth of his understanding. Daniel was the epitome of the knight in shining armour coming to her rescue expecting nothing and demanding nothing. Daniel was twice the man to the woman she was, Alessandra told herself.

Alessandra nudged Daniel back as he started to rise. Her touch sent his mind reeling with emotions. "If you don't have any plans for today, I thought we could have lunch out on the patio. Maybe go for a swim after my run."

Daniel met the emerald-green eyes he'd looked into each time he'd made love to her. The throbbing ache he may never see them again in that light made the need to put distance between them essential. "I should get going."

Alessandra squeezed Daniel's hand, and his stomach flipped. "Please stay."

As Daniel was about to turn her down, he saw the pained look Alessandra tried to disguise behind a half-smile. It told him she needed him there.

As sure as the sun beamed from a cloudless sky and birds flitted under its warm spill, Daniel surrendered to her. "Only if you promise to eat everything on your plate."

"I promise."

"While you do that, if you don't mind, I'd like to take a quick shower."

"Of course. There are fresh towels in the bathroom cabinet." Feeling better, Alessandra took a forkful of eggs and realized how hungry she was. It was the first semblance of nourishment to touch her lips in days. "Daniel?" she called to him before taking her next bite. "Thank you for everything."

With a nod, Daniel closed the bedroom door behind him.

Thirty-Eight

THE CLANKING OF footsteps on the stairs made Daniel look up. Alessandra wore a lime-green T-shirt and white shorts. Her wet hair was spooled through the adjustment opening of the baseball cap. At the end of the very toned, very long legs, she wore white running shoes.

"I see they fit." Alessandra eyed the polo shirt and tapered jeans Daniel filled well. "Did you find the bathing suit in the shopping bags?" She got a nod from Daniel. "So, will you join me for a swim later?"

"Sure." Daniel took a long, silent breath when she walked past him and wrapped him with the scent of her lavender soap.

"I don't suppose you'd like to come for a run with me."

"I didn't see a pair of running shoes in the bags."

"Another time then." Alessandra smiled when the sigh of relief bloomed on Daniel's face. "My grandmother painted those. I've tried my hand at painting but quickly discovered I didn't inherit the artistic gene." Alessandra explained when Daniel eyed the paintings on the wall.

"I've heard it skips a generation." Daniel quipped, studying the framed work closely. "She was talented. I can see her hand on all except this one. I don't think your *nonna* painted this one."

When Alessandra stood next to Daniel, he shook the thought of taking her into a long, passionate kiss there and then. "Why do you think that?"

"All the paintings relate to this property, but this one depicts a different vista. Aside from the different scenery, the paint strokes on this one go in the opposite direction. See here." Daniel pointed to the fountain in the painting, where the strokes were most visible. "I think a left-handed person painted this one."

"You're right. You know there's something familiar about it." Alessandra moved closer to Daniel. His pulse thrummed at the sensation she shot through him when she brushed her arm to his. He wasn't going to make it through the day with his sanity intact.

"This inscription, *Mea Domus Est Tua* is Latin for my home is yours," Daniel said once he regained his focus.

Alessandra raised an appreciative brow. "You know Latin?"

"High school Latin is the extent of it. The notation is odd. Normally, you say my house is your house."

"Simple mistake to make, I guess." Alessandra's eyes were still on the painting when it hit her. "Oh my God, Daniel!" She absently wrapped her hand on his arm.

Alessandra would never know the shot of want that bulleted through him. "What is it, Alessandra?"

"This is a painting of Villa Santini."

"Are you sure?"

"Positive. It's their house. See that fountain with the goddess surrounded by the pool of flowers in the oval base below.

"They're frangipani."

Alessandra's eyebrows shut up. "High school botany?"

Daniel gave her a slow smile. "My mother's garden."

"Anyway, that's the fountain standing there now. It's now flanked with blood-red poppies, but that's the fountain at the center of their circular driveway. Why would there be a painting of Villa Santini in my home? Maybe Luca put it here." Daniel gave her a side-eye look. "A thought. May I?"

Daniel took the painting down when she nodded. Carefully inspecting it, he flipped it every which way, but it wasn't until his fingertips felt their way around the back that he detected the bulging center.

"What is it, Daniel?"

"There's something in here." Daniel guided her fingers over the swell. He fought the flutter at the pit of his stomach when their hands touched. Daniel was sure he was going to have a coronary before the day was over.

"You're right. What do you think it is?"

"I don't know. We'll need to disassemble it, but I think we should get an expert to do it. I'm not an art expert, but something tells me this could be a valuable piece, if not monetarily, at least historically. I know who can do it."

"Your sister," she chimed.

Daniel nodded. "She'd be able to take it apart for you, and if it's a historical piece, she'll put a date to it. I can call her if you like."

Alessandra nodded curiously, gazing at the painting.

Thirty-Nine

THE WORDS EXPLODED from Antonio's lips. "Goddamn it, Luca, as if I don't have enough to deal with already." He shoved away from his desk with force and crossed to the bar in search of a stiff drink to calm jangled nerves.

"Please calm down, Antonio." Laine pled, easing herself into the guest chair next to Luca.

"How can I calm down, Laine. Did you not hear what I said?" Antonio's boisterous voice filled his office. "I don't think you did because if you'd had, you'd be fuming along with me. So I'm going to repeat myself for it to sink in to both of you." Antonio flicked his eyes to Luca then to Laine. "Elisa is claiming she's pregnant with Luca's child."

"I heard you the first time, but screaming and getting your blood pressure up is not going to solve anything." Laine bit back the anger for her husband. She'd unleash it when the moment was right because she was sure he somehow had a hand in the sordid situation. "Pour me a glass."

Antonio poured scotch into two glasses and walked them and the bottle back to his desk. "I knew this day would come to pass sooner or later. I mean, look at the lifestyle he leads. Women parading in and out of his life like a bordello." Antonio tossed back part of his drink. "You damn well know your name, and money attracts women whose sole purpose is to get themselves pregnant with your child. They're looking to score the lottery, and you've been very accommodating by pollinating half of Europe."

Laine reached for Luca's hand, squeezed gently. "Comments like that are not conducive to this conversation, Antonio."

"It has to be said point-blank for it to sink into your son's thick skull." Antonio swallowed heavily. "You're not a child, Luca, and whether you like it or not, you have a responsibility to us, to the corporation, to uphold the Santini name."

"That's it, Dad. Put your business priorities ahead of everything. Optics is all you ever care about." Luca snapped.

Antonio bolted forward in his chair. "I don't think you're in a position to pass judgement, Luca. Everything I've done is for the family's benefit, and I don't recall you complaining about the business when you use the private jet to whisk the woman of the week to that exotic destination. I didn't hear you complain about the company when I set you up on your six-figure salary, even though most of your time is spent farming. Need I go on, Luca?" Antonio's fiery eyes could burn a hole through bricks.

"He's your son, your only child." Laine reminded her husband.

Antonio grunted as he topped his empty glass. "That's exactly why he should know better and shouldn't be saddling me with this problem."

Laine tilted angry eyes to her husband. "I think you're exactly the person to be dealing with this."

Laine's fury-laced tone made Antonio stop his drink mid-sip. "What's that supposed to mean?"

"I'll fix it, Dad." Luca's eyes darted from his father to the floor, where the rays of sunshine from an August sun hit the white marble and dispersed into a prism of light.

Antonio rolled his eyes at Luca. "I don't think so. You've done enough. Besides, your mother seems to think it should be me dealing with this because you can't exercise self-control?"

"Stop, Antonio. Now." Laine lifted a hand to silence her husband. "And yes, you will deal with this along with your son because the situation Luca finds himself in is as much your fault as it is his."

Antonio's glass cluttered against polished wood, spilling half of its contents. "How do you figure? It wasn't me who couldn't keep his fly zipped up."

"Christ." Luca cringed.

"You set Luca up. I'm still not sure why you did, but you set him up," Laine said, levelly watching her husband as his expression changed from anger to surprise.

"I did no such thing." Antonio rushed to defend himself, although he didn't sound convincing—even to himself.

"Don't deny it. Not to me." Laine threw her husband a glare as intense as the pressure headache that settled above her eyes. "You and I both know you set your son up with Elisa as the lure. You told me Luca begged to be put on the Donatella land deal. Yet he tells me you asked him to take the project on, and when he does, Charlie magically disappears from the picture and in comes Elisa. I don't believe in coincidences where you're concerned, Antonio." Laine's forceful tone drove Antonio's gaze away from her to the glass in his hand.

"I know for a fact you've been talking to Charlie about purchasing the property. Then, all of a sudden, Elisa appears in the picture. You asked Charlie to put his daughter, or should I say that viperous, conniving, manipulative..." Laine pursed her lips to stop herself. "You put her in charge of the deal to steer her in Luca's direction. Isn't that true, Antonio?"

Luca turned to his father with a look that could freeze lava. "Is this true?" And here I thought you wanted my expertise, my input in the deal. I thought you were starting to understand me. You'd already decided to buy the property before you got me involved."

Antonio remained silent, his eyes lost in the golden liquid in his glass.

"You used your son, and you used that..."

"Devious bitch to seduce me on your behalf," Luca jumped in, his voice trembling with rage.

"Explain yourself, Antonio," Laine demanded.

There was the briefest pause as Antonio tried to weave the story in his head. "I only wanted Elisa to inject herself into Luca's life to draw his attention away from Alessandra. I gave you one task, Luca. All you had to do was negotiate the purchase of her land, but no, you had to jump into bed with her."

"I'm not one of your lackeys, Dad. I'm not one of the business deals that you play for stakes. This is my life you played with. My life you destroyed." Luca's voice broke.

Laine's heart clenched for her son. "Why, Antonio? Why would you do this to your son?"

"For Christ's sake, Laine."

"Explain yourself, Antonio."

"Fine. When you told me he was in love with Alessandra I... Christ, I didn't think he'd sleep with Elisa their first night together." Antonio shot back, regaining his footing in the conversation. "And I sure as hell didn't think he'd get her pregnant. And who..."

"He did it for a piece of land." Luca's voice rose above Antonio's to subdue his father into silence. "Isn't that why you did it, Dad? You played with my life for a Goddamn piece of land."

Fury simmering, Luca went on to tell Laine the story of Villa Cuomo of Gianni and Rosa. He explained Alessandra's reason for refusing to sell. He stressed Antonio's determination to strip Alessandra of her land—at any cost. Luca told his mother about his deal with Alessandra's grandmother, which in the end, turned out to be a ruse Antonio set in motion to take ownership of the land. There was no detail too small, too mundane as Luca told his mother everything.

Disappointment filtering through Laine's system, she said, "Is this what you've become, Antonio? This is how you guard the great Santini name by going after a helpless, desperate, old woman and her granddaughter?" Laine gave Antonio a scorching look. "If what Luca says that Alessandra and her grandmother were more than willing to allow you the use of the land. That they were willing to sell the crop to you and still you deliberately plotted to steal the land from them, then Antonio, I'm ashamed to be your wife and embarrassed to bear the Santini name." Laine's words struck Antonio with the force she meant to.

Antonio's eyes flashed distress. "Goddamn it, Laine, you're missing the point."

"I don't want to hear another word from you, Antonio," Laine said flatly with a sullen look she'd never exhibited toward her husband before today. "Honey, as much as I detest Elisa for what she's done. As against I am of bringing this girl into the fold of our family, she may be carrying your son, my grandchild." Laine's motherly tone tugged at Luca as she meant to do.

"That baby is a Santini, and that woman can't be allowed to use our family and name against us. One way or another, I don't see an alternative to this mess, which you've dropped on our laps. You'll have to marry Elisa." Antonio scowled.

"Not another word, Antonio." Laine's eyes and tone warned before turning to Luca. "I hate to say it, but your father's right, honey."

"How do we even know she's actually pregnant or that it's mine? As you said, she's a manipulative, conniving bitch who went out of her way to seduce me." Luca was quick to point out.

Antonio jumped in with a caustic laugh. "Funny how you overlooked those traits when you hopped into bed with her. And the fact that she's manipulative leads me to believe it's yours. I wouldn't put it past her to have planned the whole thing to the last detail."

"And we have you to thank for that. Don't we, Dad?" Luca's eyes shot daggers.

"I didn't get the woman pregnant." Antonio sipped, sighed. "Look, as much as I understand the hormonal aspect of this situation, and I do. I was your age once. I'm not saying I slept around." Antonio added when Laine cocked a brow.

"But this deal we're working on with the Donatella's is worth hundreds of millions of dollars to the corporation. You know that Villa Donatella was only a stepping-stone to secure the purchase of Charlie's wine division. Our board of directors expects this deal to go through, there are hundreds of jobs on the line, and Charlie is now threatening to shut down negotiations if you don't marry Elisa. How exactly would you like me to address this at our next board meeting? Don't you see, Luca, this is bigger than you and me." Antonio pointed out.

"She's not the woman I want to spend the rest of my life with. She's not the woman I..." Luca's thoughts drifted off to Alessandra, and he felt a longing for her when images of their time together swamped him. The intense emotions she brought out in him stirred then, and he felt the deep connection, the bond, which he'd never shared with any other woman, swamp him. "I love Alessandra. She's the woman I want to marry." There was real pain in Luca's eyes, and Laine reached out with a motherly touch.

"I understand that's not in the realm of possibility now." Antonio shot out. "Didn't the girl throw you out after she found out you slept with Elisa? I'll admit it's something I never expected from any of your women to do. I underestimated that girl."

"That's enough, Antonio." Laine's voice was stern and cold enough to silence him. "Honey, it's your decision, but I didn't raise a son of mine to shun his responsibilities. You have an obligation to your child."

"I know, Mom." The sadness in Luca's eyes made Laine's heart tighten, and she curled a hand around his.

"I don't see any other solution other than for you to..." Seeing the pain in her son's eyes, Laine let the sentence hang.

Giving a knowing nod, Luca went silent when the vision of Alessandra's face flickered in his mind. Luca tried for weeks to talk to Alessandra, but she refused to take his calls, and he couldn't venture to revisit Villa Cuomo. The thought of seeing Daniel in the home he'd shared with Alessandra was heart wrenching. Deep down, Luca knew he'd never win her back, and without her, nothing mattered anymore. Life had no meaning.

This mess was his doing. He'd hurt Alessandra, put his father in a compromising position, and jeopardized the Donatella deal. But in the path of this hurricane he created, Luca's biggest regret was how he'd affected Alessandra. He'd told her he would protect her no matter what, but all he did was cause her undeserved pain.

Luca would make the Donatella's and his father whole, but he'd never be able to make it up to Alessandra. It was then the idea formed in his mind.

"I'll marry Elisa," Luca wished he had a drink to wash the nasty taste the vile words left in the back of his throat, "On the condition, you legally deed Villa Cuomo to Alessandra."

Antonio slammed a fist on his desk. "I'm doing no such thing. Have you forgotten the property is overflowing with Florentia vines? Not to mention the fact that land is mine."

"You and I know it's rightly her property." Luca shot his father a murderous look.

"History begs to differ," Antonio said.

"I want the paperwork in her hands before I propose marriage to Elisa. No paperwork, no marriage," Luca said defiantly.

Laine's cautionary glare at Antonio made him close his mouth immediately after he opened it. "It will be done, honey. Won't it, Antonio?" The eyes that stared at Antonio were those of an attack dog meant to cause harm, and Antonio thought best than to add anything but a grunt to the conversation.

"Thanks, Mom. Will you talk to Alessandra? She won't take my calls." Luca's voice broke when the sense of complete loss crept upon him. "I know she'll talk to you. Let her know you're going to ensure she gets all the paperwork necessary to make Villa Cuomo officially hers. Talk to her about the grape crop. I know she won't sell it to anyone else. It's not who she is."

"Of course, honey. I'll talk to her and sort things out." Laine met Luca's pained eyes. "I'm so sorry it's turned out this way."

"Not as sorry as I am," Luca said, feeling the sour waves of nausea rise in his stomach at the thought of the finality of his life with Alessandra becoming a reality.

Forty

CLOSING THE FRONT door behind him, Daniel called out, "*Ciao*, Alessandra, are you home?"

"I'm upstairs. I just got back from my run. I'll be down after a quick shower."

Daniel's mind swarmed with images of her naked body under the rainfall of water, and his juices stirred to boiling. He'd be more than happy to step into the shower with her. That, however, wasn't in the cards—not for the moment. Alessandra hadn't invited Daniel back to her bed since that memorable night, but he was a patient man.

The consolation was that Luca was a distant memory in Alessandra's mind. She hadn't taken Luca's calls, and he hadn't returned to the house since their encounter. Better than that, Daniel, not Luca, was now the man in Alessandra's life. Albeit Daniel was a platonic man-friend, but he, not Luca, was there.

"Did you have anything to eat this morning?" Daniel shrugged out of his suit jacket, laid it on the back of the living room chair.

"Nope." The pipes moaned to life like a waking giant when she turned the water on to let it run hot.

The sound of raining water stoked Daniel's imagination some more, and the rise came fast and hard. Goddamn it, now he needed a cold shower. He was sure if he stepped into the sea's water, half would go up in steam. He'd have to settle for the next best thing, standing in front of the refrigerator with the cold air rushing at him—again. In the past couple of months, he and the fridge had become well acquainted.

"Ah, it's, umm ... eleven now." He loosened the tie that was choking him and cutting off the oxygen to his brain. "How about I, ah, make us some lunch?"

"Sounds good." Alessandra wondered how Daniel managed to get through his highfalutin negotiations when he couldn't string a sentence together during their conversations. "Stepping into the shower now, so give me fifteen minutes."

Jesus, why did she have to say that? His cool-me-down-time in front of the refrigerator just went up five minutes.

Daniel rolled his sleeves to the elbow and headed for the refrigerator with a low whistle blowing between his lips. Standing there while his hot-blooded maleness succumbed to the cold air rushing at him, Daniel wondered how much longer he could go on freezing his jewels without causing damage. Daniel was fond of his jewels.

Daniel's blood cooled, and his ego deflated he set a pot of salted water on the stove and turned the flame to high. Crossing to the pantry, Daniel reached in for a pappardelle pasta bag to add when the water came to a boil.

Vegetable and sausages sliced, Daniel set the cast iron skillet on the second burner. Daniel added olive oil and chopped garlic to the hot pan. The mouth-watering aroma of sautéed garlic instantly permeated throughout the house. The garlic golden, Daniel added the sliced sausage, zucchini, and tomatoes. Lowering the heat, he gathered the makings for garlic bread.

Daniel knew his way around Alessandra's kitchen as well as his own. He should since their Monday talk-my-ear-off dinners, which started after Luca's departure, morphed into two nights and soon enough into a nightly event.

In time, Daniel's dinner visits expanded to weekends when he and Alessandra went shopping at the market, visited with Francesco and Maria, or went for a run or swim. Afterward, out on the patio sharing a bottle of wine, they'd fall into something that felt comfortable and right.

In a few months, their relationship evolved from a business association into a friendship that went deeper than any he'd had. In Daniel's eyes, their bond solidified into something more tangible than he imagined possible. It was as if Daniel rolled out of sleep and into the life he'd dreamed of with Alessandra.

Although Daniel craved the intimacy they'd shared weeks ago, he understood Alessandra wasn't ready. As much as Daniel hated to admit it, Alessandra's heart still belonged to Luca, and he didn't want to become her fallback man. Daniel needed to be more because his love for Alessandra was solid and real, and when they came together, he wanted it to be meaningful.

Daniel was selfish. Sharing Alessandra with the ghost of Luca wasn't an option. Daniel wanted Alessandra for himself, and if it took months for it to happen, he'd patiently wait. Until then, Daniel was going to be the friend Alessandra needed.

Daniel tossed the cooked pasta into the sausage and vegetable mix and then plated it with slices of garlic bread on the side. He chose a bottle of *Nero d'Avola*, uncorked it and filled two glasses. Food and wine set on the tray, he carried it to the patio.

The air scented with heat, sea, and orange blossoms hit Daniel. Glass smooth waters reflected sunlight sparkling diamonds. It was the beginning of August, and the beach was peppered with the locals and pale-skinned tourists that flocked in search of the sun and the cooling relief of the Sicilian beaches.

"That smells amazing," Alessandra said when she joined Daniel on the patio fresh from her shower. She wore a white tank and canary-yellow shorts. Her hair spilled in wet ropes around an unpainted face. The scent of her soap hit Daniel when she walked by him and made his brain liquefy.

"I, ah, hope you're, umm, hungry." As usual, his Goddamn brain wouldn't cooperate. "I've added lots of grated Parmesan as you like." Daniel handed her the glass of wine.

"Thank you." Alessandra sat, musing how he anticipated her every need and why she couldn't muster the feelings that stirred in her for Luca for Daniel.

Many nights, she'd thought of inviting Daniel to her bed. She'd love to spend another toe-curling night with him. The man was skilled in bed, but Alessandra couldn't bring herself to do it.

It wasn't due to a lack of attraction for Daniel that kept her from taking him to her bed. Those long-lashed, blue eyes could steal any woman's heart. It was because Alessandra's desire for Daniel didn't stem out of love for him but out of sexual need.

Knowing how Daniel felt for her, Alessandra couldn't cause him heartache. She'd come to treasure their friendship too much to hurt him.

"What brings you here so early in the day? Not that I mind in the least, but knowing you, there's a reason." Alessandra twirled noodles around her fork, savoured when she got a taste. "Excellent as usual. So, do tell."

"I have news for you," Daniel said with a quick grin.

"Me too, but you go first." Alessandra's tone matched his enthusiasm.

"My sister finished dismantling your painting."

"And?" Alessandra watched Daniel bite into garlic bread. Crumbs rained over his pasta dish.

"She told me you'd be pleased with her findings but insisted on discussing it in person." Daniel chased garlic bread with wine. "Have you been to Florence?"

"No," Alessandra said, suppressing the pained expression. Florence was where Luca committed the indiscretion that broke her heart and their life apart.

"My sister's invited us to visit." Daniel took the piece of garlic bread Alessandra offered when he bit into the last of his.

"Sounds interesting, but I don't want to impose."

"You won't be imposing. She'd love the female company. Husband and two boys, remember?" Daniel detected uneasiness in Alessandra. When the implications of a trip together hit him, he said, "I hope you won't mind sharing a room with my sister."

Alessandra set her fork down on the empty plate, picked the bottle to top up her wine. "Sounds like fun."

"Good. I'll make the arrangements. I have a case I need to wrap up. It'll take a few weeks, but we can leave afterward. If you like, we can stay for a couple of weeks." Daniel took the last of his wine, refilled his glass.

"That sounds perfect. I'm looking forward to it." Alessandra brought her knees up, wrapped her arms around them. The din of children's laughter chasing lapping waves filled the beat of silence that passed between them. "Laine Santini called me last night."

Daniel set his wine glass down with a thud. "What did she want?"

"To tell me they're deeding Villa Cuomo to me." The glow of triumph on Alessandra's face didn't elicit the response she'd hoped. "Daniel, did you hear what I said?"

Daniel's suspicious mind at work, he shifted in his seat. "I did. I'm just wondering why she'd contact you instead of my office. And why she, instead of their legal team, reached out to you? And why now? I hadn't even filed the papers challenging the ownership of Villa Cuomo yet. Why all of a sudden would they decide to make such a noble gesture?"

"You know I didn't think to ask all of those questions. I was too excited about the news," she said, with an impatient hiss. "Besides, I couldn't care less to know the reasons why. All I know is Villa Cuomo is officially mine." Alessandra's tone was too enthusiastic for Daniel to damper with his suspicions. "I gave her your name. They'll be contacting you to settle the matter in the next few days."

"I'm sorry. Sometimes I can't stop my legal mind from over-analyzing. Congratulations. I'm happy for you. What about the crops, the vineyard?"

"Laine offered me more money for the crop and use of the land as long as I commit to a long-term contract."

Anticipating there was more, Daniel said, "And? As your legal counsel, I need to know everything, Alessandra."

"I, of course, agreed without hesitation. She was charming, apologetic even for ... you know." Alessandra's mind drifted, and she became lost in the red swirl in her wine glass.

Sensing her thoughts were floating on memories of Luca, Daniel aimed to distract. "Do you believe Laine's sentiment was genuine?"

"I see no reason why not. I mean, she called unexpectedly with the offer. Besides, she doesn't seem like the conniving type. She offered to pay for all the legal expenses. You'll take care of that for me, won't you?"

Daniel nodded. "All she wanted was to get her hands on your crop. After all, the harvest is weeks away." His tone had a bitter edge to it.

"She was forthright about that and hoped I understood. I told her I did and that it was never my intention to give their secret away. I even told her I'd sign an NDA stating just that."

A look of mild amusement flashed in Daniel's face. "I'm sure that set her back."

"What do you mean?" Alessandra stacked dirty dishes and cutlery onto the tray.

"I doubt anyone has ever volunteered to give rather than take from them," Daniel added his empty wine glass to the tray.

"Huh, maybe that's why she offered to take over the supervision and management of the workers, which was a huge relief. Farming is not my cup of tea. I only enjoyed it when..." Knowing Luca was a sore point for Daniel, Alessandra let the sentence hang.

When the silence lengthened, Daniel said, "You're a far better person than I am."

Alessandra's face softened. "If I learned anything in the past months, is that clinging to anger is far too debilitating and that life's too precious to be filling it with unnecessary hatred."

That there was one of the many reasons, Daniel fell deeper in love with Alessandra with every passing day. "So, do you want me to stop the research on the Villa Santini lot?"

Alessandra shook her head. "Keep digging. If I've learned anything from this experience is that I need to have something of substance to counter the Santinis just in case. If your suspicion is correct and I own a portion of Villa Santini, I need to have that proof in my hands. You know, just in case." Alessandra rose, and Daniel followed with admiring eyes into the house.

Beautiful, intelligent, and noble, was it any wonder he was crazy in love with her?

Forty-One

ALESSANDRA SIPPED COFFEE as she systematically ticked off the completed items on her To-Do list. She highlighted LOCK BACK & FRONT DOORS and LATCH WINDOWS as a reminder to do before she and Daniel left for the airport. Locking doors wasn't part of the rhythm of a small-town mentality, and it was how Alessandra rolled now.

Pausing to think what else required her attention, Alessandra's eyes drifted beyond the patio. A bold morning sun and dreamy blue sky canvassed the brackish waters. Waves chopped in against the shore and then reared back for the next pass. To the west, rows upon rows of grapevines bulging with fruit stretched as far as the eye could see. The sight of them, the land they sat on, filled her with memories as a breeze whispered warmly over her face.

It was early morning, but the beach was already crowded. The aroma of cocoa butter from oiled bodies drifted in the air that pulsed with laughter. Alessandra watched children dipping their toes in the water before running away from chasing waves while mothers, spread out on colourful blankets, kept a vigilant eye on them. A group of children scooped sand into pails to build imaginary castles.

Alessandra watched couples walking hand in hand by the water's edge, sand sliding between their toes with envy. She thought back to the times she and Luca walked the beach at sunset. Sadness filled Alessandra's eyes at the thought, and the emptiness that filled her since his departure washed over her. It had been two months since she'd asked Luca to leave, but the pain was still raw and very real.

Luca hadn't been back since his conversation with Daniel. Just as well, because Alessandra didn't want to hear Luca's excuses and had nothing to say to him. Still, Alessandra missed Luca terribly. Hot tears stung Alessandra at the thought she'd never see him again but refused to shed them. She'd shed enough tears for Luca already.

Luca had come into Alessandra's life at a time she needed him. He'd been her salvation and filled her life with hope and love. Luca replaced darkness with light and gave her reason to laugh again. No matter what life brought, Alessandra would never forget him. Luca was her first love. As much as he was the cause for them going their separate ways, she'd fallen more so in love with him the time they were apart. Absence—no matter the reason for it—did make the heart grow fonder.

Alessandra's eyes swam with grief at the thought that chapter of her life was closed. She'd never wake up to Luca's brilliant blue eyes, hear his laugh, see his bright smile, or breathe in his scent. She'd never be enveloped in his arms or feel his touch on her. Alessandra wouldn't hear Luca whisper in her ear how much he loved her while making love with her.

Something crumbled inside her.

Alessandra wondered what the future held in store. Whatever life steered her way, she'd always feel the vacuum in her heart and her life that Luca once filled. The shrill of the telephone jerked Alessandra back to reality, and she turned to head inside.

"Oh, hello, Dr. Scalia." Alessandra's stomach muscles clenched. No good came from a doctor's call.

Alessandra hadn't felt well in days. Along with a lack of appetite and an excessive buildup of saliva, sleep hadn't come easily. At Maria's urging, Alessandra had Dr. Scalia run a check-up.

Fearing the worst from the tests Dr. Scalia had run, Alessandra hesitated for a moment. "Is everything okay, Dr. Scalia? I have an appointment scheduled to discuss my test results the day after my return from Florence."

Alessandra listened intently to Dr. Scalia when he jumped into the conversation. His words came out so fast she wasn't sure she heard correctly. "Can you repeat that?" When Dr. Scalia did, everything inside Alessandra froze. "How long do I have?"

Dr. Scalia's response wasn't what Alessandra wanted to hear. Her palm went sweaty on the receiver. The telephone fell from a loose hand, and the coffee cup followed seconds after.

A LIGHT RAIN WELCOMED ALESSANDRA AND Daniel to Florence. By the time they alit the plane, hauled their luggage off the carousel, and hailed a taxi, the rain was petering out, and dark clouds were floating away. That, however, didn't impress Alessandra. Her mind was back on the conversation with Dr. Scalia and the myriad of questions it set off in her head.

The shock still reverberating through Alessandra, she wondered how she was going to get through it. There were no medical options available, and Alessandra debated going home. She could seek medical help from the doctors there and fall back on her aunt for support. There was so much to think about, but she'd have to set that aside until after the trip.

"Is everything all right, Alessandra?" Daniel asked, folding himself into the back seat of the taxi next to her. "You were quiet for most of the flight."

Needing to let air into her lungs, Alessandra rolled the window down. The September air that hit her was hot and moist. "Everything's fine. I'm just tired. In the excitement of the trip, I barely slept last night." The lie burnt on her tongue.

Daniel stared at Alessandra for a moment. "You would tell me if something was bothering you or if anything was wrong, wouldn't you?" he said when he saw the troubled look in her eyes.

"Of course, I would."

"You know you can tell me anything."

"I know I can." Alessandra gave his hand a comforting squeeze that made his eyes glaze when the sexual pull came fast and hard. He set his briefcase down on his lap to conceal his delight at her touch. She was going to be the death of him. "Daniel."

"Mmm?"

"The driver is asking for the address." Alessandra listened to Daniel give the taxi driver his sister's address. "I'm looking forward to meeting your sister, her husband, and those two perfect nephews of yours."

A warm smile played across Daniel's face as he gazed out the window. The sky was lightening from dark to blue, and beams of liquid sunshine began to slip through. "I don't know about being perfect, but they're pretty close to it. It's been too long since I saw them. I'm looking forward to spending time with them. I hope you don't mind."

"I'd be upset with you if you didn't." Seeing the delight that leapt into his eyes at the mention of his nephews, Alessandra said, "You love children."

Dimples dented Daniel's cheeks. "I plan to have an entire football team."

Alessandra cocked a brow. "Ambitious. What if they turn out to be girls?"

Daniel broke into a smile of innocent pleasure. "Girls or boys both can kick a ball."

Alessandra let out that soft feminine laugh that made Daniel weak at the knees. "Sounds as if you have it all planned out."

"What do you think of Florence so far?"

Alessandra's eyes drifted out the taxi's window framing Florence in all its beautiful splendour. Basilicas, cathedrals, and piazzas whizzed by. "It looks spectacular."

"It is where the birth of the Renaissance originated. Florence is considered one of the most beautiful cities in the world." Daniel pointed to the domed cathedral dominating the skyline. "That's *Santa Maria del Fiore*. It's the first to embody an octagonal dome. The dome took sixteen years to construct and marked the beginning of Renaissance architecture. It dates to the fifteenth century," Daniel said with pride.

"But I'm not going to bore you with the history of the Medici family who controlled the city and commissioned much of the beautiful architecture and art you see. I'll leave that to my sister and brother-in-law. They're passionate about the city, its art, the Romanesque and gothic architecture. It's what made them choose Florence as their home. I hope you brought comfortable walking shoes."

"I've come prepared. I've even read up on the city and its famous artists. I thought I'd throw some of my newfound knowledge here and there. You know, to show I'm not a complete neophyte."

They jolted forward when the driver slammed the brakes inches from the car that cut him off. The driver's animated hand gestures, complete with bottom lip biting, made Daniel and Alessandra break into a smile.

"Just promise me one thing."

Alessandra fixed a curious gaze on Daniel. "What's that?"

"If my sister or brother-in-law bore you with talk of art and architecture, you'll let me know."

Absently, Alessandra reached out to put a hand over his. The intimacy of her touch felt electric on Daniel's skin, pure joy. He shifted the briefcase a few inches. The woman was going to drive him into an early grave—cause of death, sexual frustration.

"I'm doing no such thing. They're gracious to invite me, a total stranger, to their home. Not to mention the work she's done on Gianni's painting. If all they're asking in return is for me to endure a professorial lecture now and then, so be it."

His sister was going to love her.

ADORABLE AND LOVABLE WERE THE WORDS Alessandra thought of to describe Daniel's nephews. Carmelo, five, and Paolo, seven, had a curly mop of jet-black hair and large inquisitive eyes set in a rosy-cheeked face.

Anna, Daniel's sister, was not the stereotypical professorial type. She was medium height with long ash-blonde hair, which flowed around a heart-shaped face down to her shoulders. Her olive skin was the perfect complement to the dark, almond-shaped eyes. It was no wonder Massimo, her scholarly-looking husband, adored her.

As Daniel said, Anna was thrilled to have a woman in the house and the two immediately bonded. Over dinner, boys and men didn't dare interrupt Alessandra and Anna as they rambled on without stopping for breath. Their conversation, laced with female innuendo and laughter, dominated the dinner.

Massimo cleared the table, and the women washed the dishes and tidied the kitchen while Daniel tucked the boys into bed. When Daniel finished reading the boys a bedtime story, the four gathered in the office next to the kitchen. Massimo poured *Frangelico* into four shot glasses while Anna laid out the letter she uncovered between Gianni's painting and the matboard.

"The letter is well preserved. The painting and letter are authentic, and Massimo and I agree both date back to eighteen eighty-two and are painted and written by Gianni

Santini," Anna said, shining light when she turned the desk lamp on.

"How can you tell?" Alessandra asked, scrutinizing letter and painting with an analytical eye.

"June of eighteen eighty-two is the date of the letter, and we believe the painting was done in-and-around the same time. See the greenish-blue cerulean used for the landscape. That colour only became available in eighteen sixty. Max and I have also authenticated the initials on the painting and writing on the letter as Gianni's." Anna held the magnifying glass over the area for Alessandra and Daniel's scrutiny.

"I would've never seen that." Alessandra took a sip of the hazelnut-flavoured liqueur and found it divine.

"It is inconspicuous. The writing on the letter and initials match physical characteristics and patterns to many of Gianni's letters on display at the museum. Lastly, the letter is embossed with the Santini crest, which he likely did for authenticity. Then there's the type of paper and ink used to pen the words. They date back to the late eighteen hundreds. Massimo and I can attest to the fact both these pieces date back one hundred years," Anna said, and everyone eyed the painting and letter with the admiration worthy of their history.

"What does the letter say?" Alessandra held out her glass for the refill Massimo offered.

"I've translated it for you. Gianni was very much in love with your great-great-grandmother, and he didn't trust his family and, well, read for yourself." Anna turned the translation over to Alessandra.

Amore,

I write this letter with tears streaming down my face because I plan to leave you without saying good-bye. Although we will never see one another again, I cannot bring myself to say the word to you.

I have yet to leave and already miss you terribly.

Was I not shackled and mired in the obligations brought on by the Santini name, I would be marrying you, not a woman I care not for.

I know you understand I marry her to protect you, but I need to say it because I want you to never forget it is you I love. It is you I will love for eternity.

Know I will always have you in my heart, and come what may, amore, you will always have my heart in the palm of your hand.

I will forever carry your face with me to sleep at night and wake up with thoughts of you. I will, until my dying day. You are the best of me, and I love who I am when I am with you.

I am grateful to you for making me a better man and, however fleeting, for bringing joy into my life when I brought you nothing but pain and misery into yours.

To make amends, I gift you my home, amore. It's not much, but it's something dear to me, something that will last a lifetime and be there to remind you of me when you see it, touch it, and walk on it.

My home is yours now.

I, Gianni Enrico Santini, bestow the land situated at Villa Santini, lot number 262.049, consisting of one hundred and twenty-three acres to Rosa Elia Cuomo this 27th June 1882.

I have asked my father to deed you the property, but I fail to trust him, or my mother, to do the right thing. This letter will serve as proof if my family uses trickery to strip you of ownership of the land. You are to keep this letter under lock and key. Never part with it, but you will let them know it exists.

This will not make up for the pain I cause you, but it will hopefully remind you of me—in a positive light—and of our time together.

As long as there are stars in the night sky, you will be in my heart, in my thoughts, and my memories because I will see your face in them. I pray to God that you will see me and be reminded of the depth of my love for you when you look up to them.

I wish you love and happiness for your life-long days.

Gianni

Tears stung Alessandra's eyes. "That's heart-wrenching."

"It is. I think your great-great-grandmother read the letter often. I have a gut feeling Rosa's tears caused the ink to run." Anna pointed the blots throughout the letter.

Alessandra felt a connection with Rosa she hadn't before. Both had loved Santini men and lost them, and land was the substitution for lost love. Hardly a comparable trade-off, Alessandra thought. She'd have relinquished her land for Luca's love without a second thought. Alessandra was certain Rosa would have done the same for Gianni. History did repeat itself.

"Are you all right, Alessandra?" Anna asked. When Alessandra nodded, she said, "I believe this letter will stand up in court as a legally binding document. Am I right, Daniel?"

Daniel nodded. "It will. You can easily lay claim to lot number 262.049, which is," he pointed to the lot on the survey that ran through the middle of Villa Santini. "I suggest we do it after the deed to Villa Cuomo is finalized. Congratulations, Alessandra. You will soon own Villa Cuomo and a portion of Villa Santini."

With the shock cycling through her system, Alessandra said, "This is a lot to process. I need time to absorb it all. I need time to think," Alessandra said.

Her words left Daniel stunned. What he saw in her eyes wasn't victory over the claim to her land and another that stood to make her very rich. But then, Daniel couldn't understand that claim to Villa Santini kept Alessandra tied to the man she loved so much as not to allow her to move on with her life, to trust, and love again.

Daniel's brows furrowed. "But, Alessandra, this is..."

"Something Alessandra needs time to mull over on her own time," Anna said, seeing the pained look of lost love in Alessandra's eyes that only a woman could see with perfect clarity.

Daniel had told Anna of Luca's betrayal, but it was from a male perspective and an emotional one because she now saw the love in her brother's eyes for Alessandra.

Forty-Two

WIPING SLEEP OUT of her eyes, Alessandra let the vertical blind roll to let the sunshine in. When she stepped onto Anna's bedroom balcony, the sounds and scents she'd forever associate with Florence struck her.

It was quarter to seven, and the din of foot and car traffic that already crowded the cobbled streets and sidewalks competed with one another. A stream of stylishly dressed professionals moved quickly past strolling tourists. Alessandra turned her head when the purr and throttle of approaching *Vespas* zoomed past.

Alessandra took it all in, breathed it in, as she had every day since her arrival. Florence was an exciting, vibrant city she'd cross off her bucket list but not from visiting again.

Despite Dr. Scalia's conversation, continually circling her mind and the emotional turmoil Rosa's letter left her with, Alessandra was having a good time. The food was to die for, the sights breathtaking, and Massimo and Anna were hospitable and filled Alessandra with a sense of family.

Alessandra smiled when she heard the boys' muffled groans when Anna told them to brush their teeth before they set off to school. Massimo chimed in with a stern warning for the boys to do as told and be ready to leave for school in five minutes. It was the sounds of family and home, the familiar and comfortable Alessandra thought. Her mind drifted to thoughts of her family with an ache of loss in her heart.

When the bedroom door opened, Alessandra turned and was met with Anna's smile. "*Buon giorno*, they're gone. You're safe to come down to have a peaceful breakfast."

"I enjoy the sound of your boys and family." Alessandra reached into the armoire for skinny jeans and a lime-green shirt.

Anna sleeked her flowing hair into a ponytail and picked up the brush from her dresser to brush the tail end smooth. "Only because in a couple of days you get to go back to your quiet life. I'm stuck here, remember."

"You don't mean that."

"Sometimes, I do." Anna smoothed moisturizing cream on her hands and arms. "Grab a shower, and by the time you come out, I'll have breakfast ready for you."

"I thought I'd treat us all to breakfast at the café."

"That ... how do you westerners say?" Anna paused to think, "Sounds like a plan."

Alessandra laughed. "Good. Gather the troops."

OVER BREAKFAST, ANNA WENT OVER THE day's itinerary, and Daniel crossed his eyes at the detail and precision of his sister's schedule.

"Anna, it's our second last day here. Ease up. Massimo, tell your wife..."

"Nuh-uh." Massimo raised two hands, palms out, as if in surrender. "I do as I'm told. It makes it for a more peaceful life. You'll understand when you get married."

"Good answer." Anna pinched her husband's cheek. "We have much to see still." Turning to Alessandra, Anna pointed to the itinerary to make her point.

Alessandra thought they'd covered every inch of Florence already. During the past twelve days, they'd visited the *Palazzo Pitti*, a fifteenth-century palace. They'd toured the beautiful *Boboli Gardens*, where Massimo gave a historical account of the park's statues and fountains.

Anna and Massimo took them on a *Basilica di San Lorenzo* tour at the center of the city's market district. Anna explained that the Basilica, one of Florence's oldest churches, was the earliest example of ecclesiastical Renaissance architecture and the Medici patriarchs' burial place.

They'd been to centuries-old palaces and piazzas, walked the *Uffizi Gallery*, which Anna and Massimo regarded as one of the world's greatest museums. Alessandra had to agree once she saw the stunning collection of Renaissance art by Michelangelo, Botticelli, Leonardo da Vinci and Titian, just a few of the thousands of famous artists on display.

"You're enjoying Florence, aren't you, Alessandra?" Anna asked.

Daniel jumped in before Alessandra could answer. "She is, Anna, but Christ, you need to slow it down."

Massimo's eyes aimed a now-you've-done-it look at Daniel a millisecond before Anna's eyes flashed with hot ire and her tempest descended on him.

"Don't you use the Lord's name in vain? You may be my older brother, but I can still tell you what's what. If mama knew the heathen you've become, she'd be spinning in her grave."

"You mean turning," Daniel corrected with a smirk.

"I said exactly what I meant. She's spinning, full rotations. You don't go to church anymore, and your leanings are toward atheism now." Anna crossed herself. "Sacrilege, I tell you. If..." Anna launched on her rant.

When Daniel opened his mouth to infuse his philosophical views, Massimo shot him a cautioning look. Taking heed, Daniel bit back the words.

Alternating between Italian and English, Anna's passionate lecture lasted ten excruciatingly long minutes. Both men silently ate while Alessandra watched her high-spirited friend with admiration.

When it was safe to jump in, Alessandra cautiously said, "What Daniel means, Anna, is that this won't be my last visit to Florence, and I hoped you would leave some sightseeing for the next time I visit."

Warmed by the idea of her friend visiting again, Anna folded the itinerary and set it aside. "Understood, Alessandra, no sightseeing today." What do you say about a shopping spree? Florence is known for its leather goods, and a girl can never have enough leather."

"Sounds like a plan," Alessandra said, eliciting a smile from Anna, a dumbfounded eye roll from Daniel, and a shoulder shrug from Daniel.

How a woman went from attack dog mode to mother Teresa sweetness was a mystery for greater minds to decipher.

"TO SAY FLORENCE IS AN IMPRESSIVE city is an understatement, but it's the leather goods that have me hooked." Alessandra took a spoonful of the chocolate *Tartufo* Daniel ordered at the outdoor café, where they stopped to rest.

"I'm glad you've enjoyed yourself," Daniel said, noting whatever was bothering her at the beginning of the trip wasn't.

"Very much. It's amazing how these two weeks have flown by, and thank you for coming shopping with us. It's too bad. Your sister and Massimo had to head back to pick up the boys." Alessandra wiped cocoa powder from the corner of her mouth when Daniel pointed to it.

"We'll meet up with them at dinner." Daniel took a spoonful of Tartufo from Alessandra's plate.

"Thank you for my jacket." Alessandra pulled the leather Cavalli out of the bag and smoothed a hand over the soft leather. "It's stunning."

"It's you." Daniel thanked the server when she set their espressos on the table. "And as my crazy sister says, 'A girl can't have enough leather.'"

That drew a smile from Alessandra. "So true. Thank you, Daniel, for my jacket, for the trip, for introducing me to your sister and her wonderful family." Even with the need to get home to address her medical concern, Alessandra felt a pang of regret that their trip was ending, and this time tomorrow, they'd be on a flight home.

"It's me who should thank you for making the trip a memorable one. I'd lost love for the city, and you've helped me recapture it." Daniel confessed. Alessandra was about to ask him why, when the across not from the *Santa Maria del Fiore* bells rang, their music echoing over the city. "They only toll the cathedral's bells like that when someone of importance gets married," he explained to Alessandra.

The thickset man with sun-streaked hair tumbling out of a red baseball cap at the adjacent table drawled. "Says here the man getting married is one of Europe's wealthiest, and from the sound of it, she's no slouch herself. They've closed the cathedral doors to the public until noon because of them. My wife had her heart set on touring it this morning. Now we're going to have to come back tomorrow. You know how women are when they set their mind on something."

"I've heard," Daniel said, with a dimpled grin aimed at Alessandra as she tucked her jacket into the bag.

"Well, here's the wife." Thickset-Man wound the Minolta camera strap around his neck when his wife returned from the bathroom. "Y'all have a good day now." He dropped a few bills on the table.

Eyeing the newspaper Thickset-Man left behind, the headline jumped at Daniel, and he reached for it. ITALY'S MOST ELIGIBLE BACHELOR MARRIES WINE HEIRESS Daniel read. His eyes darted to the picture of the couple and their names below. Alessandra saw Daniel's face pale.

"Is something wrong, Daniel? You look like you've seen a ghost."

"I'm... fine. I ah, we should go, or we'll be late meeting the family for dinner," Daniel muttered.

Alessandra scanned her watch. "We're not due to meet them for another hour."

When Daniel remained silent, Alessandra took the newspaper from his hand. Her eyes jumped from headline to picture to see a miserable Luca, standing next to a stunningly beautiful woman, with a dimpled smile, her arm linked with his. Alessandra felt her throat slam shut on her.

The thought of Luca marrying another woman, the mere notion he did weeks after he broke her heart, stung like acid in an open wound. She'd never felt as betrayed or as used as she did then. Alessandra felt her heart ripped out of her chest and smashed into a million pieces all over again.

The measure of pain that filled Alessandra's eyes broke Daniel. He struggled between despair and the stabbing pain brought on by the tears that fell from between Alessandra's closed lashes.

"Every word he said to me was a..." The stab of betrayal came so quickly, Alessandra swallowed her words. The sound of traffic, the Italian ballad flowing from the speakers on the patio, the smells of Florence she'd come to love grated on Alessandra's nerves.

"That sonofabitch." Hatred for the man who'd caused her and him so much pain geysered in Daniel. "Luca, the Santinis have no compunction about using people. It's what they specialize in. It's what they do, Alessandra. Luca's not worth your tears." Daniel's rage sharpened his voice.

"You're right." She'd cried herself to sleep, had carried the guilt and pain of his absence since throwing him out, deep in her.

Alessandra's mind racing, she wondered why Luca would marry weeks after they went their separate way. Luca wasn't the impulsive type, and he didn't need to jump into marrying for female attention. It was then Alessandra read the name below the photograph, and her blood ran cold.

The wheels in Alessandra's mind spun fast, churning explanations.

"Luca was forced into the marriage," Alessandra rationalized. "His father forced the marriage on him. Whom he married was important to his father, and Elisa was heiress to the winemaking business his father wants under his belt." But why so soon after she and Luca split? Alessandra mulled the question in her mind when the lightbulb lit brightly. "She's claiming she's pregnant."

"What?"

"Elisa, the woman Luca's marrying, is claiming to be pregnant. It's why he's marrying her. It's the only thing that makes sense," Alessandra said with conviction.

Infuriated by Alessandra's refusal to see Luca for what he was, Daniel snapped, "How could you still be defending him?"

"I'm not, Daniel."

"Luca Santini is a self-centred narcissist who only knows to take without caring whose feelings he tramples along the way."

"Look here." Alessandra picked up the newspaper and pointed to the name. "Elisa Donatella is the woman who seduced Luca when he visited Villa Donatella."

The comment took Daniel's breath. "Seduced him? You don't know what you're talking about." Daniel bolted to his feet, and she reached for his arm.

Alessandra chased after Daniel. "Listen to me, Daniel. Luca told me the owner's daughter, a woman named Elisa, let herself into his locked bedroom while he slept. He said he woke up to find her on top of him, naked. He claimed she intentionally went out of her way to seduce him even after he told her to leave."

"He made it all up." Daniel stopped in his tracks.

Alessandra slammed into him. "Ultimately, he decided to sleep with her, but marrying her was never his intention."

Daniel fell back onto the bus bench. "You still can't see past his lies."

Alessandra set the shopping bags on the bench and sat next to him. "I bet you this, Elisa, planned this entire thing to get him to walk her down the aisle. She seduced him, possibly drugged him, to get at his name and money."

Daniel bit back, the pain slicing his heart. "You're deluding yourself if you believe that, Alessandra."

"Think about it. Why would Luca jump into marriage so soon after? That manipulative, money-hungry bitch destroyed our lives to get at his name, his money." Alessandra realized how much like Luca she sounded, but it was the only plausible explanation.

"You're making sorry ass excuses to make yourself feel better. He used you and then cast you aside like dirty laundry." Daniel's temper caught Alessandra off guard.

Her brows furrowed in confusion. "Why are you saying these things, Daniel? Why are you so angry when it's me, Luca's hurting?"

"Because I don't believe for a moment, Elisa would do such a thing." There was pain in the words.

Alessandra set surprised eyes on Daniel, and it was then that the flash of recognition came. "Oh my God, she's the Elisa Anna told me about." Elisa was the woman Daniel fell in love with and disappeared overnight.

"Anna had no right to tell you anything about my private life." Daniel's voice was full of anger, but the wounded eyes told her everything she needed to know. "It's not her story to tell, and it's none of your business."

"No, it isn't. I'm sorry, Daniel. So very sorry. You of all people don't deserve this."

Pain, hideous pain, chocked both for very different reasons.

Forty-Three

IT WAS LATE afternoon when Daniel rolled his car onto Villa Cuomo's driveway.

"Please stay, Daniel. I'll make us lunch." Alessandra set her suitcases down in the foyer.

"I should go."

"Don't go, Daniel. I don't want to be alone." Alessandra hoped the lie would sway Daniel to stay. What he needed now was a friend, not seclusion.

Alessandra was glad when Daniel closed the front door and reached for her suitcases. "I'll take these to your bedroom."

"And I'll get working on the lasagna," Alessandra said of the first dish that came to mind that would take an hour to make. Hopefully, by then, Daniel would be amenable to stay in her guest room for tonight and for however long he wanted.

There was as much hurt in Daniel as Alessandra held inside her, but at that moment, he needed her support and being there for him felt undeniably right.

"We'll get through this, Daniel," Alessandra called out as Daniel made his way up the stairs.

DANIEL OUT ON THE PATIO WITH his thoughts and the tall glass of wine Alessandra poured him, she took to the kitchen. Aiming to keep her mind off Luca, Elisa, and the wedding, Alessandra busied herself making the lasagna.

Alessandra was adding the last layer of mozzarella cheese when Daniel walked into the kitchen. His eyes, filmed over red, added to the pain she felt in her heart.

Popping the lasagna into the oven, Alessandra turned to Daniel. "Do you want to talk about it?"

"No." Daniel started to walk away, and Alessandra clamped her hand on his arm.

"I'm here if you do."

"I know." His voice sounded drained in emotion.

"The lasagna needs thirty minutes in the oven. Keep me company until then?" Alessandra was glad when he took a chair at the table. "Top your glass up?"

Daniel didn't respond, and Alessandra went ahead, pulled the wine bottle from the refrigerator, uncorked it, and poured into their glasses. For a long while, Alessandra fell into the silence with Daniel because what he needed was a silent friend by his side as he sorted through his emotions.

Alessandra watched Daniel idly run his fork in the deafening silence of the kitchen through the stacked pasta. Thirty minutes later, Alessandra cleared the dishes with untouched food and walked them to the sink. Alessandra washed pots, plates, and cutlery in soapy water. Next, she wiped the table clean and hung the dishcloth on the side of the sink to dry.

At the table, she picked up the bottle of wine, refilled their glasses, and sat next to Daniel. "We have wine and all day to talk, and I'm sitting here until you say something, Daniel."

"I met her at the café you and I were at. There wasn't an empty table in sight. I was alone and had a seat available, and she asked if she could join me. She was armed with shopping bags, looked hot and tired, and still, she took my breath away." Daniel rotated his glass of wine as the memory filled him.

"Her hair was as dark as a summer's night and spilled around an angelic face. The large, almond-shaped eyes that stared at me held secrets and mesmerized me. I felt outclassed, but I invited her to join me."

Alessandra could see Daniel's mind cycling through long-buried memories. "She could read the great guy you are."

Daniel's lips quirked into a soft smile. "We ended up sharing a bottle of wine and talking for hours. I didn't want the moment to end, so I invited her to dinner. To my surprise, she accepted."

"And why wouldn't she? You're a great guy." Alessandra pointed out.

A soft smile played across his face. "Waiting for her in the lobby of her hotel that evening, I picked up one of those gossip magazines. I don't know why I did. I never read that trash. Flipping through it, I came across an article about her. That's when I found out she was the wine heir to *Vinissimo* wines. I knew for sure then she was way out of my league, and I wasn't sure why she'd accepted my dinner invitation. Anyway, I waited and waited and figured she decided I didn't rank because she didn't show up."

The insecure Daniel Alessandra saw before her was very different from the confident man she'd come to know, and her heart melted.

"As I got up to leave, she stepped out of the elevator. She wore a lime-green dress that exposed smooth, bare shoulders and whispered against her curves. The glint of diamonds at her ears matched the one in her eyes. She came barreling across the foyer in a flurry of dark hair and apologetic eyes. I was dazed by her beauty and shocked she bothered to show up. I figured we'd have a nice dinner, and at the end of the night, each would go our separate way."

"But, you didn't?"

Daniel shook his head. "She called me a couple of days later. She was fun to be with, spirited. I enjoyed her company. She was exactly what I needed then. Caring for my cancer-stricken mother and coming to terms with her death physically and emotionally drained me. All I wanted then was to touch life, the comfort of another human being, physical closeness. I told her as much." Daniel watched Alessandra top their glasses when she drank the last of her wine.

"I told her I wasn't mentally ready to get involved with anyone then. I think I said that as a defence mechanism. The two of us were from different worlds, and I figured we wouldn't go beyond the physical. She surprised me again when she told me she was fine with a purely physical relationship. But then I did the unthinkable."

"You fell in love with her."

"I did." Daniel's eyes flashed pain, and Alessandra reached for his hand, wrapped hers around his. "It took me weeks to gather the nerve to tell her. Shortly after that conversation, she vanished. I waited for her return. When she didn't come back, I set off to find her. I looked everywhere."

"You didn't find her."

"It was as if she'd disappeared off the face of the earth." Daniel absorbed the dull, dragging ache the memory brought.

"When my sister told me she read in the tabloids, Elisa had left the country, unknown destination, that's when I returned to Sicily. I settled into my mother's home, started my practice, and went about setting roots, a life for myself." Recounting the story drained Daniel, and he sipped on wine for liquid strength.

"You never reached out to her again?" Alessandra rose to set the coffeemaker on the stove.

"Why would I? Her actions told me she didn't want to see her, that what I thought was the most memorable six months of my life was all a mistake, and we were never meant to be. I never saw her again." Eyes drained of their usual sparkle, Daniel watched Alessandra turn the heat on the stove. Flames flashed under the coffeemaker.

"I think you're wrong, Daniel. I think she cared for you very much. The simple fact she disappeared without saying a word tells me she cared about hurting you, and her only way to deal with it was to disappear. If Elisa hadn't cared about hurting you, she would have broken it off. It's difficult to hurt face to face. As cowardly as her action was, it's what we do when we care for someone." As odd as the statement was, Alessandra said it. How could she not? The fragile man she saw before her needed comforting words.

Daniel gave Alessandra something close to a smile. "Just like you to put a positive spin."

"It's not spin. It's a fact." She set a cup and saucers on the table. "She couldn't face you, which leads me to believe there were extenuating circumstances that caused her to vanish. Meaning she didn't break it off with you because she wanted to."

Daniel laid a hand on her cheek. "As insane as that logic sounds, it makes me feel better."

Alessandra lifted her hand to cover the one on her face. "One thing I can tell you with certainty is that it's her loss."

ALESSANDRA TALKED DANIEL INTO STAYING THE night. After he headed to the guest room, she lingered on the patio.

It was a beautiful night. The moon was bright enough to see the gentle ripples on the surface of the water. The night wind singing through the trees in concert with cicadas made nostalgia swim through Alessandra. The memories she'd made with Luca flourished in her mind with painful intensity. Suddenly the depth of her pain struck hard.

The church bells announcing Luca's marriage to the world rang in Alessandra's ears. Luca was married, and if her hunch was right, he'd have a child in a few months—an heir to the Santini dynasty.

There was no undoing any of it.

Luca hurt her, her pride, her heart. The humiliation on top of the hurt was more than Alessandra could bear. Detaching from the heartache and memories was what Alessandra needed. But both clung to her like a spider to its web. Her pain had deep roots. The only way to get past it was to forgive and forget, but she wasn't ready to do either—yet.

Alessandra folded up her thoughts of Luca and replaced them with Dr. Scalia's telephone conversation. The Florence trip served as a distraction, but now back home, Alessandra needed to face up to her demons and determine the course of action.

"What am I going to do?"

HANDS CLASPED BEHIND HIS HEAD, DANIEL stared out the opened window. His mind roiling on the events of the past twenty-four hours, he failed to see the beauty canvassed in a black-blue sky. Daniel saw past the twinkling stars and the luminescent round moon that turned the room silver. Daniel didn't hear the roll of foam lapping the shore or the cicadas and crickets singing their mating song.

Daniel's mind was on Elisa and the pain of betrayal that seared through him. She disappeared from his life years ago and reappeared as Luca's bride. Goddamn, Luca had taken Alessandra from him and toyed with her emotions. Now, he was married to the woman he loved.

Daniel felt like a complete failure.

Daniel wished he'd gone home to sulk and wallow in self-pity. There, he'd be able to throw a few things against the wall and drown his sorrow in a bottle—or two—of bourbon, but he let Alessandra talk him out of going home.

Those green eyes could talk him out of or into anything, and in the end, Daniel figured whether he wallowed in his bed or Alessandra's guest bedroom made no difference. Pain travelled with you.

Daniel's mind wandered to the what-ifs. There were many, but his lawyerly mind dismissed them all. A lawyer focused on facts, not supposition. The reality was, the only woman he loved long ago tore his heart out of his chest, and the woman he now loved couldn't love him back.

Alessandra was in the bedroom next to his, a wall and varying emotions separating them. A miserable hollow sadness wrapped around Daniel's heart, squeezed it tight. Feeling empty and alone, the tears sprang to his eyes and turned his world into the blur that was now his life.

For a long time, Daniel's tears streamed down his cheek onto the pillow. As he was about to resign to the fact his life would forever be a bubbling cauldron of sadness and regret, Alessandra's sweet and sultry scent flowed into him. Like a dream, Alessandra emerged from the shadows.

Crossing to him, she sat at the edge of the bed. "I'm sorry you're hurting, Daniel. I'm sorry she hurt you. You don't have to cry alone." She wiped Daniel's tear-stained cheeks. The gentle touch of fingers over his face felt comforting. Gazing into the shadowed blue eyes, she leaned in and kissed him. "You are loved, Daniel. You are very much loved."

Daniel watched Alessandra shed her nightgown. "You don't have to do this, Alessandra."

"I want to. Let me love you, Daniel," Alessandra said the words he needed to hear.

Daniel's emotions mirrored in his eyes, he drew the bedsheet back, and Alessandra slid her naked body into the arms that stretched out in welcome. Lying next to him, she felt warm, soft, and real. The moment was real, he assured himself.

Daniel brushed the hair from her face. Teeming with love for her, he kissed her on the lips, and Alessandra met the mouth swamped with need. Feeling the curve of her mouth against his was drugging everything he'd waited for so long.

The feeling of need potent, Daniel pulled her close and covered her mouth with his. To his delight, Alessandra matched the greed and desire in his kiss and let her tongue mate with his. The pulsing heat spreading through his body felt like fire burning through dry brush.

Alessandra lifted her eyes then met his. "Close your eyes, Daniel. Enjoy my touch. Let it smooth the pain away."

Daniel's eyes fluttering close, he let himself feel. Her tender kisses on his body, the feel of her soft hands as she explored felt electrifying her skin. Her avid mouth tasted and possessed, and Daniel floated on the sensation.

Her body joined with his, the sense of hopelessness that swirled like an ocean current in Daniel faded. Relishing the moment, he thought this was as perfect as his life could be.

As the night stretched out, Daniel turned to Alessandra again and again, and each time she was there for him, willing and wanting. Daniel believed in love again.

Alessandra's head pillowed against Daniel's chest, they watched the wave of gold sunshine rise out of darkness to proclaim a new day.

Forty-Four

ENJOYING HIS ESPRESSO on the patio, Daniel tilted his face to the warm sunshine casting a glorious glow over the island. A hint of breeze teased the air, and birds made sweet music somewhere between the tree branches.

It was a perfect Sunday morning. The best, Daniel thought with a smile on his face. What a difference a day made.

Thoughts of Elisa and his pain were pushed into the deep recesses of his mind and replaced with thoughts of last night.

After Elisa, the women in his life satisfied a sexual need because none filled the emotional void she left. Several tried to become more than his bedmate, but Daniel wouldn't let them in. After a while, he gave up on love altogether. That is until Alessandra.

Until Alessandra, Daniel thought he'd never feel love again. Now, his eyes were full of light, and he believed in love again. There was no better feeling in the world.

The screen door opened, and Daniel turned to see Alessandra stepping onto the patio. Fresh from her shower, she brought with her a provocative cloud of lavender. The mink-brown hair he'd combed his fingers through last night was tied into a wet ponytail. Her skin was golden against the white of her shirt, and the cranberry-red shorts she wore rode high enough to draw his attention to long, toned legs.

Daniel rose, scraped the chair back. "Buon giorno." He wore a white polo shirt and jeans, and his windswept hair crowned his smiling face. "Coffee?"

"Yes, thank you."

Daniel poured coffee into her cup. "I made you eggs and buttered toast. If you'd like something else, I can make..."

Alessandra leaned in to glide her lips over his to ease the tension she sensed in him. "Everything looks perfect, Daniel."

"Do you like sailing?" Daniel asked when her contemplative eyes flicked to watch sailboats skitter over the water.

"I've never been." Alessandra spooned eggs onto her plate.

"Would you like to go sailing?"

"Yes, I would." With a reflective silence, Alessandra stirred sugar into her coffee, sipped.

"Or we can go down to the beach unless you'd rather go for a run."

"Whatever you'd like to do is fine by me."

Daniel helped himself to a slice of Maria's bread and topped it with her homemade jam and butter. "You need to partner up with Maria and open a café."

"I'll give it some thought."

"They found a whale on the beach."

"Sounds nice."

"What's wrong, Alessandra? Alessandra," Daniel called a second time breaking her trance.

A short silence passed between them before Alessandra said, "I'd like to talk to you about something."

The shift of uneasiness in her tone piqued Daniel's attention, and he set the cup down. "If it's about last night, you don't have to say anything. I know you don't feel for me as I do for you."

"Last night was very special to me, and I don't want you to think I came to you devoid of emotion or for any reason other than to be with you."

"As well as you know that each time I made love with you was from the heart."

"I know." Alessandra rested a hand on the freshly shaven face and looked into the sparkling blue eyes full of goodness and love. "I want you to know that last night meant the world to me. I wasn't there to lay the groundwork... That there was no motive other than to be with you and ease your pain." Alessandra's statement had his shoulders stiffening. "You know I love you. Not in the way you want me to, but I do love you, Daniel."

"I know." From anyone else, the blunt statement would have felt like a rebuke. Daniel studied Alessandra's face as she debated whether to share Dr. Scalia's news. The uneasiness that had her shifting in her seat made Daniel's chest tighten. "What is it, Alessandra?"

She hesitated as she summoned her courage. Her heart beating fast and her mind racing, Alessandra took a deep breath for calm. "I'm thinking of flying back to Toronto."

But I've just found you. "When, why?" The shock and disappointment on Daniel's face were inescapable. "I thought you were enjoying your stay."

"It's time I go back. I've secured Villa Cuomo, and it's time, Daniel."

Staggered, he ran a hand through his hair. "You never gave any indication you were thinking of returning."

"I need to get back to work. I need to get back to my life and get on with it."

"I see."

The hurt and confusion on Daniel's face smothered Alessandra in guilt. He'd been a good friend, understanding and caring, and he deserved an explanation. "That's only part of the reason. I had a call from..." Alessandra trailed off, not sure how to say the following words.

"Who called you, Alessandra?"

"My doctor, the day we left for Florence."

With a jolt, Daniel sat up straight. "Are you all right?"

"I'm not. I'm..."

His spine stiffened at her tone, but he forced himself to remain calm. "You can tell me anything, Alessandra."

She swallowed deeply. "I'm pregnant, Daniel."

The words came out so fast, Daniel wasn't sure he heard correctly. "What?"

Finding it easier to say the words the second time, she repeated them with a calm measure. "I'm pregnant. I wasn't feeling well, and I had the doctor check me out. Unbeknownst to me, he ran a pregnancy test. It came back positive."

To Alessandra's surprise, Daniel didn't recoil, wince, or give her the judgemental gaze she expected. Instead, he sat back and fell into silence.

After some time, Daniel said, "Is it his?"

"Yes. Maybe. I don't know. It may be .... yours. Jesus! This conversation sounds so wrong. This isn't who I am."

She'd been with two men, one to share her love for him and the other to escape the pain tearing her heart. Now, she didn't know whose child she was carrying.

"Understand that regardless of the outcome, I'm not holding you responsible. I'm telling you because I want you to know."

"Are you going to tell him?" Daniel forced himself to ask.

"No." Her voice was quiet, her tone adamant.

Her decision to keep the pregnancy from Luca wasn't honed out of spite but out of love for her child. Alessandra wanted a normal life for her baby. She wanted her child to be free from the burdens that the Santini name and wealth imposed.

She didn't want her child to live a life of preconceived notions because it bore the Santini name. Alessandra wanted her child steered far away from the pressures that came with the name. Besides, she was sure nothing good would come out of telling Luca or Antonio, who'd conclude she got herself pregnant as a ploy to entrap his son.

"What would you like to do, Alessandra?" Daniel asked.

"I thought of asking the doctor for my options."

The stunned look on Daniel's face came quick. "Options?"

"I've been scared and confused. Then my world caved in in Florence, and everything looked desperately dark and hopeless. Except for my aunt, Maria, and Francesco, I'm alone. I can't do this on my own."

"You're not alone. You have me, Alessandra." Anger had Daniel bolting to his feet. "I'm sorry I've been consumed in my self-pity and didn't notice you had so much on your mind. Maybe then you wouldn't be contemplating options."

"I'm not, not anymore." Alessandra rested a hand on his rigid arm and signalled for him to sit. "After last night, I woke up with a positive outlook and realized this baby is a part of me, and I'm giving her up."

A wave of relief levelled Daniel's anger, and he took her face in his hands. "You have me to lean on."

Her eyes curved in a watery smile. "I know."

Daniel crouched beside her. "Would you allow me to be in your life, to be in the baby's life?"

"Of course, but only if you want to be, Daniel. As I said, I'm not holding you..."

"I want to be in your life. I want to be in the baby's life. I want you to let me help you take care of this baby and you."

Drenched in love, Alessandra stroked a fingertip over his cheek. "I don't deserve you."

His heart soaring with newfound boldness, Daniel said, "Marry me, Alessandra."

Alessandra's green eyes popped wide. "No, Daniel, that's not the answer. This may not be your child. I want you to be a part of my and the baby's life, but only if it's yours. I don't want you taking on another man's burden. It's not your responsibility."

Daniel's eyes on hers, he said, "I love you, Alessandra. As long as there's a breath in my body, I always will."

"Daniel, I..."

He rushed to silence the words he didn't want to hear. "I have enough love for the two of us, and although I want this child to be mine, whether she is or not doesn't matter to me. She'll be our child."

"She?"

"You said she, but she or he, it'll be our child."

There was love, true and pure, in the wistful blue eyes that gazed at her. "You don't have to do this, Daniel. I've accepted my situation, and I'm willing to do this on my own."

"But wouldn't it be an adventure if we did it together?"

Here was this beautiful man with nothing but love for her. So much love, he was willing to marry her and possibly take on the responsibility for another man's child. The tears welled in Alessandra's eyes.

"Will you do me the honour of marrying me, Alessandra Cuomo?" This time the question came on bended knee.

"Are you sure about this, Daniel?"

"As sure as the day is bright and the night dark. Marry me, Alessandra."

Part III

The End

Treacherous acts brand you.
Betraying acts isolate you.
Noble acts shape everyone around you.
—M.L. Lexi

Forty-Five

Five years later

IN THE SMALL house with the quaint patio, surrounded by the olive trees overlooking the Mediterranean, on the land where grapevines of a recent past stood, Alessandra and Daniel, set up home. It was where Alessandra found the strength to pick up the shattered pieces of her life. Where she found solace and, in the process, stumbled into her new life. It was where Alessandra found love, lost it, and love found her. It was her ancestor's home, rich in history and memories—good and bad. Now it was her home and Daniel's and their boy's.

It was where Alessandra belonged.

They made some changes to the home to wash a recent past away and usher new beginnings, their new life.

The bedroom, where they'd once watched darkness give way to light, was turned into a nursery. Walls were painted bright yellow, and curtains with smiling teddies hung in place of white lace. A racing car bed, an airplane-shaped chandelier, and hand-carved rocking horse and chair—a gift from Francesco and Maria—filled the room. A wing housing, a family-slash-playroom, and an office was built.

Of all the changes, Alessandra's pride and joy was the revival of her grandmother's garden to its once colourful state. Water flowed again from the vase in the mermaid's hands into the fountain's basin. At its lip, Alessandra had her father, mother, brothers, and Rosa's names etched.

Nathaniel DiBlassio was a four-year-old healthy, rambunctious boy, but his arrival into the world wasn't an easy one. After a gruelling nine months of pregnancy, Alessandra gave birth by emergency caesarian performed by Dr. Scalia. The procedure nearly took Alessandra's life, and Nathaniel was a mere four pounds, but he was healthy, perfect, and beautiful.

Everyone said Nathaniel resembled his mother, but Alessandra saw Luca in her son's face. She was sure Daniel did too, but it didn't seem to matter to him. As Daniel promised, on the day he knelt and asked for Alessandra's hand in marriage, he considered Nathaniel as his own.

Under a star-washed sky, Alessandra indulged in a glass of wine and reflected on her life. It had been five years since Luca left, and although thoughts of him still filled her from time to time, they were fading from her memory.

There were times Alessandra had to smother the pang of guilt for not telling Luca about Nathaniel. Seeing the beaming smile on her son's face as he went about doing what he enjoyed doing allayed the feeling.

It saddened Alessandra Nathaniel wouldn't have a brother or sister, but the emergency cesarean Dr. Scalia had to perform progressed into a hysterectomy. As much as the news devastated Alessandra and Daniel, they were happy with their life.

As much as Alessandra pushed thoughts of Luca from her mind, her love for him wouldn't fade as easily because when you loved someone as deeply as she'd loved Luca, you never stopped. Alessandra was sure Daniel suspected as much, but it didn't deter him from giving her his love.

Daniel's deep-rooted love for Alessandra, in time, drew her close to him. Alessandra hoped that blossoming bond over time would make her love Daniel as she did, Luca.

"He's finally asleep. I had to read him two bedtime stories before he went down," Daniel said when he stepped onto the patio.

Grinning, Alessandra looked over her shoulder. "That's because he loves how you fall into character with every story."

Daniel crossed to her and chained his arms around her waist. Her hair smelled of strawberries, and he lost himself in it. "He told me he wants a puppy."

"He mentioned it and I told him not until he was older. I hope you echoed the sentiment." When Daniel remained silent, Alessandra turned to face him. "You promised him we'd get him one, didn't you?"

Daniel rolled his eyes to the sky. "I kind of did."

Alessandra's firm stare fizzled into a smile. "You spoil our son."

"I spoil you, and I don't see you complaining." Daniel played his mouth over hers.

"Don't try kissing your way out of this." Alessandra chided with a curled lip.

"But it's so much more fun than having a discussion, which in the end will go full circle because you and I know we'll give in to our son. We always do."

Alessandra's face softened. "We're spoiling that child. He's going to become quite the, what's the male counterpart for a diva?"

"Divo, and I know this, but aren't you having fun doing so?"

Alessandra succumbed to Daniel's puppy-dog stare. "I'll shop around for a small dog, not a large farm dog."

"You're the boss. Just keep in mind he's going to call it Pizza."

Alessandra laughed. "Pizza?"

"It's 'the most bestest food in the whole wide world.'" Daniel reminded her of their son's motto. "And he claims the dog will love pizza as much as he does."

"That's all we need, a constipated dog."

Daniel let out a soft rolling laugh and, taking Alessandra's hand, led her to the table. "Don't forget tomorrow I'm in court for most of the morning. What are you up to?"

"Maria and I are going to take a look at the two premises we're considering for our second location. Although I'd like to hold off a few more months, she's anxious to get going, claiming she has a new batch of recipes introduce."

It had been a challenge to talk Maria into believing enough in herself to share the fantastic foods she created with the public. After much prodding, Maria relented to Alessandra's idea to open *Mangia Mangia*. Between Alessandra's marketing expertise and Maria's cooking skills, the bakery-slash-trattoria grew rapidly. Two years on, demand dictated they open a second location.

"For a woman her age, Maria has a lot of energy." Daniel ran a thumb up and down the sole of Alessandra's foot.

"I can barely keep up with her. The long hours the woman puts in that kitchen would kill me." Alessandra signalled for Daniel to massage her heels. "After I inspect the buildings we're considering, I have an appointment with Signore Marciano at the bank."

"You know you could use our money to open your new location."

"I know, but getting the bank to finance the venture is the wisest option."

"My wife, the business magnate," Daniel quipped, but the pride in his eyes was unmistakable.

"Besides, you're our legal, not our financial advisor."

"And as your legal advisor, you should listen to me and pursue your ownership of Villa Santini."

"We've been over this, Daniel."

"We could have settled on a financial settlement because I know they'd never deed that parcel of land to you."

Alessandra's eyes locked with the enraged ones. "You know I'm not the suing type. It's not who I am. I already got Villa Cuomo, which is what I wanted and..."

"And you think pursuing ownership will draw Luca's attention to his son," Daniel finished the thought she refused to voice. Daniel gave her a knowing nod when her face radiated surprise and guilt. "It's hard to miss." He plowed on when she started to speak. "My pursuit for the land is not out of spite. It's for our son. It would be a financial windfall for Nathaniel when he comes of age. I guarantee you I won't bring attention to Nathaniel. The Santinis will never know about Nat. I would never do that to our son."

Taking a portion of the home that had been in the Santini family forever and held their history was Daniel's crusade because Alessandra wanted nothing from them.

"All I'm saying is consider it."

"I'll think about it," she said and proceeded to change the topic. "I think I'll take Nathaniel with me tomorrow and treat him to a pizza lunch because, as you know, it's 'the most bestest food in the whole wide world.'" Alessandra mimicked their son and made Daniel laugh.

"Why don't you stop by that boutique you like so much?" Daniel smiled when Alessandra winged a brow. "All right, the boutique I like so much. Treat us both to something special."

"If you insist."

He kissed her on the tip of her nose. "I do. Consider something red. I like you in red."

"You do, do you?"

Daniel pushed to his feet and reached for her hand. "You interested in joining me in bed and indulging in the most bestest thing we can think of?"

Her lips bowed into a smile that answered his question.

Forty-Six

IN THE BACK seat of Alessandra's car, Nathaniel sang and asked questions—so many questions. Nathaniel was a curious and bright four-year-old. As much as Alessandra loved that about her son, it terrified her. The fear that inquisitive mind would one day lead her son to question Daniel's paternity haunted her daily.

Daniel treated Nathaniel as his flesh and blood, and his name appeared on the birth certificate. That—Alessandra prayed—should dissuade her boy from doubting Daniel's paternity. Even with all the bases covered, the concern Nathaniel would eventually raise the question was always in the back of her mind because when you harbour a secret of this magnitude, you can't help but let paranoia take over now and again.

Although Alessandra had no clue what she'd say if Nathaniel posed the question of one thing, she was sure. She'd tell her son the truth—no matter the consequences. Alessandra hoped Nathaniel understood she'd kept him from his father out of love. So he'd have a normal childhood.

Talking to Nathaniel about the father, he knew nothing about iced Alessandra's blood. She wished she had her parents' listening ear and shoulders to cry on. That not being a possibility, all she could do was pray and hope the day when Nathaniel questioned her about Luca never came.

Alessandra knew better. All secrets eventually came to light, and this one was too formidable to be concealed for an entire lifetime.

"Are we there yet, Mommy?" Nathaniel asked for the umpteenth time, his excitable legs bouncing off his car seat.

"We are, *amore*." Alessandra eased her car into the first available spot.

A noon sun shot shafts of light over the island. Shoppers from the market spilled onto the sidewalk, arms loaded down with shopping bags. A long line of diners waiting to be seated formed at the entrance of *Fellini's* and the cafés in the area.

Nathaniel's ruddy cheeks dimpled. "I'm glad 'cause I'm starving."

"You are." Lifting him out of his car seat, Alessandra thought he was getting too big too fast for her liking.

"I'm so hungry I can eat the whole pizza myself." Nathaniel stood looking up at Alessandra while she finger-combed his dark curls from his face.

"Then we better order a very big pizza." Alessandra knelt to pull his socks up, then stepped back to study him. He looked like a young version of Luca in his polo shirt, jeans, and tan loafers.

Nathaniel's eager nod sent his black curls bouncing forward again. "I think you better. Besides, if we have extra, we can take it home. I know I can get hungry for pizza later."

Alessandra couldn't help but smile at his logic. "Well, then, we'll order a ginormous pizza."

Nathaniel's smile went bright as sunshine. "Yippee."

Glancing at her watch, Alessandra calculated. "We have fifty minutes to eat before we head out to meet with Signore Marciano."

"I can eat very fast," he said, linking his small hand with hers.

It took them less than the allotted time to eat lunch and even less time to talk *Signore* Marciano to sign off on her loan. The business proposal she'd submitted impressed him, and Alessandra didn't have to persuade much to get him to sign off on the loan.

Excited by the meeting's outcome, Alessandra and Nathaniel made the short trek to Tina's Boutique. Walking into the boutique, Alessandra's mind flashed to Luca. He'd introduced her to Tina and her boutique when she told him she had nothing to wear to his mother's lunch. Luca was the one to pick out the sundress Alessandra had worn to their lunch at Villa Santini because of how her tanned skin looked against the white cotton.

Alessandra never shared that story with Daniel because some things were best left unsaid. Besides, what could be the harm in shopping at her favourite boutique when Luca was making a life for himself thousands of miles away?

Alessandra couldn't pass up on the little black dress with the plunging neckline Tina had her try on. She couldn't pass up on the virginal white or the red, frilly teddy, complete with garter belts. She bought all.

Alessandra felt guilty about the extravagant purchase, but she'd get over it when Daniel saw her in them. Bags hanging from her arms and a guilty smile on her face, Alessandra swung the store door open.

"*Scusa.*" The familiar voice echoed in Alessandra's ears, and she tilted her gaze up.

It had been five years since she last saw him, but there was no mistaking the arctic-blue eyes aimed her way were Luca's. Ashen-faced, she remained shocked on the spot. For a long moment, neither spoke.

Staring into her shocked eyes, they were as he membered, green as Chinese jade, and as captivating as the stars. He'd thought of her often, so very often. Head dreamt of her on countless nights. Now standing before him, Luca wasn't sure she was real or a figment of his wishful imagination.

The intensity of their connection told him the moment was as real. It was Alessandra, and she was as beautiful as he remembered.

Emotions Luca had held inside him all the years they were apart swirled into his eyes. "*Ciao*, Alessandra."

It took her a moment to answer. "Hi," she said, careful to filter the shock out of her voice.

He was just as Alessandra remembered him. The dark curls she'd run her fingers through hung wild around his tanned face. His strong jaw bore that fashionable stubble she loved to feel against her face. He wore jeans and a cotton shirt, sleeves rolled up to the elbow.

Alessandra felt as if time had stood still, and the memories that filled her thoughts in times of aching loneliness bloomed in her mind. Alessandra thought of all their firsts. She vividly remembered their first meeting, the first time he held her in his arms to comfort her, the first kiss they'd shared, and the first time they made love.

"You look great," Luca said softly.

"You too."

"How are you?"

"Good, thank you." When the uncomfortable silence lingered, Alessandra asked, "You?"

"I'm miserable. I have been since the day I left our home. I think of you every waking minute and wish to God that I could undo what I did to you because I can't live without you. I love you, Alessandra. You're the only woman I ever will," screamed in his head, but said, "Okay."

"Good. I'm glad." Alessandra nervously tucked a strand of hair behind her ear. The simple gesture made his heart trip.

"I've missed you so much, Alessandra. There hasn't been a day I haven't thought of you," Luca almost blurted out before he caught sight of the wedding band on her finger and was doused with the hard shock of reality. "You're married."

"I am," she said, letting her ringed hand fall to her side.

Luca's mind whirled to the notion she'd married Daniel, and the expression that came over him was strangely sad.

"I should get going. It was nice seeing you, Luca."

"I hope you're happy, Alessandra. Are you happy?" he asked, then wished he hadn't. As much as he wanted love and happiness to fill her life, he didn't want to know she'd found it with another man.

Nathaniel's hand tightly wound around Alessandra's in protection from the suspicious man afflicting his mother with the discomfort he sensed. "Mommy, let's go home?"

Luca's eyes darted to the boy who appeared from behind Alessandra. His eyes filled with shock, disbelief, and confusion at the sight of the child with the wary eyes looking up at him.

Alessandra recoiled at the bewildered expression that came over Luca's face. The moment she'd dreaded was here, and the sharp claws of fear clutched at her stomach. How was she to explain the child standing before him was his son? How was she to explain she'd kept his existence a secret all these years?

Before Alessandra could calm herself to delve into the well-crafted words, the rehearsed explanation she'd committed to memory for just such an impromptu moment vanished from her brain like smoke the moment the young boy snuck out from behind Luca.

"Dada, I'm hungry." The blue-eyed, dark hair child shyly tugged Luca's hand.

Alessandra's gaze fell on the boy. Eyes widened in shock, and for a fleeting moment, she doubted her eyes. A cold chill shot up her spine as her eyes darted from the boy to Nathaniel and back in absolute disbelief.

The eyes, the hair, the smile, there was no mistaking it. Alessandra felt a punch, smack-dab in the middle of her stomach knock the wind out of her.

Alessandra's mind weaved in and out from shock to disbelief. It couldn't be. How could it possibly be? The air clogging her lungs made it difficult to breathe.

"Mommy, he looks like me," Nathaniel said, curiously eyeing his mirror image in the child across from him.

Alessandra's eyes turned to shock, the shock to disbelief and confusion at the sight of the identical boys. Her blood running cold, her mind raced, and in one moment, everything became clear. The bags in her hands fell to the floor.

"That's my child, my son's twin brother." Fury punched through the words. Alessandra hadn't meant to speak so bluntly in front of the children, but the words shot out of her like a bullet. "You have my son." The quiver of rage in the roared words drew the attention of everyone in the store, and a crowd of shoppers gathered. Whispered speculations flew from ear to ear.

Alessandra's mind circled back to the day she was rushed to the hospital to give birth. She remembered lying on a gurney as they wheeled her into the emergency room. The wrenching pain that slammed into her was unbearable. Drugs, yes, drugs, she remembered the drugs Dr. Scalia insisted she take. As hard as she tried, Alessandra couldn't remember anything afterward.

She couldn't remember giving birth to a second child. But how could she when she was out cold?

Alessandra brought her hand to her temple, rubbed at it like a genie lamp, hoping to summon up her memory. Nothing stirred in her head.

Out cold or not, how could she not know? She was their mother. She'd given life to them, carried them in her womb for months.

But no one told her, not Dr. Scalia or not his nurse or the sonographer, that there was a second baby. How could she know if she was never told?

The room suddenly felt suffocating as the implication became clear. As fury punched through the shock, the anger took form deep within sprang hot. Alessandra looked up at Luca with a cold, steely glint in her eyes.

"You kidnapped my son."

NATHANIEL DIDN'T UNDERSTAND WHAT KIDNAPPING MEANT or what was going on with all the screaming grownups. Seeing his mommy cry made Nathaniel sad. He'd never seen his mommy cry. He didn't like it. Although daddy told him everything was fine, Nathaniel decided he was never going to make her cry.

Nathaniel wasn't sure how his mommy knew the tall man the boy that looked like him called Dada. He'd never seen him before. Mommy told him the tall man was an old friend. Nathaniel liked him. The tall man was nice to him.

The man talked to him for a while. He asked him what he liked to do and called him young man, not baby, as his mommy did or little man as his daddy did. Then the man told the boy that looked like him, who he called Riccardo, to stay and play while he went out to talk to the grownups. Nathaniel was happy when he did because he liked Riccardo. He liked him a lot. Riccardo did everything like him and liked everything he did. Nathaniel thought that was funny and fun.

Riccardo even loved pizza as much as Nathaniel did. It was why the woman named Moma, who came with the angry-looking man and the pretty lady, served them the leftover pizza they brought home from the restaurant. Nathaniel enjoyed eating pizza with Riccardo in his playroom.

For the first time, Nathaniel had pizza twice in one day. He could eat the bestest food in the whole wide world with his new friend all day long. After they finished eating, Moma sat in a chair and watched them play. Nathaniel hoped Riccardo liked his toys and his house by the water because he wanted to invite him to play with him often.

Nathaniel wanted to stay friends with Riccardo.

Forty-Seven

AFTER SEEING NATHANIEL and Riccardo together, the shock reverberated through everyone in the room. There was no doubt Riccardo was Nathaniel's twin brother and that Luca was his father.

"That's my child, my son." Alessandra heard the rise of her voice but made no effort to control it. She didn't care whether she was following Santini protocol or not. She wanted to be heard.

Alessandra wanted Luca, Antonio, and Laine to know the depth of her anger, the violation she felt at what they'd done to her. Kidnapping her son was reprehensible, an unspeakable assault on her and her family, and at that moment, she had nothing but contempt for them.

The anger pulsing inside Alessandra's for the child kidnapped from her womb compared to nothing she'd felt before. It had her believing what Daniel told her about the Santinis' sense of entitlement that they would take anything they wanted by any means.

"Please have a seat, Alessandra. Let's discuss this rationally," Laine said, with a calming tone when Alessandra began to pace the living room.

Alessandra's eyebrows lifted in disdain. "You kidnapped my son, you don't want me to get the police involved, and now you want to discuss this rationally? Is that what you'd do if you were in my shoes, Mrs. Santini?" Alessandra shot a fiery glare at Laine. When Laine didn't reply, she said, "I didn't think so. My son will remain with me, and I want all of you out of my house. Not only will you never set foot here again, but I will go to the ends of the earth to ensure you never see either of my son's—ever." Alessandra's tone was defiant, her eyes fearless.

"Alessandra, you can't mean that." The distress in Laine's tone was discernible.

"Try me." Alessandra's anger all-consuming, she couldn't wrap her head around anything other than revenge.

"Please sit down, Alessandra. I'll get you a drink to calm your nerves." Daniel put in.

"I don't want a Goddamn drink. I want them gone from my home. They're not welcome here. And I never want them near my children." Temper had whipped color into Alessandra's face.

"Please, Alessandra, sit down." Daniel took her by the hand and guided her to the couch.

"Daniel, is it? I wouldn't mind a drink, something strong. Why don't you bring the bottle over? I think we're going to need it. At least I am," Antonio murmured, cursing Elisa under his breath.

There was no doubt in his mind Elisa orchestrated the kidnapping. The Goddamn woman was trouble. He sensed it the moment he met her, but he never imagined she'd go as far as kidnapping a child to entrap Luca into a sham marriage.

Antonio paid Elisa handsomely to pursue Luca. In return, she vowed that splitting Luca and Alessandra in return for his commitment to purchase Villa Donatella—at her price—was the extent of her interest. He should have known better than to dismiss his instincts when his warning-meter went off.

"You have to believe me, Alessandra. I knew nothing. I would never do anything to hurt you." Luca's blue eyes were steady on Alessandra's green eyes.

"I don't care whether you knew or not. All I know is my son was kidnapped from my womb, and the fact he's been living under your roof makes you all complicit." The icy stare Alessandra fixed on Luca could freeze a raging fire.

Slamming the brandy bottle on the coffee table, Antonio tilted his gaze to Alessandra. "That's a serious accusation. I don't know if the courts would agree with you, considering anyone can see the boys are Luca's sons. From where I stand, the fact Luca wasn't aware of the existence of at least one of them makes it not only morally reprehensible but a legal matter." Antonio's expression was the picture of righteous indignation.

"This doesn't involve you, Dad. It's between Alessandra and me." Luca's tone was sharp, his eyes unyielding. "Don't you think you've done enough already?"

"She's accusing us of kidnapping." Antonio's voice boomed in the small living room.

"If you don't keep quiet, I'm going to ask you to leave." Luca shot a warning glare at his father. Because of him, they were here. Because of Antonio, Luca was married to a woman capable of kidnapping his son to make her fairy tale pregnancy a reality.

"Luca's right, Antonio. This has nothing to do with us. I'm sorry we've injected ourselves into the moment, but he, they're our grandsons, Alessandra. I hope you understand."

The acknowledgement Laine hoped to get from Alessandra didn't come. "I have one question, Alessandra. Why didn't you tell Luca about Nathaniel?"

Alessandra set hard, unwavering eyes on Laine. "I don't have to explain myself to you, to any of you. I will take my son, and if you refuse to give him to me, I'll get the authorities, the press, anyone who can make this public and mar the almighty Santini name. I'm not threatened or intimidated by you." Alessandra's protective motherly impulse permeating infused her with formidable strength.

Luca jumped in before allowing his father the opportunity to do so. "Alessandra, you can get anyone you like involved. I'll support you every step of the way, but before you do, let's try to resolve this between us, for the children's sake. Can I speak to you alone?"

"You and I have nothing to discuss. Whatever you need to say, you say with my husband present." Alessandra lobbed out the words with the burning edge of her rage to hurt and scar.

"This is outrageous. How could you say there's nothing to discuss? These are my grandchildren, and I'm not allowing you to take them." Rage and arrogance rang deep in Antonio's voice when he slammed his glass against the armrest and sent brandy splashing.

Alessandra turned to Antonio. "You're being very arrogant, Mr. Santini, considering the dubious circumstances you're in right now. And as always, you're being presumptuous. Stay out of this. This has nothing to do with you, and if you don't keep quiet, I'll..."

"Alessandra's right, Antonio, be quiet." The fierceness in Laine's voice tempered Antonio's hostility.

Alessandra turned to Luca. "This is exactly why I didn't tell you about Nathaniel. For one, your father would have assumed I got myself pregnant to get at your precious money and name, which doesn't impress me as much as it does him. Two, I didn't want Nathaniel to have to endure a life of acceptable socialization under your father's thumb. I didn't want him to have to conform to the social convention expected by him in your world." Alessandra saw Laine wrap a hand on her husband's arm when he opened his mouth to speak.

"I didn't want to succumb my boy to a life, which the almighty Santini patriarch demands of him. I wanted Nathaniel to enjoy his life without pre-determined expectations, to do what little boys enjoy doing. I wanted my boy to do with his life as he chose, not as your father expects."

"How dare you," Antonio broke in abruptly.

"This is the last time I'm warning you, Antonio. Be quiet, or I'll ask you to leave myself." Laine cautioned.

With tears spilling from her eyes, Alessandra said, "I'm sorry I didn't tell you, Luca. I am, but I wanted Nathaniel to enjoy being a little boy. It was because of your father I didn't tell you. My decision was in the interest of my son." When she fell into Daniel's arms to be comforted, Luca's chest tightened.

The pained expression on Luca's face broke Laine's heart. At Luca's inability to speak, Laine met Alessandra's eyes with quiet patience and spoke to her mother-to-mother. "I can understand why you made the decision not to tell Luca about Nathaniel. I do, Alessandra. Our lifestyle, although a privileged one, is demanding and takes some amount adjustment."

"Pfft, some?" Alessandra hissed knuckling tears from her eyes.

"And you're right when you say my husband is a hard man, overzealous at times." Laine shot Antonio a warning look that quashed the oncoming protest. "But you have to know Antonio loves Riccardo, and I know he will love Nathaniel as much. All of us will. And you must believe me when I say we'd never dream of causing them harm or unhappiness. They are your children. But they're also Luca's, and as good a father as I sense Daniel is, you can't deny Nathaniel, his biological father."

"How can I ever trust you, people, after this. You kidnapped my child from my womb. That proves your money is far-reaching and that you'll go to any lengths to get what you want. My children aren't for sale, and they're not safe with you." Alessandra's tone was ice cold.

"We had nothing to do with this, Alessandra. I can assure you. This is all Elisa's doing," Luca said, struggling with the seething anger in him at himself for bringing pain into her life again.

"She's your wife, therefore your family." Alessandra charged at him.

She wasn't family and only his wife on paper. There was only hatred and animosity in Luca for Elisa, so much so, he hadn't touched the vile woman, but for that one time. Luca wanted to be nowhere near the contemptuous bitch.

Appearances were maintained for the sake of the families and business. Luca financed Elisa's expensive lifestyle to ensure she wouldn't take Riccardo from him as she'd threatened to do if he didn't. Luca wanted to explain his hell to Alessandra, but it wasn't a conversation for today.

The sick ball twining tight at the pit of Luca's stomach, he said, "Believe me when I tell you Elisa will be dealt with."

"You're damn right she'll be dealt with because I'm charging her with kidnapping," Alessandra shot back.

"I encourage you to do so, and you can count on my support when you do," Luca assured.

"Our support," Laine put in, and Antonio silently nodded. "I guarantee you I will personally see Elisa's dealt with under the full extent of the law."

"Thank you, *Signora* Santini. We'd be grateful." Daniel, who until now had remained silent, voiced.

Only then did it dawn on Alessandra how difficult the entire exchange must have been for Daniel. Being in a room with Luca, discussing Luca's sons, talking about Elisa in such a negative light had to cut deep.

Alessandra's sympathetic eyes tilted to Daniel. "I'm sorry, Daniel. Are you okay?"

Daniel's blue eyes said he wasn't, but his emotions were irrelevant then. "It's clear to everyone that Nathaniel and Riccardo are everyone's priority. Luca and Alessandra need to discuss the boys alone because if I know Alessandra, Riccardo is not leaving this house."

Alessandra reached for Daniel's hand. "I want you with me."

"You need to talk this out with Luca. You'll have privacy on the patio. In the meantime, I'll speak to Mr. and Mrs. Santini about the legal options we have to pursue the matter against Elisa," Daniel said.

Understanding the implications Daniel's proposed action was to have against the woman he once loved, Alessandra laid a hand on his shoulder. "Are you sure?"

"I'm fine. You go ahead and talk to Luca." Daniel gave Alessandra a smile of encouragement, but watching Luca follow her to the patio, he had to force himself not to run after her.

Daniel's heart sank deep in his chest when the overwhelming feeling of loss flooded him. Daniel stood to lose his son, the life he built with Alessandra. He stood to lose the woman he loved, but setting her free was what he needed to do, not because Alessandra's happiness was essential to him, or because it was what you did for someone you loved, but because he needed to know the depth of her love for him.

Forty-Eight

ALESSANDRA MADE HER way to the edge of the patio marking a safe distance between Luca and her. Understanding she needed the space, Luca stayed back and fell into the awkward silence that felt like elongated seconds that stretched into eternity.

Lingering there filled Luca with the familiar scents of her potted blooms and her perfume. The intensity of the memories they'd shared on that patio left Luca feeling as if it happened that morning. The realization she was recreating those memories with Daniel was sobering and crushing.

It was a long while before Alessandra turned to face Luca and, with a calm tone, said, "Please, have a seat."

As Luca drew close to her, Alessandra felt the emotions she'd cast aside stir. The love for him she'd buried sprang up like a violent geyser. She still loved him. Not in that all-consuming, naïve way she had when they first met, but she loved him. Even after everything that transpired between them, the heartache he caused her, the love in her for him was strong.

"I'm sorry for everything, Alessandra. I'm sorry for hurting you. I know it doesn't make up for what I did, but you deserve an apology." Luca was glad he finally had the opportunity to say the words he'd wanted to say for the past five years. "And I hope you believe me when I tell you I had nothing to do with this that I had no idea what Elisa did. I'd never do anything to hurt you, to hurt our children."

"I believe you," she said, casting her eyes to where a handful of boats swayed gently on smooth water as egrets flew past en route to distant places. "I'm very sorry I didn't tell you about Nathaniel. It wasn't out of spite that I didn't. I did it to protect my ... our son. I hope you understand."

"I do." Luca followed with a stretch of silence before he said, "Riccardo is smart as a whip. I guess he takes after you."

A smile softened her lips. "So is Nathaniel, and he's a caring, loving boy."

Luca saw her eyes light with pride and turn the soft shade of green he loved. He wished he could touch her. "How could he not be? You're a great mother."

The comment crept up through her defences and made her eyes fill, but she blinked the tears away. The guilt she'd worn like a second skin for lying to Nathaniel, which had her doubting she was a good mother, dulled. "Thank you for saying that."

"It's the truth. Anyone can see Nathaniel's a happy child." Luca started to reach for Alessandra's hand but pulled back when she lowered it to her lap. "Although the boys have been apart, I know they'll come together and get along splendidly," Luca said, and Alessandra nodded. "I want to be in their..."

Before he finished, Alessandra jumped in. "You will be in their lives. They're your sons."

Luca had a strong urge to chain his arms around Alessandra, to taste the petal-soft lips. "And I'll make arrangements for you to get the financial support you need." Luca volunteered to fill the awkward silence because Alessandra knew he would never shirk from his responsibility, not because of his wealth, but because it was the type of man he was.

"Thank you. The boys will appreciate it."

"And I promise my father will have no input in their upbringing other than to be a grandfather."

Softening her expression, Alessandra said, "It's all I ask. I know both your parents will be loving grandparents."

"Of that, you can be sure. How are we going to sort out visitation and...?"

She jumped in. "We'll sort it, but if you don't mind, I'd like them to live here with Daniel and me."

At the mention of Daniel's name, Luca's first instinct was to say no, but he couldn't bear to hurt Alessandra again. "If that's what you want. We can get our lawyers to draft the papers."

"If you think it's necessary."

His gaze locked on her. "I don't. I trust you."

"Thank you. Then we won't. They'll spend time with you and visit your parents as often as they like. They're the only grandparents the boys have." Alessandra's offer didn't surprise him. It was who she was.

"Mom and Dad will appreciate that." Luca's eyes caught sight of her wedding ring, and he felt the tightening at his throat choke him. "Are you happy, Alessandra?"

She nodded. "Daniel's a good man, a good husband, and a great father. He loves Nathaniel as his own. And he'll love Riccardo as much."

Not the response Luca wanted to hear, but he was glad she was happy. She deserved no less. For a long silent moment, their eyes held. Sensing his thoughts, she answered the unasked question.

"I do love him," Alessandra told Luca. Seeing the pained look on his face, she decided to finish her thought. "Not as I love you, and I think he knows it."

The words hung heavy in Luca's heart, and the floodgate burst open. "I miss you terribly, Alessandra. I've thought of you day and night. There's a huge emptiness in me only you can fill. You're the only woman for me, the only woman I've loved. I'd do anything to get you back." At his words, her gaze faltered. "I'm sorry. I shouldn't have said that."

"No, I'm glad you did. All this time, I've felt you didn't feel anything for me, that I was just another notch on your bedpost." There was a beat of hesitation. "But I don't know how to respond to that." Alessandra's weary voice was almost a whisper.

"Tell me you miss me too and that you want me back." Luca's eyes implored.

Suddenly she was caught in a furious storm of emotions, and the words flowed out of her. "I miss you, Luca. I miss you so much, and I too want us back to the way it used to be."

DANIEL CAME TO A FULL STOP at the screen door. He felt something inside him break when he sensed he'd walked into a moment meant to be shared by two people, not three, and he was the intruder.

Locked in the chain of Luca's arms, Alessandra slanted a look at Daniel. He could see sadness, possibly regret, in the tear-filled eyes that stared at him. The aching notion of finality clawed at Daniel, and he turned to walk away.

Forty-Nine

WHEN ELISA STOOD firm on her denial of kidnapping Riccardo, Antonio spared no expense and hired Tomas Burgos to dig up the truth. Tomas didn't disclose to his client his connection to Elisa—professional or otherwise. Tomas didn't tell Antonio Elisa had hired him to dig up information on him and Luca. Tomas made no mention of Elisa's past connection, not because confidentiality lay at the root of his reputation, but because it was the perfect scenario for him to strike back at her. Being paid handsomely by Antonio Santini for the opportunity to get his revenge on the deceitful, scheming bitch who used him, then tossed him aside like a used dishrag was a definite win-win

It was a painstaking and gruelling few weeks of interviews and document chasing, but true to his word, Tomas came through. His report was thorough, detailed, and concise. More importantly, it proved Elisa's involvement in the kidnapping scheme.

Tomas managed to turn Dr. Scalia's nurse against Elisa, the sonogram technician, and the second-rate doctor when he promised to ask the court for leniency in return for her cooperation. Not that Tomas could, but Nurse Marla was running scared enough to believe him and told him everything.

In her sworn statement, Nurse Marla revealed Elisa was never pregnant. She told Tomas, Elisa initially planned to fake the non-existent baby's loss weeks into the marriage, and Dr. Scalia would corroborate the outcome. As Elisa's lover, she could manipulate Dr. Scalia into doing anything. Having been in Dr. Scalia's shoes, Tomas understood how persuasive the bitch could be.

Nurse Marla explained that Elisa believed reputation meant everything to Antonio Santini and banked the baby's loss would gain her the empathy needed to avoid Luca from divorcing her, which she knew he'd do at the first opportunity,

That plan turned the tide when Elisa steered her jogging friend, Alessandra, to her "fiancée" Dr. Scalia, when she felt ill. Elisa, having befriended Alessandra for the sole purpose of information gathering on Luca, steered her to Dr. Scalia for a checkup. When lover boy discovered Alessandra was pregnant with twins, he reported it to Elisa and the scheme to kidnap one baby formed in her head.

Nurse Marla explained that by Elisa's reasoning, the loss of a baby gave her a temporary reprieve, but an actual baby guaranteed her ties to Santini money forever. The promise to her lover he'd be well compensated for his contribution and silence made, Dr. Scalia promised Nurse Marla the same, and the plan was set in motion.

The twin's existence was withheld from Alessandra and all medical records. On the day Alessandra was rushed to the hospital to give birth, Dr. Scalia deceptively pumped her with drugs and hurried her to the operating room for an unnecessary cesarean.

All went as planned. The babies were delivered, and the mother was fine. That is until Alessandra's hemorrhaging got out of control. In the end, a hysterectomy had to be performed to save her life. It took a lot of dancing around the truth and more document falsifying, but money was made readily available to make it happen. And it happened.

"Money is far-reaching," Nurse Marla told Tomas when she admitted to taking the five-figure bribe for her part.

Antonio turned over Tomas's report to the *Polizia di Stato*, and Elisa, Dr. Scalia, the sonogram technician, and Nurse Marla was taken into custody. Although their destiny was yet to be determined, everyone involved, including Tomas Burgos, was pleased to see Elisa behind bars.

To add insult to injury, Johnny and her brother refused to take Elisa's call or offered to post the half-million-dollar bail.

"THE MAN DOES EXCELLENT WORK," ANTONIO said, handing the copy of Tomas's report to his wife when she reached for it.

"How could Luca not know Elisa wasn't pregnant?" Laine flipped through the pages.

"I asked the same question of your son. He told me they slept in separate rooms and that he was never intimate with her during their marriage in the hopes it would have her pushing for a divorce."

Laine's eyes widened. "He didn't share her bed not once in five years they were married? I know he wasn't involved with anyone. Are we talking about our son?"

"Shocking, I know, but it will work to his advantage when he files for the annulment. He suspected she was lying about the pregnancy and aimed to make her walk away from the marriage when she didn't have the baby. When Riccardo came into the picture, Luca kept up the ruse of their marital bliss for the boy's sake."

"And yours." Laine gave her husband a chastising gaze. "God, there's a lot here that woman did to get to us," she said, sifting through Tomas's file.

Nodding, Antonio got to his feet and crossed to the bar. "Elisa was willing to do anything necessary to get her hands on our money. Brandy?"

"Yes, please." Laine took the handed glass and watched Antonio eased a hip onto the corner of his desk. "I think Luca also stayed away from Elisa because he's desperately in love with Alessandra. She's certainly made an impact on his life."

"She has. She's ten times the woman Elisa could never be."

Laine heard the guilt ooze from Antonio. Alessandra, the young girl he conspired against and considered to be from the opposite side of the tracks, taught him an invaluable life lesson he'd soon not forget. Money wasn't the be-all and end-all in life. Moreover, Alessandra proved to be the noble woman she was when she handed Antonio Gianni's painting and letter and told him it rightly belonged to him.

"She's quite the woman." Laine handed the file back to Antonio, who locked it in their vault.

Contemplatively sipping on brandy, Antonio said, "Yes, I'm happy to welcome her into the family."

"I hope you've learned your lesson because I don't doubt Alessandra will not think twice about keeping those beautiful grandchildren from us if you so much as to inflict your misguided principles on them. As much as I love you, Antonio, I will choose my grandchildren over you any day." Laine's forceful tone told him she meant every word.

"I promise you I won't disappoint you anytime soon. I already have to make amends to Alessandra and Luca for what I've done. I won't be able to stand it if you disown me too."

"I'm not turning against you. It's a warning. I'm in this with you for the long haul. Remember, it's for better or worse. As for Luca, you need to give him time. No matter what you've done to him, you're his father. As Alessandra has, your son will forgive you too. It'll take time, but he will. I will tell you that you deserve his anger."

"I know. I deserve everything lunged my way. I accept the error of my ways, and I'll do everything in my power to regain my son's trust and respect." The sincerity in Antonio's tone told Laine he meant what it.

"It's certainly refreshing to hear you sound so contrite."

"It's a first for me. I need to get used to the taste of crow, which, by the way, is not pleasant. Anyway, I'm glad Luca and Alessandra sorted things out between them."

"Me too."

"And I'm glad you backed me when I suggested we give ownership of Villa Santini, lock stock and barrel, to Alessandra."

"I wish you would have done it sooner and not waited for a tragedy to do the right thing." Laine pointed out.

With the sting of remorse in his voice, Antonio said, "Me too. It's another one of those mistakes I deeply regret making."

"You know Alessandra's not going to relocate the family here. She has no desire to live in this—what is it she called it?—imposing home," Laine said, looking around and thinking of the house in those terms for the first time in her life.

"I figured as much. I'm hoping to talk her into letting us live here. I want to stay close to the children."

"I'm sure she'll let us stay for as long as we want, but it's her call, and we'll do as she says." Laine gave her husband a long, thorough look.

"Agreed." Pushing to his feet, Antonio took the glass from Laine and offered his hand. "Want to come to bed with me, grandma?"

Enjoying the sound of her new title, she let out a rich laugh. "I do, grandpa."

Epilogue

WITH NATHANIEL AND Riccardo tucked in their beds, Alessandra stepped onto the patio and watched him. He was everything she wanted, and she was grateful to have him back in her life. She'd never hurt again because he'd never bring pain into her life. Of that, she was sure.

Suddenly the air smelled only of her, and he turned to face her. For a long silent moment, their eyes held as if nothing else existed, as if nothing else mattered. She was everything to him, and he was thrilled she'd chosen him.

She was all he'd ever wanted. Her love shaped him, and to be back in her life was the best ending he could ask for. Although he was the one she chose to share her life's journey with, it felt like a dream.

He closed the gap between them. When he was close enough, his fingertips traced lightly over her cheek. She was real. She was *his*. The thought of it felt magical. He'd never again make her heart ache. He'd cherish and treasure her, love her for as long as there was a breath in his body.

She stepped forward into him. Holding her tight, he savoured the dreamlike feel of her against him. Above them, thousands of stars winked, and an orange moon cast a flowing ribbon of light on a sea plunged in black. In the dreamlike scenery, swamped with love, his lips met hers. He took her into a deep kiss that spoke of love and every emotion coursing in him. It wasn't the first kiss they'd shared, but it was the first one since she chose him, and to him, it was the most extraordinary kiss.

Her arms chained tightly around him, her eyes met his. "I love you."

The words floated like a melody, and his breath released on a shudder of joy. Nothing had ever felt as good or as perfect. This, he thought, was as complete as his life could get.

He rested his brow against hers. "I love you so much. I have from the moment I set eyes on you and always will. You and the boys will always be the best part of me."

Slowly, he trailed a lazy line of kisses down her neck, inhaling the scent that would forever fill his days. His mouth crushed down on hers and desperately took in the taste of her. The erotic slide of his tongue unleashed a passion dormant in her for so long. It was a passion he welcomed.

Pressing her needy mouth to his, her kiss soothed every ache and filled his heart with the love he'd waited for five long years.

He pulled back just enough to look into her face. In her eyes, he saw what he hadn't these past few years. She wanted him, all of him.

Alessandra rested her hand on his cheek. The eyes that looked at him told him she would love him tonight and forever and that they would always be together.

"Take me to *our* bed," Alessandra said.

On those words, Daniel swept her up to carry her into the house. Tonight was the beginning of their history.

If you liked *The Noble Woman*, look for M.L. Lexi's other novel: *The Determined Woman*, available as eBook and paperback.

Special Excerpt from

THE DETERMINED WOMAN

Prologue

Spring 2007

THAT ONE ACT set everything in motion, and the consequences were still reverberating all these years later. Now, things Isabella thought would remain inside her forever had to be told.

On a long breath, she dropped her weary body into the plush leather of the Kensington recliner. The golden liquid in her glass sloshed dangerously close to the rim. Resting her head against the chair, she squeezed her eyes shut and struggled for calm.

Isabella wasn't under the delusion this moment would never come. She only hoped it wouldn't, but the repercussions of a single vile act could go on and on for years and touch many lives. As hard as Isabella tried to keep the painful experience from reaching her family, the time had come when it would.

Isabella's expression shifted as her daughter's angrily lobbed questions came to her—again.

How could you do this to me, to daddy?

How could you lie all these years, and with such ease, Mother? What else have you been lying about?

Do you know how betrayed and broken I feel knowing the person I love and trust most in this world has lied to me my entire life?

My whole life has been a lie.

The anger hot and pulsing in Bianca's voice as she came at Isabella with the questions, accusations, and hate, her response was to run away—far away from her daughter. Escaping, shrouding herself from everything and everyone was what she needed, and in the darkness of night, Isabella made the two-hour drive to her northern retreat.

No matter how long Isabella had mentally prepared for when the moment came, when it did, it felt like a detonating hand grenade to her system. The shameful, ugly secret she'd kept buried in the deep recesses of her mind for the twenty-three years of her daughter's life, her entire married life now had to be told.

Isabella was bone-tired, but as much as she needed to lay her head down, her racing mind wouldn't allow sleep to come. She did the next best thing. Isabella fueled herself with the remaining brandy in her glass.

Swooping to the bar, she slopped brandy into her glass then crossed to the window. The first light from a rising sun peeked from between the treetops. Isabella cast eyes to the natural, unspoiled surroundings of Lake Rosseau. Spring was beginning to show her face in the small Canadian town, and fields and forests framing the lake were steeped in the budding green heralding the season. Canada geese migrating from their winter sojourn filled a vivid blue sky.

In the deafening silence, her father's words rushed at her.

Secrets are like walls, Isabella. They will protect you and those around you from the pain they can inflict and the harm they can spawn, but only temporarily because no matter how shocking or terrible those secrets are, eventually, they always come out.

Hers now had.

The warmth of the living room suddenly felt stifling, and Isabella stepped out onto the terrace. The air against her face, cool and moist, carried the pungent peaty smell of damp earth and dew from the previous week's rains. The sounds of dawn were all around. Within the shelter of trees that sprang up majestically toward the sky, a soft wind rustled through their leaves. Birds joined in the chorus of birdsong, and creatures stirred.

The soothing and utopian panorama she escaped to when she needed recharging from her busy life today did nothing to calm her restless mind. Today, her heart ached too much. It ached for her daughter and her unsuspecting family. Resurrecting the long-hidden event from her past was going to cause deep hurt.

She prayed her daughter, husband, and son would understand and forgive her. At the thought, they may not, a frightful chill cut deep, and Isabella wrapped her hands around her shivering body.

"How could I have been so careless?" she thought, eyeing the envelope—the cause of all her problems—sitting on the coffee table. Twice she'd attempted to read its contents but hadn't found the courage to do so.

She should have locked the Goddamn thing in her office safe when her assistant handed it to her, but there were so many distractions. The ringing telephone, the tantrum from her Vice-President of Sales complaining about late shipments, and her secretary's urging words to get to the boardroom for the meeting she was running late for had her dismissing the envelope. Although Isabella thrived on such chaos, the contents of the envelope, which was about to change her family's life, had her mind distracted, and she rushed off to her meeting, leaving it on her desk for Bianca to find.

Isabella couldn't fault her daughter for the screaming match she'd incited or the accusatory and hurtful words Bianca hurled when she so much as handed her the DNA report she'd requested without her knowledge.

Guilt compressed in a tight ball in the pit of Isabella's stomach.

The should-haves whirled in Isabella's head. She should have done this or that, but it was too little too late, and her impulse was to run to avoid Bianca's demands for answers, for the truth.

Not that she blamed her daughter. If she were in Bianca's shoes, she too would have demanded an explanation, answers. She, also, would have flung the hateful words Bianca hurled like daggers aimed to wound because she and her daughter were alike. The thought, however, didn't lessen the fact Bianca's hurtful words cut Isabella deeply.

You're my mother, the person I trust unconditionally, and now you're nothing but a lying, deceiving— I will never trust you again, Mom, and I couldn't hate you more right now if I wanted to. I hate you. I hate you. I hate you.

Isabella hadn't known a hurt like that of a child telling their mother she hated her.

Her daughter's words echoing in her ears with the intensity they were meant to, Isabella imagined the depth of Bianca's pain, the feeling of betrayal when she read the report.

No one escaped the past, Isabella thought. A shiver cut through her like a serrated knife, and she wrapped her arms around her body for warmth. Closing her eyes, she opened herself to the memories and the lie at the heart of it all.

Also By M.L. Lexi

Coming Soon

Visit us at www.mllexi.com to read excerpts of upcoming releases.

Author contact: mllexiauthor@gmail.com

Visit our website at mllexi.com

Visit our blog at mllexi.blog

Email us at mllexiauthor@gmail.com to receive emails whenever M.L. Lexi publishes a new book. There's no charge or obligation and your information will remain confidential.